D0396590

Bliss House

LAURA BENEDICT

PEGASUS CRIME
NEW YORK LONDON

For Ann Arthur Benedict, my favorite Virginian,
and Cleve Benedict, her Prince Charming

⌒

BLISS HOUSE

Pegasus Books LLC
80 Broad Street, 5th Floor
New York, NY 10004

First Pegasus Books cloth edition June 2014

Interior design by Maria Fernandez

ISBN: 978-1-60598-572-5

10 9 8 7 6 5 4 3 2 1

Printed in the United States of America
Distributed by W. W. Norton & Company, Inc.

From case file 8214.P of the Virginia State Police, Homicide Division. Listing from the records of *Powell Company Properties*:

**OWN A TREASURED PIECE OF HISTORY IN THE
TIMELESS FOOTHILLS OF THE BLUE RIDGE MOUNTAINS**

Built in 1878 by industrialist Randolph Hasbrouck Bliss as a country retreat, Bliss House is one of seven American homes designed by the prominent black French architect Jean-Paul Hulot. Its serene setting among sixty-two acres of orchards, pastures, and ponds, gracious formal gardens, and rambling woods offers the ultimate in pastoral privacy. A yellow-brick Second Empire gem, Bliss House features 9 original bedrooms, a generous kitchen with butler's pantry, paneled study, theater, formal dining room, salon, partial cellar, and rooftop storage space, 8 full & 2 half-baths, and central air. Stone patios, mansard roof, nine working fireplaces (including the kitchen), and original cherry moldings throughout are among the many period details. Once an inn, Bliss House also offers six servants' bedrooms with a separate kitchen, living area, and entrance, plus a detached four-car garage with a second-level apartment.

Located forty-five minutes from Charlottesville and Interstate 64, near historic Old Gate, Virginia, settled in 1744 on the James River. Bliss House invites endless possibilities: spa, inn, private residence, or luxurious business suites.

Attractively priced.

Chapter 1

A Generation Ago

The blindfold kept Allison from seeing, but the chilly air around her smelled sweet and damp. There were flowers nearby—roses, she guessed—and the *drip drip drip* of water. They might be underground, even in a cave.

How thrilling!

Michael, her lover, stood close, touching her neck, her shoulder. When he touched her breast, she giggled.

He shushed her with a whisper.

Why do we have to be so quiet?

Nothing in her life was ever this quiet. Rattling dishes, noisy customers, the gossip of the restaurant's kitchen staff filled her days. At night, she listened to records or watched television, hung out at her mother's house, which echoed with the shouts of her half-brothers and neighborhood kids, or she went dancing in bars near the university. It was only since she'd met Michael that her life had turned quiet. Slower. They never went dancing, and he often brought takeout when he came to see her in her two-room apartment. He'd told her that making love with her felt like the most important thing he'd ever done. That they didn't need other people around. And while she thought the notion that their sex was important was kind of silly, she never told him because it might have hurt his feelings.

He helped her sit down on something soft. A bed, perhaps.

Were they in his house? She'd asked him more than once where he lived, but he would only tell her that he lived with his family, not too far away. She sensed that he didn't have a good relationship with them. Not everyone had a mother like hers, who loved her enough to not get into her business—especially since she'd left home. She knew she was lucky that way.

Tonight, before they left her apartment, he'd told her he had a surprise for her. She'd looked up at him expectantly, hoping they were going somewhere special like the Grange, the big resort hotel a few miles outside Charlottesville. When he'd called to set up their date, he'd told her to put on something pretty, and she'd dug out a ruffled yellow sundress from the back of her closet and tamed her unruly hair as best she could.

"I know this sounds weird, but I need you to ride in the back of the car. On the floor."

When she told him there was no way she was going to do that, he had asked her to please, do it for him. It wasn't so much, was it? And didn't she like surprises?

So she'd found herself on the floor in the back of the Cutlass as they drove through the night, her dress crumpled beneath her, and her long red hair clinging to the picnic blanket he'd laid on the back seat. She'd tried to convince him that she could sit beside him with the blindfold on, or just close her eyes, but they both knew she couldn't do it, which made them laugh. He kept the blindfold up front with him.

Before they drove away, he put a Boz Scaggs cassette in the stereo, and gave her a vial of coke and the tiny spoon he always carried in his pocket.

"It's kind of a long drive," he said. "I want you to enjoy the ride." His smile didn't quite reach his brown eyes, which were sometimes hard for her to examine under the shadow of his brow. Even though he was nineteen, a year younger than she, Michael seemed older than a lot of the university guys she met. The difference was in the things that he *didn't* do, immature things like getting stupid-drunk, or tearing at her clothes when they made out.

At first she'd tried to guess in what direction they were headed by paying attention to which way the car turned and watching the streetlamps outside the window. But when she opened the coke, she had to concentrate to keep it from falling off the tiny spoon, and quickly lost her orientation.

After the coke, she got antsy—her mother was always telling her not to fidget—and poked her head up to take a quick peek out the window. Because she was only just a hair over five feet tall, she had to shift, getting onto her knees to see anything. But she made too much noise, and Michael admonished her, his voice loud over the music.

"Hey! Don't look!"

She ducked back down, laughing nervously. He'd never sounded angry with her before.

"You'll spoil the surprise," he said. "I just want you to be surprised."

Chagrined, but still feeling playful, she told him she was sorry, and promised to be a good girl. She hadn't been able to see a thing outside the window, anyway. The streetlights had disappeared, and she had only seen her own face, pale and curious, staring back at her from the glass.

By the time he stopped the car, the Crosby, Stills, and Nash tape that had replaced Boz Scaggs was nearly over, and she was feeling carsick. The last few minutes of the drive had been slow, down a gravel road, but he still wouldn't tell her where they were. He bent over the front seat to tie the blindfold for her.

"Hold your hair. Just like that, to the side. I don't want to hurt you."

It was more of a command than a request, but at least he was being gentle with her. When they had sex, he was also gentle. But always, when he came, she had a sense that he was holding something back, hiding a part of himself. Was it frustration? Anger? He didn't like to talk about himself or his feelings. Some guys were like that. And that was okay with her. She had secrets of her own, so she didn't push or question.

With the blindfold snugly settled, he'd led her away from the car, solicitous about where she walked. She clung to him so she wouldn't fall. She was high enough, excited enough, that she didn't ask any questions. If he wanted to play some games, she could stand it. The sex he thought so important was good, even if it was getting a little predictable. If he tried to hit her or hurt her the way that some guys she'd gone out with had, or the coke stopped coming, she would stop seeing him.

The night smelled like the woods, and she could hear peepers and a single distant bullfrog. It was so reminiscent of night on her grandparents' farm in West Virginia that she felt sad and nostalgic and happy all at once.

She'd been in love, once, in high school, and this felt almost like that. At least when she was high like she was now. Michael—not Mike, *never* Mike—wasn't perfect. Sometimes he didn't call her, then showed up at her door again without warning or apology. Before tonight, she hadn't heard from him in two weeks. The first week of waiting to hear from him had been painful, and just a couple of days earlier she'd had a bowling date with a guy who worked at the jewelry store next to the restaurant. He'd been bugging her for months, and she was feeling bored and angry with Michael. She hadn't decided whether to tell Michael about the date, but she'd gone to make him jealous, so she thought she might. Then he'd called her out of the blue like he hadn't been away at all, and she hadn't been able to stay mad. Plus, he had her for sure when he pulled out the coke.

Now that she was sitting—wherever they were—he turned her head slightly so he could reach the ties of the blindfold.

"Let's see how quiet you can be."

The velvet blindfold fell into Allison's lap.

Such a strange, unsettling room! Were they in some castle chamber? That was the first impression she had, maybe because of the damp, chilly air. Like so many other little girls, she'd bought into that fairy tale dream of marrying a prince and living in a castle. But this place felt too claustrophobic to be part of a castle, and wasn't at all romantic. Even the candle flickering in a niche carved into the rough, blank wall seemed to lack warmth. But the adjoining wall was covered by a set of heavy curtains hanging from a thick wooden rod. They were the kind of curtains she'd imagined hanging in a house like Thornfield in the novel *Jane Eyre*; curtains that would keep out not just the cold, but the creatures that roamed the moors at night. She could make out deer and horses stitched into a black or dark blue field. Without much light beyond a weak, amber bulb in a single electric sconce on the wall, and the candles, it was hard to make out colors. The bedspread on which she sat was a different design, but equally elaborate, and the bedposts were tall, only inches from the ceiling. A high bedside table held a vase with red roses, a simple wooden box, an ashtray, and a tarnished silver candelabrum with lighted candles standing in three of its five arms. A pile of threadbare towels sat on a wooden folding chair pushed up to a table that looked as though it could barely seat two people. The furniture looked to Allison like things out of a museum. Only a covered plastic bucket, a metal cooler in the corner, and the rust-stained pedestal sink looked like they were from the current century.

"This place is weird," Allison said. "Do you live here?"

Michael got up from the bed and opened the wooden box on the bedside table. Because of his height and the restricted dimensions of the room, he looked like a giant trapped in a walled cage. If he wished, he could easily have pressed his palm against the ceiling.

Pulling out a perfectly rolled joint, he lighted it, took a hit, and handed it to her. She didn't much like to smoke pot when she was doing coke, but the whole evening had turned surreal, and she was thinking she could use a little help to relax and settle her stomach.

Michael lay down near her, resting his head against her thigh. She'd thought he was handsome, but now she noticed that his nose was just a bit too large for his face, and his chin was too round compared to the sharpness of his nose and the size of his jaw.

Why didn't I notice that before?

He looked different from how he looked back in her apartment. She shivered. At the last moment before leaving the apartment, she had grabbed a sweater that her grandmother had crocheted for her. But the sweater did nothing to break the chill of the room.

"What do you think of it?" Michael asked.

"It's . . . I don't know," she said. "It's really cool, I guess."

A look of disappointment crossed his face. "You don't like it. I should've known you wouldn't like it."

"That's silly. Of course I like it."

He took the joint and sat up again to flick the ash in the crystal ashtray on the table. He seemed anxious in a way she'd never seen him act before.

"I hoped you would. What about the flowers? You like them, don't you?"

Allison laughed. "What's up with you? Why are you being so weird? How come you don't have a TV in here? Or a phone? You don't even have a telephone."

He offered her one last hit off of the joint before he took it back, and crushed its cherry in the ashtray. When it was out he laid it carefully aside.

"You ask a lot of questions," he said, getting up.

Allison lay back, resting on her elbows. "Are we in your parents' basement or something?"

"Something like that." He stood over her.

With a mirthless smile, he lifted her up a few inches, only to drop her again farther back on the bed. She weighed less than 110, and he was at least six feet tall and almost 200 pounds. He often just picked her up and moved her if she was in his way or wanted her somewhere else. It was a dumb jock kind of thing to do, and she had known the dumbest jocks in high school. Sometimes it bugged her the way he treated her like she was some kind of doll, but usually she thought it was pretty funny. And she liked that he wasn't dumb. In fact, there were times when he said things that made her feel like she wasn't very smart.

"Hey, don't be mad, okay?" She held out her arms for him, and smiled. But her smile died when she saw his eyes.

"Why did you turn out to be such a stupid cunt?" he said.

Before she responded, Allison waited just a moment to make sure she'd heard him right. But it wasn't just his words. He was kneeling over her, and his face, so close to hers, was ugly and distorted.

"What did you just call me?" She shoved at his chest, putting him off-balance for a moment. But he didn't fall. "Get away!"

"Did you think I wouldn't know?" He snatched at the skirt of her dress, roughly pulling it up to her waist. "I can smell him on you! I can smell your nasty little cunt already. Ever since you got in my car tonight. You stink like dead fish."

Allison flushed with embarrassment. Fear.

"He didn't touch me . . ." was all she could manage. She'd always been a terrible liar. If she'd made out with the other guy, it wasn't any of his business. Michael had abandoned her like she didn't even matter.

"Look, you're not even wearing underwear, like the whore you are. Wanting to make it easy for me. Just like your whore mother. Shitting out those little bastard brothers of yours."

She tried again to push him away, but he was able to hold her down with one arm as he slid his pants off. Now her terror was mixed with an angry shame. Her mother's second husband hadn't been her husband at all. But nobody knew that, did they? He couldn't know! And what did it have to do with her?

"What's wrong with you, Michael? Stop it!"

She screamed as loudly as she could, but Michael didn't stop. When he entered her, it felt nothing like it had before. The size and shape of him was the same, but that was all. Even more disgusting to her was how he slipped so easily inside her—she'd been ready when they arrived in the room, excited because of the coke, because of how he'd breathed, warm and tingling, on her neck. How horrible it was, as though she'd been anxious for this. Oh, God, the shame! He pounded against her so violently that her head banged repeatedly against the bed's immovable headboard. Squeezing her eyes shut, she screamed and screamed.

No one came for her. There was no panicked knock at the door, no shouted promise of help on the way.

As he climaxed, he gave a triumphant, inhuman roar that filled that sepulchral room and silenced Allison with her own fear. She lay there, willing herself to be somewhere else. Anywhere else. Or dead. When it was over, he rolled onto the bed beside her, shuddering with each breath, heat radiating from his body.

Her dress and body were soaked and stinking with his sweat. She lay quietly, waiting for whatever was going to happen next, afraid to make a sound. If she did, he might be reminded to come at her again. She couldn't think of a time when they'd had sex twice in one night, but this was a different Michael.

After his breathing slowed, he got up from the bed. Was he talking to himself? Praying? He was saying something she couldn't make out, as though he were talking to someone—but not her.

Though she was loath to move, she rolled carefully onto her side and tried to cover herself with her dress. If only she were lying on her own soft bed, in her own apartment, maybe then she could bear it. She might feel hopeful then, like she might be able to save herself. But in this place—this strange, awful place—she saw little reason to hope.

Michael tucked in his shirt and did up his pants and belt. His lips were moving, but she couldn't make out anything he was saying.

"Michael," she whispered. Her throat was scratchy and dry from screaming.

He wouldn't look at her.

"Michael, I don't understand."

Still without looking at her, he turned on one of the sink taps. The water stuttered out, a rusty orange color, and he let it run until it was a narrow stream. Finally he splashed some water on his face and, dripping, grabbed a towel from the chair to dry himself. When he was done, he smoothed his hair back and tossed the towel at her. It landed, covering her arm, but she didn't move to take it.

"Clean yourself up," he said.

He went to the door, then turned back to her, took a disposable lighter from his pocket, and tossed it too on the bed.

"For the candles. And if you do something stupid, like start a fire, it will only kill you. It won't hurt anyone else."

As the door shut behind him, Allison—propelled from the bed by the sudden realization that he was going to leave her behind— grabbed the doorknob and pulled. But she was too late. She heard a bolt shoot into the doorframe, probably from the brass lock a few inches above the doorknob. Pounding on the door, she screamed for him.

"Don't leave me here! Michael!"

Remembering the curtains on the other side of the room, she ran to them, thinking she could break the window if it, too, was locked. She slid the curtain along the wooden rod.

But there was no window. Only a gray, unbroken expanse of wall.

Chapter 2

Present Day

Standing a few feet behind her fourteen-year-old daughter, Ariel, in the hot Virginia sun, Rainey Adams watched her staring up at Bliss House. If it had been possible to will Ariel to love it as much as she did, Rainey would have done it in a heartbeat.

It was a house from Rainey's dreams, rising from its bed of tattered gardens on two stories of firm yellow brick, its face boldly pushing forth from between two shallow wings. The third floor was a mansard crown of aged gray slate, relieved by several chimneys and windows set deep into shadowed cornices that made them seem secretive even in the afternoon light. The lower floors were layered with shutterless arched windows taller than a man and punctuated with iron accents whose points looked more dangerous than decorative. But the creamy white trim and pale stone outlining the house's edges lent Bliss House a tentative air of softness and kept it from looking too severe. Too guarded. From the outside, one of Bliss House's primary architectural oddities—a dome crowning the central well of the house—was barely visible. Overall, the house gave an impression of contradicting itself, as though it weren't sure of what sort of house it meant to be.

Rainey, though, was certain it was meant to be hers. While she'd found it intimidating on seeing it for the second time in her life (the first having been when she was only eight years old, and then she couldn't go inside), it was like nowhere she'd ever lived before, and she found that she wanted to cling to its immutable presence. It was solid and old and beautiful and challenging, all at the same time.

Ariel needed the stability a place like Bliss House could give her. Rainey needed it, too. As an interior designer who spent much of her life making homes for other people, she'd always believed that the atmosphere of a house was shaped by the people who lived in it. Yet here she was, looking for comfort and strength from a thing made of bricks and mortar. She and Ariel, like the house, had been damaged by their sad—even tragic—histories. But she had plans for the house beyond the critical repairs and renovations that she'd already done. She would heal it, as it would help to heal the two of them. It would be a home where Ariel would feel safe, and together they would bring the kind of happiness to Bliss House that would make it worthy of its name.

Overwhelmed with a feeling of hopefulness, Rainey reached out to touch her daughter's hair, but then quickly drew back her hand. "What do you think? Do you like it?"

It was a ridiculous question, and she knew she was opening herself up for the worst kind of derision. Ariel had become an expert at taking advantage of her eager desire to make things right between them. All she had to do was turn and fix Rainey with one of her practiced, uncaring looks with eyes that looked too much like Will's eyes. In life, the three of them had been a solid, happy unit. In death, the man they had both lost was always between them.

"You're kidding, right?" Ariel leaned awkwardly on her cane, a scowl aging her once-delicate features. She hid her thinned, cropped hair beneath a slouchy patterned cap, and her scars beneath clothes that hung loose on her slight frame.

Rainey bit her lip to keep from asking Ariel if she meant "kidding" as in *this-has-got-to-be-a-joke*, or "kidding" as in *this-is-the-coolest-place-I've-ever-seen*. She'd been expecting a strong reaction to Bliss House—one way or the other—from Ariel, who had refused to even look at pictures of it before they arrived in Virginia.

Ariel started forward slowly. The accident—yes, it was an accident, even if Rainey herself was responsible—that had claimed Will Adams, Ariel's father and the center of Rainey's world, had also left the entire right side of Ariel's body burned and badly scarred. Two years earlier, she'd been a lithe twelve-year-old who was already several inches taller than her mother. She had loved gymnastics and ballet, and wore her then-lush black hair knotted in a taut bun at the back of her head. Her porcelain skin had been free of the blemishes that plagued other girls, and her blue eyes—like her father's—were alternately full of harmless mischief and solemnity.

That girl was gone, replaced by an angry, unforgiving teenager who had spent too much time in and out of hospitals, and stabbed her walking cane into the ground as though every step were a punishment. She saw every mirror as an enemy. Her depression and anger turned the time she and Rainey spent together into a shared silent cage that seemed to grow smaller with each passing day.

Rainey was finally used to her daughter's wrecked beauty, the fierce red flesh along her jaw that spread like a chafing hand over her right cheek. She longed to gently touch the scars that ran from Ariel's face and down her arm to the back of her hand. She missed the giggling girl who looked so much like her daddy, missed the intermingling of their hair—Rainey's so blond and Ariel's so dark—as they read or played computer games together, or cuddled on the couch to watch a movie. Missed looking into her daughter's eyes and seeing something, anything, besides hurt and contempt.

To My Adorable Mommy, I Love You Soooooooo Much!!!! Ariel had written in bright gold on the last Valentine she'd given Rainey, over two years earlier. Yes, she missed so much about her baby girl.

"It was hard to get good pictures of the front of the house," Rainey said, following Ariel. There was a pebble in her open sandal. The driveway hadn't yet been repaved and was a minefield of small rocks and three-inch-deep potholes. "You'd have to go way back down the drive, and out there the trees get in the way. It will be clearer in the winter."

What will winter be like here? She hadn't thought about things like snow removal or even about the cost of heating such a monster of a house. Before buying it, she'd only been in Old Gate once, and by that time Bliss House had been sold to a doctor outside the family. But then it was sold again to become a successful inn run by a married couple, the Brodskys, whose ownership had ended in a tragic murder. Before it was sold the first time, Bliss House had been in Rainey's mother's family for over a hundred years. Now it was hers.

In a better market, Bliss House might have cost her half-again the one-point-four million she'd paid for the house and land. Between her own trust fund and Will's life insurance, she had a very manageable mortgage and, if she acted carefully, they could live quite comfortably for at least the next ten years. Ariel would be out of college by then—if she would even go. They hadn't exactly been diligent about home schooling.

Will would never have believed she could let things get to this point. God only knew Rainey could hardly believe it herself.

When they reached the landing below the front door, Rainey looked up to the distant rooftop. Barely five feet two inches in her shoes, she suddenly felt insignificant. Beside her, Ariel seemed much younger than she was, and more vulnerable. It was as if they were two tiny, fragile dolls about to enter a massive new dollhouse.

Two ragged, broken dolls.

Chapter 3

The first night Ariel lay in her new bed, in her new room in the strange house, she dreamed like she hadn't dreamed since long before the accident.

She walked with her father through unfamiliar woods, looking for a comfortable place to share the picnic lunch her mother had packed for them. Ariel was hungry and tired. The straps of the heavy backpack she wore dug cruelly into her shoulders. But her father laughed when she complained that she wanted to take it off, the sound of his voice echoing through the gold- and red-painted trees. She loved her father's laugh.

"Don't open it, Button," he said, ruffling her hair. "It's full of fire."

The dream-logic of his answer made sense to her, and she trudged on, breathing heavily over the noise of leaves crunching beneath their feet. They headed downhill, the weight of the pack propelling Ariel forward so forcefully that she stumbled. Spying a stream in the distance, she stopped thinking about her burden and ran. Sunlight cast shards of silver on the water, and she couldn't wait to get to it so she could splash the water on her face.

Once she broke through the trees, she saw that the sky beyond the stream was vast and cloudless. Falling to her knees on the muddy bank, she shrugged the pack onto the ground. The water was cool on her skin, and she gathered it to her again and again, heedless of the way it soaked her sleeves and untethered hair. She felt as though she could kneel there forever, and never be thirsty or weary again. Finally, she sat back on her heels and wiped the water from her face with the dry hem of her shirt.

Looking up, she found the sunlight was brighter. It spread without shadow, but instead of bringing warmth, it was spreading cold, and she shivered. She turned around, and saw that the woods had disappeared—and, with them, her father.

"Daddy?"

She scanned the pale tundra that, only a moment before, had been a forest blazing with color.

Beside her, the backpack shifted. Something was moving inside, wriggling against the canvas. She reached out to touch the pack, but drew her hand back, afraid, as the clip securing the cord at the top of the pack began to slide off all by itself. The pack opened a few inches, and tiny tongues of flame darted out, reaching for her.

She struggled to her feet, but the flames shot forward, growing longer and longer, chasing her as she ran toward the flat, frozen landscape. She screamed for her father. He had to be near!

"Daddy, where are you?"

The sound of her own choked words awakened her as she struggled to break free of the dream.

The walls of her new bedroom were bathed in a mellow gold light, and the air—like the air in her dream—had turned brutally cold. It was a winter cold, not the welcome chill of a late summer night. A curtain across the room stirred, and Ariel saw that the window was open. She groped for the blanket folded at the end of the bed. Finding it, she pulled it to her. Why was the room so bright? She didn't remember the nightlight that her mother had plugged in the night before being so strong.

"I'm right here, Button."

Ariel turned her head to see her father sitting in the chair nearest the bed. He leaned forward to smile at her. It was a sad smile.

In that split second of recognition, Ariel felt a weightless thrill in her stomach, like that moment before the plunge down the first hill of a roller coaster. How many nights had she awakened in the darkness, wanting to see his face?

The thrill quickly faded.

This can't be real.

"Shhh. You're all right," he said, rising from the chair to stand over her.

Ariel held out her arms to him. "I want to be awake. I want you to be here, Daddy."

Her friends had always wanted to come to her house to see her dad because they thought he was cute. Even though he was a lawyer, he kept his wavy black hair—so much like her own—a little long. Because he almost never got angry or said mean things, he always looked young, and not wrinkled like some of their fathers. But it was his eyes that made so many people like him. Cheerful, blue eyes, the color of her friend Melody's blue finch. Now, he was dressed in his weekend clothes—khakis, a bright red polo shirt, and the embroidered canvas belt with the ducks on it that Grandma Adams had made for him before she died, and that her mother teased him about.

"You see me. I'm here."

"But you'll go away," she said, sounding like a very young child.

His eyes were darkened by the shadows in the room, and they didn't look as happy as she'd first thought. Still, she wanted to memorize every bit of him. To remember.

"No. I won't. I promise, baby girl."

She was still reaching out for him, but he wouldn't come close enough. If only he would gather her into his arms to keep her warm. But she knew if she tried to touch him, he wouldn't really be there.

"Go back to sleep," he said, his breath making clouds in the air. "I'm watching you."

Ariel, shivering and not really wanting to go back to sleep, lay back on the icy pillow.

"Stay, Daddy." She was so tired that she barely heard herself speak.

Her father leaned down and rested a hand on her leg—the leg that a piece of metal from the house had nearly cut in two. Did she feel the pressure of his hand? She wasn't sure because her eyes closed, and she no longer felt anything.

Ariel woke up on her stomach, her face mashed into the pillow. The room was stifling with humidity, and she'd kicked off the covers to the foot of the bed. A sheen of sweat had pasted her tank top to her back. With a tiny pang, she remembered the cold of the night before. With the memory of the cold came the memory of her father. She quickly rose up on her hands and knees, the heat and sticky sheets forgotten.

The chair was still near the bed. Empty. But she could feel that he'd been there. Something had changed. Despite the heat and the sweat, she felt better than she had since the accident.

Chapter 4

Rainey washed her cereal bowl and spoon and put them on the drain board of the sink to dry. Most of the maintenance work on Bliss House had been done before they'd arrived, supervised by Gerard Powell, the husband of the real estate agent who had handled the house purchase. Repairs to the aging slate roof, the doors, stairs, and floors of all the usable rooms refinished, walls painted, and the heat pumps replaced. But she hadn't been able to bring herself to do much of anything to the kitchen. The only things that were different from the day she'd come out from St. Louis to close on the house, three months earlier, were a new microwave and an electric stove that replaced the professional eight-burner gas range the former owners had installed.

All her life she'd had a passion for things old and quaint and unusual. Her passion, along with an artistic eye and years of training, had led to a comfortably profitable interior design career. Their house near St. Louis, just over the Missouri River, had been custom-built for them, and she had filled it with the antique treasures she couldn't bear to pass on to clients. Eighteenth-century Irish tables, a set of Welsh chairs, thirteen gilt-edged mirrors from a Louisiana Creole plantation house, a trundle bed from a Kentucky barn that was two days from being demolished. Even her kitchen had been furnished with cabinetry salvaged from a dowager house near Forest Park. They were strings to the past that tugged at her because her own past had been so rich and full of love—like Ariel, she had been an only child, adored by her parents.

"But an antique gas stove?" Will had said, pausing as he pried open pistachio nuts—a quick after-work snack he washed down with a local micro brew. He wore the somber gray suit he'd put on for court, but had loosened the plum necktie she had laid out for him that morning. He wasn't wild about the color, but she loved it because it made his eyes look as blue as the day she'd met him, fifteen years earlier.

"Can't we just get one that looks retro?"

"Look at the molding on the doors. It's gorgeous," she'd said, her voice full of a proprietary awe that Will knew well. She ran her fingers over the stove's pristine cream-colored front. "It'll last another seventy-five years." She wasn't listening to him. A few days later, Will simply nodded when she told him the technician was scheduled to do the installation.

As always, Will had trusted her.

It wasn't her fault that the technician had rushed the retrofitting of an electronic ignition into the stove. It wasn't her fault that he was about to miss a payment on his truck and had to get to the credit union before it closed. It wasn't her fault that their house was so tightly built that Will hadn't smelled the gas filling the house before he unlocked the door. People from two miles away had reported the explosion. What none of them had seen was the second floor of the house rise, only to collapse onto the ground floor, crushing what hadn't shot away in the initial blast. But Ariel, who had been down at the mailbox, had turned to look back at the house at the explosion's initial roar. Ariel had seen more than enough.

The kitchen in Bliss House was in the shape of a T, and much more suited to a busy inn or a family with servants than a woman living on her own with a fourteen-year-old. Here in the long galley there were two deep, adjoining sinks with ridiculously long drain boards, and a food prep counter with open shelves above and below for pans and bowls. The racks on the walls already held a few knives and the other cooking tools she'd been able to find. There was also an industrial dishwasher with two brand new plastic dish racks sitting ready to slide automatically through it, but she'd yet to turn the dishwasher on. She'd never run anything like it, and, actually, she was a little afraid of trying it.

Around the left-hand corner of the galley was the part of the kitchen where all the cooking was done. There was the pitiful stove, a new microwave, a plate-warmer, a substantial refrigerator, more open shelves for pantry goods, and a handsome five-foot-long marble counter for making dough or candy. Rainey's mother had made hard candy for gifts every Christmas, and she had romantic visions of doing the same with Ariel. Around the other corner was the butler's pantry, with its gas fireplace (all of the fireplaces in the house had once burned wood, but now they were fitted for gas), rows of elegant glass-fronted cabinets, and a broad antique Irish table she was told was original to the house, where she and Ariel would eat most of their meals.

In the butler's pantry Rainey was dismayed to find that there was no order in the way the moving people had unpacked the sets of dishes and glassware she'd recently bought.

The moving company had sent a pair of workers—a muscular African American woman with close-coiffed gray hair and a sallow white man of about fifty who smelled of breath mints—who arrived just after the half-filled moving van had come and gone. They asked no questions and kept their heads down, diligent, the whole time. They spoke to each other in whispers, as though they were in a church. Rainey had tried to be friendly, offering them coffee, but their reticence had made it clear that they just wanted to get their work done and get out.

The truth was that, uncommunicative as they were, Rainey had liked having them around. With every passing hour in the vast house, she worried that she'd made a huge mistake. She had imagined living an idyllic, healing sort of country life for a while, then maybe—when Ariel was ready—turning most of the first floor into a studio where she could meet clients. But the house would need even more work if she were to do that. And she would have to start socializing to get those clients.

She sank onto the window seat at the end of the butler's pantry with a heavy sigh. The sun was warm on her skin, and she rested her head gratefully against the glass. She felt chilled all the time now. Always petite and small-boned, she'd lost fifteen pounds that she could hardly afford to lose. When a client back in St. Louis had recently told her how great, how *thin* she was looking, Rainey had seen a glint of envy in the woman's eyes that sickened her. Did she really want to spend the rest of her life being beholden to people who were so vain that they could envy a woman who couldn't eat because she'd accidentally *killed her husband?*

She looked up at a sound from another part of the kitchen, and saw Ariel heading for the refrigerator, wearing a nubby pink bathrobe Rainey had bought for her to wear at the rehab facility. Its sleeves were already too short, but the rest of the robe looked too big for her. Her hair was long enough that it was hard to tell where it no longer could grow behind her left ear, but Rainey knew the scarred flesh was there.

Ariel took milk and an apple from the refrigerator and pulled a box of cereal from a shelf. When she turned, she noticed Rainey.

"Hey, honey," Rainey said, not wanting to startle her. She wanted to help her—God, how she wanted to get up to help her—but she made herself stay in the window seat.

Unfazed, Ariel asked her where the bowls were.

"Here," Rainey said, finally jumping up. She had at least organized the Portmeirion china that she'd ordered for everyday use right away. She grabbed a bowl and dug out a spoon from the chaos in the silverware drawer.

"Sit down," she said, putting the bowl on the oak tabletop that separated them.

Ariel glanced around, but didn't say anything else. Rainey was glad to see some curiosity in her eyes.

A shadow changed the light in the room for only a second, and Rainey saw her daughter's face darken. Ariel was looking out the window.

"What is it?" Rainey turned around. She hurried to the window, but it looked straight onto the herb garden, and not out to either side. "Did you see something?"

Rainey turned back to Ariel, but she was gone. From the sounds she heard coming from the dark hallway leading to the back stairs, Ariel was already making her slow, labored way back to her room. Calling after her wasn't going to get her back. Rainey sighed.

Out in the mudroom, whose entrance was in the front galley of the kitchen, someone was knocking purposefully on the porch door. Ariel had seen whoever it was through the window and fled. As Rainey crossed the kitchen to answer the door, she was less curious about who was there than how her daughter had just been able to enter and leave the kitchen without using her cane.

Chapter 5

"I've wanted to meet you in person for the longest time, dear Rainey. Notes and Christmas cards every few years just aren't the same thing." Roberta "Bertie" Bliss stood behind a chair at the table in the butler's pantry. "May I sit?"

Rainey colored, totally off her game. "Oh, I'm sorry, Roberta. Of course." She gestured to Bertie, as well as the solid young man who had followed in her wake.

"You *must* call me Bertie. Everyone does, except the Judge, of course."

Judge Randolph Bliss was a remote cousin of Rainey's. It was his family Rainey and her mother had stayed with on her childhood visit to Old Gate. Her mother had driven her out to see Bliss House, where Randolph had grown up, but they hadn't gone inside because the family that had bought it wasn't home. The house had imprinted itself on her memory. Just being close to it gave her a strange sense of belonging.

Bertie was a comfortably upholstered bottle-blonde, girlish down to her pink-and-white, floral capri pants and sleeveless white eyelet shirt, pedicured toes, and petite handbag festooned with pink fabric flowers. Though she was in her mid-forties, some seven or eight years older than Rainey, the only lines on her face were laugh lines at the edges of her teal green eyes and pink (again, pink!) lacquered lips. But there was something else about Bertie's mouth: the corners looked red and flaky beneath her heavy foundation makeup, as though beneath all the pink and white of the outer Bertie, there was someone less smooth and moist and girlish, someone wiser and more serious trying to get out. The most significant thing about Bertie, though, was that she wore her feelings on her face. Bertie Bliss would be a very bad poker player. Rainey liked her instantly.

The young man with her was her son, Jefferson. He wore a stiff denim jacket over his broad torso, even though the outdoor humidity was already punishing. Rainey was startled to see much of her own father in him: a strong, angular nose and deep-set eyes. His neck was long, his Adam's apple prominent. There was an air of restrained confidence (or perhaps arrogance?) and intelligence about him. His pink scalp—not nearly so pink as anything adorning his mother—showed through the military buzz of his blond hair. Despite the threat of his bulk, Jefferson Bliss had a ready smile that held none of the frantic energy of his mother's. Rainey had been charmed by the way he'd nodded politely and responded to her proffered hand with a warm handshake.

"I think I know where the tea is," Rainey said, almost to herself. "And the kettle." She hadn't made any coffee that morning, and in fact had no idea where the coffee maker might be. *Somewhere on the shelves in the galley*, she thought.

"Moving is such a trial," Bertie said. "Though it's not like I've ever moved anywhere myself. Only from Mother's house to the house Randolph and I bought when we got married. Practically everything of mine fit in my little car. Mother insisted we take some of the furniture she had stored in the attic." She smiled at the memory, revealing a row of dainty, even teeth. "We had some men move all that for us."

Rainey started for the stove, hoping she really had seen the kettle on a nearby shelf.

"Do you want some help?" Bertie said, barely pausing. "Jefferson, you get up and help Cousin Rainey."

Jefferson stood up quickly, scraping the chair hard against the tile floor.

Rainey tried to wave him back but, seeing the enthusiasm on his face, she knew she had to give him something to do. He was much older than Ariel, but she couldn't help but compare her daughter's sullenness to Jefferson's obvious desire to please.

"There are mugs in that cabinet right behind you," she said. "Would you get out three? Spoons are in that drawer." She pointed. It occurred to her that Bertie would expect teacups with saucers. Something about the floral pants spoke to that. Mugs or teacups? When had she ever in her life worried about something so unimportant? Maybe the formality of the house was getting to her.

By the time the tea was served and drunk, and Jefferson and Bertie had eaten most of the gourmet oatmeal raisin cookies she'd bought to tempt Ariel, Rainey had heard all about Randolph's mother's slow death from lung cancer, Bertie's opinion of people who didn't train their dogs, the sad state of affairs of afternoon television, and Jefferson's first year at UVA. This last bit was shared with a great deal of pride mixed with a small amount of chagrin, because Jefferson—self-conscious about the fact that the university was founded by Thomas Jefferson—had decided to refer to himself as "Jeff" at school.

"Such foolishness," Bertie said. "*Jeff.* If I'd wanted him to be called Jeff, I'd have put that on his application for Tiny Woodlands preschool years ago, and that would've been that."

Jefferson gave Rainey an abashed grin and looked away, out the window.

Rainey listened for a sound from upstairs, knowing it was unlikely that Ariel would even leave her room while there were strangers in the house.

"Jefferson, honey," Bertie said. "Be a dear and get the bag we brought—you know the one I mean—from the car."

"Sure, Mom." He pushed his chair back under the table and nodded to Rainey before leaving the room.

As soon as they heard the door shut, Bertie grabbed Rainey's hand. Startled, Rainey instinctively resisted, but Bertie held fast.

"Cousin Rainey," she said, leaning close, so that Rainey could smell oatmeal cookie on her breath. "You can tell me the truth. Aren't you and that little girl of yours scared to death to be living here? I couldn't believe it when I heard it was you who signed a contract on the house."

"I never believed those stories," Rainey said. It was almost the truth.

"Everyone says it's the wickedest house in the county. You know that thing that happened to poor Mrs. Brodsky."

"You mean her murder?"

Bertie nodded enthusiastically. "And Mother Bliss. She didn't talk about it much until after they moved out, of course, after Michael disappeared. But after Randolph and I got married, she made me promise not to let Randolph buy the house again after she died. She made me swear. Shouldn't that be a warning? Randolph won't hardly even talk about it."

Rainey stood to clear the tea things away. "People are always making up things about old houses. I've been in enough of them to know." What she was doing here with Ariel wasn't anyone's business but her own. Still, she bit back her words. She wasn't sure what kind of influence Bertie had in the town, and while she wasn't ready to become part of the social fabric, she didn't want to become a total pariah, either.

"But the evidence! It wasn't just murder, you know. Peter Brodsky chased his poor wife through the woods and killed her with an axe. Why do you think no one has lived here in almost five years?" Bertie shook her head. "And long before that . . ." Bertie's voice trailed off and she fiddled with one of her bracelets.

Rainey stared down at her. "Go on."

For Bertie to go on would mean that she had to admit that she truly believed in . . . what? Ghosts? Evil spirits? Even Bertie couldn't bring herself to buy into the lore one hundred per cent.

"You know," Bertie said. This time, the pout of her bottom lip had disappeared. Hardened. Yet she wouldn't say it. "What Mother Bliss said."

Bertie's face—with its too-fair foundation, plump cheeks, and carnation lips—was made for gossip and ladies' luncheon chatter, not fear and frustration.

Rainey smiled and relaxed some, wondering if anyone ever took Bertie seriously. "Hundreds, maybe thousands of people have lived in or stayed at Bliss House. Have you seen how all the bedrooms have little brass plaques on their doors? They've got names like Dolly Madison and Pocahontas. I can't imagine anything bad ever happening in the Pocahontas Suite, can you?" she said. "In fact, that's where I'm sleeping myself. Ariel picked the E. A. Poe suite. I haven't the slightest idea why."

"Oh, the Brodsky people did that," Bertie said thoughtfully. "Now, Ariel. Where is she?"

She'd obviously decided not to push Rainey on the subject of the house, which Rainey thought was wise. But how long would it be before she tried again? She guessed that Bertie didn't let her politeness get in her way for any longer than she really wanted it to.

"She's only fourteen. Shy," Rainey said, playing along. "You know teenagers. I never know when or if she's going to make an appearance."

For the first six months after the accident, people whom Rainey didn't even know exhausted her with sympathy and questions about Ariel. But, finally, even Ariel's friends stopped calling the condo they'd eventually moved into, and only texted Ariel infrequently. Rainey didn't blame Ariel for being self-conscious, and she couldn't do anything to speed her grieving process. She could barely even handle her own grief, and kept telling herself that Ariel would heal in her own time.

"She'll want to meet other young people," Bertie said, regaining her bearings. "At least before school starts next month. She'll need to get in with the right children. And what *about* school? You know the choices are sadly limited here, unless you're willing to drive to Charlottesville every day."

Rainey heard a quick, polite knock on the mudroom door, which then squeaked open. Whatever other qualities Jefferson had, he had timing in spades.

"Come on in, Jeff," Rainey said, leaning out into the galley.

Jefferson smiled broadly at the sound of his nickname. He carried a large yellow gift bag with green and white ribbons fluttering from its handles.

The gifts turned out to be a giant tin of Virginia peanuts and a locally crafted pottery bowl for her, and a gray and ivory buffalo check newsboy cap for Ariel.

When Rainey saw the cap, it was her turn to bristle. What did they know about Ariel? How did they know about the hats? It bothered her.

"Jefferson picked out the little hat," Bertie said, as though reading her mind. "I wasn't sure, but he said many of the girls on campus wear them."

Jefferson nodded. "I hope she likes it."

Rainey thought he might blush, but he simply looked friendly. Confident. If he wasn't genuinely a nice kid, it was a hell of an act. She hoped he'd be a good influence on Ariel. "She'll love it," she said.

"I'm sorry, but we need to go." Bertie's bounce had returned. "I have garden club this afternoon." She stood and smoothed the eyelet top over the well-secured flesh of her belly. Rainey noticed that her sandals sported pom-pom flowers similar to the ones on her handbag.

"You didn't have to come around back, you know," Rainey said. "Let me show you out the front door." She stopped. "I'm sorry. I should've taken you on a tour. Did you want to see the house? We've got furniture being delivered left and right, but things are still a little bare."

"Oh, you know, I would," Bertie said, her eyes wide. "But I'd really like to be surprised, later, when we have more time. I read all about your business on the Internet. You're a famous decorator out there in St. Louis!"

What else had Bertie read? How much did she know about Ariel's injuries? Rainey had gotten a card from her just after Will's funeral. She'd responded with a thank-you note, but they'd never even so much as chatted on the phone before.

"It'll be a few weeks before the house is presentable. But I'll certainly have you back," Rainey said. "And Randolph, and you too, Jeff."

Jefferson preceded Bertie out the door, but Bertie hesitated. For an awkward few seconds, Rainey thought Bertie might be anticipating a hug and didn't quite know what to do.

"Not to pressure you or anything, dear," Bertie said. Her carnation mouth still wore its dainty pout. "You'll have lots of invitations. Everyone wants to meet you, though they all want to give you the space you need, of course."

"I appreciate that."

"Housewarmings are a big tradition here in Old Gate," she continued. "They're nice because no one worries if the house isn't *just so*, if you know what I mean."

Rainey's laugh was slightly nervous.

"I'd think about two weeks would be about how long a person would want to wait," Bertie said. "I mean, you wouldn't believe the number of people in town who've never set foot in Bliss House. Of course, their parents might have, years ago. There were people who came here for parties and things."

31

Two weeks?

As she shut the door behind Bertie and the very quiet Jefferson, she realized she had agreed to give a party for a number of strangers in a house in which she'd only spent a few nights. It wasn't at all what she'd imagined herself planning when she'd gotten out of bed that morning. Worse, she had no idea how Ariel would react.

Chapter 6

Gerard Powell drove his pickup carefully over the grass, well out of the way of the paving company trucks and equipment laying asphalt on the drive leading to Bliss House. He parked beside Rainey Adams's Lexus crossover near the entrance to the formal gardens on the eastern side of the house.

Getting out of the truck, he was confronted with the slow-burning stink of asphalt, which was never pleasant but was particularly nauseating in the stifling July heat. He gave a brief wave to the paving crew foreman, whom he knew slightly. The man nodded back, but didn't rush over to talk. There was no need. He was there to do the job, and if there weren't problems, there weren't any questions. Gerard hired only the best, most professional sub-contractors. His clients paid for it, sure. But he made certain they knew what they were getting when they hired him.

Early on, his extremely youthful appearance had concerned a lot of clients, but his gregarious wife, Karin, who (not coincidentally) was often also their real estate agent, gave her promise that they would be more than satisfied. Now, even though he was in his late thirties and far more successful than most of the well-padded, good old boy contractors in the area, Gerard was still narrow-hipped and slender. He kept his wiry brown hair cropped close and usually covered—to Karin's dismay—with a ball cap. If his lips were a little thin and his nose on the narrow side, they only served to emphasize the intensity of his hazel eyes. The effect disarmed most women. Men who weren't yet familiar with his reputation were usually swayed by Karin. Too swayed, sometimes.

As he ascended the broad brick and stone stairway leading to the newly-installed mahogany front door, he noticed some damage to a strip of mortar dividing a row of bricks. He ran his finger down the mortar, following a long, jagged crack. It continued around the top of one brick, widening irregularly as though someone had tried to chisel it out, loosening the brick. He made a mental note to have one of his people come over and fix it.

Gerard reached for the door handle, then stopped himself. He wasn't yet used to anyone being at home in Bliss House. He, his crew, and subs had had the run of the place for months. The access had given him a proprietary feeling about the place—not that Bliss House would ever let a single owner fully imprint herself on it. Bliss House was a house unto itself, like a person with an oversize, overwhelming personality. He wondered if Rainey Adams was up to dealing with it. He didn't know her well enough to guess, but he doubted it.

He took his hat off and rang the bell.

⌒

Rainey and Gerard sat at a card table in the Lee Suite, the rooms she'd set up as a temporary office. She was self-conscious about having Gerard in so intimate a space, but she'd wanted to get as far away from the front of the house as possible. The downstairs ceiling fans had done little to keep the stench of paving materials out of the house, and she had set out at least a dozen burning candles—vanilla, mostly—to combat the smell. One of the candles flickered between them like a table decoration in a restaurant.

Gerard slid a paper-clipped sheaf toward her, photocopies of the set in front of him.

"Here are the current change-orders," he said. "I'm guessing there will be a few more after you've been here another few weeks. We'll handle those as they come along."

Rainey looked over the list, conscious of him watching her. She'd always had a reputation for driving hard bargains with contractors. Many of her clients—if they didn't have an architect directly involved with their projects—relied on her to deal with them. Their satisfaction rested on her. As did her commissions.

Despite being put off by the high-pressure sales tactics that his wife, Karin, had tried to use on her when she was negotiating for Bliss House, she'd liked Gerard immediately on meeting him. It was a mystery to her how this quiet, outdoorsy man had settled on the charming but aggressive Karin as a soul mate. But the night she'd gone to dinner with them, just after the closing of the house sale, she'd watched Gerard's eyes follow Karin as she greeted half the patrons in the restaurant. She bestowed air kisses on the women and touched the arms or shoulders of the men with playful familiarity. Karin wasn't classically beautiful, but she dressed her well-toned body in expensive body-skimming knits and kept her glossy red curls restrained just enough to imply trustworthy respectability. She had an aggressive sensuality and smiled with abandon. But Rainey had worked with enough women like her to understand that her charm was just a veneer to make her aggression more palatable.

"The cost of the plumbing changes alone could feed a family of four for a year," Rainey said, laughing. "You probably think I'm a little crazy taking on a place this . . ." She glanced out the door to the hallway, taking in the space beyond. "I know we could've done both the house and the business in a smaller place."

Rainey watched a flicker of discomfort cross his intelligent face.

"People do things for a lot of reasons," he said, shrugging. "I didn't think it was any of my business." He paused a moment. "Karin told me the house had been in your family. It's pretty common knowledge by now. That kind of information gets around Old Gate fast."

Rainey laughed. "That's for sure."

She found herself wanting to tell him more, about how she needed something new in her life, yet at the same time something familiar. A safe kind of challenge. Something to fill the huge space Will had left behind in her life and in her heart. She had known the minute she'd walked into Bliss House that she'd found exactly what she was looking for. But she wasn't sure how much to share with Gerard. He wasn't her friend, not really. Since leaving St. Louis, she'd felt as though she'd lost her bearings when it came to dealing with people. She hated how insecure she felt. How lost. A complete break with the past and the person she'd been before was exactly what she'd wanted. Only she hadn't counted on how much work it was going to take to build a new life. New friendships. New intimacies. Her only constant, the only important link to her old self, was Ariel. And their relationship was in tatters.

Gerard went over the changes line by line. She was smart about the business, and when it came to discussing tile choices and paint qualities she was intensely focused. He wondered, though, about the dark circles beneath her eyes and how thin she was. He was used to fashionably thin women—Virginia was full of them—but Rainey Adams seemed even less healthy than when they'd met several months earlier. She'd been grieving deeply then, and had been pale, but still driven and energetic.

"About the garage and the apartment above it," he said. "I know you don't want to do anything else about the third floor yet . . ." Here, he gestured to the ceiling, indicating the rooms above them. "But the carriage house is in really bad shape. Will you be using it anytime soon?"

"No," Rainey said. "Maybe for storage. Later. For a house this size"—she waved a hand, indicating the house around her—"the storage is weirdly limited. Only that sad half-basement. There's hardly room for anything besides the boiler. And the stairs to the rooftop storage sheds are so narrow, I don't know how anyone got anything up there."

Rainey started to go on, but was interrupted by a loud noise from out in the hall. At first, Gerard wasn't sure what he heard, given the constant grind of machinery from the driveway. He saw the horrified look on Rainey's face at the same moment he realized it had been a scream that they'd heard.

Rainey upended her chair onto the floor and pushed past him, running from the room.

"Ariel! Where are you?" Her voice was pure panic.

He'd never seen the daughter, Ariel, and hadn't even been certain she was actually now living in the house. Hers had been one of the rooms whose bath they had completely redone, but it had been finished well before their move-in date. Karin had mentioned Rainey was planning to homeschool her daughter, and that it seemed odd to her because the girl was high school age.

The cry had come from one of the back hallways.

"Baby?" Rainey was ahead of him, beyond the gallery, in the hallway to the servants' quarters. She knelt at the foot of the stairway, bending over someone. He hurried to see if he could help, nearly tripping over a fuzzy lime-green hat covered with lilac peace symbols.

"Is she okay?" he asked.

There was another pained cry from the girl. Gerard saw the ends of a pair of black ankle-length leggings and two bare feet poking from behind Rainey. One of the feet looked like any young girl's foot—toenails painted a vibrant turquoise—but the other foot and ankle were a dull mass of warped scar tissue. A couple of the toes looked as though they'd fused together, and the nails weren't visible.

There was an arm, too, wrapped around Rainey's neck. The skin was almost purple in the shadows, the hand stiff and awkward as a claw. Staying well away, Gerard pulled his cell phone from his pants pocket. "I'll get the EMTs here," he said.

"It's not necessary. You should just go," Rainey said, her voice full of emotion. "Really. I'm sorry. I'll call you later."

His gut told him that he shouldn't leave.

"If she fell, then she shouldn't be moved until we make sure she's not badly hurt."

Rainey spoke quickly to her daughter in a voice too low for him to hear. He finally saw a side of the girl's head—a length of spiky black hair, a long patch of pinkish skin, a drooping eye that looked fearfully at him, then looked away.

"I'll handle it." Rainey was impatient, and working very hard to remain composed. Polite. "I'll call you."

It took every ounce of self-control he could muster to keep from going closer to see the girl. He tried to picture what she might look like as a whole person. What he'd seen of her was grim enough. Karin's confusion about home schooling was now sadly answered.

"Don't hesitate," he said. "Please."

Rainey didn't respond, but gathered the girl closer to her. Gerard turned to go, regretting the heavy tread of his boots as he returned to the suite to gather his papers. As he made his way down the main stairway, he was conscious of being watched, but Rainey and her daughter were nowhere to be seen. If he'd been a less practical and sensible sort of man, he might have convinced himself that the stars painted around the ceiling's oculus had arranged themselves into curious eyes that watched to make sure he was leaving.

Chapter 7

Ariel stared out at the gardens from the sofa in her mother's bedroom, the late afternoon sun warming her face. She rested her head against the sofa's overstuffed cushions, her bruised legs extended along its length. A mug of hot peppermint tea—her favorite—sat on the nearby table.

The garden was overgrown, and sun-burned brown. Even the boxwood maze was yellowing, starved for nourishment. She could clearly see the maze's beginning, end, and square center with its stone Hera standing on a pedestal, cradling a peacock in her arms. At the outer edge of the garden were the crumbled remains of a wall. She thought of the book *The Secret Garden* and wondered what that wall had once enclosed. Maybe it had had a door that led to someplace altogether different.

She'd never want her mother to know, but she was glad they'd moved to Virginia. She'd been glad from the moment her mother said she thought it was a good idea to get away from St. Louis. Ariel knew there was nothing there for her anymore. Her friends didn't *really* want to hang out with her—burned and hideous as she was—and she'd been grateful when their lame, pitying phone calls and texts stopped. And she certainly didn't miss the barely furnished apartment her mother had taken near the hospital. Its walls were blank and the long communal hallways were blank and it looked out on a thin stretch of trees that separated their development from another very like it. None of her things from home were there because they'd all blown up and burned with the house. No pictures of Ariel as a toddler (not that she'd ever want to see them again), no old report cards, no baby dolls her mother had stored away in the attic for her to sneak up to visit and sometimes hold, even though she was getting too old for that.

She tried not to think about those things, and almost never did, except for times like now when she was tired. She tried not to think about lying with her father in the hammock behind their house, listening to the birds and squirrels playing in the trees, as she played with his hair, as black as hers, winding the thick waves into curls around her fingers. She tried not to think about his laugh when she imitated her annoying art teacher or read him silly jokes from an issue of Reader's Digest from the subscription that one of his elderly clients sent him for Christmas every year.

Her mother had said that her father would've liked Bliss House, but Ariel wasn't so sure. It was so big, and her father had never wanted to live in a big house. Her mother had even had to talk him into moving out to St. Charles County and building the new house. Ariel heard them talking when they thought she wasn't around. It was a longer commute for him, he said, and he thought the Kirkwood house was just the size they needed for the three of them. *Cozy*, he called it. Her mother had laughed.

"I don't think I've ever heard you use the word *cozy* before."

Her father had laughed then, too.

"What if we need more room? Did you ever think of that?" Her mother's voice had dropped, and Ariel had heard nothing more.

Ariel had never asked for a brother or sister. She'd been happy with their life just the way it was. And then they had built the house and moved, and there was no brother or sister. Now there never would be.

Though she liked Bliss House from the beginning—if a person could like a house the way they liked a person—it still seemed endless and strange to her. But that didn't matter because her father was here. Somewhere.

That morning, she had decided she wanted to get a better look at the third floor, and so had gone upstairs without telling her mother.

The rooms above were different from the rows of bedrooms on the second floor. There were only four rooms up there, two of them small bedrooms, and the other two—facing each other across the open gallery of the well of the house—were larger than any of the other rooms in the house. One was laid out as a theater and contained an ornate oak proscenium stage rising two feet above the floor. The only furniture was a stack of metal folding chairs on a cart. Deep inside the stage was a child's puppet theater, a few trunks, and an old standing mirror whose surface bore rough patches the color of tin. Because the theater room was on the western side of the house and had tall windows, it promised to be stifling hot late in the day, and probably freezing in the winter. There was a fireplace, but Ariel couldn't imagine it could heat such a big room. It wasn't a friendly room. The tall windows, the cold metal chairs, the darkened stage . . . who would perform in a place like this? It didn't seem like it would be any fun.

Across the gallery, in the ballroom, the button light switch beside the door made a soft clicking noise when she pressed it. The seven or eight electric sconces came on, but their light was dim. The room didn't have a single window.

She walked barefoot over the floor (miraculously, without her cane!), feeling as though she were in another world. She stayed close to the wall, her fingers sliding lightly over the wallpaper which was covered with palanquins, pagodas, and bent, bearded men, and dainty Japanese women in robes with flowing sleeves, their heads demurely bowed beneath mere suggestions of tree branches heavy with blossoms. When she was close to the doorway, she could see that everything was drawn in black or gold on a field of red, the gold glittering as though it were real. The women's faces were similar though not identical to one another, and their robes varied in design. Each old man was exactly the same, and wore a round cap and carried an elaborate snake-headed cane.

Seeing the canes caused a twinge inside Ariel, and she raised her unblemished hand to the ruined side of her face. She had much more in common with the old men than she did the beautifully dressed, perfectly-formed women. Only lately, she'd begun to feel better. Much better, physically and emotionally. It was as though the house had some power to heal her, a healing that had begun when her father—or his ghost, or her dream of him, still her father!—had touched her. That such a thing was technically impossible made no difference at all to her. The doctors and therapists had all made such a big deal about her healing being *her journey*. Her journey had taken a turn for the strange, but she didn't care. She felt better, and that was what was important to her.

The ballroom's ceiling was slightly lower than in the other rooms in the house and directly in the center of it there were two thick metal rings. The metal was dull, and looked as old as everything else on the third floor. Her mother suggested that they might have held chains for a cradle or a swing, but Ariel didn't have a good feeling when she looked at them.

The fireplace mantel was almost a foot higher than her shoulder, and when she bent to look inside, she could smell the faintest odor of ash and woodsmoke. *When could there have last been a fire here?* She touched one of the tall metal panels that reached as high as the underside of the mantel and stood like guardians on either side of the opening. Both were covered with bursts of pom-pom flowers in relief. Chrysanthemums.

Tired from exploring, Ariel went back to the center of the room and eased herself to the floor to sit. She'd been doing so well without her cane that she'd left it down in her bedroom. But now it occurred to her that she might have trouble standing again without it.

Stretching out, she rested her ruined cheek against the floor. The bare wood felt cool and soothing on her skin. The door was open, but she was utterly alone in the quiet room. Even the sounds of the driveway construction in front of the house had faded away. It felt like some kind of blessing, this aloneness. Maybe she could just stay up here, and never go downstairs again.

Downstairs, her mother was busy making more plans for the house and her business. Ariel didn't like the idea of living in a place where strangers could show up at any time, wanting to buy things, or have meetings to make plans, or complain. Their house in St. Louis hadn't been like that. Her parents had had parties, and her mother had stored things for her clients and made phone calls down in her basement office, but she'd also had the shop in town. Their house was always their home. Ariel was tired of how hard her mother was trying to make their lives different.

It had only been a few weeks, but already Missouri was fading in her memory. Occasionally one of her friends—*former* friends, that is—texted her, but she never answered. By now they all probably thought she'd changed her number or had forgotten about them, and that was fine with her. She was a freak, and freaks didn't have friends. It didn't matter what the stupid therapists or her mother said.

Ariel sighed and closed her eyes. One thing she did miss was touching and being touched by her mother. Her mother's touch hurt her now, as though the burns on her body had never healed. As though she hadn't had a single skin graft. It was like the burns had seared deep into her bones, bruising them forever.

"Daddy," she whispered. "I want to go home."

It had been more than a week since he'd come to sit beside her bed. The memory of that night was fading, and she felt like she was losing him all over again.

As she lay there, the hurt of missing him causing a deep, real pain somewhere in the area of her heart. The room filled with a low rumbling, not so different in tone from the machines outside, and the floor vibrated beneath her. The sound rose slowly, slowly, as though coming from very far away. When she heard footsteps pounding across the floor, she tensed, afraid. Something, someone, hit her leg, then bounced away. She thought of gym class, boys wrestling and fighting.

The light in the room hadn't changed, and there was enough light to see that she was still alone.

"Daddy?" She sat up. The room was freezing cold.

The sounds stopped for a moment, and she heard whispering near her good ear. *Kids*, she thought. She couldn't make out what they were saying, but the room seemed to be filled with them.

Something poked her—hard—in the side.

Maybe a finger, maybe a stick.

Please let it be my imagination.

She rolled onto her hands and knees to get up. She was cold, but the air in the room was motionless, as thick as swimming pool water.

Another poke, this time on her thigh. And another. Harder. More insistent, like someone was trying to provoke her.

Ariel finally got to her feet. Panicking, she flung out her arm at whatever—whoever—might be there. *Nothing.*

She ran for the door, but before she could get out, she felt a painful jab at her chest, just below her collarbone. Something was trying to force her back into the room. Her body was weak from the surgeries and lack of exercise, but she fought back, and kept moving ahead.

Behind her there was the sound of another scuffle, and more thumping on the floor. A hand—surely it was a hand!—pressed firmly between her shoulder blades, pushing her toward the door. The air coming from the hallway was warm and she couldn't wait to be warm again.

I'm going. I'm going. Please let me go!

The push hadn't quite been a shove, but it wasn't gentle.

Free of the room, she hurried to the nearest stairway and a narrow window with its strip of fragile blue sky facing it. The sounds behind her folded back into the distance with every step she took, though there was a kind of static hum in her ears that wouldn't quit.

Reaching for the railing, she grabbed it with her good hand, almost laughing with relief. As she took the first step down to the second floor, something—a hand, or maybe a rope or a snake of some kind—wrapped itself all the way around her ankle and pulled.

Finally she'd screamed, bringing her mother and the contractor running to find her.

⌒

Her mother had been coming by the bedroom every twenty minutes. This time she was carrying a tray. Ariel smelled chicken noodle soup, and her mouth began to water.

"Do you feel like you could eat?" Rainey set the tray down on the table in front of the couch. Beyond the table, a cable cartoon channel on the television burbled constant, mindless chatter at low volume, reminding Ariel of the voices from the ballroom. It wasn't an unpleasant sound, but the similarity sent a ripple of tension up the back of her neck.

"I don't want the TV on anymore," she said, turning her face to the window.

"Sure, honey." Rainey pressed the power button, and the room was quiet.

⌒

Ariel hadn't said what she'd been doing up on the third floor, and Rainey didn't want to ask. She watched the sunlight play over her daughter's hair, picking up some of the brown highlights in the black.

When she'd found Ariel lying on the landing, she'd felt like her heart was going to tear from her chest. If Ariel had died too . . . Rainey shook her head to get rid of the thought.

"What?" Ariel said.

"Turn this way." As Rainey reached out to touch her daughter's face, Ariel predictably pulled away, her eyes filling with suspicion.

"Please, Ariel. I'm your mother, for God's sake. I won't hurt you." It was one of those rare moments when she remembered that Ariel was only fourteen years old and still in need of serious parenting.

The sharp note in her mother's voice startled Ariel and threw her back into the past:

Get your coat, Ariel. You're going to be late for school!

Ariel, please turn off the light and the radio when you leave your bedroom—or are you planning to pay the electric bill yourself next month?

Ariel, honey, move your milk away from the edge of the table before you knock it off.

Ariel relaxed her shoulders, making her seem slightly less defensive. "What are you doing?"

"Just looking." Rainey took Ariel's scarred chin in her hand. Maybe it wasn't so scarred. It had lost some of its leathery appearance, and the scar tissue was almost transparent instead of an angry red. The damaged area seemed less significant as well, as though it had receded a bit.

The burns had been so significant that the skin grafts hadn't made the difference Rainey had hoped for. They'd come to Virginia after Ariel had healed from the last round of operations, when the doctors said Ariel had needed a break from the surgeries. Even as they suggested that further healing would be limited, the doctors had encouraged her to start living her life again.

Ariel's running from her life the same way I'm running from mine.

"I think Virginia agrees with you," Rainey said, brightening. "I think that's a good thing, don't you?"

Ariel shrugged.

"I guess so," she said. But she turned away from Rainey because she thought she might laugh or smile. Give herself away. *Give her father away.*

Chapter 8

Bliss House glowed. The paneled walls of the central hall wore a gloss of candlelight, and there were flowers everywhere. Rainey had brought in armfuls of tiger lilies from one of the ponds on the property and arranged them with lavender and eucalyptus for the hall and salon. Gracious mounds of hydrangeas filled the dining room. In the midst of the scents of flowers and food and wine, and the sound of a hired pianist playing their new grand piano playing in the salon, the big house seemed to sigh with pleasure. *This* was what it had been born for. *This* was what it had missed for so long. Rainey was certain that Bliss House wasn't meant to be lonely, though she'd thought she needed to be alone here. Maybe she'd been wrong. Having people around her again made her happy.

Every so often she looked up to see if Ariel was watching from the second floor gallery. Back in Missouri, a much younger Ariel would've drifted among the guests, the center of attention, perhaps doing a ballet turn for one of the admiring old ladies.

Getting the bartender and two servers up and running had kept her busy right up to the minute that Bertie arrived—early, as promised—closely followed by Randolph, her husband (whom everyone called the Judge, as though he were a character in an old western), and Jefferson. Both father and son wore dark suits, but only the judge looked at ease. Jefferson had given her a wry, amused smile, as though he wanted to say, *I know these people with me are crazy, but I can't get away from them!*

Resplendent was the only word for Bertie, who was dressed in gold-flecked, blue and green harem pants, sandals shaped mostly from gold links and disks that jingled when she walked, and a diaphanous tunic of pale blue that did little to minimize her generous bosom.

Randolph had greeted Rainey—whom he hadn't seen in almost thirty years—with a cool, firm handshake. His surprisingly dark, lively eyes took Rainey in approvingly.

"You wore a green sundress, and you'd just gotten over the chicken pox," he said. He turned to Bertie. "She was lovely even then, Roberta. Only as big as a minute."

"You tossed me into the pool," Rainey said, laughing. He was in his fifties now, almost twenty years older than she, and she remembered being intimidated by his height and roughhousing nature. There had been a sense of mystery about that visit, too. While they were there, she had wondered about Randolph's older brother, Michael, whom her mother had told her about. He'd disappeared many years earlier while he was getting his art degree at nearby UVA, so she'd never had the chance to meet him. When she got older, her mother told her that Michael had been into drugs and had left a note behind saying he was tired of meeting his family's "ridiculous expectations." But Rainey had only been eight years old when they visited, and no one but her mother mentioned him to her.

Why hadn't she put it together that Randolph was probably at least ten years older than Bertie? His hair was ice-gray and neatly trimmed, and his body was still athletic, though not particularly muscular. Rainey saw the familiar in him: his towering height, and the prominent Bliss nose and rounded chin of her maternal grandfather. Seeing Randolph's face, she was plunged back into her childhood and the happy hours she'd spent at her grandfather's side, watching him work on his stamp collection or following him through the St. Louis Art Museum as he taught her about paintings and history. His words had set her on the path to design. She didn't know Randolph well at all, but the resemblance alone was enough to make her like him all over again.

"I promised Rainey I wouldn't let her hire anyone but the best bartender, but you know Douglas needs warming up before the party really gets started," Bertie said. "Would you pretty please ask him to make me an apple martini?" She stood on tiptoe to kiss Randolph's cheek.

"Anything for you, Cousin Rainey?" Randolph said. "I remember you were very fond of lemonade, but maybe you're an apple martini fan, too?

Rainey laughed. "Scotch for me. But maybe in a little while, thanks."

He smiled and headed for the bar.

Guests moved easily through the dining room where the light buffet was set, and the downstairs salon, and the central hall where she'd put the bartender. It was a genial crowd.

Bertie had made sure Rainey invited everyone she considered proper Old Gate society, including members of the Chamber of Commerce and most of the Old Gate Historical Society. There was Bertie's garden club, too.

One of the garden club women cornered Rainey near the buffet saying, "We would just love to get our hands on your formal gardens." Rainey could hardly believe this golden-curled beauty with her French-manicured nails and honeyed voice had ever so much as repotted a begonia. "My mother talks all the time about how charming they used to be. Before the—well, you know. The Brodsky people." She seemed flustered by her own mention of the Brodskys, and took a nervous sip from her glass of chardonnay.

Was everyone in Old Gate afraid to talk about the poor Brodskys? At least Karin Powell hadn't been so disingenuous.

"Maybe you have some old photographs?" Rainey changed the subject for the woman's comfort.

"Oh, you know, Mother just might. I'll make a note to ask her." She smiled broadly, obviously relieved. "It's just so nice to see that you're taking care of the house. It's such a piece of history."

"I get the feeling that history is important around here," Rainey said. Ethan Fauquier, the amateur historian who owned Fauquier's Books in town, had already done his best to impress her with his knowledge of local history. He had promised to tell her more about Bliss House, as well.

"Important?" The woman looked stunned. "If we don't protect it, it will just be lost forever by people who don't care."

Rainey wondered how upset people would be when she turned the house into a more complete showcase for her business. She'd already gotten a sense of where the Brodskys, lowly innkeepers, had fallen on the Old Gate social map.

"You're a Bliss, honey," Bertie had told her. "You're nothing like those horrid motel people."

What would Will have made of the party? He'd been Midwestern through and through: no BS, no subterfuge or ancient historical agendas. Rainey had been raised to be alert to the deep concerns of the people around her. She knew there was much more going on in this very room than anyone was saying.

Bertie introduced her to Nick Cunetta, a local lawyer who had been in solemn conversation with another man, a professor named Henrik, down from UVA. A twenty-something young woman, Martina, was the third member of the group. She announced to

Rainey that she was studying in the archeology department at UVA and gave Rainey a challenging look, as though Rainey might not believe her.

Nick Cunetta put his arm around Bertie's shoulders, causing her to giggle and the girl, Martina, to curl her matte-stained lips into a hint of a smile.

"Ah, my Bertie." Nick pulled Bertie close and nipped her ear with mock salaciousness.

A little rough, Rainey thought. Glancing around for Randolph to see if he was watching, she saw him near the bar with Karin and Gerard Powell. Karin's hand—nails tipped in a luscious bronze manicure—rested on her husband's arm. She leaned slightly forward, laughing, her cleavage displayed as though it were on the evening's menu. Rainey had tried hard to like her, but settled for cordiality. That Karin was a good businesswoman was all that mattered. But it hadn't hurt that she'd gotten Gerard's services as well. How they'd ever become a couple, she still didn't understand.

Rainey turned back to look at Nick. Surely he wasn't being anything but familiar and friendly with Bertie.

How does anyone take him seriously?

As elegant as his black silk polo shirt, sports coat, and grey pants were, he wore his shiny black loafers without socks. Will would've taken in his dark tan, glossy black curly hair (not so different from Will's own), careless manner (*very* different from his own), and heady gin and tonic, and pronounced Nick Cunetta *louche*. She could almost hear Will whisper in her ear: *Ten to one he's personal injury.*

Thus far she hadn't met a single man for whom she felt the slightest attraction, and definitely wasn't to the point where she was thinking about another relationship. God knew she still thought about Will every day, and even felt closer to him here than she had in the months after the accident. But it was Ariel who took most of her concentration.

"Nicholas, you're shameful," Bertie said, playfully pushing him away. "What would the Judge say? And in front of Rainey, too. She hardly knows you."

"I think that the judge would say . . ." Here, Nick lowered his voice an octave and attempted to mimic Randolph's distinguished drawl. "You're a fine, fine woman, Roberta Bliss, but you're just too fine, just too much woman for one man."

Everyone laughed, perhaps pretending his words had nothing to do with Bertie's plump, soft figure. Bertie laughed along, though Rainey saw a shadow in her eyes. Bertie—for all her chatter and occasional pretense of confusion—wasn't stupid.

Rainey couldn't stand to see Bertie hurt. Bertie was kindness itself. She put a hand on Bertie's arm.

"Bertie's my consultant for all things festive," she said to the little group. "I think one of the women in the kitchen has wandered off, Bertie. I'm hoping she hasn't taken the silver."

"Oh, but she's very good," Bertie said. "She's probably just outside smoking. Nasty habit."

Was it Rainey's imagination, or had she looked pointedly at Nick, whom Rainey had seen smoking a half hour earlier on the dining room patio? She hoped so.

"If you're worried, we'll find her," Bertie said, leading Rainey away.

But in the kitchen they found that nothing at all was amiss, and Bertie looked momentarily confused. The catering woman was right where she was supposed to be.

Chapter 9

There was a part of Ariel that wanted to go back into the ballroom, despite what had happened to her. She had stayed away almost two whole weeks, and what better time to do it than when the house was full of people. *Safety in numbers*, she'd always heard. Would they experience anything strange? Probably not. Everyone would think she was crazy. *Poor little crazy deformed girl.* She hadn't even told her mother exactly what happened on that awful morning.

What was her mother saying about her to the people downstairs? They had to be curious.

The music from the salon drifted up to her, mingling with the conversation and the clinking of glasses. Chopin. Her mother loved Chopin.

Her mother had come upstairs to bring her a plate of party food before the guests arrived. The halter dress she wore was such a pale, lovely green that it might have been fashioned for one of the flower fairies in the framed illustrations on Ariel's bedroom wall. She was wearing lipstick and eye shadow and smelled of the Chanel No.5 that Ariel's father had put under the Christmas tree every year.

Now, as Ariel watched her mother from the gallery balcony, laughing and going from guest to guest, she wanted to ask her why she was trying to look so pretty. Why did she want to smell so good? Was she hoping that some other man would love her?

Ariel pushed away the thought. She had always loved her mother's parties. Everyone was always so happy.

Are you watching, Daddy? Doesn't Mommy look pretty?

She fingered the fragile edges of the silk robe she'd found hanging in one of the third floor bedroom closets the week before. It was a creamy beige color and covered with lucious white peonies whose petals were edged in a pink so dark that it was almost red. The robe hung loosely on her, and when she sat down, she felt like she was sitting in a puddle of silk. Tonight, she'd taken off her clothes to put it on, and it felt as soft as water against her skin.

Where are you, Daddy?

At a sound from the other side of the gallery, Ariel scooted on her bottom into the shadows behind her. Someone was at the entrance of the ballroom, his back to her, his hands positioned to push the pocket doors aside. There was no way she was fast enough to move out of sight if he looked over his shoulder. She pulled the robe closer.

Why would he want to go in there? Is he lost?

He turned around, but didn't seem to see her at first. He wasn't very old—in fact, he looked only a few years older than she was—and she had the feeling she'd seen him before. He took a drink from the beer bottle in his hand and walked over to the railing to look down.

"Nice party," he said. The dome above them carried his voice to her so clearly that he might have been standing beside her.

Is he talking to me? Ariel reddened as though she'd been caught doing something wrong.

"I hated parties like this when I was a kid," he said. "Is that why you didn't come down? Do you hate them, too?"

"Why do you want to go in there?" Ariel asked.

"I've been in every room in this house," he said.

Now she recognized him. She'd seen him out the window with his mother, Bertie. They were cousins of some kind. *Jefferson.*

"Can I come over there? It's an okay party, but it's kind of boring."

"You shouldn't be up here."

Instead of heeding her, he started around the gallery. With every step he took, Ariel felt the knot in her stomach tighten.

"Hey, I brought you a hat. Did your mom give it to you? I got it up by school. You should come up to UVA and look around some-time. Everyone who's a Bliss goes there." He paused a moment, his brow furrowing. "Only I guess your mom didn't."

"Don't!" she said. "Go back downstairs."

"Don't freak out. I'm not going to hurt you."

That was how everyone approached her now, like she was some kind of helpless child, or a scared animal.

For the briefest of seconds it occurred to Ariel that maybe he wasn't real, that maybe something horrible had happened to the real Jefferson and this was only his shadow. She hadn't seen him come up the stairs. Again, she pressed herself against the wall.

The chandelier hung below them so that its light cast shadows over his face.

She could hear the Chopin less clearly now.

"I don't understand," Jefferson said. "What's wrong?"

"Go away!" Ariel was panicked. *Should I scream?*

He was close enough that she could see the label on his beer. It was the same kind her father drank when they had barbecues at the house. He had liked to drink a beer as he floated on a lounge in the pool, and the summer before he died, she had swum beneath him and turned the thing over. His beer bottle had bobbed away to the deep end, but her father had just laughed and playfully dunked her in response.

Where are you, Daddy?

Jefferson squatted beside her. The way he had come right over to her, she had expected him to have a crazy look in his eyes. But his eyes weren't threatening at all. They were nice eyes. Now that he was so close, she felt suddenly self-conscious. She turned her face away.

"Hey, it's okay." He touched her shoulder. His voice was low and gentle. "I know all about the house," he said. "I know about you."

Chapter 10

Walking from room to room with a tray, Rainey picked up the few things the caterers had missed, and shut off lights.

All evening there had been people—people she didn't know—coming in and out of the house, laughing and drinking. The women in gauzy summer dresses, many of the men in navy or seersucker blazers, like something out of a Fitzgerald novel. In memory, their faces were a blur, but she hoped that when she had some time to reflect she would remember them all. Their future here depended on it.

The party had gone well until just before ten when she'd gone into the dining room to discover a few remaining guests pretending not to listen to Karin and Gerard having a voluble argument out on the patio. She casually shepherded them out into the hall under the lame pretense of showing them the grandfather clock she had restored. Eventually Karin came back inside alone, got another drink, and entered the salon, all smiles. Within moments, she had launched into a story about an Art Deco swimming pool rumored to be buried in the woods beyond the crumbled garden wall, and was imploring Rainey to resurrect it. Gerard never returned to the party, and Karin went on with her evening as though he didn't exist.

Seeing Karin's controlled, rather triumphant manner, Rainey suddenly decided that, whatever the fight had been about, Gerard had probably been in the right. She sensed something icy and untrustworthy at Karin's core.

Now, Rainey found an abandoned shoe beneath a dining room chair: a woman's high-heeled gold sandal that certainly hadn't come in on the foot of someone wearing khakis and a navy blazer. She wondered if it belonged to Martina, who had come with the professor of something-something. The professor hadn't been bad-looking, with his gray ponytail and intense blue eyes. But they'd been a little too intense, a little too sympathetic when he'd asked her how she'd been doing since losing her husband.

Lost, as though Will just wandered off or I left him at the grocery store.

She'd been grateful when his attention had turned back to Martina, in her flirty smock dress and—no—Martina had been wearing expensive, scuffed red cowboy boots. The shoe had to belong to someone else. She set it on the sideboard, unsure what to do with it. Also, she wondered, who loses just one shoe at a cocktail party and doesn't notice?

Starting for the kitchen, she stopped to inspect the few inches of layered wallpaper that—just that evening—Karin had shown her was lifting from the wall.

"You'll want to glue that back down," she said as though Rainey, a decorator, knew nothing at all about things like wallpaper. "It will just keep peeling if you don't." By that time, Rainey had noticed a precise, controlled edge to Karin's words. Some people's speech got messy when they drank too much, but others' got more careful. And Karin's wineglass had been refilled several times.

The peeling wallpaper was a grand textured design of leafy bamboo that must have complemented the British Colonial furniture that someone told her the Brodskys were fond of. Beneath it were the fine barbs of a lushly painted peacock feather. The brilliant gold and blue surrounding the dark iris of the feather's eye was as vivid in the mellow evening light as it had surely been the day it was painted. Setting the tray beside the errant shoe, Rainey peeled another couple of inches away. At the edge of the feather was a field of iridescent blue. Perhaps a midnight sky? The Victorians and Edwardians had been fond of mystical touches like peacocks and feathers of all sorts. On first walking into the house she'd felt the absence of the clutter that must have filled it when it was first built. But she wasn't fond of clutter herself. She hadn't yet bought everything she planned to acquire, but had managed a few good paintings and ceramics. There was time. Plenty of time to make the house hers.

"What's that?"

Rainey jumped. Ariel stood beside her wearing a voluminous silk bathrobe that Rainey had never seen before. Her hair was wet and lightly-curled from the shower.

"Where did you get that robe?"

"I asked you first," Ariel said. She leaned forward to touch the torn wallpaper. "Weird."

With her daughter so close, Rainey could smell the watermelon-scented shampoo she always used, but something else as well. Something floral. Tuberose? No. Sweeter. It was peony. Like the flowers on the robe. Rainey recoiled.

"It's something Karin Powell showed me," she said. "I wish you had come down to the party for a little while."

Ariel scoffed. "No, you don't. Not really." As she turned away, Rainey had a glimpse of how she might look as a woman. Dignified. Hardened. But perhaps it had been the grown-up bathrobe that had put the strange image in her mind.

Rainey let Ariel's snotty comment slide. Forgetting about the shoe, she picked up the tray and followed her daughter across the empty front hall that, just twenty minutes earlier, had echoed with laughter.

"I'm hungry. Is there any food left?"

"Ariel, where did you get the robe? Please tell me."

"Found it in a closet." Ariel ran one hand over a sleeve. "It's pretty."

Rainey had a fondness for vintage clothes, and the robe, while in good shape, looked to be at least thirty or forty years old. How long had it hung in the house? In what room had Ariel found it? Rainey didn't remember seeing a robe in any of the closets. But, truthfully, she hadn't checked the house's dozens of closets carefully. Ariel had obviously been exploring without her again, which wasn't necessarily a bad thing, despite the fall down the stairs. Still, she couldn't help but wonder who had owned the robe. Someone much older than Ariel, obviously. It was a woman's robe. A woman with a taste for expensive things.

"Honey, I know you're hungry, but would you double-check the salon for glasses first?" This elicited a very teenage-like sigh from Ariel, who swept the hem of the robe around her with a dramatic flourish as she limped off—again, without her cane.

It was Rainey's turn to smile. Even this slight change in Ariel's attitude was welcome. Given that her daughter hadn't left Bliss House since they'd arrived, it followed that Bliss House was somehow good for her. Maybe soon she'd even feel secure enough to venture out a bit more.

After the last of the party detritus was cleaned up, Ariel sat on a stool at the galley's counter, a stack of leftover miniature salmon, chèvre, and cucumber sandwiches in front of her. Rainey thought to sit on the other stool, but changed her mind. It was enough that Ariel was willing to sit in the same room with her for more than five minutes. She contented herself with fixing Ariel a cup of herbal tea, then unloading the few serving pieces and silverware belonging to her that the caterers had run through the dishwasher. As she worked, she told Ariel about the party, and the way Bertie had interrupted her every time she tried to talk, and about the funny harem pants she'd worn, and how embarrassed her son, Jefferson, had looked when they arrived. Ariel even laughed once or twice, a guileless, childish laugh. It was almost like the worst parts of their past had never happened.

Chapter 11

Gerard sat in his truck, parked halfway up the drive leading to Bliss House. He was smoking his third cigarette of the night from the weeks-old box of Marlboros he kept in the glove box. Both he and Karin liked to have a cigarette or two when they'd had a few drinks. It was one of their secrets. He'd switched the radio off and rolled the window down. A bright symphony of crickets flooded in, drowning out every other nighttime sound but that of two barred owls calling to one another in the woods.

Bliss House sat ahead of him, its windows blank with moonlight.

He twisted his wedding ring around his finger, unused to wearing it. Most of the time he left it in the tray on his dresser because anyone who insisted on wearing a wedding ring on a construction job risked losing a finger. But Karin liked him to wear it when they were out together, even though she herself hadn't been able to remain faithful to him for more than a few months at a time during the fourteen years they'd been married.

Had he finally stopped loving her? This feeling—or this absence of feeling—was new to him. He'd accepted her as she was, sex addiction and all, and endured the judgment of people who thought they knew better how they should live their lives. After all, their relationship on the business end of things had made them quite rich. But tonight, when he saw her with a drink in her hand, and later another, he decided she'd bullshitted him for the last time.

If I don't love her, why in the hell am I here?

He got out of the truck, shutting the door quietly behind him so that the latch made only a half-hearted clicking sound. He finished the cigarette and smashed the glowing butt beneath his heel.

Ahead, Bliss House looked solid and satisfied, but lonesome and empty of life.

Not so lonesome.

There was a single car—Karin's Cadillac convertible—parked beneath the trees, in the shadows of the driveway, about twenty yards from the front steps.

Chapter 12

The roses in the vase had dried, their petals dropping to the tabletop when Allison touched them. So she didn't touch them anymore.

She'd given up trying to remember what was day and what was night. It didn't matter here in this place of no time. For the first little while, she'd worried that the room would become a place of no air, as well. When she'd seen that there was no window behind the curtain, she had panicked beyond all reason and begun to hyperventilate, which landed her on the floor, slumped against the bed. How long she was passed out, she didn't know. It might have been seconds, or hours. But it didn't matter. She woke to the same stillness, the same anonymous walls and gritty slate floor.

If anyone had asked her before she was kidnapped how she might act, she would've said she would spend all her time trying to think of ways to get free. But it hadn't been that way at all. She was bored. Mind-numbingly bored. She'd counted the animals on the curtain (87 deer, 52 horses, 35 small dogs) several times until she felt that she finally got it right. Half or partial creatures didn't count. Only whole ones. You couldn't count half of a horse or the hindquarters of a leaping deer as creatures. She'd washed her sundress in the sink countless times, using the bar of Ivory soap that Michael insisted she use to wash herself, then wrapped herself in the bed sheet for comfort, and wished for underwear. She'd made herself remember all the words to all the songs they'd sung in her high school chorus, singing—in her own thin and wavering voice—the solos she had never gotten.

She waited. Waited for Michael's return. Waited for him to decide to let her out. Waited for someone to come looking for her.

She hadn't told anyone—not even her mother—anything about Michael. Not even his name. The first night he'd spent with her, she'd checked his pockets while he slept. All she'd found was a fold of cash, his car keys (no house key), and a second, empty vial that had once held some coke. He was mysterious and good-looking. It had seemed like such an adventure!

Michael, who always had cash. Michael, who always had coke. Michael, who always told her how pretty, how smart she was. Michael, with his vague promises about the future, and the things they would do together.

"Have you ever been to London?" he'd asked. He'd brought a book about the Tower of London to her apartment, with pictures of the crown jewels and armor and the other treasures displayed there. There were pictures too of the cells where criminals, queens and nobles and even children, were held prisoner. It looked like a place where frightening fairy tales might come to life. The thought of traveling with him had thrilled her, and she'd imagined they might get married and honeymoon in London, and maybe see Ireland, too, where her mother said her father's family was from. There would be girls like her there, girls with unruly red hair and brown eyes and fair skin that had to be protected from the sun. And Michael would take care of her, and give her nice things.

Now, she realized that those dreams had only seemed possible because of the coke, which had made her stupidly optimistic. The certainty that the coke would always be there, and Michael would always make her happy, had betrayed her. Everything he'd said, everything he'd done, had been calculated to win her trust.

She was the princess locked in the castle. Except that her shit smelled up the room from beneath the lid on the bucket. Though she could hardly smell it anymore because she was getting used to it. There was less, though, than there had been before because she didn't feel like eating much. He was still bringing her food: bread and peanut butter (she had to spread it with a plastic spoon), peaches and bananas, candy and soda. Like she was a fourth grader on a school field trip. Not even the pot he brought her made her hungry—not like it had before she'd been locked up.

For a while she'd tried to stay away from it, to keep herself alert. Then Michael had shown up and started their time together (his words) by pulling her to him more roughly than usual. When he tried to kiss her, she resisted. (Of course she had resisted! She still had her dignity then.) So he had punched her in the jaw. Neatly. Quickly. Confidently. What did it matter to him if she was hurt? It only made things easier for him.

She soon understood that he liked it when she didn't cooperate.

He did everything confidently now. Gone was the sometimes-shy guy. Gone was the considerate gentleman. Gone was the man who might have taken care of her.

⁓

She couldn't remember making a plan. She just acted, and it cost her a broken collarbone.

When she heard him unlocking the door, she'd hidden under the bed.

"Allison, you're being silly," he said when he didn't see her. "Come out."

He rustled a paper bag, like he was trying to get the attention of a child, or an animal.

Pressing her cheek to the floor, she could see the door was closed behind him.

There were often noises outside that door. Footsteps. Slow footsteps, like a guard walking back and forth. Once, she'd woken to a woman's laughter and she'd run to the door to pound on it, and tried to rattle the ancient doorknob that would never move for her, no matter how she tried, no matter what she hit it with. When she got no answer, and was exhausted with calling for help, she found that the laughter had been replaced with something far more distressing: heavy, regular breathing, like a giant was sitting just outside. It wasn't a human noise, but animal, and the sound of it had driven her back, away from the door, and she had climbed onto the bed and made herself as small as possible until—with a bristling, sweeping sound—it moved away.

Now, Michael was pacing like that unseen creature. She could see his feet in their fine brown leather boots. Boots she had admired so much until she'd found herself in that room. Until she had felt the broad toe of that boot kick her in the left side only a day (three days? a week?) before.

When he stopped pacing, he addressed her again: "It's on the table. Make it last. You'll need it."

He opened the door.

She moved faster than she'd ever thought she could, launching herself across the gritty-smooth floor to grab him—mid-step—by the ankles. It didn't work exactly as she thought it would, but she got him off-balance so that he stumbled against the door, shutting it. As he fell forward, his body twisted, and he cried out.

Allison, barefoot, climbed onto his back and stood on his shoulder.

Please, God! Let the door open!

But Michael's prone body blocked it, and as much as she pulled, she couldn't get the thing open.

"You cunt!"

Michael bucked beneath her, unhurt. She'd surprised him, but that was all. But when he started up from the floor, she was able to pull on the doorknob. Three inches! Four!

Please, God! Thank you, God!

With one bare foot braced against her captor's leg, Allison got her hand through the door. Her forearm. It was working! Outside the door, the air was cool. Drafty. She would be in her own little apartment soon. No. She would go straight to her mother's house. Never mind the silly, noisy boys. How much did she want to be with her mother and never leave her again? She would be happy to share her. She'd been a fool to move out in the first place.

Then Michael rolled onto his side, and she almost fell. But she righted herself quickly—God was with her!—and had her shoulder through the doorway.

In the hallway, she saw another larger, heavier-looking door she would have to get through. *No! It can't be!* The enormity of the information came over her just as Michael slammed this door against her. Crushing her. She heard a "crack," and wondered for a curious second where it had come from.

After she fell, he pulled her inside the door again. When the door clicked shut, she felt something inside her shut as well. As he kicked her repeatedly, she retreated into that shut and shuttered place and watched from its dark, safe interior.

Chapter 13

At first, Ariel thought it was her father who awakened her. She lay, eyes wide open, listening hard. Outside the window, the sounds were the ones she heard every clear night: trucks on the distant highway, the crickets in the grass that told her summer was hurrying to a close.

"It's like they're saying goodbye," she remembered once telling her father as they sat together on their darkened patio.

This sound was inside the house. Not rhythmic, but insistent. Someone running. Voices, but not happy ones.

I won't be afraid.

Her father had said he would be there, watching over her. She pushed back the light cotton blanket and slipped into the robe that smelled like flowers. The top of it clung to her body, while the skirt floated behind her, making her feel graceful. *Graceful.* Why hadn't her mother said anything about how much better she was walking? First the cane had gone, and now she had almost no pain at all.

She stepped out into the hallway and looked up to where she thought the sounds had come from. Moonlight filtered through the clerestory windows around the base of the dome, tracing shadows everywhere. Maybe there were people from the party who had stayed behind, hiding upstairs. The idea filled her with a strange mixture of fear and delight just as Jefferson's sudden appearance upstairs had. Could it be him?

The footsteps stopped.

"Jefferson?" Ariel whispered. Her voice was small, but sounded loud to her own ears in the vastness of the hall.

But what if I'm afraid?

Across the gallery, she saw the faint glow of a nightlight beneath her mother's door, and she had an urge to run to her mother's room and climb in bed with her, as she had when she was a very little girl. Back then, her father was always there, his comforting, solid presence balancing her mother's warmth.

She had two choices: to run and hide in her mother's room, or to go upstairs alone. She pushed the thought of the ballroom out of her head. These noises were different. Definitely not children.

Someone else was whispering. She strained to make out the words.

Moving quietly down the hall to the staircase to the third floor, she listened. Someone was moving around up above her. Jefferson hadn't admitted to being in the ballroom, and now she regretted not making him confess. He'd asked for her phone number so that they could text one another. She'd thought at the time he was just being nice. But if he was here, in the night, that was a different matter.

Is he looking for me?

When she put a foot on the staircase, it creaked. She wished she'd brought the flashlight her mother had put in her room for emergencies, but knew if she went back for it, whatever was upstairs might be gone when she returned.

Glancing back out to the gallery, Ariel caught a flash. She hurried back to the railing.

The shimmer came from the third floor, and for a moment she thought it might be a flag of some sort, or a swath of fabric. It shone, but was almost transparent as it quickly took the form of a young woman.

She was older than Ariel, maybe about Jefferson's age, and so thin that her mane of red hair overwhelmed her body. The loose, pale garment she wore looked familiar to Ariel, but she couldn't see it quite clearly. That she was barefoot comforted Ariel somehow. It seemed so normal. Maybe it was someone from the party who had been too drunk to drive home.

The shimmer around the girl didn't reach very far into the darkness, but Ariel could hear men's voices coming from somewhere upstairs. She could tell by the attitude of the girl's body that those voices were making her afraid.

If they're real. If they're not a dream.

The girl leaned back against the railing, a sleeve of her robe— *yes, it's a robe. . . .* the *robe*—hanging over it like a curtain. Ariel could hardly process what she was seeing. It was happening fast, but she couldn't look away. In a blink, the girl had climbed up to sit on top of the railing.

The house was so quiet that Ariel could hear the ticking of the clock down in the hall. Her heart pounded. She thought of those seconds just before her father died, the leaden hush that had surrounded them. Like the universe holding its breath.

Slowly, so slowly, the girl leaned back into the air.

The robe floated like a rain-laden cloud around the girl, and moonlight glanced off of it like tiny flashes of lightning. Her arms were a perfect V. Her mouth and eyes open wide. Knowing. Accepting. She might have been crying out, but the only sound Ariel could hear now was the blood pounding in her own ears. Before she could look away, she saw something else: someone, a man she thought, standing at the railing where the girl had gone over.

Ariel flung herself back against the wall so she wouldn't have to see the girl hit the ground far below her.

⌒

When Ariel awoke on the floor, her head cradled in the crook of one arm, she had a single perfect moment of forgetfulness. But as soon as she felt the worn hardwood beneath her palms, she remembered what had happened. Hardly any time had passed at all. The moonlight was no longer so strong, but dawn was still a long way off.

"Mommy," she whispered. The glow of the nightlight from beneath her mother's door hadn't changed.

What will I say? Was I dreaming?

She willed herself to look.

Standing safely on the second floor gallery, she saw that there was definitely a woman or a girl lying on the big oriental rug below. She was barefoot, and had similar hair to the girl in the robe, but she wasn't nearly as thin and was wearing a tight dress that was hiked to her hips. Even from where she stood, Ariel could tell she wasn't wearing panties. One of her legs was twisted at a distressing angle, and Ariel winced, imagining the pain. But she knew the woman wasn't feeling pain or anything else. She was too still for that. Her eyes were open.

This wasn't the girl she'd seen fall from the third floor.

"Button." Again, a whisper. One that she heard clearly.

Ariel looked across the hall to see her father standing just outside her mother's bedroom door.

It can't be you, Daddy.

He mouthed something to her that she couldn't understand and put a shushing finger to his lips.

He had come back!

But Ariel's flush of happiness at seeing him quickly retreated. Her father was dead, and death was all around her now. She turned and ran back into her room, slamming the heavy door. Crawling into bed, she gathered every sheet, every blanket within reach into a nest around her.

For a long time she lay there, shivering, her eyes squeezed shut. Finally, the nighttime sounds from outside her open window overcame her panic, and she buried her face in her pillow to cry until she slept.

Chapter 14

Rainey woke up feeling happy and motivated. She was a natural worker whose habit of waking up early had annoyed everyone from her mother to her college roommate at the art institute to Will and Ariel. Having daily projects to look forward to made her feel alive. She didn't have many mornings like this now, and she wanted to savor the feeling. The party had been the sort of success that she could build on.

As she toweled her hair from the shower, she stood, naked, in the window overlooking the garden's boxwood maze. The yellowed leaves worried her. A large number of the bushes were dead, and the rest were so overgrown that they would have to come out. The whole thing would need to be replanted if the maze was to be restored, and Ariel would be well into adulthood before it would be fun for anyone but a young child. Gerard had arranged to have all the junky trees that had spontaneously rooted near the house taken out, but a hot Virginia summer was not the best time to do major garden renovation. Before Rainey first looked at the property, Karin had arranged for routine yard maintenance. But the results of such limited care were brown and grim.

Baby steps.

This morning her primary project was to go into town and try to familiarize herself with it beyond the asphalt between the grocery store, the DMV, and the hardware store.

Although Old Gate had been founded in 1744, most of its public buildings and houses had burned down before the end of the eighteenth century. Ethan Fauquier, the bookstore owner from the party, had said it was the best thing that could've happened to the town. It was able to reinvent itself from a rough-edged village buried in a remote southern Virginia valley to something more sophisticated. After a year of wrangling among the town's prominent families and politicians, it was decided that a young Italian protégé of Thomas Jefferson would redesign the town.

The result was remarkable: All the main streets of Old Gate radiated out like spokes of a wheel from a single octagon that held within its confines the courthouse, the Anglican church, a town hall, and an expanse of green reminiscent of villages in both New England and Mother England. Those main streets were connected by smaller streets that were exclusively residential, creating a complex web of the commercial, the official, and the private. And so there were small pockets of houses whose residents knew each other very well, and because the houses were often so close to commercial establishments, there wasn't the usual acrimony between business people and regular citizens. Careful zoning kept everything attractive and harmonious.

Rainey didn't find it particularly easy to get around Old Gate, but then she hadn't had much practice. Most of the buildings and homes near the town's heart were neo-classical, like the ones Thomas Jefferson himself built. But it was fun to see the progression of the town, to ease around gentle corners to discover an unexpected classical antiques shop next to a contemporary restaurant, or to drive along ever-lengthening avenues of lovely old houses. The longer the avenue, the later in time the houses were built.

She was anxious to visit the bookstore and speak with Ethan Fauquier again. He'd promised to tell her more about the history of Bliss House as well.

Rainey dressed and left her bedroom. On impulse, she called across the gallery to Ariel.

"Ariel, how about some pancakes? Come have breakfast." She knew it was probably futile, that Ariel wouldn't even have stirred. If that were the case, she would just surprise Ariel with a tray in her room.

She was halfway down the stairs when she noticed something below her, in the hallway.

Was it a pile of clothes?

Rainey stopped to stare, too stunned to make a sound. There was no mistaking Karin Powell. She recognized the dress and the hair and the long, pale legs. She wanted to think that perhaps Karin had simply mistakenly stayed behind after the party. Falling asleep somewhere? But no. She hadn't passed out. There was something wrong with her leg. The angle wasn't right.

Karin Powell's eyes were wide open, staring past Rainey to the starry ceiling above them.

Rainey couldn't force herself to go all the way downstairs to get closer to Karin. She was afraid, and her stomach churned so that she thought she might vomit. Karin was dead.

For Ariel's sake, Rainey stifled a scream, and ran for her phone back in her bedroom. Stumbling inside, she realized that she wasn't able to talk or even think about talking. She ran for the bathroom, where she retched for what seemed like an hour before she could make herself stand up and call the police.

⌒

"Ariel. Honey." Rainey tried to be gentle as she shook her daughter's shoulder to wake her, but her own body was trembling. She'd called the police, and they were on their way. She'd even gone so far as to find Gerard's name in her contacts, but something made her stop before she pressed the "call" button. It was the one thing she couldn't bear to do.

Ariel groaned and threw an arm across her face to block out both Rainey and the sunshine streaming in the windows.

"Mommy, stop." She tried to shrug her mother away.

"Baby, wake up! The police are coming . . ." God, what was there to even say?

"There's been a horrible accident." Rainey squeezed her shoulder again. "Honey, you must get up. It's Karin Powell. I don't know what happened. In the front hall."

Ariel tried to sit up, but the memory of the night overwhelmed her, and she fell back onto the pillow.

"It's okay," Rainey said, worried by the shock in her daughter's eyes. If only she could keep every bad thing away from her. Death seemed to stalk them. *Why won't it leave us alone?* "Nothing's going to hurt you. You're safe."

Ariel stared up at her mother, still overcome. How could she trust her mother with the truth of what she'd seen?

Rainey stroked her hair. "The police are on their way." She looked away, out the window. "Gerard. I can't tell him." Her voice fell to a whisper. "He loved her so much. Everyone liked her."

"What do I do? I don't know what to do." There was a childish desperation in Ariel's voice that Rainey hadn't heard since she was six years old.

"I didn't know she was still here," Rainey said, almost to herself. Then, "You don't need to do anything, baby. They'll take her away. Quickly. I promise."

"But I was *there*, Mommy."

Stunned, Rainey stared down at her.

"I saw her—I saw somebody—fall from the third floor gallery." Ariel pointed up. "I wanted to tell you last night. I just couldn't. I'm so sorry, Mommy. I was scared."

"You saw it, and you didn't come to me?" Rainey's voice sounded sharp to her own ears. But they might have done something! Might have saved Karin. They had spent the night with Karin dead or dying just a few feet from their bedrooms. The idea horrified her. What could Ariel have been thinking? It was bizarre. Had Ariel become so isolated that she'd lost all sense of human empathy? No. It couldn't be.

Seeing tears in her daughter's eyes, she softened. She couldn't bear to see Ariel so fragile. Again.

God, why are you doing this to my baby? To us?

Rainey pulled Ariel to her. Holding her shaking daughter made her feel strangely calm, even though their lives were about to be torn apart. *Again.* "You're not alone. Ever."

"They're going to want to talk to me, aren't they?" Ariel pressed her face against her mother's chest.

No, Ariel wasn't going to be involved in this mess if she could help it. She'd suffered enough for two lifetimes. Whatever had happened to Karin Powell had nothing to do with her daughter. If Ariel had seen anything—*please, please, let her have been dreaming*—it must have been the very end of Karin Powell's long, long process of disintegration. People didn't just wake up one morning and decide to kill themselves later that evening, right after a party. It was all very sad for Gerard. Only God knew how well she understood the sadness of it. But Karin Powell had nothing to do with them or with Bliss House. Bliss House had obviously just been convenient.

Chapter 15

Ariel stood on the edge of the bathtub looking down on the brown summer grass from her bathroom window. A woman in an EMT uniform was smoking a cigarette and talking to a male cop. The cop said something, and the woman laughed, but then covered her mouth as though remembering laughter was inappropriate.

The morning breeze felt good on Ariel's face. She knew she shouldn't be looking out, in case someone saw her. She was supposed to stay in her bathroom until everyone was gone, and had even made a kind of nest for herself in the linen closet. She would do anything to avoid talking to the police.

How long did it take to make a body go away? Her mother had said she didn't think it would take too long because it had clearly been suicide.

Except . . .

There had been someone else there. If the girl she'd seen fall hadn't been a girl at all, but had been Karin Powell, then the man she'd seen might not have been a stranger. Was it Jefferson? Or no one at all?

The only thing she could be completely sure of was that it was her father she'd seen outside her mother's door.

But Daddy would never hurt anyone, would he?

The EMT dropped her cigarette in the grass and stepped on it. It was a good thing her mother wasn't watching. She complained when she found cigarette butts left by workmen in the yard. It was not only disgusting, she said, but it was a fire hazard. Their Missouri house had been close to the woods, and brush and leaves on the ground could easily catch in a dry fall.

Had the nearby woods caught fire when the house exploded? Ariel had never gone back to where their house had been. If the woods were gone, then the tree house her father had built her was gone too. She scanned the trees nearest Bliss House as though she might see it there, reborn.

Below her, the cop pointed to the butt smoldering in the grass. Shrugging, the EMT ground it out harder, and bent to pick it up. They left, heading toward the front of the house. Thinking the police might be coming inside to search the way her mother had said they might, Ariel slid down off of the tub. As she went back to her hiding place in the linen closet, she chanced to see her own face in the mirror. If it weren't for the small but significant healing she saw there, she knew that she would be feeling worse. Far worse.

Chapter 16

State Police Detective Lucas Chappell had no love for Bliss House, and he wasn't at all happy about being inside it again. While the house had certainly improved cosmetically since he'd been there five years earlier, it still wore a palpable air of malice. If anything, it was stronger now, more intentional. The house didn't want him or anyone else there. The immediate scene of the murder in the case he'd worked on back then—the murder of the innkeeper's wife by the innkeeper himself—hadn't even been inside the house, but in the surrounding woods, over a hundred yards away. Still, the house had been an issue. The innkeeper, who was now on death row, had told them it had driven him mad. Only a handful of old-timers in Old Gate admitted to believing him. But everyone involved in the investigation understood the house had been a factor.

The house's history explained why, when there was a suspicious death like today's, the county sheriff almost immediately called in the state police. It was just Lucas's dumb luck that his partner, Brandon Stuart, was on vacation, leaving him on his own. At least this time he was in charge of the investigation, and it wasn't the first time the locals had worked with a black detective.

"When the photographer finishes up, Mrs. Adams, we'll have the medical examiner and the tech team come in. They should only be here a few hours."

Rainey Adams was keeping her composure, but she still looked as shaken as anyone who had found a body in her front hall might be. He had looked over the county officer's notes before coming into the house. Lorraine Adams was a 36-year-old interior designer, but looked much younger (an unnecessary note from the too-eager local officer) and had moved into the house less than a month earlier with her fourteen-year-old daughter. There had been some sort of party at the house the night before, but all the guests had gone by eleven P.M. The dead woman had been a guest, the real estate agent who had sold the house, and also happened to be the wife of the contractor who had done the renovations.

It hadn't been an enormous renovation, but the house looked more solid and less tatty than it had looked before. Lucas had lived in Virginia all of his life, and he was used to the way people held onto things. They found immense value in longevity. Longevity meant stories. Sometimes he felt he had lived so many of those stories that he was a part of the soil, the very air of the state.

"I started to call Gerard, her husband," Rainey said. "But I couldn't do it." She bit her lip. She wore no makeup, but she was neatly dressed. That made sense. She'd told him she'd awakened, showered, and was on her way to make breakfast just before walking into this mess. Karin Powell had obviously been dead a while, so it would've been a very cool thing for her to go to bed, then rise and shower before calling the death in. The tiny woman in front of him didn't appear that calculating, but he'd been fooled before.

"It's taken care of," Lucas said. He touched Rainey's elbow. "Wouldn't you be more comfortable somewhere else? Why don't we go into the kitchen?"

81

It wasn't until Rainey was making tea for them both that she wondered how the detective had known to press the decorative panel in the hallway to reveal the disguised kitchen door. People usually had to have it pointed out to them.

She could hardly focus. The whole thing was complete madness. Why had Karin been in the house after the party at all? If there really had been someone with her, how could she not have heard? Rainey wanted to know, to understand. But the important thing at that moment was to protect Ariel.

Was this her fault, too? Death had followed them here, halfway across the country.

"I've been in the house before," the detective said, as though reading her thoughts about the door. "Used to be in these old houses that the kitchen would be in the basement with a dumbwaiter to the dining room, or outside the house completely because of the summer heat. But I saw you're an interior designer, so I imagine you know plenty about houses." He tucked his notebook into an inner pocket and held out his hands for the mugs she'd taken from the cabinet. His green eyes were serious. Rainey sensed he was trying hard to be friendly. He set the mugs on the table.

Both his demeanor and appearance were meant to inspire confidence. He appeared comfortable in his European-cut, dark khaki suit, and his shoes bore a perfect military shine. Above his crisp white shirt and somber tie, he was immaculately shaved, and his hair was cropped close and razored neatly around his ears. At one point she'd seen the back of his head and noted that his hair was thinning near the crown, even though he might have been a couple of years younger than she. He was tall, maybe even over six feet, and his high cheekbones gave him a look of arrogance, though Rainey knew she wasn't in any kind of shape to be critical or make any kind of judgment. He didn't smile. It wasn't a day for smiles.

"Gerard said he thinks the galley part of the kitchen used to be something else," Rainey said. "There's so much to know about the house."

"This house has been a lot of things," he said, looking around. The tension in his voice got her attention.

"What do you mean?"

"Last time I was here was five years ago."

Rainey stared at him a moment. *Five years? Of course, the Brodskys.* She wouldn't own Bliss House if it hadn't been for the murder. The thought struck her with its full force. Another woman's blood had helped her become the mistress of Bliss House.

Mistress of Bliss House. It sounded absurd in her head, and the weight of it felt crushing. The massive house, the history she hadn't considered thoroughly. Why hadn't she thought more about what it meant to live in a house where a murder had been committed? She'd uprooted Ariel and had just run away to Bliss House, assuming it would be a haven. What in the hell had she been thinking?

"I need to sit," she said, fumbling to pull a chair away from the table. Her pulse was racing.

The detective leaned down slightly to get a closer look at her.

"It was a mistake for us to talk so soon," he said, frowning. "I'm going to get one of the EMTs to look you over."

"Wait." Rainey put a hand on his forearm. "There's something I need to tell you. It's about my daughter."

The detective nodded and sat down.

"Ariel's not . . ." What was the word she was looking for? Whatever it was, it wouldn't come.

Seeing the question in his eyes, Rainey hurried with more of an explanation. "Ariel may have seen Karin fall. But she didn't even recognize her. She'd seen Karin's picture, and maybe seen Karin from a distance. I don't know. From the way she talks about it, she might have dreamed the whole thing."

"If she had a similar dream, it sounds like it was a big coincidence, don't you think? Did she say if she dreamed that there was someone *with* Mrs. Powell?"

Rainey shook her head. "Nobody else. I'm sure. I'm so sorry. I know it sounds strange."

"It would help if I could speak to her. Could you bring her in for a statement?"

She cut him off.

"Absolutely not!" The idea of taking Ariel to a police station sent a spike of anxiety through her. "I can't do that to her. She's not even fifteen yet, and she won't leave the house."

"I don't understand."

Was it just skepticism in his eyes, or did he already think she was lying about everything?

Rainey clasped her hands together. "She was in an accident," she said, trying not to rush her words. "Not here. In St. Louis. She was badly burned, and she doesn't go anywhere unless it's to the hospital or to see a doctor. That's just the way it is."

She barely listened to his expression of sympathy, and spoke quickly when he'd finished.

"Can you wait to talk to her here? Will you come back tomorrow?"

～

Lucas followed Rainey Adams out of the kitchen, and watched her hurry up the front stairs to her daughter's room. He lingered near Karin Powell's body, which the ME had finally covered completely, and looked up through the well of the house, past the bronze chandelier hanging from the hand-painted dome. He'd seen the ceiling up close, with its sparkling stars painted on a field of deepest blue, like some kind of primitive planetarium. There were constellations he didn't recognize. It had always puzzled him as to why someone would want it to appear to be nighttime in their house, twenty-four seven.

He couldn't help but admire the restoration work the Adams woman had arranged. The Brodskys had let things run to disrepair in the last years of the inn, an obvious result of their increasingly deteriorating mental states. The floors hadn't been stripped or polished; the drafty windows and peeling caulk and paint had never been repaired. Several of the stairs leading onto the roof were completely rotted through. Their fussy furniture hadn't quite suited the dignity of the old house, either. Because Bliss House did have a dignity that wouldn't be denied.

Now the bulky walnut secretary that had served the Brodskys as a check-in desk was gone from the south wall, as was the stark white brochure stand and the loveseats and several sets of overstuffed floral chairs that had been scattered around what the Brodskys had called the Great Hall. Now the hall wore a mellow shine in the early-afternoon light, giving the house an appearance of comfortable, substantial warmth, if not luxury.

An appearance.

In his gut, Lucas knew there wasn't one thing wrong with Bliss House. *Everything* about it was wrong.

Karin Powell had jumped—or had accidentally fallen, or been pushed—about thirty feet, from the third-floor gallery. One of the techs was still dusting the railings for fingerprints. Not a huge height to fall from. Five years earlier, Karin Powell might have landed on a sofa or chair. Even now, she might have gotten away with a broken limb or two if she'd landed well. But the medical examiner, Silas Hamrick, had shown him how she'd landed solidly on her back, breaking several ribs but leaving her face unmarked. There was no blood outside the body, but rigor was quickly setting in, pulling her cheeks away from the front of her face and mouth so that she looked as though she were trying to smile. While Hamrick was doing his preliminary examination he'd discreetly covered the woman's groin with a plastic sheet. Lucas was aware that many women chose not to wear underwear as a regular thing, but the fact that she had died so boldly exposed gave the scene a lewd, suggestive appearance.

"If it was suicide," Hamrick said, "it was a risky way to go. Not reliable."

Not reliable. It would have been an even dumber way to murder someone. And the Adams woman claimed to have slept through it all.

But just the fact that she'd made such an outrageous claim made her seem less likely to have been the one who committed the murder. Or perhaps she just wasn't very smart. He was anxious to talk to the daughter, but he'd caved in to the mother's request that he come and talk to her the next day. Something about the way she'd been so protective about her daughter had gotten to him.

The medical examiner had gone, and techs who would take care of the body were hanging around outside, waiting for the husband to show up before they took it to the morgue at the hospital. It had been Lucas's call to have them wait. It made a difference for some people to see where a death had occurred. Plus, he was interested in seeing Gerard Powell's reaction.

He made himself go upstairs, feeling the oppressive weight of the place with every step. At least Rainey Adams had had carpet runners installed on the stairs, so that his footsteps no longer echoed in the vast hall.

He nodded to the female tech dusting the second floor railings.

"All done upstairs," she said. "So far, it's pretty clean down here."

"Let's do the doors on this side, too," Lucas said.

She didn't demur or even blink, but went back to her work.

The Brodskys had lived in the house's servants' quarters. The bedrooms lining the second floor gallery still had brass plaques centered on them at doorknob height: Dolly Madison, Mr. Washington, E.A. Poe, Pocahontas Suite, Maybelle Carter, Pearl Bailey, Robert E. Lee. An eclectic Who's Who of Virginians, one of the Brodskys' attempts to cement themselves as a historically recognizable part of the neighborhood.

In life, the Brodskys hadn't been significant—historically or otherwise. In death, they'd simply become notorious, like the house itself.

He had had an officer do a casual search of every room except the daughter's. His own search was more to re-acquaint himself, distasteful as it was.

The stripped and shredded mattresses, the mice running through the place, the trash cans overflowing. The smell of mold and even—God help them—excrement. The odors in the Brodskys' quarters like a disused abattoir. The crude writing. The smell of death everywhere. And then Mim Brodsky's chest of drawers. Perfect, as though encased in glass or frozen in time. Soft things, tenderly laid aside. Silk scarves and lingerie. Infant clothes and photographs of their children when young. You could imagine her turning the pages, touching each photo as though sealing it for all time.

He and the tech had tied a piece of yellow crime scene tape around the railing where the medical examiner had determined that the woman had probably gone over. It was directly opposite the front of the house, midway between the daughter's and the mother's bedrooms and up one floor. The third floor gallery ran all the way around the inside of the house, unbroken by stairs. There was a double set of stairs at the back—one set that had been used by the servants, and one for the family. At the top of each set was one of the strange little hallways that showed up between a few of the rooms. Hallways that each ended in a single narrow window, presumably there to keep the house from being too dark.

Rainey Adams' bedroom was the kind of room his mother was always bookmarking online and in magazines. A late-nineteenth century planter's bed, with four tall turned posters with delicately carved pineapples at their bases, and a mass of pillows nearly covering the headboard. An ivy-patterned couch set in front of two tall windows overlooking the formal—now yellow and wild—garden. Rich oil paintings of houses and architectural landmarks hanging above the fireplace and arranged in groups on the walls. The scent of some herb or flower everywhere. Definitely a woman's room. Lucas was uncomfortable on the pale cream rug with its apricot flowers and green tendrils that seemed to continue to the walls, disappearing in the lush garden wallpaper. There were women's clothes hung in the enormous pediment-topped armoire and carelessly strewn along the floor. The trail led to the bathroom, which also overlooked the garden.

As a cop, it was his job to know about Rainey Adams, but he was self-conscious standing in front of her dressing table, his gloved fingers gently moving her scattered jewelry and bits of scrap paper with notes jotted on them: *Buy paper towels! Get shutter nailed back—tell G. P.O. Box!*

G for Gerard? He wondered what sort of relationship she had with the contractor. Was there something there? He took out his own notebook.

It wasn't the room of a calculating, obsessive woman. In fact, there was a sense of relaxed disarray about the room that he didn't feel in any other part of the house.

He had just come out of another bedroom—one that looked as though it was being set up as an office—when he heard his name spoken downstairs. He leaned over the railing to look. The outline of Karin Powell's body emerged from the plastic sheet like a piece of macabre artwork.

"Somebody looking for me?" he said.

One of the sheriff's deputies stood just inside the open front door, which had been open all morning, filling the house with flies.

"He's here," the officer said.

The victim's husband. Maybe the murderer. He couldn't help that his thoughts went there. Husbands had a bad rep when it came to being suspects. Mostly because they were so often guilty. Right now he didn't have a single bit of evidence to call it a murder, a suicide, *or* an accident. He had next to no information. Just a bad feeling, and a worse location.

Chapter 17

Gerard Powell looked down at his wife's supine body, the exposed side of her face revealing a smear of fiery red lipstick that looked as though it had been applied by an overeager child. *Still*, he thought. *She's finally still.*

In life, Karin had been in constant motion, so charged with internal energy that he was sometimes reluctant to touch her, lest his own calm be completely shattered. There had been a time when that energy had captivated him, and he saw in her everything he wasn't but thought he needed to be. In those early days, they would lie in bed, cuddling and talking about how, together, they were like one perfect person. She offered him momentum, and the encouragement and incentive to build amazing, revolutionary things—churches and houses and bridges that looked like no others, projects full of life and light and beauty. He could see them in his head, and even got out his drafting tools again to draw them, with Karin standing close, her slender fingers gently massaging his shoulder or absently stroking his hair, the curve of his ear. He was her rock, the lodestar on which she could focus so that she could tame and control the roiling creative and sexual mania that kept her pacing, moving, talking, planning. She couldn't quite put what she wanted to do into words, but she'd believed that one day she would do exciting, important things. Maybe design gorgeous clothes, or upgrade her dull old general studies degree to an MBA and make them a ton of money by starting a company that would be on the Fortune 500. But she complained that the MBA classes didn't move fast enough, and she'd started selling cosmetics and made easy money and lots of local connections. Her talent for sales led her to a real estate license. Her listings were pricey properties, the kind that sold even when the economy was poor.

After a while Gerard found that Karin's manic drive enervated rather than encouraged him. The drawings went away, and they never spoke of them, as though they were a kind of embarrassment. They were, to him. He fell back on contracting because he was good at it. He was organized and quality-conscious and had ideas his clients—often also Karin's—liked. He was, they said, unflappable. Flexible. The business suited him, and he didn't have any real regrets.

He felt the detective watching him, and was self-conscious. How was a person supposed to act when his wife lay dead in front of him? What could he say? It wasn't true that he was unflappable. He had a habit of thinking before he spoke. Now, he could hardly speak at all. There was a knot in his chest that made him feel like he'd swallowed one of the tennis balls their Golden Retriever, Ellie, liked to chase.

Ellie was going to miss Karin. She'd been sulky that morning, wandering from room to room looking for Karin, who had been home only briefly to change into party clothes after work the previous day.

"Mr. Powell?"

Gerard raised his eyes. Was he expected to say something?

"Is this woman your wife, Karin Powell?"

"Yes, she's my wife," Gerard said, his voice strained. He swallowed hard. It seemed like an incredibly stupid question for the detective to ask. Yet even as his wife lay there dead, he glanced at the detective and wondered if his wife would've tried to have sex with the man. It was an absurd habit developed within the absurdity of his life with Karin—mentally appraising nearly every man he met against Karin's standards for possible lovers. Standards he knew all too well. With his commanding, forthright manner and cool good looks, the detective was the kind of man who might have initially appealed to Karin. She had a taste for authoritative men and hadn't been shy about telling Gerard he needed to be more aggressive with people. That she wished he'd be more forceful *with her.* More than once, he'd tried to indulge her fantasies about being dominated. But he got no thrill from tying her up or handling her fair, beautiful body roughly, and had only disappointed her, driven her into the bed of some new lover who could give her what she needed. This man, the detective, was definitely handsome, but he was still just a state police detective. Karin preferred her lovers to be powerful. And if they weren't powerful, they needed to at least be younger. More malleable.

He'd learned to tell himself that it was only her addiction that made her unfaithful. She'd been working on it, making a show of taking her addiction medication—at least up until the past few weeks. They'd been so close to changing their lives.

"I'm sorry," the detective said.

I'm sorry too were the words that came to Gerard's lips, but he left them unspoken.

He watched as a pair of flies landed on Karin's bountiful hair, and half-expected her to push up from the floor and brush them away, complaining about the humidity and the nearby farms and the smell of manure spread on the fallow fields.

"I understand you had two cars here last night. Do you know why your wife might have remained here, or even come back, after everyone left the party?"

"If she did, she had a reason." Gerard looked up, apparently taking in the upper floors.

Lucas watched him. It was a good time to push Gerard Powell a little, while he was off-balance. His wife's death hadn't really hit him yet.

"Was your wife under any unusual stress?" He paused a moment and spread his large hands in a gesture of appeal. "Listen. We can go outside and talk. We don't have to stay in here unless you want to. I know this is tough."

"Nobody wanted this listing," Gerard said. "Karin didn't, at first. She thought about it for a long time."

Then her practical side had kicked in and her apprehension about the house went away completely. "I can make it work," she'd told him. She'd spent a lot of time in Bliss House before it was sold—*soaking up the history*, she'd said. Now she was lying in the hall beneath the star-painted ceiling, narrow beams of sunlight stabbing the air around her.

Gerard didn't have a problem with the house. A couple of his workmen had been reluctant, but they worked because they needed the money. He lost a single carpenter who quit because he'd felt a hand or something pressing hard on his back and turned around to find no one there. The rest, though, had sucked it up and gotten the job done quickly. There was a lot to like about the house, and Gerard knew things about it that he suspected no one else alive knew. Things he hadn't even told Karin. Now it was too late.

"Can I touch her?" He was numb. Touching her might make him feel something. Karin no longer looked human, but like a bizarre wax figure someone had posed on the floor as a joke. Despite the heat streaming through the open front door, she looked cold. Frozen. At least they had closed her eyes. In his head, he could still hear her voice.

"Really, Gerard?" she'd say. *"Would you look at the mess my hair is? I'll never get the knots out of it. And my nails are wrecked. I'm going to have to go to the salon at the beginning of the week. Like I have time for that."*

"I'd like to let you, but no."

Gerard thought it was to the detective's credit that he looked regretful.

"In these circumstances, the ME is required to do an autopsy before the body is released."

Lucas watched Gerard's reaction carefully. He didn't look surprised or alarmed, but gave a curt nod.

"Let's go outside," he said.

Chapter 18

Rainey put her hand on the front door handle, but rested her forehead against the cool, smooth surface of the door a moment before opening it to the detective waiting on the other side.

The past twenty-four hours had been a blur of phone calls from Bertie and media types. The reporters she'd ignored with caller ID, and she'd put off Bertie by saying that Ariel was too upset. It wasn't far from the truth.

Ariel was more distant than ever. She'd stuck to her room, watching movies and sleeping or reading, and their conversation was limited to what she might want to eat. The hats had been replaced by a tangerine hoodie that she kept zipped up to the neck and covering her hair. Not satisfied with hiding in her room, she was retreating even further. Rainey imagined her melting away, disappearing into herself, and leaving Rainey behind. Neither mentioned Karin Powell, whose presence was between them as though she were there in the flesh. Just like Will. Two ghosts.

Rainey had made sure that Ariel had seen a decent therapist—Lynne Pogue—after Will's death, and had suggested, when she'd taken up a tray with some breakfast that morning, that Ariel should give Lynne a call if she wanted to talk. But Ariel had barely lifted her eyes from the movie on her laptop and mumbled a thank you for the breakfast.

Since the police had gone the day before, Rainey had felt utterly alone. Worried about Ariel, worried that they had made a horrible mistake coming here. She'd wandered through the house, arranging and rearranging the furniture in the salon and the unoccupied second floor bedrooms. But she avoided the third floor. Imagined Karin Powell's footsteps on the stairs. How had she not heard her?

⁓

Lucas stood in the front doorway of Bliss House, but Rainey Adams didn't seem disposed to let him in. He'd even called first to set up the time. Now he was short on patience.

He'd released his people from the scene early the previous evening after nearly taking the entire house apart, looking for something, anything, that would explain why Karin Powell had died in Bliss House. He'd told Rainey they were looking for a note, or some evidence that someone besides Rainey, Karin Powell, and Ariel had been in the house after the party. They were also looking for Karin's belongings. Her purse with her identification had been found in her car, but they hadn't found her keys or her phone yet. Or her other shoe. They had confirmed with Gerard Powell that the shoe Rainey had found belonged to the dead woman. Now he needed to talk to the daughter. The day before, the Adams woman had asked him to wait on the interview because the daughter was upset. He wondered if that was the only reason.

"She's in the library, Detective," Rainey said. "Please don't let this take too long."

The last time Lucas had been in the small library off of the living room—or *salon*, as Rainey called it—its shelves had been stuffed with faded paperback books and case after case of VHS tapes of old films. The Brodskys hadn't quite caught up with the whole

DVD revolution. The room had also contained an old Siamese cat who—apparently oblivious to the chaos around Mim Brodsky's murder—had greeted him with a grouchy cry from a cat-hair-covered loveseat and went quickly back to sleep. But this time, what he saw when he followed Rainey into the study pierced his heart.

The girl sat in a broad leather chair, her legs hidden beneath a long skirt in the same way her face seemed to be hiding beneath her orange hood. Even so, he could tell she was tall for her age. She looked up from the book she'd been reading, and he thought he could see a challenge in her blue eyes. He tried to keep looking at her eyes because he didn't want to stare at the ruined skin on her neck and right side of her face. Her right eyelid drooped, too, so he tried to focus on the left. On the job he'd seen a lot of exploded motel meth labs and catastrophic car accidents, so he was no stranger to burn victims. But he'd never seen the beauty of a child so destroyed. Looking at her face was like looking at heaven and hell at the same time.

Still, he refused to look away. One of them had to be a grownup.

"Ariel, this is Detective Chappell. You don't have to talk to him any longer than you want to, sweetheart," Rainey said. She perched on the wide arm of her daughter's chair like a lioness guarding her cub.

"Then I can go back upstairs now?" Ariel stared back at him.

Lucas came forward, thinking he'd shake her hand, but he suddenly put his right hand in the inner breast pocket of his sport coat, feeling for his digital recorder. He would've been reaching to shake her damaged right hand, which rested, palm up, in her lap.

"What are you reading?" He laid the running recorder on the table and sat in the chair opposite hers.

The question took her by surprise, and she glanced down at the book. He thought she would answer, until she turned to look up at her mother. *Ah, not so brave*, he thought. *Running to mommy for cover.* He could tell without looking at Rainey that she was about to jump down his throat.

"Let's make this as brief as possible for both of us, okay? That works for me, too," he said. "Yesterday must have been tough, with all the police and technicians here."

He opened a case he'd brought from the station and set up a small digital machine on the table. "First thing, I need to get your fingerprints, and your mother's. We have to be able to exclude your prints from everyone else's."

Rainey was first. Her hands were ice cold, and she was silent as he pressed and rolled her fingertips over the machine's screen. Ariel couldn't disguise her curiosity, and rose to her knees in the chair so she could watch.

When her turn came, she made a crack about her prints being in the system for the rest of her life. Lucas simply smiled.

Rainey stood close by. He heard her breath intake sharply when he gently took her daughter's damaged hand and rested it on the scanner. The skin felt slick and soft, but he kept his face neutral. He figured that it must really suck to be a fourteen-year-old with her kind of problems, and didn't blame her for being out of sorts.

When they were done, the girl retreated to her chair, her mother again at her side. Lucas didn't get the sense that it was a comfortable arrangement. The girl seemed solitary, and not very affectionate.

"Ariel, did you know Mrs. Powell? Had she ever spoken to you?"

Ariel shook her head.

"I'll need you to answer for the recording, if you don't mind."

"No," she said.

"Had you seen her before the party?"

"Mom talked about her, and she showed me a picture of her online. I don't see a lot of people in person."

"Not even that night?"

"I might have watched some of the party, but I wasn't sure who she was. After the party, Mom showed me the pictures she took with her phone, and she was in a couple of them. Am I done?"

Rainey put a hand on her daughter's shoulder. There was a world of sympathy in her eyes when she looked at her. Lucas wondered how much sympathy a kid could stand.

"So you never saw her around the house at any other time? Did she come upstairs during the party?"

"No." Her answer was vehement.

"How do you know, if you weren't watching the whole time? Did anyone else come upstairs or to your room, maybe to say hello or to bring you something?"

The girl started to answer, but then hesitated when her mother stood up.

Some of the hair in Rainey's ponytail had come loose and hung in blond wisps on both sides of her face, making her look younger and more disheveled than he imagined she usually was. Her peasant-style blouse hung wide and loose over her short denim skirt. She looked like her clothes were a size too big, as though she'd recently lost weight. If she wore a size two, he would've been surprised.

"She never met her," she said. "Most of the people in the house didn't even know Ariel was here."

Lucas kept his voice controlled.

"Mrs. Adams, we've got a lot of questions to answer here. You can imagine that Mr. Powell will want to know why he woke up two days ago to learn that he's now a widower. Please, let your daughter speak for herself."

The air in the room seemed to still instantly. The color drained from Rainey's face.

Ariel put a hand to her hood as though to protect it, or herself, and looked anxiously from her mother to him.

Then he remembered what one of the deputies had told him the evening before: that Rainey Adams had come to Virginia after her husband had died in a gas explosion at their home. It was obviously the reason the girl was disfigured, the accident Rainey Adams had referred to. He felt his face flush. *Damn, I'm an ass.*

"Sorry," he said, hoping he didn't sound as lame as he thought he did. "I'm just trying to cover all the possibilities here."

"Really?" Rainey's voice was stiff. "I don't think so. I think you're harassing us because that's how you get your thrills. Has this been fun for you?"

"I chose my words carelessly, Mrs. Adams. We're just looking for answers."

"Ariel gave you answers. She doesn't know anything."

He looked at the girl, but she'd turned her face to the window. From that angle, he couldn't see any scarring on her face at all. She was just a shy, slightly gawky fourteen-year-old.

"Your mother says you saw Mrs. Powell fall from the balcony. Tell me about that."

"I don't know what I saw," she said quietly.

It was a start. He waited. To her credit, her mother didn't jump in. She sat watching her daughter.

Ariel shifted in the chair, but still didn't turn around.

"It was foggy. Like in a movie, or something out of focus. It didn't look like Mrs. Powell. She was younger. Not as pretty."

Out in the hall, the grandfather clock chimed the half hour.

"When I first woke up, I heard talking. And noises like someone running."

"Inside the house?" Lucas said.

"I knew it wasn't outside, so I went out of my room. I looked over the railing to the front hall first."

Now she turned to him. Lucas paid close attention to her words, not wanting to be distracted by her scars. He leaned forward a little.

"Then I looked up, and I saw her kind of balanced on the railing, but it was hard to see because of the fog or whatever it was. She raised her arms up in the air and then she was falling. She looked at me."

There was a sharp intake of breath from Rainey Adams, who touched her daughter's arm, obviously concerned. But the girl stopped her with a slight, impatient gesture.

"Had you ever seen her before?" Lucas asked.

Ariel shook her head. "No."

"How was she dressed?"

She hesitated so briefly that, if he hadn't been paying attention, he might have missed it. "A nightgown. A white nightgown."

"Are you sure she was looking at you?"

"Why shouldn't she be sure?" Rainey asked.

"That's how I knew it wasn't Mrs. Powell," Ariel said. "Like I told you, this girl was younger. She had red hair, but she was a different person."

Lucas had wanted to see how confident she was, and he had his answer. She was utterly convinced. But it still didn't make any sense.

"After she fell, what did you do?"

She blushed. "What do you mean?"

"You didn't call for help, or go down to see what happened?"

"That's enough!" Rainey said. "She answered your questions."

"Mrs. Adams, please. Her recollections are important."

Ariel leaned slightly toward her mother.

"Did you see anything else? Anyone else?" He still wasn't satisfied.

"We're done, Detective." Rainey stood. "She doesn't have anything else to say."

Ariel shook her head and whispered, "Nobody else. There wasn't anyone else."

"Thank you," he said. "I guess we're done, then. Later today I'd like to send a couple of officers to look more thoroughly for Mrs. Powell's keys and phone."

Anticipating an angry response, he raised his palm a few inches. "Outside," he said. "You won't even know they're there." He stopped the recorder and quickly packed away the fingerprinting equipment. "I can see myself out. I'll be in touch."

He left Rainey standing by the girl's chair looking calmer, but still on the defensive. There had been no point in continuing.

Passing through the front hall, he glanced up at the dome, two stories above. Except for the rhythmic ticking of the clock, the place was as stuffy and solemn as a church. He had almost reached the front door when he heard hurried footsteps behind him.

"Detective?"

Rainey stood in the center of the hall, illuminated by a shaft of sunlight from overhead. He steeled himself for another tirade about him harassing her daughter.

"Ariel wanted me to tell you that she ran into her room and shut the door after seeing the girl. She was afraid. You can understand that, at least, can't you?"

There was a grudging plea in her voice. He knew she was in a difficult spot. While there was still the possibility that she was involved in Karin Powell's death, he felt pretty sure it was a remote one. He didn't want to be swayed by the fact that the daughter was messed up, and she was attractive and obviously vulnerable. The prisons were full of attractive people who'd committed crimes during difficult periods of their lives. She looked almost like a child herself against the enormous scale of Bliss House. What was she doing here, anyway? It wasn't the kind of house in which to bring up a damaged girl like Ariel Adams—especially alone. Then he chided himself. Rainey Adams was a grown woman. It would be foolish to underestimate her.

"Of course," he said. "You take care, Mrs. Adams."

When he shut the door behind him, he couldn't help but feel relief at the warmth of the late morning sun. He'd had enough of that damned house for the day.

Chapter 19

Rainey and Ariel ate a cold, silent lunch in the kitchen an hour after Detective Chappell left. Rainey didn't feel much like eating, but she was trying hard to set a good example for Ariel, who was looking gaunt. It may have been Ariel's sad lack of sun exposure that was making her good skin look so transparent. She still refused to go outside. Two summers earlier, she'd been on the country club swim team and had started golf lessons. Will had taken her out every weekend to hit balls, and the pro at the club in Hilton Head, where they had a condo, said she showed real promise.

"I was thinking of going into town later," Rainey said. "But I worry about you being here alone."

"Why? Just because somebody died here? I'm not scared. Not anymore." She took the top slice of bakery sourdough off of her turkey sandwich and began to eat the avocado and turkey with her fingers. Rainey didn't say anything to stop her. She was using her right hand to eat. It looked awkward, but it was something new.

"Of course, that's not what I meant," Rainey said. "I just thought it might be too soon, that you might not want to be by yourself. You could always go with me. Maybe wait in the car while I run some errands?"

"That would be a *no*. I wish you'd stop asking me. I don't want to see the stupid town. Plus, now people will stare at us even more because of Mrs. Powell."

"We'll have to see your new doctor up in Charlottesville soon," Rainey said.

Ariel didn't answer.

"I made the appointment for three weeks from now. That's the soonest they could work you in."

"You might've asked me." Ariel dropped a piece of turkey to the plate.

"The doctor isn't negotiable, honey. You know that." Rainey moved a veggie chip around the plate with one finger. "Besides, I think she'll be pleased when she sees you've made a little progress since we moved here." She laid a hand on Ariel's arm and gently squeezed. Ariel didn't pull away.

"They said I wouldn't heal any more," Ariel said, her voice low.

"Doctors don't know everything, honey," Rainey said. "You're doing just fine."

Ariel stood looking out the French doors in the dining room that opened onto the big side patio. Her mother waved as she passed by from the garage, her huge sunglasses hiding her eyes.

"Are you sure you're okay here for a little while?" Rainey had asked her. "You won't be scared or weirded out?"

"I might take a nap."

"I'll stop in at the library, or maybe that bookshop on the square. Bertie says they have a little of everything. I liked the owner, even if he did talk a lot."

"No more vampires," Ariel said. "Maybe some mysteries. Or a book about haunted houses. That would be cool."

"Really?"

Ariel shrugged. "Whatever."

Her mother had said she'd made a "little" progress. Why didn't she want to admit how much she'd healed? Before going back to the kitchen, she went to the mirror in the downstairs powder room. Tilting her head to the side a bit, she ran her fingers down the scarring on her neck. The flesh had become more supple and sprang back when she pressed it. There was a change around her eye, too. It opened wider, and tiny lashes had begun to grow along its lid. When she smiled at her reflection, it was an easier, less painful smile. Pretty soon her mother wouldn't be able to deny what was happening to her.

Satisfied, she continued on to the kitchen, where she opened the refrigerator to find some of the lemon bars and tiny cakes left over from the party. She was suddenly very hungry.

Chapter 20

The afternoon Will died, Rainey was on the highway driving home from the shop when Joyce, a neighbor, called her screaming that something had happened at the house. Joyce was so distraught that Rainey had a hard time understanding exactly what she was saying. But the word *explosion* came through clearly and, a moment later, the distant sound of sirens through the telephone. Joyce tried to convince her to stay on the call while she went outside, but Rainey hung up before Joyce was out the door. As her call to Will's phone connected, Rainey told herself that Joyce didn't even have a direct view of their house, so how could she know? But she voice-dialed Will right away, just in case.

She drove recklessly through the traffic, taking advantage of any breaks, no matter how risky, as she half-listened to Will's lighthearted voice telling her to leave a message and that he would get back to her later. Not waiting for the beep, she called Ariel. Will was always careful about being on the phone when he was driving. He and Ariel were together, and Will probably didn't want to answer. Ariel would surely tell her that they were almost home and would let her know if they saw what Joyce was upset about. But after a single ring, she heard Vivaldi's "Summer Adagio," and

Ariel's high, sweet voice laughingly saying that she was probably in dance class and would call back the minute she had a chance. Finally, Rainey hit the app that would locate them—or at least their phones. After a full, agonizing minute, the same message came back for them both:

LOCATION NOT AVAILABLE.

That was all Rainey would remember of her drive home.

Ten minutes later she was on their street, driving way too fast, and approaching the curve from where she first might see the house. Knobby clouds of gray smoke drifted through the neighborhood like dull, unseeing creatures.

Yes, there's a fire somewhere. That doesn't mean anything.

A rotund man wearing a helmet and an open fireman's jacket waved her down from beside a fire chief's pickup slanted across the road. Rainey braked to a hard stop about ten feet away from him and yelled out her window for him to *get out of the way!* When he shook his head and called out that she needed to turn around, she answered, her voice filled with desperation:

"It's my house! Someone called and said it's my house—I have to get to it!"

"It's not safe past here," he said, coming over to her window. "We've evacuated most of the neighborhood because of the possibility of more explosions. You need to turn around."

Rainey didn't consider obeying him for even a second. Before he could continue, she hit the gas pedal so that he had to jump away or be injured. She swung around his truck without looking back or even glancing in her rearview mirror.

Rounding the curve, she nearly plowed into a solid bank of fire trucks, police cars, and EMT trucks. There was a narrow path between them, no doubt for more emergency vehicles. Unwilling to be stopped, Rainey left the road and drove into the grass. The house lots were all an acre or larger and were mostly open lawns, so she didn't have to drive over anyone's landscaping—not that that would've deterred her. But when she reached the edge of her next-door neighbor's property, she stopped the car, stunned.

The scene was unreal, like something from a disaster film. Their house—the house that she and Will had spent a year planning and another nine months building—was an unrecognizable, steaming shell. Only two soaked, blackened masses of wall remained atop a pile of rubble. It didn't didn't even look like a house anymore, but some kind of antique ruin. There were three fire hoses going, one of them from the top of a ladder truck, its water aimed at the smoking trees at the back of their property. The sky was filled with vapor and smoke. The only color was in a small, uncertain rainbow in the arc of one of the plumes of water.

Then she saw the Jeep. She was too far away to see any detail, but it looked as though the windows were gone, and some large piece of debris lay on its hood.

Will and Ariel had beaten her home.

She wanted time to stop just then. She wanted to stop it and rewind herself like a cartoon, back out of the neighborhood, onto the highway, and all the way back to the shop where she was showing a new client a damask fabric for the too-large sofa the woman had selected, where she could have called Will to have him pick her up so the three of them could have dinner out together, instead of coming home.

But it was only a flash of fantasy that bloomed in her brain for the length of a single inhalation, the time it took for her to open her car door into the stinking, leaden air filling the yard.

No one seemed to notice her as she flew across the neighbor's driveway, and then what was left of her own lawn, toward one of the several groups of uniformed responders. She somehow knew—God, she knew!—that Ariel was at the center of that cluster of uniforms, those men and women who seemed to be both hurrying and moving in slow motion all at once.

She screamed Ariel's name.

One of the cops stepped in front of her, and she propelled him backward a foot as she ran into him. He grabbed her arms.

"Let me see my daughter!" Rainey struggled, reaching toward the group.

"Wait," the cop said. "You can't be in this area, ma'am."

"This is my house! And that's my husband's car. Where's Will? Where's my husband? Is it him?"

"You don't know . . ." the cop said. But his voice wasn't calm. And it was bad if this man, taller and broader than Will, with a brusque, paternal demeanor, was upset.

Rainey looked up at him.

"Let me see. God, just let me see. Please."

"Your house?" he said.

Some of the others had taken notice of her, but barely paused in what they were doing.

She looked toward the house and saw a man with something laid over his outstretched arms as he walked toward another group of uniforms. They were gathered near a black plastic sheet spread out on the grass. Her mind registered the image and the shape of the thing he carried, but her brain seemed to refuse to reach any conclusion about what it might be.

I know. It's black and burned, but I know. And the smell . . . the smell of cooked meat.

"Oh, God, no. No. No. No," she whispered.

Every muscle in her body seemed to relax at once, and she collapsed against the cop, who caught her.

I won't!

Rainey took that second of surprise to free herself from him. She ran to where she thought Ariel was, pushing between an idle EMT and a man who was a neighbor she'd only met once.

They were all silent. The cop hadn't even yelled after her. The rumbling of coursing water and diesel engines receded. The only sounds Rainey heard were the EMT talking brusquely into the radio attached to his shoulder, and the reply from the doctor on the other end. But even their voices dropped into the background.

Rainey's head was filled with Ariel.

Stripped of her clothes, Ariel was like some frail creature driven out of the burning woods. Her eyes were closed, her face almost unrecognizable. Was she asleep? Not dead, surely! They had put an oxygen mask over her mouth and nose, and Rainey watched her daughter's chest for signs that she was breathing. It was as though she had been drawn into halves—her left side was still fair and healthy-looking. Her left hand was even raised in seeming defiance, resting beside her cheek. But the rest of her . . . Was this even her daughter? Flesh melted and black, her thigh a raw mass of red. Her right arm, pinned by her side, her hand almost unrecognizable.

A second EMT was working to wrap some sort of large bandage over her leg, almost like a blanket.

Rainey fell to her knees, covering her mouth, afraid of what might come out. A scream. A wail of agony. Any of the people watching her might have thought that she was praying. But inside her head, she was cursing God.

The people who weren't working on Ariel fell away. Rainey didn't notice them go. The sounds returned. After a few moments, when the EMTs had Ariel wrapped and were transferring her to a gurney, the cop who had tried to stop her from seeing Ariel helped her stand.

"My husband?"

The cop shook his head. Rainey didn't react. She already knew.

"We'll talk at the hospital," the cop said. "There'll be a social worker there. Just be with your daughter."

"I can go with her?"

When Ariel was carefully loaded into the ambulance, and the techs were ready to go, the cop helped Rainey inside.

She didn't look back, but only watched her daughter's face as they sped away, leaving Will and the remains of their house behind.

109

Chapter 21

The bookstore was bright and sunny, all wood floors and sleek pine bookshelves and book-laden tables spaced comfortably for browsing. Several people sat in canvas sling chairs near the window, sipping coffee and reading in the air-conditioned sunshine. Brahms played quietly from the overhead speakers. An enormous sense of freedom washed over Rainey, and she wished she could grab a book and sit in one of the chairs herself for an hour or two. But this was not the day for it, and Ariel was home alone.

Before she could get a sense of where the books Ariel might like would be, a young man with extravagant, shockingly white-blond hair approached her. A chunky gray and white striped cat lounged contentedly in his arms. As the man scratched its chin, it tipped its head backwards and embraced his arm with its forelegs, purring loudly.

"What can I help you find?" he said.

Now that he was closer, Rainey saw he wasn't as young as she'd thought. His white hair, caught and bound up in a pony-tail, was cut through with wiry strands of silver, and there were deep, white lines around his eyes that were accentuated by the tan on the broader planes of his face. His loose, comfortable clothes didn't hide the fact that his body was athletic and taut beneath them. But her attention was immediately drawn to the complicated tattoo on the arm embraced by the cat. She'd seen plenty of tattoos—mostly on artist and musician friends at design school—some of them gorgeous works of art and others quite extreme. This one, a lynx or some other kind of exotic feline surrounded by fantastic blue creatures with yellow eyes, repelled her.

When he cleared his throat, she realized she'd been caught staring. She covered with a smile.

"Young adult. Something new for my daughter."

Hearing Rainey's voice, the cat startled and twisted out of the man's arms with an irritated growl. Rainey backed up.

"Strange," he said. "She's usually very calm." He motioned for Rainey to follow him.

After showing her to a table piled with new releases, he left her to make up her mind. Rainey had to guess which ones Ariel had already read. She worried over them for a good ten minutes before picking up two paperbacks and a hardcover—the latest in a series about an adolescent pair of girl detectives. None of them were about haunted houses. At the cashier's desk, she also picked up a famous North Carolina novelist's book that had just come out. She couldn't remember the last time she'd had the focus to read an entire novel, but maybe it was time to try again.

"Anything else we can help you with today?" The man with the ponytail pulled the pile of books toward him.

Rainey picked up a four-dollar dark chocolate bar from the rack beside the register and set it on the counter.

"Had you pegged for milk chocolate. Win some, lose some."

Rainey smiled and handed him her credit card. He looked vaguely familiar to her, but of course she hadn't ever been in the bookstore before.

He swiped the card through the machine. "Thank you, Ms . . ." He looked at the name on the card. "Adams." He handed Rainey the card. "Let me get some more bags. We're out of them up here."

He disappeared behind the pair of swinging doors behind the register, and was gone much longer than Rainey thought it should take to get bags. She slid the chocolate into her purse and looked at her watch. She felt guilty about leaving Ariel alone, and an idea had come to her when she had passed Gourmet Away, the shop that had catered most of the food for the party.

When the man came back, he wasn't alone. Rainey was pleased to see the small, bespectacled man in a bowtie who preceded him.

"Mrs. Adams!" he said, his voice barely above a whisper. "Ethan Fauquier. We spoke at your lovely party?" Making a little moue, he took one of her hands in his and pressed it firmly. "This is such a sad day for us to meet again."

Rainey still couldn't decide how old he was. He might have been forty or sixty. His skin was virtually unlined; his light brown hair was thin enough that she could see some age spots showing through near the front. In his yellow shirt and rumpled blue seersucker suit, he was the picture of a relaxed southern gentleman.

He took the bags from the man with the ponytail. "I'll finish up here, DeRoy."

DeRoy nodded and disappeared through the squeaking swinging doors.

"DeRoy's a far-distant relative of yours, by marriage. On Judge Bliss's mother's side. So, not blood. But then most everyone in this part of Virginia is related if you go back far enough."

Was it her imagination, or had DeRoy looked at her differently—more critically—before leaving? She thought she saw a certain smugness in the way he turned his back on her. And the other patrons? Were they looking at her too?

"How *are* you doing? You must still be in shock over poor Karin Powell. Everyone here is."

"Well, yes. It was a shock. It's all very new." *New? Where did that come from?* If she'd known people would so easily realize who she was, she would've stayed home until Karin's death wasn't so fresh.

Ethan spoke so quietly that Rainey had to lean forward to hear him.

"No one who knew Karin—and *everyone* knew Karin—can imagine for a minute the thing that would lead her to take her own life. But people do have depths into which we cannot see." He shook his head. "I hope the press hasn't been bothering you too much."

"I considered Mrs. Powell a friend, too, Mr. Fauquier. I hope you'll understand I'm uncomfortable talking about what happened the other night. It's all a little overwhelming."

She hoped that sounding vaguely helpless would shut Mr. Fauquier down. How strange it was that people would now know who she was because someone had killed herself in her house. Ignoring the phone calls hadn't been enough. She'd drawn attention to herself by coming into the bookstore.

"You'll have to forgive me," Ethan said, obviously sensing her unease. "It's a terrible habit I have. Being the owner of the only bookstore in town is a little like being the only bartender. People tell me things. Then other people come by and expect me to have information that no one else has. I gather information like a squirrel gathers nuts. Historians are the worst sorts of gossips." He paused for a moment as he expertly tied the small stack of books together with a raffia string. "Given that Bliss House has such a notorious reputation, everyone suddenly wants to know about it again."

"I can imagine," Rainey said.

Will he ever stop?

"Most houses of any age, big or little, have a history of deaths of all sorts, of course. Poor Mrs. Brodsky—lovely woman—didn't pass inside the house, you know, but there were several other deaths that were looked at as questionable. Starting with Amelia Bliss, the first

113

Mr. Bliss's wife. Everyone thought she'd killed herself because she was heartbroken about the death of her poor little girl." He shook his head sadly. "But what they found out later . . ."

Rainey interjected. Hearing a litany of terrible things that had taken place in her beautiful house was upsetting her even more. At least he had mostly stuck to the house's architectural history at the party.

"I need to get back to my daughter. We'll talk another time, maybe?"

He got the message and smiled at her, revealing a set of too-white dentures. "Of course, of course. You get these books to your little girl, my dear. I know they'll cheer her up. We'll have lots of time to talk. I'll mail you the historical society information that we talked about the other night."

After putting the stack of books into the small shopping bag, he showed her to the door and held it open. A wave of humidity washed over them, but she was happy to escape into the heat.

"There's so much for you to know about the area, and your fascinating house," he said. "It's a rare treat, Bliss House. Rare."

Chapter 22

Rainey programmed an address into her GPS and pulled out of the parking space. She'd spoken with Ariel and was now much calmer. Ethan Fauquier, with his stories about her house, had shaken her badly, and she'd considered just going straight back home. But Ariel had only sounded a little sleepy and wasn't at all combative or upset. No one had called the house or come to the door to bother her, so Rainey felt comfortable telling her she'd be home within the hour. The house to which the GPS was guiding her was only ten minutes away.

Beside her on the seat was a glossy box filled with individual food containers: a chicken, rice, cranberry, and walnut casserole; a cucumber salad; a sourdough baguette; a selection of hard cheeses; and a small chocolate torte. At the last moment, she'd grabbed a bottle of Pinot Grigio from the shop's cooler and included it in the order.

Her experience of losing her own husband hadn't been like most deaths. She'd spent the first weeks of her widowhood at the hospital with Ariel, sporadically retreating to a nearby hotel to shower and catch some sleep. There had been no stunned relatives sleeping on her couch (she had no couch, anyway), looking either for solace or to make sure she was okay. Both of her parents were dead, and Will's mother was in a nursing home. No casseroles or gourmet fruit baskets. Only the occasional glass of wine, pressed on her by her closest friends when she could get away from the hospital. By the time she had a memorial for Will, she had moved into a sparsely furnished apartment. She'd given a lunch afterward at Will's favorite restaurant.

Everything had felt wrong, and too late.

Gerard and Karin's house couldn't be seen from the road, and Rainey wasn't sure what to expect as she drove up the twisting gravel drive. The trees met overhead, their branches and leaves creating a shifting pattern of sunlight and shadow on her car.

Finally, the tunnel of trees ended, bursting onto a broad, sunny landscape of grass and scattered trees that took Rainey's breath away. Gentle hills hugged the property, making it seem secluded yet wonderfully open at the same time. The house was low and long, all wood and creekstone and glass, like a mountain lodge. Its rooflines followed the ridge behind it so that it blended into its background as though it were a natural formation. Stone paths wound through the tall grasses, butterfly bushes, and rhododendrons planted in front. The yard at one end of the house was completely shaded, and filled with more rhododendrons and bushy oak leaf hydrangeas. There was nothing stiff or formal about the place. She wondered what part Karin had played in the design. Knowing Karin, Rainey had imagined a house that was grand in a different, more polished way. Maybe even marble stairs leading up to the door. Definitely columns. She mentally chided herself for being so uncharitable about someone who was dead. It wasn't like *she* lived in a modest cottage. And, of course, Gerard had probably done the design himself. She'd forgotten that he was also an architect.

She stopped behind one of the several cars that were already parked in the arc of the driveway. One of them was Karin's Cadillac, and another Gerard's work truck. By the time she got to the door, she wasn't at all certain what she was doing there.

The entrance to the house was in shadow, and almost like a room itself. The underside of the tall porch roof above Rainey was copper, not yet turned verdigris, and there were two beautifully turned teak benches on either side of the door. Pots of shade flowers bloomed all around her.

When the door opened to her knock, she felt reality shift. Was this Karin? *Yes, and no.* This woman's red hair was cut into a shapely bob that swung just above her shoulders, but she had Karin's frank manner and startling green eyes.

"Yes?" The woman's attitude wasn't particularly friendly, and she gave no indication that Rainey should come inside.

"Is Gerard in?" Rainey said. She smiled, but not too broadly. She was used to aggressive people like Karin, and this woman was obviously a sister or other relation. Her skin was clear, her eyes lucid. If she was someone close to Karin, why weren't her eyes red from crying, or her face puffy? Maybe it was Rainey's imagination, but she felt like the woman suspected her of something terrible. "I just wanted to drop some food off for him."

The woman glanced down at the neatly-packed box with its perky pink *Gourmet Away* sticker on top.

"I'll make sure he gets it," she said, opening the door a little wider. She gave Rainey something short of a smile, as though she were about to do her a huge favor by taking the package off of her hands.

"It's okay, Molly. I'm here." Gerard appeared at the woman's shoulder.

The woman turned to him. "It's not a great time. We should be inside with Mom." She looked back at Rainey with undisguised irritation. Rainey wondered why someone would bother to be so unpleasant to a complete stranger.

Grief, of course. It does terrible, strange things to people, Rainey thought to herself, trying to be understanding.

"I'll be there in a minute," Gerard said firmly.

The woman didn't bother to excuse herself, but simply walked away, back into the house. As she went, a large yellow Golden Retriever whined and tried to push past Gerard, but Gerard held it fast by the collar.

Aside from looking tired, Gerard seemed very much himself—nothing like a man who had lost his very reason for living—and definitely more composed than even the woman he'd called Molly. Rainey recalled the loud argument he had had with Karin that horrible night. The word "selfish" had been hurled more than once, but she couldn't remember if it had been his word or Karin's. He'd never struck her as the selfish type. Karin, though, had seemed to be all about Karin.

"I thought I'd bring some food by," she said. "It's not much. Just a little dinner."

"Smells like Gourmet Away's cranberry and walnut chicken. We pick that up a lot."

Rainey smiled. She didn't quite know how to answer or what to say next. They hadn't exchanged more than a few words the previous morning. Someone else had come by Bliss House to get Karin's Cadillac and hadn't come to the door.

"Karin's family is inside," he said. "They got here last night."

She wondered if Gerard was going to ask her in, yet half-hoped he wouldn't. But she needn't have worried. He didn't move from the doorway.

"If you're concerned about the project, I have to say I don't really know when things will be back on schedule."

Rainey couldn't believe what he was saying. "Oh, no. Did you think I'd come out here for *that*?"

He continued as though she hadn't spoken. "And there's the police. Who the hell knows what the police think." He looked down, into her eyes. "What is it that *you* think happened? You were home, weren't you? Your girl was home. Maybe you both know." His voice sounded normal. He might have been talking about grades of lumber or project estimates. Yet his words chilled her.

"That's not fair, Gerard. How could I know anything about it?"

There were no problems with the gas line coming into the house, Mrs. Adams. It was something—possibly an appliance—inside the house.

"You don't know what goes on in your own home?" he said. "The police said they were questioning your daughter. What did she see?"

"Please, Gerard. We told them everything. Don't be angry with Ariel. She didn't see anything that would help. What can I do so you'll understand how sorry we are?" She glanced involuntarily down at the box in her arms. It was getting heavy, and the smell of the food combined with the agitation she was feeling was making her nauseous. "Karin was a lovely, lovely woman."

Now there was silence between them, except for the occasional whines from the dog. Rainey could hear sobbing from the inner reaches of the house, and a deep male voice offering comfort. She couldn't bear it any longer.

"I'll go," she said. "I'm sure they'll find some answers."

She wasn't quite sure who *they* might be. The police? Where would they find those answers? Bliss House was empty of Karin Powell. She was dead. Rainey had stood outside her bedroom, watching, as the medical examiner's technician and police eased Karin's body into a bag and onto a stretcher to be wheeled out of the house. There was no question that she was gone forever.

She took a step over to one of the teak benches and set the box down on it.

"Lovely," she whispered.

Was it the bench she referred to? Or Karin? Neither of them knew. It had just slipped out.

Rainey didn't hear the front door close behind Gerard, and she didn't look to see if he was still standing there as she drove away.

119

She suddenly felt foolish for bringing what might have looked like a romantic dinner to a man who had just lost his wife. What had she been thinking, bringing him wine? But there was more. Gerard had suggested she was hiding something, that Ariel had seen something more. Worse, there was the subject of what Rainey herself knew. What *she* might have done, or caused. Although she hadn't really been hiding anything important, she felt like he'd seen through her. It made no sense at all because there wasn't a thing that she could have done, or anything else she could have told him except for Ariel's vision of the girl, but what did that have to do with anything? Nothing about this was logical.

Chapter 23

Ariel awoke, stiff, in the big leather chair. The study was like a tiny, protected cove in the vast house, and she was nearly as comfortable there as in her own bedroom. She'd fallen asleep over a biography of Joan of Arc that her mother had been bugging her to read for months, lulled by the sunshine coming in the window and the ticking of the clock out in the front hall.

Thirsty, she went to the kitchen for water and came out with both water and a grape Popsicle from the freezer. She felt like she was probably too old for Popsicles, but her mother kept buying them, and she kept eating them. She thought of the swing set they'd had in their back yard in Kirkwood, before they'd moved farther out of town to the new house and her mother had opened her shop. How many Popsicles had she eaten in the four-person swing with the twins from next door? Purple, orange, red frozen syrup melting down their hands and arms. Too busy or too lazy to run to the house and turn on the hose, they'd wipe their hands in the grass and go on playing, their fingers dotted with grass clippings and dirt and the occasional mashed ant.

It was easier to think about those friends, the ones she'd known several years ago, than the ones she'd left behind when she got out of the hospital.

Would they even recognize her if they saw her? *Maybe.* She knew she was looking more like herself every day. In the hallway, she stepped into the powder room, turned on the light, and leaned close to the mirror. If she turned a certain way, her skin looked perfect. But that wasn't the horror-show side. Tilting her chin just a little, she could see how new, pink-white skin was replacing the textured scar tissue.

What will the Charlottesville doctor say?

She'd be some medical miracle. Maybe she'd even be written up in medical journals. And what about dancing? She looked down at her feet.

No, not quite yet.

Behind her, all signs that the police and Karin Powell's body had been there were gone. Ariel went to the place where Karin's body had lain, the wool rug rough on her bare, tender feet.

She walked in a wide circle, spiraling in closer and closer, until she could look up and see right where the woman had leaned back on the balcony railing.

Maybe she'd been wrong. Maybe she *had* been dreaming.

But what about Daddy?

Looking up at the balcony and the strange star-filled dome in the ceiling, she felt frozen. The hall was drafty despite the heat outside, and she could feel the tepid air conditioning moving through the house, between the floors, and down over her body. Sounds started coming to her from a distance.

Please, not from upstairs. Not from the ballroom.

She wasn't afraid of the rest of the house, but whatever was in the ballroom confused and worried her. It had seemed to both want to hurt her and save her. It felt dangerous. Unpredictable.

There was a shout from outside, and something knocked against an outer wall. Ariel ran to a window. Two people, a man and a woman wearing uniforms, were running in the garden. The man was shouting something she couldn't hear, and the woman was talking into a radio. Ariel pressed against the window, standing on her toes, though her right foot hurt when she did that. She saw nothing. She finally remembered that the detective had told them that someone would be coming to look for evidence outside.

When she stepped back, she realized she was breathing hard.

I won't be afraid. Daddy is here. Daddy is watching.

The police were out of sight now, and she strained to hear their voices. That was one thing about Bliss House. When the doors and windows were closed, it was sealed as solidly as a tomb.

Someone pounded on a door at the rear of the house.

Ariel looked out the window again for the police, but she could neither hear nor see them. There was no way they could've made it to the back of the house without her noticing. She had no weapon, not even her cell phone. The closest phone downstairs was in the kitchen.

I shouldn't look. I don't want to.

But even as she thought it, she knew she would go.

⌣

Jefferson took the soda Ariel handed him, flipped the tab on the top of the can, and drank like he might never get another one. When he finished, he turned to release a large burp behind his hand. His short hair was drenched in sweat and stood, spiky, where he'd run his hands through it.

"Sorry," he said. "I didn't mean to scare you."

"You didn't," Ariel said.

He tore several paper towels from the roll hanging over the counter and ran them over his forehead and the back of his neck. Ariel could smell the sweat and grass.

"Your mom's not home?"

"She went to the library, and maybe somewhere else. She didn't say." She liked that he was there but was a little afraid of him after how strangely he'd acted the night of the party. With what had happened to Karin Powell, she hadn't thought about Jefferson very much, and he hadn't texted her even after he'd asked for her number. When she'd reached the mudroom door, his smiling face had seemed to fill the glass. He'd looked anxious, though, and had even glanced over his shoulder as she let him in.

"How come you're here? Do you want to talk to her?"

"Not really." He drained the last drops of soda and crushed the can between his palms. Ariel had never seen anyone do that before. "So, have the cops figured anything out?"

"Was that you they were running after a minute ago?" Ariel said. "Why didn't you just come to the front door?"

"I hate talking to the police. They already asked me a bunch of questions about the other night. I told them I didn't know anything. Did they talk to you?"

"I didn't tell them anything." The only other time she'd talked to the police was after she'd come out of her coma in the hospital. She couldn't help but link their presence with death.

"Because you don't know anything, anyway."

"What do you mean?" She had no idea if she could trust him, but he'd told her he knew that things happened at Bliss House that couldn't be explained. His father, Randolph, had lived here when he was a kid, and had told Jefferson he was glad that none of them lived here anymore. Plus, Jefferson knew about the ballroom. But that didn't necessarily make him trustworthy.

"Did you see what happened to Karin? Did she hang around after the party?" he asked. "Come on. You were watching every-thing that night." He smiled. The red flush had just about gone from his face, but he still smelled of the outdoors. Ariel didn't think it was such a bad smell.

"Why would I tell you something I didn't tell the police? That would mean I lied to them." Did he hear the shaking in her voice? She suddenly knew that she was going to tell him everything.

Jefferson laughed. "Touché. But it's not like *you* did anything to her, is it?"

"Sure," Ariel said sarcastically. "I pushed her backwards off the balcony. I decided I don't like Bliss House after all. She was a terrible real estate agent, and I wanted revenge because there are spiders in my bedroom. What do you think?"

"How did you know?" Jefferson said.

"I was kidding," Ariel said.

"So how did you know?"

"How did I know what?"

Jefferson leaned toward her an inch or two. "That she fell backwards. You said she went off backwards."

"I don't know that she did. Did I say that? Maybe I heard the police say it." Ariel knew she had said it, but why did he care? She felt her face flush—or most of it. Some of the scar tissue barely had any feeling in it.

He crossed his arms over his chest. "Bunch of dumbasses. They wouldn't know the truth if it came up and chewed their faces off."

"How come you didn't text me?" Ariel said, changing the subject.

"So you saw her fall," Jefferson said, ignoring her question.

"Maybe."

"It's okay," he said. "You don't have to tell me. It must have been pretty creepy. I mean, this house is creepy enough at night without someone about to off herself in front of you. It's not like you and your mom have any kind of protection. It's got to be hard, just being the two of you. Aren't you afraid?"

Ariel held onto the edges of her hood, suddenly self-conscious. She'd been standing there talking to him, forgetting that she looked like a freak show. He was talking to her like he'd forgotten it too. Still, she was embarrassed, and looked at the floor.

"I think there might have been other people here when it happened."

"No shit. Really? Did you see them?"

"You'll laugh," she said.

"Listen, I'm not going to tell anyone and get you in trouble. Who would I tell? The police?" He stepped closer to her, and his voice was low. Quieter. "Karin was good people. I just want to know what happened to her."

"I don't know," Ariel said, looking down at the floor, conscious of how close he was standing. How closely he was watching her.

He touched the front of her hood, near her left cheek. "You were afraid, weren't you?"

No boy had ever stood so close to her before, and she couldn't decide if she should move away or not.

"It wasn't . . ."

She stopped when she heard the doorbell chime its soft xylophone notes from the hall.

"I need to see who that is."

Instead of stepping aside, Jefferson put his hands on her shoulders, stopping her.

"What?" Ariel's head was filled with a profound confusion. Maybe fear.

Should I be afraid?

"I like you, Ariel. Don't you like me?"

Now her confusion turned to anger. He was playing with her, again. But before she could pull away from him, he pressed his mouth onto hers.

She held her breath, stunned. His lips were warm and soft and unexpectedly gentle, and she was torn between kneeing him in the groin and letting him continue to work his lips against hers. What should she do? Was he trying to French kiss her? It felt good, but not quite right.

Just as she identified the troubling rush of feeling between her legs as not really troubling at all, it was over.

The doorbell rang again.

"Somebody wants in." Jefferson took a step back. He wasn't smiling, but there was a look in his eyes that said he might start laughing at any moment. Was he just happy or was he laughing at her?

"Go on," he said.

Ariel hurried from the room in a minor state of shock. What did it all mean?

"You haven't seen anyone besides Deputy Taylor and myself near the house in the last ten or fifteen minutes?"

The deputy doing the talking was an African American woman, taller and stockier than the white male officer beside her. He was all sunburn and brushy mustache. The woman wore her hair in a thick, braided bun at the back of her neck, and the collar button of her uniform shirt was unbuttoned, probably because of the heat. Ariel looked hard at her, her own happy mood broken. She'd seen the flicker of shock in the officer's eyes when she first opened the door. It happened every time she met a stranger, and she couldn't get used to it.

Maybe soon I won't have to. How awesome would that be?

"I haven't been outside," Ariel said.

"Did anyone come to the door? Any strangers?"

"My mom isn't home. You should probably wait until she gets back." There was no way she was letting them into the house. She wanted to get back to Jefferson. Alone. Though that idea was a little intimidating to her. What would happen next?

"She left you here on your own?" The two deputies exchanged quick, puzzled glances, which irritated Ariel a lot. It wasn't like she was ten years old.

"So I probably shouldn't let you in, right?"

Before either officer had a chance to answer, Ariel saw her mother's car coming up the driveway.

"There she is."

Ariel pointed with her ruined hand, bringing it within a few inches of their faces, just to freak them out. The male officer took an involuntary step back, then quickly looked to where she was pointing. His sunburned neck and ears turned an even more satisfying red.

⁓

Rainey followed Ariel into the house. After talking to her, the deputies had gone toward the woods, through the garden, to continue their search. One of them had a metal detector.

"What if it had been someone else?" Rainey couldn't keep the panic from her voice. "It was stupid of me to leave you alone. You should've called me."

"You were already coming up the driveway." Ariel didn't mention Jefferson, even though she couldn't see a reason why it would matter to her mother if he was there. She wasn't sure if she wanted him to still be in the kitchen or not.

Rainey unpacked one of the bags on the hall table and handed Ariel the tied stack of books. "I know. But that doesn't excuse my not being here."

Ariel ran a finger over the books' spines, her hand shaking a bit. "They didn't have any about hauntings?"

Rainey hesitated. "Not that looked any good."

"Sure," Ariel said. She guessed that her mother didn't want her to read anything scary because of the dead woman. Parents could be such worriers.

"Let's go put this stuff away." Rainey picked up the other bags. On the way to the kitchen, she couldn't help but look at the place on the rug where they'd found Karin's body, and it slowed her. Recovering herself, she asked Ariel if she was hungry.

Now it was Ariel's turn to hesitate. Should she mention Jefferson, or take the chance that he might be gone?

"What is it?" Rainey asked.

"Nothing. I just didn't eat any lunch yet."

Rainey laughed over her shoulder. "Well, I may be a terrible mother, leaving you all alone in this big house out in the country, but at least I came back with éclairs from the bakery. Does that score me any points?"

Her mother had such a pretty laugh. Everything about her mother was pretty. No wonder everyone liked her. Ariel wanted—really wanted—to stay angry with her mother, but it was getting harder.

"I probably need to taste one, first," she said.

Rainey went through the dining room to get to the kitchen, still not much liking to use the disguised panel door in the hall. The kitchen was empty, but the air was disturbed and she had a sense that someone had just left the room. Whether that person was alive or dead, she wasn't sure.

A moment later, seeing that Jefferson was gone, a relieved Ariel grabbed the bakery bag from her mother and dug for an éclair.

Chapter 24

"God, it stinks in here," Michael said. "Light another candle. And tie up that bag from your bucket and put it by the door."

He'd stayed away longer than he ever had before. All the fruit was gone from the cooler. Allison hadn't eaten any of the bread, or the peanut butter. She only wanted the peaches.

Before he'd brought her here, the roadside stands had just started to sell them. The first peaches he brought her had been small and soft and covered with light red skin that faded to gold. Definitely local. But these last had been harder and hadn't ripened well at all. He'd probably gotten them from one of the bigger grocery stores that shipped them in from Texas or Mexico, out of the Virginia season.

Why hadn't she ever begun to count the days? No. She knew why. There was no day here, just as there was no night. It never mattered.

"My stomach. I had diarrhea," she said. "I always do, now."

Suddenly tender, he put a hand to her cheek. "Poor thing. I'll bring you Pepto-Bismol or something."

She knew he was lying. Pretending, like he always did. He didn't care at all how she felt. If he did he wouldn't leave her here. Shrinking away, she said nothing.

He smiled. "You're such a flirt, Allison."

"I smelled something from outside," she said, hoping to distract him. "Smoke. Was there a fire?" She had definitely smelled smoke. There were two tiny vents up near the ceiling, and she had gotten in the habit of climbing on top of the dresser to press her face against one of them.

He looked confused for a moment, and then his face cleared. Sometimes she forgot what he looked like when he wasn't sweating over her.

"Someone was probably burning brush."

Immediately, she regretted asking him. It had been her secret. A message from the outside to let her know she wasn't completely alone in the world. If there was a fire, she knew that there must be other people close by.

"Wash yourself," he said. "I brought you another towel." He pulled a thin towel with a green stripe down its middle from the backpack he'd brought, and tossed it onto the tiny sink.

Ignoring him, she moved to the niche that held an unlighted candle. How many had she burned? She'd lost count. This one was ridiculously ornate, with orange, yellow, and white stripes, and wax curls decorating its sides. She'd made similar candles with her cousin when she was a kid and they'd sold them to ladies in the neighborhood. Just the sight of this one plunged her further into dull misery.

When she was done with the candle and the bucket, she came back to stand in front of him, and, without comment, began to take off her clothes. She dropped her panties on the floor and moved them to the side with a desultory kick.

"Where's the romance?" He laughed. "Remember when I showed up at your apartment and you did that little striptease thing? What about that?"

131

She bent to pull off the socks he had finally given her to wear as well. (He'd taken her sandals that first day.) Already, they were wearing thin.

"You need to wash your hair again, too." He tried to run his fingers through it, but they became quickly tangled. "I used to like your hair. Maybe I'll cut it for you."

Moving to the sink, she turned the water on. It trickled out, just like always. Each time she turned it on, she wondered if it might be for the last time. Where did it come from? It had a heavy, mineral taste to it that reminded her of well water.

Shivering, she cupped her hands beneath the rusted tap until there was enough to splash on her face, and did it again, and again.

As she stood there, not wanting to ever lift her face from that stained, ancient sink again, she felt him press against her backside. He'd unzipped his pants, or taken them off. It didn't matter to her which. She kept the water running, cupping it into her hands, drinking it, letting it run onto her chin and neck, as he rubbed against her.

He kneaded her buttocks and gave a contented moan. Then he slipped one hand between her legs, fitting his middle finger into her vagina. She was dry, and his fingernail was sharp. When he moaned some more, she knew that he had his other hand on his cock. He slipped a thumb into her anus, and she understood that that was what was going to happen today. She had healed from the last time, but it still ached deep inside.

After a couple of minutes, he pulled away and told her to get onto the bed. She didn't want to look at his face—she never wanted to look at his face anymore, couldn't believe that there was ever a time when she had looked forward to seeing it when she opened her apartment door—but there he was, sunk down on the end of the bed. His face was red and slack and his eyes had lost their focus. He was no longer there in the room with her. She knew it wasn't the same place she would be going in her own head. How strange that neither of them wanted to be in that room.

Squeezing her eyes shut, she tried to keep her hold on the bed as he entered her. But when he tore his way into her body, she screamed and screamed.

He didn't even bother to stop her.

Chapter 25

Tuesday mornings were for doing laundry. Bertie tucked one of the telephones in her apron pocket as she went down to the basement, thinking she might try calling Rainey one more time.

Most of the women of her status had someone in to both clean and do the laundry, but Bertie found a sense of peace in doing the family laundry herself. It made her feel closer to the Judge and her Jefferson, and the Judge had had the ancient laundry area in the basement remodeled when Jefferson was a baby so it would be more cheerful for her. For years, Jefferson had played with his trucks on the well-scrubbed tile floor while she worked. Since he'd come home from UVA for the summer, he'd resumed dropping his laundry down the chute so she could take care of it like she had before he left home. It was no trouble, and she thought she might as well get used to doing it again. The Judge didn't know it, but Jefferson would be going back to UVA under academic probation, and he might be forced to leave if the fall semester didn't go as it should.

The Judge hid it well, and appeared to give Jefferson all the encouragement a father should, but Bertie knew Jefferson was a disappointment to him. The Judge had been at the top of every class he'd ever attended, and had known what he would do with his life since he was ten years old. But her Jefferson was in love with life, just like she was. He saw beyond books and making money and hundred-year-old traditions. He'd loved to explore their house and grounds and the woods and trails around Old Gate. She'd taken him on trips, too, that the Judge didn't want to bother with. In addition to all the Civil War sites, they'd seen Yellowstone, San Francisco, New York City, and had even been out to the Grand Canyon, where they'd spent an exciting, dangerous night camping with a group and guide in the canyon's basin. Jefferson understood adventure, just like she did.

Even now, when he was supposed to be relaxing during his summer break, he was out of the house all day and most nights. She didn't ask where he went. He needed his freedom, and he was happy. That was all that mattered to her.

She took the laundry from the chute and sorted it into loose color piles on the floor, then removed the Judge's shirts and set them aside. Laundry was one thing, but ironing the Judge's shirts to his strict preferences was a different matter. The cleaners did a much better job than she could.

Pulling the phone from the pocket of the apron she wore to do housework, she started to dial Rainey's number but stopped halfway through and ended the call, worried she might be intruding. She felt such a kinship with Rainey, and wished that Rainey would let her meet Ariel. It was a shame they weren't related by blood because then she might have a real claim on Rainey's time. There had been talk in Bertie's mother's and grandmother's generations that Randolph Hasbrouck Bliss, who had built Bliss House, had fathered a number of children on the wrong side of the blanket. It was hinted that her great-great-aunt Flora might have been one of those children, but there was never any proof and the possibility was only spoken of among the women of the family.

Practically everyone born in this part of Virginia was, in some way, related to everyone else, she knew. Black or white, it didn't matter. The boundaries of flesh and emotion had never been as clearly drawn as people liked to pretend they were. It gave Bertie a daring little thrill to know that she and her own husband were tenuously linked in history, as though they were living characters in a great Gothic drama.

It would've been so much easier for Rainey to get the advice she really needed if the Judge's mother were still alive. Charlotte Bliss had had a fondness for Rainey, an understandable fondness that Charlotte had explained to her when Bertie was a young bride, and which had bonded Bertie more closely to her mother-in-law. Charlotte also had very strong opinions about who should and shouldn't live in Bliss House. Rainey definitely would have been on the "should not" list.

Rainey had treated Bertie so kindly—almost like a sister—that she harbored a hope that they might become best friends. She had plenty of friends in Old Gate, of course, but she knew in her heart that not even her closest friends took her seriously. She didn't mind being a little ridiculous, with her fondness for flowers and sunny colors that made her feel happy and adventurous. And she knew she wasn't the smartest person on the planet. College at Randolph-Macon had exhausted her after three semesters and she had come home one early March afternoon and declared that she wasn't going back. Her parents had told her it was just as well. In fact, her father's words were: "Good on you, Bertie. You'll save me ten thousand a year." But when serious things like a death came up, she wanted to show that she was just as valuable as anyone else. Besides, she understood about Bliss House, about what Rainey and that dear child were up against.

She'd tried to talk to the Judge about it. He'd gone to the party reluctantly, because he had made it clear from the beginning that he didn't want anything more to do with Bliss House. He'd told her that she should stay out of the business of the woman's death, and that she needed to keep Rainey Adams at arm's length. But Bertie was scared for Rainey, and the girl too. She had to do something.

Resolving to finally do something, she decided to skip the phone call and go right over to Bliss House to see how Rainey was doing. The Judge didn't even need to know.

When the first load of laundry was in the washing machine, Bertie bent over the large basket beneath the chute to make sure she hadn't missed anything. A single sock was curled in the corner of the basket. As she plucked it out, something fell back into the basket with a tiny *click*. She felt around for whatever it was, and brought it into the light to get a better look.

The thing was small and thin, rough to the touch on one side, smooth on the other. She held it closer, wishing she had her reading glasses with her. Turning it over, she almost threw it to the floor. It was part of a fingernail. Bright and bronze and definitely not hers.

Chapter 26

Detective Lucas Chappell drummed his fingers on the restaurant's pocked wooden tabletop. It had been slightly more than forty-eight hours since Karin's body had been found. He had a team interviewing both the guests from the party and the woman's friends, but by interviewing the family—including Gerard Powell, the husband—himself, he'd learned that the couple's marriage was way more complicated than it had looked on the surface. It definitely warranted a closer look. Because the evidence didn't point to a straight-up murder, the case wasn't imbued with a strong sense of urgency. But that could change at any moment. Right now his primary goals were to get some food and to get on the phone with the medical examiner.

The service at the Lettuce Leaf was slower than usual. Despite the brutal August heat, the Shenandoah Valley was packed with families trying to sneak in a last vacation before school started. Every café in town was stuffed with overweight, sunburned men, women in flip-flops, shorts, and t-shirts, and bored teenagers texting on phones that cost more than his first car. Finally, Lucas caught a server's eye, and she immediately started toward the table.

"How are you, Kyleigh?" he said.

He knew servers ate it up when you remembered their names without looking for a nametag. Being nominally vegetarian, he ate at the Lettuce Leaf whenever he was within ten miles or so of Old Gate because they had a particularly good hummus burger.

Kyleigh was a bouncy sort of young woman, with a heart-shaped face and a talent for applying false eyelashes that made her look perpetually wide-eyed and expectant. Her breasts neatly filled out her bright white Lettuce Leaf t-shirt, and her tiny denim shorts exposed a pair of well-shaped legs that were both tan and athletic. He guessed that she was about twenty-two.

"Ugh," she said. "I made this huge dinner for my boyfriend last night, and he only ate like five bites of it. So frustrating! And how are you? Can I get you something to drink?"

"Hayseed Summer Lager, and a glass of water. Did he make it up to you?"

"No. He did not. He told me he felt sick, like I poisoned him or something."

"You can't do any more than try," Lucas said.

"I know, right?" she said, giving him an exaggerated blink. "For specials today, we've got a white bean vegan chili with cilantro, served with rosemary caraway bread, also vegan, and mushroom and Gruyére quiche with a melon salad, but that's not vegan. I mean, the quiche isn't. You want me to come back in a minute?"

"Give me a hummus burger with your homemade chips."

As she walked away, he watched her, her brunette ponytail swinging with her lilting gait. She was cute and he sensed that, in another couple of visits, he could make her forget the ungrateful boyfriend for at least a few hours if he chose to. Then he wondered what the boyfriend was like. It was a diversion from the paucity of information he'd gotten from the medical examiner about Karin.

He'd been frank about his sexuality with his work partner, Brandon, when they started working together two years earlier. Brandon was straighter than straight and had a pretty blond wife named Gayle and a new baby. Lucas knew it puzzled Brandon, and probably worried him, that he didn't discriminate between men and women when it came to his love life. Though he did differentiate: while he didn't mind being with men who were his own age or slightly older, he definitely preferred women who were younger.

"What the hell do I care who you date?" Brandon had told him. "Well, with the exception of my wife, of course. Maybe that part-time guy down in records, too. He's got a body odor problem, and that would show a serious lack of judgment."

Once they'd been partners for a year or so, he'd tried to be funny by asking Lucas if he would "do" a particularly good-looking guy who had waited on them in a restaurant. Lucas had stunned him by answering honestly and in detail. It wasn't a question he asked a second time.

With some time to kill before his lunch arrived, he got Hamrick, the medical examiner, on the phone. He confirmed that the marks on Karin Powell's neck indicated someone had had their hands on her firmly enough to leave bruising, but hadn't caused her death. A significant but not problematic amount of alcohol and Lorazipam in her system, but not enough of either to suggest an overdose.

"Anxiety?" Lucas asked. He kept his voice as low as he could, even though the people at the tables around him were well-occupied with their own concerns.

"Likely," Hamrick said.

"The prescription bottle was in a makeup bag in the car. A box of laxative pills was in there, too," Lucas said.

"Well, that could've been a diet thing."

"Nice," Lucas said. He did a fast mental inventory of what was in his own medicine cabinet. What would a detective make of his medication, shaving habits, or preference for waxed dental floss? He couldn't help wondering. It came of having too much experience of the lives of the dead.

"And then this . . ." Hamrick said.

"What?"

"There were signs she was pregnant."

"Okay." Lucas said.

"The thing is, she wasn't pregnant when she died. She *was* pregnant. Recently. But there are no signs that she ever gave birth."

"Miscarriage? Abortion? What?"

"She has all the signs of having had a recent abortion. We're testing for the amount of pregnancy hormone in her blood," Hamrick said.

Stressed out and pregnant. Or not. A hell of a combination. It made sense that she wouldn't have been taking the Lorazipam when she was pregnant, unless she knew she was going to get rid of the baby. It was a notion that seemed cold-hearted to him, but he pushed the judgment aside. There wasn't room for that kind of thinking in his job. It had been her business. He had to stay focused on the facts.

"I need to know how long ago the pregnancy ended," Lucas said. "Also if the anxiety meds were connected in some way, and if she was on them when she died."

"Pregnancy could be a motive for suicide *or* for murder," Hamrick said.

Children were always a complication. It was as though the diapers, the doctors' appointments, the weird sleeping and eating schedules weren't enough. They had to mess with everyone's heads, too. They never arrived at just the right time, or for exactly the right reasons. Damned if they didn't come out already well-versed in human flaws and steeped in drama. Lucas had no desire to ever have one of his own.

"We don't know if it was the husband's or not?" Lucas said.

"How the hell would I know that?" Hamrick said. "That's y'all's job. I just open them up."

"I don't suppose there was any DNA from the baby? What do you think?"

Hamrick sighed. "Sorry, she was clean. No reputable clinic would keep the fetal tissue around for more than a day or two, at most."

"Let me know when you get more," Lucas said.

"Hey," Hamrick said. "She was missing two fingernails. Not real ones, but the kind that they temporarily fuse to the real nail. And don't expect this to be easy. I don't believe in a lot of hocus pocus bullshit, but both my old man and my grandfather were docs around here most of their lives, and their notes go way back. Some of the stuff they dealt with at that house was nasty enough to rot the paper the notes were written on."

"So you told us after Mim Brodsky's murder."

"Then, my friend, don't bother acting like any of this surprises you. Bad things have been happening around that house for a very long time. The Brodsky murder was only the most recent. Bliss House is like one of those celebrity rehab shows. You have to keep watching it or you miss the big meltdown. Everyone's waiting for it to happen. Then when it does, people act like they want to know why and how and all that stuff. Mostly they just want to be certain that it won't happen to them."

Some surprises were more surprising than others.

Lucas hung up the phone.

Gerard Powell's exact words that morning had been: "My wife was a sex addict who screwed pretty much any man she was interested in—married or single, bi or straight, any time she felt the need to do it. She might even have done you, Detective. You never met her, did you?"

There had been a challenge in Gerard Powell's eyes, but Lucas didn't rise to it. He'd never been married, but he could imagine it would've been hell to come home to someone like Karin Powell. He just shook his head, not bothering to tell the husband that his wife hadn't been his type.

The interview with the rest of the family members at Powell's house had been brief. They all lived out of state, and Karin Powell had only been in frequent touch with her sister, Molly. The father had made a lot of noise after Lucas had offered his condolences and told them his team was working as hard as they could to get answers. He knew they were in a hard place: their child had died before they had. Worse, no one had any answers about *why*. Molly, who looked disturbingly like the victim, had hovered over them, looking irritated. She had nothing but soft words for Gerard Powell, though. To Lucas, she looked like she wanted to be a comfort to her brother-in-law in the worst way.

It wasn't until they were alone that Gerard Powell had brought up his wife's addiction. Did the parents know? Lucas thought that they—and certainly the sister—must. It wasn't the sort of addiction that was easy to hide.

A server who wasn't Kyleigh brought his lunch to the table. But Kyleigh soon followed with a pitcher to refill his ice water.

"You want another beer?" she asked. "It's awfully hot out there today. It's like one of those spa saunas back in the kitchen." She ran the back of her free hand across her forehead. "So crazy. But I guess it *is* August."

"No, thanks, Kyleigh. It all looks good to me."

She must have heard more in his words than he meant to imply because she blushed prettily before moving on to the next table.

It didn't seem a bad thing to him to let a girl like Kyleigh feel flattered. But given the case that was beginning to consume him, he couldn't help but compare her to the Adams girl. What would *her* life be like in five or ten years? Unfortunately, her sad situation and her injuries had little bearing on whether she was a truthful or trustworthy person. He hated to be suspicious of a child, but he couldn't help himself. Something wasn't right about her. She was steely and angry and he knew it was unlikely that she would open up to him anytime soon. Which left the mother. If he was patient, maybe he could get to her.

Chapter 27

Rainey walked from the carriage house, slowed by the cloying noontime humidity. She'd spent most of the morning stripping wallpaper in the dining room and had begun to feel claustrophobic, so she'd taken a short walk to clear her head. The scent of honeysuckle and the sound of a thousand bees at work drifted from the banks of bushes along the driveway. She'd loved the house they'd built back in Missouri, but it didn't have the privacy and the natural beauty that the land surrounding Bliss House had. She imagined Will walking with her along the sunny drive. He often held her hand when they walked outdoors. Before he died, the possibility that she might have to grow old without him had never occurred to her.

She liked to think of him here, exploring the place with her, letting her bounce ideas off of him about how it should look.

Stopping in the sunshine, she closed her eyes and listened to the droning of the bees. So frantic, yet peaceful at the same time. The sun was warm on her face. Will might have kissed her in that moment, his hand firmly cradling her head, his fingers messing up her hair. She would pretend to be shocked that he would kiss her so frankly in a place where anyone watching from the house could see them. He might squeeze her breast playfully, daring someone to notice, making her laugh and blush.

What if Ariel sees us?

You had the talk with her, right?

But we're her parents!

Then he would kiss her again. Harder.

Their physical connection had been instant and deep and lasting, and she felt stirrings that went beyond memory. She'd been without him for so long! How easily, unthinkingly they'd touched one another in the four-poster bed they'd shared since the day they returned from their honeymoon. The bed that had been so lucky for them. The bed in which they'd lain breathless and spent and happy.

Rainey.

Will's voice, whispering her name. Despite the hazy distance of the sound, the word itself was brutal to her ears. She'd heard Will's voice before, in the brief, thick moments of gloom between sleeping and waking. It would always be there, she knew, as much a product of her guilt as her love.

When something—or someone—touched her hair, Rainey brought her hand to the back of her head and opened her eyes. The sun seemed to have dimmed.

"Will?"

There was no one near. She felt dizzy. Disoriented. Bringing her hand back around, she discovered a fat bumblebee crawling on her index finger. She started to shake it off, but realized that she wasn't afraid. The bee was as weightless as a thought. If she hadn't seen it, she wouldn't have known that it was there.

Then: a woman's laughter. Confident laughter, low and suggestive.

The driveway, the gardens, the grass stretching back to the far-off orchards . . . all desolate and shimmering with heat. Ariel was inside the house, napping. But Rainey sensed that someone was nearby.

I won't be afraid. For Ariel's sake, I won't be afraid. And she had heard Will's voice. How could she be afraid if Will was nearby?

"Will?" She couldn't believe she was actually calling his name, but it felt so right. So natural.

Ariel was in her room, right above her, so she didn't want to say his name too loudly. The laughter had seemed to come from behind the house. She didn't hurry, even though she wanted to.

He touched me. God, it's been so long. But I remember!

The windows she passed were blank with sunlight, and she could see her own solitary figure reflected back as she walked. When she reached the corner of the house, she opened the iron gate leading to the herb garden behind the kitchen and went inside. As she ran a hand over the unchecked stand of lemon verbena to release its fresh, sharp scent, the bumblebee—had it been on her hand the whole time?—dove into the leaves, then quickly shot out again, into the air above her. She followed it with her eyes. Up, up. As she lost sight of it, she noticed the woman in the window.

Rainey put a hand to her mouth. The window was in the servants' quarters that jutted from the back of the house. In the glass above an open second floor sash, she saw a pale, naked woman with burnished red curls, whose image was mixed with the vast reflection of the sky. Her hair was gathered into a sumptuous ponytail resting over one shoulder and tied with a thick blue ribbon. Her face was a mask of pleasure: lips parted, wet and open, glistening in the sun. Her eyes were closed, one hand holding fast onto the window's frame, the other nearly hidden in the apex of her thighs. But there was a man, too. Rainey could only see his outline behind the woman. He slipped a hand around her, seeking and finding one of her voluptuous breasts. The woman's breasts were the sort that Rainey had always wanted to have, that she found fascinating in their unfamiliarity. Her own were firm but almost pubescent. Even with Will she'd been self-conscious about their petite size.

What kind of woman could stand in a window like this and let herself be watched? But Rainey couldn't look away. Both she and the woman were completely absorbed. Transported. The woman's breath clouded the sun-warmed glass, clouding and fading, clouding and fading as she breathed, as the man's other hand came around her other side, sliding down her hip, covering her hand, mimicking its rhythmic movement. Whatever he was doing caused the woman's mouth to open wider, and Rainey saw more than heard her fractured gasp of delight.

As the woman bent in the throes of her certain orgasm, the loosely-tied ribbon fell, so that her hair spilled around her, hiding her face and her breasts, and Rainey saw the too-familiar contrast of hair to skin. She almost cried out in disbelief, but didn't. If the woman heard her, she might leave the window, and the whole scene might disappear. It was as if she'd seen the whole performance before and wanted it to play out again. She could feel the heat flooding the woman's body as though it were her own.

The black-haired man behind the woman pulled her tight against him, at first burying his face in her mass of hair, then emerging to cover her shoulder, her neck with lingering kisses. He squeezed both breasts, roughly fondling the nipples, and the woman gave a little scream, her chin shooting up. Her eyes opened, and Rainey could see that the woman was now looking down at her. Rainey blushed, caught in her own puzzled excitement, but still couldn't look away.

A cloud passed over the sun, and Rainey saw the woman's face clearly. It was Karin Powell, looking very much alive.

The man put his hands on the woman's shoulders and spun her so that Rainey could see her only in profile. He stepped forward, never more than a few inches from the woman who was—impossibly!—Karin Powell, his torso shining with sweat. He was handsome. More gloriously handsome than anyone she'd ever seen. Dropping to his knees, he roughly parted Karin's legs. When he wrapped his arms around her thighs and buried his face between them, Rainey blushed.

I shouldn't be watching. But I must, must watch, because I know . . .

If she were telling herself the truth, she knew she would want to be in that window herself, with them. With him. Because she felt she knew him.

She was certain she knew those arms, the feeling of those hands on *her* breasts, and the feeling of his penis deep inside her. And the way her thighs burned after he'd rubbed his unshaven cheeks against them. Of course she'd never minded because he was hers, and she, his.

But it couldn't be Will. It couldn't be Will because he would never be with another woman. It couldn't be Will, because Will was dead.

Rainey couldn't force her voice above a whisper.

"Who are you?"

Rainey stumbled as she ran through the kitchen garden. First, she tried the door that led directly into the servants' quarters, but it was locked. Hurrying to the mudroom door, she opened it and rushed through the back of the silent house and to the servants' staircase. The stairs to the servants' rooms were steep and narrow, but she hardly noticed because her feet felt light. She had to know. She had to see who it was.

When she reached the second floor, she wasn't sure which way to go. She was all turned around, and breathing heavily. A tickling rivulet of sweat ran down her back. Everywhere she looked the doors were closed and looked exactly the same.

She opened the doors to one room after another. Empty. Empty. Empty.

Putting her hand on the doorknob outside the last room, she quickly drew her hand back and touched her own throat for warmth. The doorknob had been as cold as ice.

"Hello?"

There were sounds coming from inside. No voices, but a kind of high, electric hum. By now her body felt electric as well.

Karin Powell was dead. Will was dead. There must be strangers in her house!

But the effects of what she'd seen lingered inside her. She'd felt the woman's breath on the window as though it had brushed her own cheek. No one touched her anymore.

Braving the icy doorknob, she turned it and pushed open the door. A rush of cold air flew at her from the room, as though it would send her backwards. But she kept moving forward.

A pair of windows on the far wall cast their suddenly gray afternoon light across the bare floor. The cold of the room chilled the sweat covering her chest. The air was crisp, but smelled so heavily of sex that she could barely breathe.

Empty.

Rainey walked slowly to the window that looked down on the herb garden. Even against the light, she could see the traces of fog etched on the glass. And in the center of the fog, the letter R.

For Rainey. For me.

Chapter 28

Someone was calling her name, but Rainey didn't want to wake. Her left cheek was pressed hard against the duvet on her bed where she had collapsed, and her head felt heavy with sadness. Keeping her eyes closed against the shaded light of her bedroom, she willed whoever it was to go away and leave her alone. It wasn't Ariel. Ariel would've simply come to find her. No, it was someone else. Someone who had let herself into the house.

"Rainey, honey, are you here? Ariel?"

Rainey finally recognized Bertie's voice. Of course Bertie would let herself in. Bertie never meant anyone any harm. But she was stubborn, and Rainey knew she wasn't going to go away.

⁓

Bertie was dressed in a snug pink sateen skirt, pink espadrilles, and a broad straw hat accented with a peony blossom as big as a luncheon plate. Her face was nearly hidden by the stems of the globular potted plant she carried ahead of her like a sacrificial offering.

"The Amish produce stand just put these out," she said, handing the giant chrysanthemum to Rainey. "I just love fall blooms.

Especially golden ones. They'll open in a couple of weeks, I would think."

"Thank you," Rainey said quietly. "They'll be beautiful in the kitchen."

Bertie brushed a scattering of potting soil from her otherwise spotless white top, causing the flesh of her exposed upper arm to jiggle a bit. Then she looked at Rainey and smiled.

"You know, those silly Italians think that chrysanthemums signify death, but don't you worry about that. Everyone else—everyone sensible, that is—knows they mean friendship." She hurried back to close the front door, shutting out the midday heat. Then she followed Rainey as she carried the flowers toward the dining room.

"Where . . . ?"

Rainey stopped and turned back to her. For a moment she thought Bertie was talking about the woman and man in the window, but then she realized she was asking where Karin fell. "It happened over there." She tilted her head, indicating the area near the back of the hall. "There wasn't any blood."

Bertie sighed. "If I were Catholic, I'd cross myself," she said, hurrying to catch up. "I would anyway, if I could be sure of doing it right. I've heard that if you do it backwards, you can accidentally conjure up the devil."

Rainey wasn't sure she heard Bertie correctly, but was a little afraid that she had. She didn't strictly believe in the devil, but only the presence of something malicious and evil could explain what she'd seen—imagined she'd seen?—in that window. What she'd felt inside that room. A shudder moved through her.

Bertie, who had been following closely, put a hand on her arm.

"I'm so sorry. I know it must've been awful for you. It was careless of me to bring it up. Randolph is always telling me I don't know when to stay quiet."

Rainey was touched by the concern in Bertie's eyes. But she couldn't tell anyone what she'd seen. Who would believe her? It might have been the heat plus her grief and shock all muddled together.

"No worries," she said, covering Bertie's soft hand with her own. "It's just something we have to get used to."

Bertie brightened. "The thing to do is to get your mind off of it. What are you doing in here?" She hurried into the dining room, the lining of her skirt rustling busily. "Oh, you're taking off the wallpaper. Look how much you've done already!"

"I needed to do something," Rainey said. "I can't open my design business for a while. It wouldn't seem right."

She couldn't imagine clients visiting Bliss House anytime soon. Human nature would lead the curious there to waste her time looking at the crime scene—if the location of a suicide was even called a crime scene. It would be even worse if the police finally decided that Karin had been murdered. She wished she knew for certain what was true and what wasn't. Only Ariel might know for sure, and even though they'd been communicating more, Ariel had become totally silent on the subject. She, like Rainey herself, seemed to want it all to go away.

For Rainey, the immediate answer to any degree of stress was any kind of work. There were fabric and lighting suppliers to contact, and antiques-hunting trips to take. At least Virginia and the surrounding states were rich in the kind of furniture she liked to use in her favorite projects. The trips would be fun—a way to get familiar with the people and the landscape—and she looked forward to maybe taking Ariel with her. But that part would hinge on Ariel's willingness to go. She was making some progress, but how much healing would she require of her body for her to feel good about leaving the house? She hadn't even yet agreed to see the new doctor in Charlottesville.

"I think you should call in some professionals, dear," Bertie said. "It's such a big job. I don't know that you should be up on a ladder that tall. And what if the rest of the mural under there is in terrible shape? You might not even like it. Randolph's mother couldn't bear it. Her son, Michael—Randolph's brother—restored it. But after he disappeared, she couldn't bear to look at it. Could hardly bear to be in the house at all, poor thing."

"We've had enough professionals around here the past few days," Rainey said.

"What about Ariel? Children can be so nimble."

"I'm not nimble."

They turned, both surprised to see Ariel standing in the doorway to the kitchen.

"Hi, baby," Rainey said. She wondered why Ariel had chosen that moment to make an appearance. Perhaps she sensed that Bertie—with her sunny smile and guileless manner—was safe to be around.

Bertie's smile was warm. She'd taken off her hat and her bleached blond hair curled girlishly around her face. "Honey, I know you'd want to do whatever you can to help your mama. You're a nice girl, aren't you?"

"Help her do what?" Ariel said. "What are you doing in here?"

"Ariel, remember I told you about Bertie?" Rainey said. "Bertie, this is Ariel."

"I've wanted to meet you ever since your mama sent out your birth announcements, and here it's taken all this time." Before Ariel could answer, Bertie had her arms around her, hugging her tightly. Ariel looked stricken, but she didn't push Bertie away as Rainey was afraid she might.

When Bertie stepped back, there was an awkward moment. Ariel blushed and looked down at her feet.

"I'm taking down this ugly wallpaper," Rainey said. "I showed you. Remember? At first I thought the last people who lived here put it up. But I think it's older than that." She ran her hand over the exposed wall, with its hundreds of peacock feather eyes staring out at them. "What do you think of the mural?"

"I think it's bizarre, and totally your style."

Rainey laughed. It was so much like something the old Ariel might have said. Ariel had always been curious about people's *styles*. Just months before the accident, they'd done her room in 1960's Mod, with enormous graphic flowers on the walls, beanbag chairs, brightly painted Danish furniture and a furry arctic white rug splashed across the wood floor. When Rainey had ordered furniture for Ariel's bedroom in Bliss House, she'd chosen simple wood pieces with contemporary but not trendy lines. Ariel could make it her own when she was ready.

"I'm not sure why, but it just fits the room," Rainey said. "I'm sorry you don't like it."

Ariel suddenly addressed Bertie. "Is Jefferson with you?"

"Do you know Jefferson?" Bertie brightened further. "I didn't know you'd met him."

Rainey watched her daughter closely. Ariel's voice faltered as she spoke.

"Mom told me about him. I guess I saw him. Out the window or something. Tell him *thank you* for the hat."

The hat she wore today was pink crochet, with an orange flower. It was pulled down over her forehead and ears, so that she had the look of a very young flapper. She looked from Bertie to her mother, then abruptly backed into the kitchen, leaving the door swinging behind her.

"I told you she's shy," Rainey said. "You'll have to excuse her."

"Why, she's just a baby! She looks somewhat like you. Especially her cheekbones. But I bet she favors her daddy."

Chapter 29

With her mother busy, Ariel spent the rest of the afternoon searching the hallways and rooms at the back of the house looking for . . . she didn't really know what she was looking for.

That first night she'd met Jefferson he'd said something about the house that bothered her. He'd said that he understood about Bliss House, and knew why it was different from every other house he'd ever been in.

"It's like the way the Greeks talked about God," he'd said. "A dual nature. It's not just one house. It's one house with two natures." The gold light from the chandelier had framed his head like a fuzzy halo. "Like you."

The Greeks? Maybe he had been trying to show off because he was in college and she wasn't.

"What do you mean, *like me?*" she said.

He'd put his hand to her scarred cheek. His palm and fingers felt cool, damp, and, most of all, very large. She couldn't back away from him because she was already sitting flush against the wall.

"This part of you is ugly," he whispered.

She held her breath.

"And this part of you is beautiful." He moved his hand so the back of it rested against her undamaged skin.

She'd reached out with both hands to push him away, and he'd fallen back on his heels. When he laughed, she could smell the beer on his breath.

"I bet you're drunk," she said. "You should go back downstairs. I bet someone saw you come up here. They'll come looking for you."

"I'll hide. They'll never see me." He smiled. "It's like a magic trick. Bliss House is like one big magic trick. First you'll see me . . ." He held open his hands in front of her to show her that they were empty. "Then you won't."

He put one of his hands to her hair, and when he took it away, he was holding her father's cufflink. The one she kept in a box on her dresser.

She grabbed for it, and he let her take it.

"That's mine," she said, holding it tightly in her fist. "What you just said didn't even make sense."

"It was a joke," he had told her, looking kind again. "I didn't mean to scare you. But you really don't need to worry. No one ever sees me coming."

Just like I didn't know you were going to kiss me.

She'd hardly been able to stop thinking about it, because it had felt so good. Did he want to be her boyfriend? She suspected that he really had just wanted to tease her. Mess with the burned girl. The idea made her angry, and she felt like she was already confused enough.

What does he want from me?

Now, as she crept from room to room, she pushed Jefferson from her mind and was left wondering about the Brodskys. Her mother hadn't told her much, but she'd discovered online that Mr. Brodsky had killed his wife with an axe out in the woods beyond the garden. She'd seen pictures of them: they were old people, maybe sixty. Mr. Brodsky had almost no hair and his mugshot had shown him with his jaw slack, his mouth open, like he was about to drool. He looked stoned. Or crazy. The picture of Mrs. Brodsky looked like it was taken on the dining room patio. She was smiling into the camera, her white-blond hair pulled back in a low bun. Her face was thin and bony, but she had friendly eyes and was wearing makeup and a pretty yellow blouse. She looked a lot like one of Ariel's mother's clients from St. Louis.

Mr. Brodsky was in a prison for crazy people. *If he ever got out, would he come back here?* The thought sent a chill up her body.

This part of the house was much warmer than the main part of the house. Her mother had the thermostats set higher back here, since they didn't use it. There were six bedrooms, three bathrooms, a sitting room, and an eat-in kitchen without a refrigerator or stove. Ariel didn't know what the rooms had looked like when the Brodskys had lived here, but now the walls—constructed with row after row of narrow boards—were all painted a startling white, with pale green trim. The pale green was one of her mother's signature colors, and was in her logo and all her printed material. It was even the color of the dress she'd worn the night of the party.

To Ariel, the rooms looked like they might have been in a sunny, old-fashioned cottage. They weren't frightening or unpleasant. The first time she'd looked around by herself, she'd even found the pretty robe in one of the shallow closets, and today she'd found a blue satin ribbon that she'd missed before on one of the window sills. So far, nothing in Bliss House—even Karin Powell's death—had frightened her as much as the ballroom had. And still she knew she would go back inside it. It was waiting for her, like a puzzle to be solved.

Every so often, she went to stand on the second floor landing to listen for her mother's voice. But each time it was Bertie's drawl she heard. Bertie seemed nice and hadn't freaked out at all the way Ariel thought she would when they met. She wanted to think that Jefferson was like his mother: sweet and kind of silly and not dark at all. But as much as she didn't want to admit it, she suspected that, inside, he wasn't sweet at all.

In one of the bedrooms, she climbed to the top of a stepladder the painters had left behind, and sat, thinking. She told herself that it was probably a stupid idea to imagine that there might be something—or even *somewhere*—hidden in the walls of Bliss House. She'd read a lot of books about houses with secret passages and creepy histories. But she had seen her father, and she had seen a woman who was not Karin Powell fall from the third story balcony. And then there was whatever had happened to her in the ballroom, when someone, or something, grabbed her. Her imagination wasn't that powerful, was it? Her mother might say so. But for her the answer was *no*. It had been much more than her imagination.

Chapter 30

"Yes, it's certainly beautiful," Bertie said. "But I don't think I like it."

After Rainey had poured them both some iced tea, Bertie had told her that she was happy to visit while Rainey worked on the wallpaper. At first Rainey had demurred, but Bertie insisted, and Rainey decided that maybe being alone right then wasn't the best thing. She needed some company.

Rainey stepped back, holding the third strip of wallpaper she'd managed to remove from the wall that day. Whoever had put it up had managed to do a reasonably good job hanging it. They hadn't used permanent glue, at least. She was methodical and slow in her peeling and scraping, much to Bertie's distress. Bertie seemed to be afraid that the whole wall would come down, but Rainey had been lucky. There was very little damage to the mural underneath.

There was less of a blue field than she'd thought when she'd pulled away the first corner the night of the party. Each square foot contained at least twenty-five or thirty eyes. Despite the remaining traces of paper and glue, she could feel the delicate paint strokes beneath her fingers.

"All eyes," Bertie said. "I never knew. Only that Michael restored it when he was a teenager."

"Do you think it's the same all over the room?" Rainey said.

"Rainey, I need to talk to you," Bertie said. "I'd decided that I wasn't going to say anything, because I hoped everything was going to be okay. But since that poor woman died—well, I think that mural is the least of your troubles here."

Something in Bertie's voice made Rainey want to tell her to be quiet, to just go away and not say anything else. Like a comedienne playing a tragic role, a serious Bertie instantly took her attention and unsettled her. Beneath her hand the wall felt warm and tremulous, as though the feathers hid something very real and alive.

"The Judge's mother never wanted to live in Bliss House," Bertie said. "In fact, she didn't like being a part of the family at all. *Her* family had been in Virginia since just after the Revolutionary War. Randolph Bliss—the first one—didn't get here until just after the Recent Unpleasantness."

"The what?" Rainey said.

Bertie looked quizzical a moment. "Oh. You know, the War Between the States. Or, as my mama called it, the War of Northern Aggression."

"You mean the Civil War?"

"You didn't grow up around here." Bertie gave a dismissive little wave of her hand. "Old people talked about things differently. It wasn't *me* who used the term. It was my mama."

Rainey turned back to her work, unsure how to respond.

"The first Randolph Bliss came down here from New York right after the war with a lot of money, and he made a lot more money buying and selling people's land, mortgaging it. Exploiting them. But he went back home after a year or two, and people thought they'd seen the back of him forever. He was *not* a nice man."

"I thought a lot of people did that," Rainey said. "I guess it's not a very proud beginning for the family. It's kind of ugly."

Bertie leaned forward. "I feel like you've been misled, Rainey. You shouldn't have come here at all. Especially not to Bliss House."

"I don't understand," Rainey said. If she hadn't had the steamer wand in her hand, she thought Bertie might see it trembling. "Does the family have a reputation as bad as the house's?" She gave a lame little laugh.

"You grow up around here and you hear about these things all your life, like they just happened yesterday," Bertie said. "I didn't feel like I knew you well enough to tell you that you shouldn't have bought this house. You were so anxious to live here. And you'd already been through so much."

As she spoke, Bertie arranged her tea things around her as though making a little picture of them. Rainey waited.

"Randolph Bliss came back in the late 1870s, and he seemed to have changed. He was excited about living here and started getting friendly—well, as friendly as he could—with the local families. You know he built the first library in town? Then he brought that French Hulot fellow here, and they started building Bliss House," she said. "You have to understand that there weren't a lot of people building such grand places around here back then. Even the wealthiest people built frame homes. You had to make the brick on site, or at least nearby, and there wasn't the free labor that, say, Thomas Jefferson had earlier in the century."

Rainey interrupted her. "You mean slave labor?"

"Well, of course that's what I mean," Bertie said. "Nobody around here is proud of it. It was barbaric. And there were hardly any people in Old Gate who owned slaves, anyway. Old Gate was a very Christian, Anglican town. The Anglicans hardly ever approved of slavery."

Rainey doubted that Bertie was right about the Anglicans, but she nodded, relieved that there was no stain of slavery on the house.

"It's what went on inside the house," Bertie said. "About two years after Randolph Bliss arrived, he went back north again for a few months. He put someone in charge of the house and farm—it was mostly apple and peach orchards then—and when he came back six months later, he brought a wife, Amelia, and two children with him. No one had known one thing about them before. Don't you find that strange?"

"I guess," said Rainey. "But you said that nobody liked him. Why would he tell them anything?"

"I'm not being clear," Bertie said, wringing her hands. She looked out the window as if looking for inspiration. Or courage.

"Maybe we should talk another time," Rainey said.

I don't want to hear any more. Not now.

"No," Bertie said, hitting the table firmly with her hand. "I'm not going until you've heard what I have to say. You can throw me out afterwards and never speak to me again, if you want. I'm worried for you. I'm worried for Ariel."

"I know Bliss House is . . . different," Rainey said. "But that's what drew me to it. And it's been strangely good for Ariel. She's actually speaking to me again." She shook her head in disbelief. "Do you know what kind of miracle that is?"

"Of course it's a miracle," Bertie said. "But it's God who sends miracles. Not this house. There was a young woman who died here, and her death was definitely not His work. Neither was the Brodsky woman's death. There were others, too. You need to be watchful." She covered Rainey's hand with her own. "You have to take care of your baby girl."

Rainey was struck by the intensity of Bertie's emotion. It made her uncomfortable, but at the same time she was grateful. It had been a long time since someone who wasn't Ariel had cared enough to contradict or argue with her.

"Bliss House is especially unlucky for little girls," Bertie said. "Some of the ones born into it never grew up to be women." She cleared her throat. "They say there was something wrong with one of the children—a daughter—he brought back with him. Almost no one outside the house saw her. There was a lot of talk from the servants. They said she had fits, laughing or screaming for hours at a time, and that Randolph and his wife kept her chained for her own safety up in the ballroom. The room with the rings coming out of the ceiling. Those were for the chains. Then she was gone, and no one knows what happened to her."

Rainey had avoided the ballroom after looking at it once during the tour of the house, and she'd only looked in twice since they'd moved in. The mustiness had repelled her, and the rings in the ceiling—bizarre. Karin Powell had made a passing comment about the room being great for storage, or even a potential media room because of the lack of windows, but neither of them had wanted to linger inside.

"Those rings," Rainey said quietly. "Why in the world are they still there?"

Bertie shook her head. "As far as I know, everyone who's lived here simply kept the door closed. Even Randolph's mother didn't like to go in there, or let any of the children use it for play. I've never even seen it."

"I'll take you up there if you want. There are lights instead of candles, now. But I can't imagine a young girl living in there, much less being chained up. I don't know if there were even electric lights then. It would've been awful. There's a fireplace, but she must have been so cold. So alone."

Bertie wrapped her arms around her broad bosom. "I'd rather die than go in that room."

Her words hung between them for a moment.

"Later, Amelia died. Some say it was of a broken heart because of her daughter, some say she killed herself with laudanum because Randolph had shamed her with so many other women. We have a portrait of him at the house," Bertie said. "If you spend enough time in town, you'll see some of his features on the faces of strangers. He remarried, of course. Those men always did."

"It's tragic," Rainey said. "Karin Powell told me that there had been many deaths in the house, but that's true of all old houses, right? It doesn't have anything to do with Ariel and me." Why was she defending the house? Was it because she'd felt Will's presence out in the driveway? It couldn't have been him with Karin Powell in the servants' wing. The whole thing was ridiculous.

Something else—*someone else*—was here.

It wasn't her, Ariel had said. *It wasn't Karin Powell who fell.*

"But years and years of tragedy, Rainey?" Bertie said. "Randolph's mother was a tough woman, and even she eventually gave up living here."

"Every old house has some sadness attached to it," Rainey said, trying to convince herself. "If our house near St. Louis had survived, there's no way I could still live there after Will died."

Bertie shook her head. "Why, of course you couldn't."

"What happened with Karin was a coincidence." Rainey put the hot steamer wand down and shut off the machine. "There was obviously something wrong with her. You know how high-strung she was."

"What if it *was* the house?" Bertie said. "Or what if someone killed her?"

"Karin was sick. That's all. And I'll tell you this, because I know I can trust you: Ariel *saw* her, Bertie. At least she believes she did. She also believes there was someone in the shadows, watching, but I don't think there was anyone else there. Ariel's just a young girl who woke up scared in a place that was strange to her. As for Karin—I think this house was *convenient* for her."

"Don't you see?" Bertie said. "That proves it! You both need to leave here. If it's a question of money, dear, I can help you."

Rainey sat down in the chair closest to Bertie's and took her hand. She could see the intense worry in Bertie's face.

"You're such a sweetheart to care about us like this. I'm looking out for Ariel. She's safe. But if I ever feel she's really in danger, we'll leave here, okay?" She squeezed Bertie's yielding hand. "I promise."

She hoped she sounded more convincing than she felt.

Chapter 31

Lucas leaned back in his chair, listening to one of the investigating deputies who had spent the past twenty-four hours interviewing party guests and friends of Karin Powell. He knew that they didn't much appreciate having to provide support to a visiting detective, but it had been their own sheriff who had asked the state to step in. Right now, his own supervisor was satisfied to continue investigating it as a suspicious death. But she was a hawk on the budget and had made it clear that she could pull the plug at any time.

Nearly everyone from the party, with the exception of the guy who owned the bookstore and Gerard Powell, had gone home with a significant other or a family member after the party.

"So, what about the professor from Culpeper?" Lucas asked.

The deputy, Tim Hatcher, was a tall, enthusiastic kid with a serious cowlick at the back of his head that tended to bob whenever he nodded. Which was often. "He's covered. A grad student, Martina Manly, walked out with him to his Porsche around ten-thirty and drove him back to his condo in Culpeper. She told me what they did next, but . . ." He blushed.

"What? Was the professor there to comment on the details, or was the girl just showing off for you?"

"Something to do with her red cowboy boots," Hatcher said. "The professor—who wasn't present for the interview—apparently has a, uh, thing for boots." Finally regaining his composure he said quickly, "Neither of them was more than acquainted with Karin Powell."

"Is there a consensus on what time Gerard Powell and his wife had their big fight?"

The deputy looked back in his notes. "Ten o'clock. He didn't come back inside, but she did."

Lucas was feeling impatient. Maybe it was because of the August heat, or the two other, more clear-cut cases on his desk at the post that needed attention. Brandon had another three days and a weekend to go on his vacation. He couldn't return to work soon enough for Lucas's taste.

"I get the impression that Karin Powell liked a show," he said. "Strange that no one saw her leave."

"But she didn't really leave, did she?" Hatcher said. "I guess the husband probably didn't want to know the details. Since they were fighting and all."

"What do you mean?" Lucas asked. Though he knew exactly what the deputy meant. He'd obviously heard—from his fellow cops or the people he'd interviewed—that Karin Powell slept around. Polite reticence was a lost art.

"It's messed up," Hatcher said. "The way people live their lives, sleeping with whoever the hell appeals to them. Like freaking alley cats. You know?" He blushed again, and Lucas almost smiled. The kid wasn't going to be able to hold onto his naiveté for very much longer and remain a cop.

Lucas was about to comment when the intercom on his desk interrupted. Gerard Powell had arrived for his second interview of the day.

⌒

"I don't mind coming in," Gerard said. "I want answers just as much as you people do. More, I guess."

"There's a nice volunteer lady who comes in every morning to make us coffee and sweet tea," Lucas said. "You want something? Deputy Hatcher here will surely oblige."

The deputy gave a curt nod that set the cowlick off, but he couldn't quite make eye contact with Gerard Powell.

Gerard shook his head.

"I never drink sweet tea myself," Lucas said. "I had a babysitter put it in my bottle from the time I was old enough to hold onto it. I've had to cap half my teeth." He indicated the chair on the other side of the desk. "Have a seat."

He closed the door.

"I'm recording this just like I did this morning. I want us to have all the details straight."

When everything was set, Lucas sat forward in his chair, doing his best to imply a sort of professional intimacy. He wasn't thrilled about this particular discussion. The deputy sat in a chair by the door, looking a little too interested.

"We have the results of your wife's autopsy, Mr. Powell. We wanted to give you a heads-up before we moved on anything further."

"Sounds good," Gerard said. He picked up a pen from the desk and began to fidget with it. He didn't take off his ball cap, leaving Lucas to wonder if he ever took it off—he certainly hadn't when he'd come to see his wife's body.

Lucas opened the folder on the desk. "Still no final determination as to whether or not her death was a suicide. She was in excellent health, and there was no sign of disease or visible trauma, beyond injuries sustained in the fall. The medical examiner does note evidence of a recent gynecological procedure."

He glanced up occasionally as he read from the report to get a reading on Gerard, and left out the part about the bruising for now.

"Significant enlargement and thinning of the uterus, with swelling around the cervix, indicating a recent pregnancy."

He paused.

"Procedure?" Gerard seemed confused. "She was pregnant, yes."

"You didn't mention that when we talked earlier."

"I didn't think it was anyone else's business. She was dead, and so was the baby. It wasn't like you weren't going to find out." He sounded resigned.

"Were you happy about it?" Lucas asked.

"When I was a kid, I used to have a hard time being patient," Gerard said, still fidgeting with the pen. "I was always running around spouting off about everything I thought, heard, or saw. I was really bad at keeping secrets, you know? So I'll tell you right off because I know you're wondering if it was my kid: I had a kidney problem when I was a teenager, and they pumped me full of chemo drugs for two months. They saved the kidney, but they killed my sperm production and recommended that I have a vasectomy. Whatever sperm I might produce could be deformed or something. Satisfied?"

The room was quiet enough that they could hear telephones ringing in the bullpen outside the closed door, and someone's radio playing Dolly Parton's classic "9 to 5." The deputy coughed, and said a quick "Excuse me."

"Damn," Lucas said. "That sucks. How old were you when you got the chemo?"

"Eighteen."

"So you're saying that your wife was pregnant, and that, for medical reasons, it couldn't have been your child. I guess I'm a little surprised that the pregnancy wasn't a bigger issue for you."

"My wife is dead. I'm way past the pregnancy thing."

Something about Gerard Powell was starting to bother Lucas. At first he'd thought he was just cold and dispassionate. Now, watching him, he saw the man was in a huge amount of pain. He had acted as though it didn't bother him that his wife screwed around. That he couldn't satisfy her or give her a child. That kind of act took a lot of fortitude. Or was his disconnection just the way he handled guilt?

"We hadn't planned on having kids, but when she came to me about it, I told her it was fine with me if she wanted to keep it. We'd be a family, and I'd love it just like I loved her." Gerard dropped the pen on the desk and leaned back in the chair. He finally took off his hat, and ran his hand over his wiry brown hair.

Karin Powell hadn't cheated on her husband because he was unattractive, Lucas noted. If that had been the measure, she would've been as faithful as a dog. She and her husband were in the same league when it came to looks.

Gerard continued, "But from the look on your face, I'm guessing you don't believe me."

"You must be a very understanding man, Mr. Powell," Lucas said.

"I'm not a moron. I didn't want my wife to die. Maybe you would dump your wife for screwing around, but my wife had an addiction she'd struggled with since she was a teenager. I'm not saying anyone else would choose to live the way we did."

Lucas got up to pace.

"Why would you assume that we think you're responsible for your wife's death? We're just talking about her health, here. We have to look at both her physical circumstances and state of mind."

"I already gave you her psychiatrist's name," Gerard said.

"There are just a couple of other things," Lucas said. "She had Lorazipam in her car."

"For anxiety," Gerard said. "It's not uncommon, I gather. She had a couple of different prescriptions, but, really, stress was her drug of choice." He looked pointedly at Lucas. "Along with sex, of course. With me. With other people. But you knew that."

"Tell us when you knew about the abortion."

Lucas watched Gerard carefully. Finally, he saw what he had been waiting for. The guy had had no idea.

Chapter 32

Gerard drove home on autopilot, certain that he wasn't going to find any answers there. He felt like he'd only just started grieving her death, only to have her die a second, more painful time.

They'd fought at the party because she'd been drinking. She had promised to drink no more than a couple of glasses of wine a week while she was pregnant. By the time he pulled her aside to ask what in the hell she was doing, she'd already had three. Yet she'd fought him instead of telling him what was going on. Hadn't told him that the kid he'd finally accepted, the kid he'd actually been looking forward to, was gone like it had never existed.

He'd never understood how she could have been so careless as to become pregnant. It wasn't like her. He'd found out about the first affair—at least he had assumed it was the first—a few months after their wedding. He'd accidentally knocked over her purse in the kitchen one Saturday morning while she was in the shower. The pills were in a small plastic folder that looked like a cheap business card case. It had taken him a few moments to figure out what he was looking at, but not more than a few seconds to know what it meant. She didn't need birth control pills if she was only having sex with him.

Her addiction wasn't a secret. In his heart he'd known it had only been a matter of time.

After putting the packet on the counter where she would see it, he'd left the house for the rest of the day. When he came home drunk, and angrier than he should've been, Karin's car was gone.

That night, he awakened in their bed at two o'clock in the morning with a murderous erection, and Karin's moist, gentle mouth on him. For the next hour they made love that bordered on brutality, and in the morning it was as though nothing had changed. It had stayed that way. Over the years he wondered what she'd seen in him that led her to believe he would be okay with what she was doing. He couldn't name it himself. It felt like weakness, sometimes. Other times, it made him feel rational. Powerful. Even, perhaps, merciful.

Since her death, he'd looked carefully through her things. She'd been open with him about so much, but she knew well how to keep a secret. When she was deep into an affair—even an affair he knew about—she kept all evidence of it away from him, as though pretending it wasn't happening. This was the only time he wanted to know the name of her lover: this man who had given her what he couldn't.

When she'd first told him about the pregnancy, she brought up the subject of an abortion, but there was something in her eyes that told him it wasn't what she wanted. And he'd seized on it. He'd seen an opportunity to make her cleave to him in a way she never had before.

"You're sure you want it?" she said.

"I want you," he said. "I want whatever's a part of you."

The teary look of happiness in her eyes was something new. Different from the way she responded to a big commission, a new piece of jewelry, or a new—God help them both—lover. Still, he knew it was risky. She could be manic that way, incredibly excited and passionate about something, then suddenly regretful. It was part of the cycle.

But he'd been willing to take the chance. Trusting her. Something had happened. *What?*

⌒

When he got home, he found Molly standing at the kitchen sink, cleaning up the lunch dishes. Seeing the back of her, looking so much like Karin, gave him a guilty twinge of pain. But where Karin's energy had come from a place of boundless determination—even in her weakest, most troubling moments—Molly's came from an angry tension he could never understand. She was successful in her own way. As a cookware buyer for a major catalog and store retailer, she pursued her work as though it were some kind of holy mission. She had no lightness and very little humor in her. It made her less attractive than Karin, who was always down for a laugh, and revealed itself in worry lines on her forehead and around her mouth. She was three years younger than Karin, but looked five years older.

"I made Dad take Mom on a drive out of the valley. Anywhere," she said. "They needed some time away from the house."

"Good idea." Gerard opened the refrigerator, knowing he should eat something. He was rarely hungry these days, so he had to make himself search out food. Ellie came to sit beside him, looking for a treat. She wagged her tail hopefully.

"If you're looking for something to eat, there are six kinds of chicken casserole. I put a couple in the freezer, too," Molly said. "What is it with people and chicken casserole?"

"Their hearts are in the right place, I guess," Gerard said. He pulled out the box with the chicken dish Rainey Adams had brought by. At least he knew what to expect from it. Rainey had a sensibility about her that he liked, and he felt vaguely sorry about having treated her so badly when she'd come to the door. What he'd wanted from her was information. Not sympathy or food. He still wondered about the strange, secretive daughter. Surely she knew something.

He pulled a dog treat from the jar and tossed it for the now-drooling Ellie. As always, she caught it in her mouth, then carried it to her rug by the kitchen patio door to gnaw it in private. He heated up the casserole in the microwave and poured himself a mug of the coffee from the pot nested in the coffeemaker. Karin's father made several pots throughout the day, so it was always relatively fresh.

"Dad wants to know when they're going to release Karin's body," Molly said. She bit her lip after she spoke. It was such a bald, ugly phrase: *Karin's body.*

"Detective Chappell said the medical examiner's office would let us know." Gerard spoke in between bites. "We'll need to tell them what funeral home will be picking her up." He knew his in-laws had discussed it a lot, but he hadn't given serious thought to a funeral. Karin knew just about everyone in the county, so there would be a crowd of both the concerned and the curious. Certainly the man who had fathered her child would show up. Would he be able to find him in the crowd, pick out the one man who had changed everything?

"I think you should let me and Dad handle the arrangements," Molly said, her tone suggesting she was expecting an argument.

Gerard shrugged. "If that's what you all want. We can talk about it, sure." In the end, it was just a body. Karin, the woman he had loved, was gone. He had no attachment to the empty shell left behind in Bliss House.

"Why didn't you care more about her?" Molly said, not bothering to hide her irritation. "She should've left you a long time ago."

Gerard put down his coffee mug.

"Quit playing me, Molly. If you and your Dad get what you want, what else is there?" Ellie, sensing the tension, got up from her rug and came to lean protectively against his leg.

"I want to know what happened to her, you bastard. I want to know why my sister is dead, and no one—not even you, who saw her every damned day—knows why. I want to know why she didn't tell me what was going on." Molly's eyes filled with tears. "She used to tell me everything."

"Did she tell you she had an abortion within the past couple of weeks?" Gerard said.

The stunned look on Molly's face gave him his answer.

"Don't even say that. How could you say that?" Her already fair skin blanched to bone white. "Karin was pregnant?"

Gerard was silent, watching her face as the possibilities and implications flew through her mind. He didn't dislike Molly, and hadn't wanted to cause her more pain. But she had pushed him. He had been pushed so far lately that he felt like there were no longer any boundaries around him. Anything could happen, and he didn't like it.

"You son-of-a-bitch!"

Molly came at him, her palms out, ready to push him or hit him. Her eyes were narrowed, angry and fierce.

Gerard got off the stool he was sitting on, nearly tripping on the worried Ellie, and grabbed Molly by the upper arms. They wrestled, knocking over two of the stools. She was screaming at him the whole time.

"You killed her! I hate you! You killed her, you impotent bastard!"

Finally, he pinned her to the floor, straddling her. She was still bucking, trying to push him off. Ellie stood a few feet away adding to the noise with short, sharp barks.

"Stop it, Molly," he said. "Stop it. Don't say that. Stop it, please." A part of him wanted to cry with her, to lash out. But against whom? Karin? Himself? Realizing he was gripping her too tightly, probably bruising her, he pulled away. He stood, but Molly still lay on the floor, sobbing.

Breathing heavily, he took a long look at her to make sure she wasn't seriously hurt. "What a fucking mess," he said. What had brought him to this? He was disgusted with himself, with Molly, with—*God help them all, again*—Karin.

Calling Ellie to him, he left the kitchen, and then the house, slamming the door behind him.

Outside, Ellie, sensing his intentions, ran across the clearing ahead of him, toward the foothills at the back of the property.

Chapter 33

"Roberta, you're acting like I don't know you at all," Randolph said. He slid his tie from beneath his shirt collar and tossed it onto the bed.

Bertie picked up the tie and took it to the closet to hang it on the built-in rack. She might not share a bedroom with her husband (that had ended years ago because of his unbearable snoring), but she did take pride in keeping it as neat as she kept her own. For a regimented man, her husband was surprisingly untidy when it came to his personal spaces. She and Jerilyn, his secretary of twenty years, had commiserated about it many times.

"Why go over there and then try to hide it from me?" he said. "You're not a child, and I'm not your keeper. I just suggested that you not get too close to Rainey and her situation. When people stop talking about what happened the other night, when the Powell woman is finally laid to rest, you can perhaps start fresh with her."

Bertie sighed. "I'm worried about her. I know you don't like to talk about her and all the things that have happened at that house, and I promised I wouldn't bring them up. *I promised.* But don't you think she has a right to know everything?"

"You *did* promise," Randolph said.

"But the nightmares. Sometimes I think about the way you screamed, Randolph. Do you remember how you screamed? The things you said in your sleep?" she said. "It nearly scared me to death."

"You promised," Randolph said, underscoring his words with a cold, patronizing smile. "I appreciate that promise and expect you to keep it. I couldn't go on dealing with all the ugliness I have to deal with everyday—the sickos who rape their stepdaughters, the drug dealers who think nothing of poisoning their customers, the parents who rent out their children for drugs. Without you keeping our life at home calm and normal, I couldn't continue."

"If the poor woman *was* mentally unbalanced, then maybe it didn't have anything at all to do with the house. Rainey told me that dear Ariel thought there was someone else in the house, too. Maybe someone else saw her and knew why she did it. Maybe someone even killed her."

"Fantasy," he said. He went inside the closet to finish changing his clothes. "A pathetic child looking for attention."

"I didn't mean to upset you," Bertie said. "Your opinion matters very much to me, Randolph. I just know that if I were in the same position, you wouldn't want me to be alone."

"You mean if I were dead?" he said from the closet. "You're a very different kind of person, Roberta." He came out tucking a polo shirt into the khaki pants he'd put on. Once they were zipped, he came over to where she sat on the bed and leaned to kiss her on the temple. "You've been a lot more sheltered than Rainey. You and Jefferson haven't been exposed so harshly to the world the way that Rainey and her daughter have."

"True," Bertie said.

"Speaking of our son, have you seen him today?" Randolph put his watch back on.

"Not since breakfast."

"What do you think he's doing with his time?"

Bertie laughed. "I think it's a girl. Somebody local, maybe. I wish I knew. He doesn't tell me anything anymore."

"Why would you say it's a girl? I haven't seen any evidence of that. Not since that Marcus girl he took to, what? Was it the prom? Hard to believe it was only a year or so ago."

"I keep telling myself it's healthy that he has his own life," Bertie said.

"When is dinner? I want to go in the back yard and hit some golf balls," Randolph said. "And I think you're wrong about there being a girl. Sure of it."

"Here, let me have your placemat," Bertie said.

Randolph lifted his financial magazine from the table, and she pulled the placemat away to wipe off both the glossy surface of the mat and the cork underside before sliding it back in place.

"Book club tonight," she said. "I'll be home around ten. We're meeting at that new wine bar just off the square. The one with the deck on the roof that they had to get a special permit for? Conversation *al fresco*. It's a book about finding love in Provence. So romantic. It's very well written, and full of recipes."

Randolph murmured an assent, but she knew he wasn't really listening. He only read law commentaries and magazines about golf and business. She occasionally bought him books on American history, but she suspected he only read them to make her happy. She'd heard him say that he'd read all the history he could ever need at UVA and William and Mary. She couldn't imagine that a judge would get bored reading about American history. It seemed unpatriotic.

"Would you want to take me and pick me up?" Bertie disliked driving at night.

"Not unless I absolutely have to," Randolph said from behind his magazine. "Can't you ride in with one of the girls? I've got an early case tomorrow morning, and I want to go for a run first thing."

Bertie looked up from the sink. She listened.

"That's Jefferson's truck," she said. "I bet he'll be looking for dinner." She glanced around the already-tidied kitchen and then at the clock to gauge how much time she had before she needed to leave. She didn't really have time to get everything back out to make a salad to go with the pork chops she'd set aside for him. But she automatically began pulling veggies, dressing, and the foil-wrapped chops from the refrigerator anyway.

Won't hurt to be a few minutes late.

When Jefferson came into the kitchen trailing a draft of perspiration and gasoline, she sent him straight to the sink.

"Wash up, dear. I've already cleaned up the dinner table. Let's set you up here on the island."

"Hey, Mom," he said, stopping to kiss her on the cheek. "What's to eat?"

"Nice of you to join us, Son," Randolph said, putting down his magazine. He offered him a non-committal smile. The kind that Jefferson—and Bertie—found hard to read.

"They're blasting up on Beartrap Mountain," Jefferson said. "I heard it when I was out at the western end of the county today. I guess the permits went through."

"The discussion ended a month ago," Randolph said. "Guess you hadn't heard."

Jefferson ignored the dig. Bertie wished that Randolph wouldn't be so hard on their only son. He wasn't *too* awful, but she thought it wouldn't hurt him to be a little more loving when he spoke to him.

"What were you doing way out there?" Bertie said. She put the pre-shredded lettuce in a salad bowl, and reached for the package of mushrooms.

"Went to see a guy about a ragtop Jeep. I'll go out and pick it up tomorrow. I'm going in on it with a couple of guys. If we get rains as good as we did last fall, it'll be great for mudding. Nothing pro or fancy. Just some old school hills and runs."

"Really?" Randolph said. "I've told you about the old Willys I had. Vintage 1962. No glass in the windows. Tires as big as we could get back in the seventies. We were limited, of course."

Bertie liked to hear Randolph talking about something that made him happy, especially with Jefferson.

"You ought to come by," Jefferson said. "You know. If it works out."

"I wouldn't mind," Randolph said. "I just want to make sure you've got time to be messing around with that stuff this fall. School's a privilege. Your grades are the priority."

Bertie felt Jefferson glance her way, but she didn't look back immediately. It was time to change the subject.

"Can you heat up your own pork chop, honey? I have to get into town," she said. "Book club."

"Sure. You want me to drive you in?"

"Oh, no. It'll do me good to drive a little at night. Besides, it's not even dark yet. Will you be home, later?"

At the other end of the room, Randolph was silent, but hadn't yet gone back to his magazine.

"No plans here," Jefferson said. "I don't have your busy social schedule."

"Your father and I were talking this afternoon," Bertie said. "I told him you've been gone so much because you must have a girlfriend you didn't want us to know about. Didn't I, Randolph?"

"She did," Randolph said. "I told her she was mistaken."

Jefferson laughed. "What makes you think that, Mom?"

"I just never know when you're going to be here."

"All you have to do is ask me." He leaned down to kiss her cheek. "Why would I try to hide anything from you?"

"I just thought maybe there was somebody you knew from school. A mother notices things."

"What? You mean like hickeys?" Jefferson made a show of pulling down the collar of his loose-hanging polo shirt. "Hey, you haven't checked me over in a while."

Bertie flicked him with a dishtowel. "Don't be vulgar, Jefferson. I didn't mean anything like that."

"Still, a pretty damned good example," Randolph said. "I think we've seen them before, haven't we, Roberta?" He chuckled.

Bertie wondered if her husband wasn't secretly proud of their son's exploits. She hoped Jefferson was staying away from the wrong kinds of girls. She knew what some girls were like. They hadn't changed since she was a teenager. Back then, she'd heard rumors about even Randolph being seen with girls who smoked and drank a lot. But he'd been much older than she, and he'd stopped all that when it was time to get serious about marrying the right kind of girl. The kind of girl who could make Sunday dinner for his mama, the kind of girl he would never be ashamed of. It had never been a struggle for her to be the kind of woman he needed. It was what she'd been born to, and she'd made damned sure that she kept her mind and body pure, and her fingernails clean when she wasn't working in the garden.

"You boys would keep me here all night!" she said, reaching behind her to untie the *Have You Hugged an Episcopalian Today?* apron she'd put on to do the dishes.

"Then you should probably act more like you don't like it, Mom. Hey, is there any of that mint jelly you had for the lamb left?"

"The Easter lamb? I threw that out months ago."

She started to hang the apron on its hook near the oven, but stopped suddenly as though she'd remembered something.

"Oh, if you're not seeing somebody, then why did I find *this* in the laundry?" She produced the detached cosmetic fingernail from the apron's pocket. "Here." She held the bit of fingernail out to Jefferson, who opened his palm.

"Ugh. That's weird," he said.

"What is it?" Randolph said.

Jefferson held it up between two fingers for his father to see.

"It's one of those fingernails women get put on," Bertie said. "Now, don't try to deny it, Jefferson. You know I eventually find out everything anyway."

"That belongs in the garbage," Randolph said.

"It's such an odd color," Bertie said. "Who would wear such a thing?"

Jefferson handed it back to her. "Yeah. Throw it away."

Bertie opened the garbage can.

"Maybe it's you who's keeping the secrets, Mom. We should keep an eye on her, Dad, don't you think?"

Chapter 34

"Are you sure you want it in *here*?" Rainey said, taking in the muted, heavy atmosphere of the room. Ariel had brought in an MP3 player and speakers and set them up on two TV tables they'd brought from the apartment. During Ariel's initial recovery, they had communicated little, and eating in front of the television had soothed them both, filling up their silences like a friendly, chatty stranger. "There are so many other empty rooms, honey. Much sunnier ones."

Ariel walked determinedly backward, trying not to reveal that she was struggling under the weight of her end of the mirrored panel, which she was going to use to set up a sort of private dance studio. She'd founded it hanging in one of the repainted rooms at the back of the house. She hadn't wanted to ask her mother for help moving it, but it had been too heavy for her alone.

Lying in her bed that morning, she'd been thinking about Jefferson and the way he acted, like he belonged in the house. Then it occurred to her that maybe he hadn't been going *into* the ballroom when she saw him the night of the party, but coming out of it. *This* was the room she needed to be in, even if it made her feel afraid.

There was a secret here. She'd gone to her mother right away to tell her she wanted to use the room, before she had a chance to change her mind.

"You're not using it for anything, are you?" Ariel said.

"That's not the point," Rainey said, slightly out of breath. "It's just so gloomy. I'll worry about you up here all by yourself."

They reached the part of the room where Ariel wanted to put the mirror, and they carefully turned it and leaned it against the wall.

"Phew. That was heavy," Rainey said.

"I thought you were glad I wanted to try to dance again," Ariel said. "Or were you just humoring me?"

"That's not fair," Rainey said. They had been getting along so well, and she regretted questioning Ariel about the room. But what Bertie had said about it bothered her. If there was such thing as bad karma, this room had to have plenty of it. That it was on the third floor in particular bothered her as well.

"When will you order the barre?"

"I'll do it before I go to bed tonight," Rainey said. Ariel had asked for a portable barre, one that didn't have to be mounted to the wall.

As she watched her daughter set up the speakers, she had to admit that Ariel was moving more gracefully. The limp was still noticeable, but she was using her right hand much more frequently. God owed the girl some kind of break, didn't He?

Still, she was anxious about leaving Ariel in the room alone. Bertie had been so insistent. So serious.

"Ariel."

Ariel looked over at her, hearing something new in her mother's voice.

"What do you think you really saw that night?"

Seeming to ignore her, Ariel sat down and extended her right leg for a stretch. She wore leg warmers that covered the tops of

185

her feet, and with the ballet slippers she'd been wearing around the house for a couple of days, Rainey could see very little of the scarring. Ariel still hadn't put on much weight, but the way her body curved gracefully over her leg—without any outward sign of pain—was very encouraging.

She raised her eyes to look at Rainey.

"I think that girl *wanted* me to see her instead of Mrs. Powell. It was like I was watching a movie of something that had already happened." Ariel breathed into the stretch another moment then slowly came upright. "But I don't think you'll believe me when I tell you the other thing."

Ariel had been waiting for the right moment to tell her mother about seeing her father. It was time, but she felt like doing so would cause her to lose a part of him. He belonged to her now. Not her mother. If he had wanted her mother to see him, he would've shown himself to her.

"We don't lie to each other, honey," Rainey said. "We never have before."

Ariel knew she didn't have to tell her everything. No matter how angry she got with her mother, she didn't really want to hurt her.

"Okay," she said.

Rainey felt a chill of anticipation, and knew that Ariel was right. Whatever her daughter was about to say, she would be afraid to believe it.

"It was after the girl fell. After I passed out or whatever, and then went to look over the railing."

Stop, Rainey thought. *I don't want to know.* The shadows cast by the sconces seemed to flutter against the wall.

Ariel got up and went out to the gallery. Rainey followed.

"He was standing over there." Ariel pointed. "Daddy was standing right down there, in front of your bedroom."

Rainey realized she'd been holding her breath, and let it out with a sigh.

"Your father?"

Ariel nodded. "And he was here before. The first night we slept here."

"Ariel . . ."

"He loves us, Mom. He wants to be with us. Don't you understand?" Ariel was excited. Relieved to have the burden of the secret gone. "It's like we came here so he could come to us. It couldn't have happened anywhere else. There's something special about this place. Look what it's doing for me!"

Rainey stared at her daughter. She couldn't disagree that the house seemed to have changed her, but not nearly as much as Ariel thought it had. This, though, was something very different. Since they'd moved in they'd danced around the issue of the supernatural. The woman Ariel saw who wasn't Karin. Bertie's fears. Rainey's own sense of the presence of people who weren't there. She'd pushed it all to the back of her mind, letting it be overwhelmed by her need to settle somewhere. To be in control. But now, Ariel had seen Will. Just as she thought he might have been with her outside that afternoon. And Karin and the man in the window. The man she refused to believe was Will.

"Honey," Rainey's delicate hands curled themselves into tight fists. "Listen to what you're saying. It must have been a dream."

"No! I wasn't dreaming. Why won't you just believe me? It was Daddy. It was Daddy and he touched me. Daddy's here to heal me."

"Baby, why didn't you tell me when it happened?" Rainey couldn't disguise her frustration. She wanted Ariel to be wrong. Just as she wanted to be wrong about Karin Powell still being in the house. It hurt her heart to think that Will might really be here, and that she hadn't sensed it earlier. Worse, Ariel hadn't trusted her with something so important.

Seeing her mother's disappointment, Ariel shrank back. She had thought she was prepared for her mother's disbelief, but when she saw her mother's eyes harden, she knew she hadn't been prepared at all.

Rainey couldn't help herself. She could hardly even see her vulnerable, injured daughter clearly. The tension of fighting back the pain and stress of two long, terrible years was suddenly too much for her to bear.

"How dare you." Rainey's voice was tinged with cruelty. "You go for weeks without so much as mentioning your father, punishing me. Every day, punishing me, acting like you hate me. And just when I think you've forgiven me, you pull some crap move. I changed everything for you! I gave up everything your father and I built in St. Louis so you could have a new start, a new life, and you never say *thank you* or *I love you*. Your father's memory doesn't belong to you, Ariel. He was the man I loved years before you were born, and you don't get to pull this selfish, crazy bullshit on me!"

Hearing what her mother really thought shocked Ariel out of her surprise. A surge of angry emotion came over her.

"*You're* the one who's selfish," Ariel said, awkwardly rising to her feet. "You pretend like you did all this for me, but you really did it for yourself. You couldn't face anyone back there because you know it was all your fault. You and your stupid stove. You don't get to see Daddy because he hates you! He loves me, and he hates you!" She pressed forward into Rainey's body space, using the height she'd inherited from her father to intimidate her mother.

It worked. Rainey's guilt reasserted itself, and she backed away. She and Ariel were alone in the room, but she felt the carefully limned eyes of the kimono-clad women and stern, identical bearded men painted onto the wallpaper on her. The big room felt smaller than it had when they'd first come in. The two queer metal rings hung dully above them.

"You don't know what you're saying. I'm worried that you're sick, Ariel. I don't know how to help you. I don't know how to be your mother anymore." Anxious to get out of the room, she turned her back on Ariel—something she'd never intentionally done before—and hurried to the doorway.

"Then stop being my mother!" Ariel said, meaning it. She followed Rainey and slid the open half of the pocket door closed with a violent sweep of her arm.

Rainey stumbled as the heavy door crashed against her shoulder, and she cried out. Alone in the gallery in the fading evening light, she felt physically ill, like she'd been exposed to something toxic. Something deadly. And the only other living person in the room had been her daughter. The daughter who might never forgive her. Never love her again.

Behind the closed door, a Beethoven symphony flared to life, filling the room like revenge.

Chapter 35

It took several minutes for Ariel's breathing to return to normal and the pounding in her ears to stop. She leaned against the wall, letting the music fill her head. Never in her life had she screamed at her mother as she had just then. She'd felt it coming for months but never imagined that she could let it actually happen. It was only at that moment, *in this room*, that she'd had the strength. Her mother was wrong. She wasn't sick. She'd never felt stronger in her life.

Turning her head, she could see her reflection in the mirror. The light wasn't very bright, but the changes in her face were right there. Changes her mother refused to acknowledge. Changes her mother refused to see because she didn't want to.

She doesn't want me to get better!

Her mother used to brag about how close they were, how well they understood each other. There'd even been a time when they wore matching dresses, and Ariel had wanted to be a designer, just like her. Now, Ariel finally understood how much better her life would be if her mother had been the one who died in the explosion. She and her father never would've come to this house, but that would've been okay. They would have found someplace perfect.

Her father understood her, and she wouldn't be so afraid to be out in the world.

She felt like she could stay in the ballroom forever.

Sitting back down on the floor, she examined her reflection more closely. Today, her right eye was looking even better, and her leg didn't hurt at all. She wasn't so hideous anymore, was she? Jefferson had said that part of her was ugly, but he was only being honest. He cared about her enough to be honest. And he'd said that he liked her. That was something, wasn't it?

She put her left hand in the pocket of her long sweater and traced the engraved initials on her father's cufflink—the one her mother had found in the car, weeks after the accident, and that Jefferson had found in her room. She closed her eyes. When the bandages had just about covered her entire head after the explosion, the doctors hadn't been sure if she would be able to see out of her right eye. Her left eye was blurry after they woke her from the coma, so that she would lie in the hospital bed with both her eyes closed. Listening. She learned to distinguish each nurse's or orderly's footsteps. She knew the difference between the sounds of the meal trolley, the laundry cart, and the cart with magazines and books and candy that the volunteers brought around.

The night of the party, she had listened to the music, and heard the clinking of glasses and silverware, and the startled laughter of the women downstairs, and even bits of conversations. She'd heard a door click shut, and then she'd seen Jefferson.

So, he hadn't been trying to get into the ballroom. He'd been coming out.

Why?

Ariel opened her eyes and saw the fireplace.

Aside from the things that she and her mother had brought in, the fireplace was the only other thing in the room besides the walls and the lights. That afternoon, she'd gone around the room, knocking quietly on the walls, listening for hollow spaces behind

191

them. There had to be some kind of secret entrance, some way that Jefferson could come and go without anyone seeing him. The only doors in the room were the pocket doors leading to the hallway. But she hadn't checked the fireplace carefully, only pushed on the bricks at its back.

The opening was framed with a rectangle of red tile, which in turn was bordered by tall bronze panels decorated with bursts of chrysanthemum blossoms in relief. From a distance, the flower blossoms looked like fuzzy creatures drawn by some ancient artist. She loved the photographs she'd seen of the ancient animal drawings on the walls of the caves at Lascaux. *Someday,* her father had promised, *we'll go to see them.* She had since learned the caves were closed to the public, but she liked to think that her father might have found a way to get them inside.

As she squatted down in front of one of the panels, she heard something brushing the floor behind her. The sound only made her work faster. She pushed at the panel, thinking there might be a spring mechanism behind it, but it had no give at all. Inside, she started to shake, and her hands went cold. It had to be here! She felt around the panel's edges, hoping to find a latch of some kind. It was mounted away from the wall, but it wouldn't move.

Ariel.

She looked over her shoulder at the sound of her name. Who was calling her? It sounded as though it were coming from far away. A woman's voice, but not her mother. No. Her mother wouldn't dare come back so soon.

The second panel seemed to be mounted just like the first and didn't move at all. She told herself she could bear the disappointment. There was such a small chance that something was actually there, anyway.

This time she ran her fingers very slowly along the outer edge of the inch-thick panel, pressing every couple of inches. And that was when the metal gave way, about a foot from the top, and she heard a quiet *click* inside the wall.

As she pulled the panel toward her its left side disappeared into the darkness, making an opening on the right that was narrow, but definitely wide enough and tall enough for a person to enter without much trouble. Peering into the shadows, she felt an anxious thrill. There wasn't much light from the lamps. Her excitement dissipated when she saw two solid stone walls inside. Had she just discovered an old, incredibly lame storage space? A place for brooms or coal? Then she felt a damp breeze on her face that came from right beside her. She leaned farther into the opening. There was a break in the wall and a few impossibly steep stairs made of stone just inches from her foot. Then total darkness.

Ariel.

The voice again. Not from behind her, but from the passage.

Ariel was torn. Afraid, but desperate to know what was inside.

Ariel.

Or maybe it was her mother after all? Ariel ducked out of the opening and hurried to one of the pocket doors and opened it. The setting sun had filled the hall with golden, mellow light. She listened.

There was music coming from the salon. Like Ariel herself, her mother retreated into music when she was very upset. For a moment, she felt a disturbing kinship with her mother, but willed it away as quickly as she could. She was still so angry.

Quietly closing the ballroom's door behind her, Ariel made her way to the stairs and tiptoed down to her room. Every so often she stopped to listen, but the music continued and there was no sign of her mother.

In her room, she dug the flashlight her mother had given her for emergencies out of her bedside table. When she left again, she closed her bedroom door so her mother would think she'd left the ballroom and perhaps gone to bed.

Ariel pulled the panel closed as tightly as she dared, fearing she might never be able to open it again. Never escape.

There was room for only one person to use the stairway at a time. She kept the flashlight focused near her feet and moved slowly, sliding her free hand along the wall for balance. As she descended, the light coming from the open panel above her got fainter.

She'd never been one to be afraid of bugs or spiders, but here was a place untouched by sunlight, or any light at all that she could see. If she were in a cave, there would be camelback crickets, and big cockroaches. Maybe bats. She was nervous; every cobweb, every faint disturbance in the close air of the passage made her jump.

She reached a landing, but there were no doorways, nothing built into the wall to tell her where she was. As far as she knew, she was nowhere at all. What if she stayed in here forever? What if she fell, unconscious? She might actually die before anyone found her.

Selfish. That's what she was. Her mother had said so.

Was this where the murmuring and the running footsteps that she'd heard the first time she was in the ballroom had come from? The idea of something—or somebody—hiding deep inside the house did frighten her. But she wasn't about to give up and go back.

The stairway ended as abruptly as it had begun, and she emerged into a low hallway or tunnel, facing a wall. To the left, there was a deep blackness that went far beyond the reach of her flashlight. Six or seven feet to her right, the tunnel ended in a tall, broad door. Going to it, she put her hand flat against it and pushed. It didn't move. The space was small enough that the flashlight lit up the entire door and its simply carved frame. There was a row of tiles above it, but there were no hinges or handles on its face. Nothing to indicate that it should open. She puzzled over it, feeling around the frame gingerly, mindful of any creatures that might be living around it. There was nothing but a coarse dust that soiled her fingers and made her cough into her sleeve.

As she stood waiting for some inspiration that would help her open the door, she thought about what might be on the other side. Laying her hand flat against it again, she felt a slight vibration that rose and ebbed in intensity. She had a sense of something huge and powerful.

Daddy? Are you here? Daddy, are you watching?

How much she wanted him beside her at that moment!

Something thudded against the other side of the door, and she jumped back with a cry, dropping the flashlight. It blinked out as it rolled away, and now she stood in utter darkness.

Falling to her knees, she felt around the gritty floor.

Pleasepleasepleaseplease let me find it.

She could only hear the sounds of her own panicked breath, and her hand sweeping over the dirt.

Then there was light. It was faint, timorous: a pearly cast of air like the fog that had obscured what she'd seen the night Karin Powell died. At the same time she was overwhelmed with a scent she recognized: flowers. A fresher, more alive version of the smell surrounding the robe she'd found.

As she put her hand on the flashlight, she whispered a quiet *thank you* and clicked it back on.

Since she'd made no progress on the door (she didn't even want to *think* what might be on the other side of it), she decided to continue on in the tunnel, to see what was at its end. Still worried about bugs and bats, she started slowly, keeping the flashlight pointed straight ahead. The dirt walls were smooth and damp. The tunnel canted uphill slightly, but she couldn't figure out where she was. Surely somewhere well beyond the house.

Who had put this tunnel in? It was definitely at least as old as the house. Had it been built by free men or slaves? Probably free men because Bliss House had been built well after the Civil War.

She was tired. The farther she got from the stairway, the worse she began to feel. Her foot and leg ached. The side of her face began to itch. She'd almost forgotten what they had felt like when she'd first arrived at Bliss House. Now she remembered. The thought terrified her as much as imagining what might be behind the tunnel door.

Chapter 36

Allison had had a change of heart.

That was how Michael described it. He praised her. He brought her things: a blunt plastic crochet needle and some skeins of lofty blue yarn. (No scissors, not yet. Just a tiny hook-like blade that was made for thin embroidery yarn. Someday, he said, he might trust her with some small craft scissors he'd seen at the store. But not yet. Not now.)

Her change of heart had made him kind, sometimes. Allison lived for those times.

But most nights—days?—he showed up with hell in his eyes, and she couldn't help but shrink away from him. *Hell in his eyes.* That's how her grandmother had described the rabid dog that had attacked one of her uncles when he was small. "Like hell had found its way up to the living."

That was Michael.

When he was kind, he touched her tenderly. Sometimes she cried, and he embraced her for a few moments before telling her to take off her gown. He'd brought her a series of nightgowns, calling them *peignoirs*, with a funny laugh. They were chiffon or silky polyester, and he gave her a small bottle of jasmine flower lingerie soap to wash them in. He put a couple of nails in the wall (he had brought a hammer, yes! but had guarded it jealously) so she could hang them up to dry. She didn't even have a mirror to see what she looked like in them, but just put them on, shivering. It was always damp and chilly in that place. The only things that were at home there were the hideous cave crickets that startled to life when she lighted the candles.

When Michael left, she stripped off whichever gown she was wearing and wrapped herself in the smelly wool blanket spread beneath the ornate bedspread. It was the thing that made her the angriest, the way he made her put on those stupid nightgowns.

He stole her dignity every time he came into the room with his nasty demands. It was the pretending that she hated the most. But she did it, didn't she? She did everything he asked her to do. And as long as she could get the coke, as long as he kept bringing that with him, she could almost bear it. It was her only source of relief.

What Michael didn't know was that she'd had no real change of heart. She was in neverending pain. Both from the constant, light cramps in her gut and from the collarbone break that hadn't healed properly. She could barely lift her arm. She certainly couldn't fight him. But the pot helped a lot. The coke helped even more.

⁓

When she heard the key turn in the lock, Allison went into shut-down mode. He wasn't allowed to see what she was doing. Even if he asked nicely, she refused to show him the afghan she was working on. They both knew he was humoring her, and at any minute he could make her show it to him or even take it away from her. But if he made her show it to him, she knew that she would have to somehow make him pay. If he looked at it, it would be spoiled.

She felt the flutterings of dread. What would he be like today? Or was it tonight? He thought it was funny to make her guess if it was day or night outside. Finally, he would tell her one thing, and she would believe him. Then, before he left, he would tell her that he'd lied and told her that it was sunny outside when it was actually night. She had stopped asking, but sometimes couldn't help herself. She hadn't yet had a period since he'd brought her here. She was waiting for that. That would tell her how long it had been. It came, like clockwork, every twenty-seven days.

She stuffed the half-unraveled afghan into the pillowcase he'd brought the yarn and needle in, making sure that none of it hung out. She shoved it beneath the bed and waited.

Nothing happened.

Cautiously, Allison went to the door and put her ear against it.

Something was happening out in the hallway that she had only glimpsed once. Voices. Voices that rose in volume. Men's voices. Women's. A child screaming, screaming, screaming.

Allison ran back to the bed and covered her ears, but the voices got so loud that she couldn't shut them out. Around her, the candles sputtered, one by one, drowning in their own melted wax. Worse, the single light bulb in the sconce flickered and went out. It couldn't be a coincidence! Something wanted her to be alone in the dark. And the darkness was absolute. She might have been in a coffin, or a mineshaft a thousand feet below the ground. If hell was aloneness, a complete separation from God and life and every living thing, she was now well and truly in hell.

Where was Michael? Was he coming in? Had the voices out in the hall done something to him? She screamed his name, over and over.

The bed began to shake beneath her, and she had to take her hands away from her ears to hold on.

She cried, "Hail Mary, hail Mary, hail Mary, hail Mary . . ." Before she could finish the prayer, the bed began rising from the floor. A few inches or a foot? She only understood that it was moving, tilting. Unbalanced, she crawled, feeling her way to the edge.

"Michael, please!" she screamed. "Please!"

But the only answer was the ragged chorus of voices from the hallway.

Except . . . a single, bright voice in her head: "Allison! Watch— are we flying? Look at us!" She squeezed her eyes shut against the darkness, and could see another place, another time, entirely: a beach, the tide pushing against the shore, stick-legged birds running like wind-up toys back and forth, chasing the endless thread of water that teased along the shoreline. And everywhere sunshine. Lovely sunshine.

It was the voice of her brother, Kyle, who was just six. She couldn't see him because she was giving him a piggyback ride. Feeling his small arms gently crossed around her neck, she found she could even smell the sun-drenched, muddy, candy-sweet scent of him. It made her ache for home. But it was a happy ache, and when the bed on which she precariously knelt gave a final jolt and slammed against the wall, her heart and her mind were far, far away.

The door opened. The light on the wall was still out, but the person coming into the room carried a small lantern that gave the room a peaceful glow. He closed the door behind him, but didn't bother to lock it. Holding the lantern closer to her face, he could see that she was sleeping.

He put the lantern on the table beside the bed. The way the light fell illuminated a crack in the bed's elaborately carved headboard, which he had always disliked. The men and women carved into it were gathered around some creature that lay helpless on its back. It wasn't like any creature he had ever seen in life, and the carver had given the creature an expression of defiant exhaustion. It knew it was about to be murdered by the humans whose faces wore aspects of unguarded lust, but it wasn't begging for its life.

The light also fell on the face of the girl. Allison.

She was better-looking than he'd been led to believe, and appealingly vulnerable in her sleep. He felt sorry for her. He ran one finger over a faded bruise on her left cheek. The bruise made him angry, but he wasn't surprised to see it.

Feeling his touch, Allison stirred and whispered something unintelligible.

He stood by, watching, until she opened her eyes.

When she did, she simply stared up at him, not showing any sign that the balaclava he wore to hide his face alarmed her in any way. What had happened to her in this place? He didn't know the specifics, but he knew the person who had caused the bruise, so he suspected that seeing a man in a ski mask was probably novel for her but pretty far down on the fear scale.

She didn't speak, but only reached—with some difficulty—for the nearby blanket, pulled it close over her body, and turned away. Perhaps she thought she was dreaming.

Taking the hairbrush and chocolate from his back pockets, he rested them carefully, quietly, on the bedside table, and left the room. He couldn't free her. She would tell, and there were too many people who would be hurt. But he could be kind to her.

He locked the door behind him.

Allison didn't move, but she wasn't asleep.

Chapter 37

Lucas found Nick Cunetta sitting in a booth near the back of the Waffle House, reading something on his phone. He looked comfortable, like he spent a lot of time in places like the Waffle House, despite wearing clothes that were more appropriate for a New York boardroom. Lawyers in places like Old Gate tended to all look the same: prosperously but conservatively dressed, their suits never costing much more than their Cadillac payments, an indifferent shine on their shoes, and ties chosen by their matronly wives.

But Nick Cunetta didn't look local. Given the time of the evening, there was no sign of his tie and he'd opened the top couple of buttons of his Egyptian cotton shirt. Lucas could see the edges of a T-shirt beneath the collar. Old school. Nick Cunetta wasn't satisfied with the barbershop a block over from the courthouse, but preferred to have his thinning black hair (that had a wave to it that he didn't much care for) styled—along with a subtle manicure—in Charlottesville. He also preferred Italian shoes: Prada if he could get them, Ferragamo if not. He drank red wine or craft beers, never cocktails. Lucas had personal experience of all these details. A few months earlier, he and Nick had hooked up in Charlottesville a couple of times after meeting in a bar. But that was as far as the relationship had gone.

When Lucas got to the table, Nick put down his phone, letting it slide a few inches in Lucas's direction.

"Good to see you again, Detective," he said. "You want coffee or something?" He signaled to the nearby waitress.

"Sure," Lucas said, sitting down. "I'll pay for mine."

Nick sighed. "Ah, so we're all business tonight. Fair enough. Is that why you didn't want to come by the house? We could watch a ballgame together or something."

"We can do this at the sheriff's office if you want, Nick. I just thought we'd be more comfortable here. I appreciated the call."

The waitress came over to take Lucas's order and refill Nick's coffee.

When she was done, Nick wrapped his hands around the cup as though for warmth. The Waffle House was thoroughly air-conditioned but not that cold, Lucas thought.

"Thanks, Lena," Nick said, giving the waitress a quick smile. He leaned back in the booth and looked at Lucas. His eyes were shot with red. "Really, it's good to see you, man. Deputy Fife was fine. A good kid, but—in my experience—crap on the witness stand," he said. "There were a couple of details I wanted to share with you personally once I heard you were working on Karin's case."

Lucas pulled out his notebook and held it up for Nick to see. Nick nodded.

"It's nothing that won't come out eventually," he said.

Lucas opened the notebook. "Why don't you tell me what your relationship to Karin Powell was."

"Two people living in a small town who sometimes got bored living in a small town," Nick said. "She wasn't brilliant, but sharp enough. Within a year of getting her real estate license, she had a quarter of the listings in the county."

Lucas didn't doubt that. Her face was on a billboard on one of the highways leading into town, and those didn't come cheap. The list of people who might be interviewed about her was getting longer with every hour.

"Suicide?" Lucas asked.

"No fucking way. If you knew Karin at all, you'd know she wasn't the type. I've seen a lot of desperate people, and Karin didn't have that kind of desperation in her. She was a good person, but I think she would've taken somebody else out before she took her own life."

"How close were you?"

Nick shook his head. "It was hard to tell with her. Sometimes she texted me six times a day, and then I wouldn't hear from her for two weeks. You'd be surprised how easy it is not to run into people even in a town the size of Old Gate. And what's with the question about suicide, anyway? I heard about her bruises. Somebody messed her up, didn't they?"

"Do you think it might have been related to her social activities?" Lucas said.

Nick scoffed. "She liked her entertainments, but she didn't stray that far from straight sex, no matter who she was with."

Lucas made a note. "What do you know about her relationship with her husband?"

"*Mister* Powell was too busy playing *Bob the Builder* to notice if a tree fell on him," Nick said. "*Mister* Powell was oblivious."

"What do you think of him?"

"I think he's a nice guy who had his hands full with a complicated woman. I think he didn't much like the fact that she had a particularly difficult addiction, but for whatever reason he was willing to live with it. He's the first one I would look at, I guess, although if he lived with her situation all those years, I don't know why he would snap all of a sudden. No. Him killing her is about as likely as her jumping off that balcony in a state of despair," Nick said. He took a sip of coffee.

The sun had finally dropped, and dusk was coming on. The waitress raised the filtering blinds on the broad window near their table, throwing the last of the sunlight across their faces. Despite his careful appearance, Nick looked weary. Karin Powell's death had hit him hard.

"Did you talk to her at the party?" Lucas asked.

"Only in passing. She wasn't in great shape. She was distracted, but she had her game face on. Earlier this week I had to take her out of town for the day so she could get her act together."

Lucas knew he was taking a chance, but he said what was on his mind anyway. "You were the one who took her to get the abortion?"

"That's why I called you. I heard the autopsy was finished except for the final toxicology report." Nick sighed, took a sip of his cooling coffee. "She wouldn't tell me whose it was."

"Any thoughts?" Lucas's own coffee wasn't cold, but was stale. There obviously wasn't much call for decaf at this particular Waffle House.

"Here's what I know," Nick said, leaning forward. "Her decision to terminate was sudden. She'd just told me a few days before that she was pregnant, and that—and this I find hard to believe—Gerard was happy about it. Then she calls me up and asks if I can drive her to have a procedure. She wouldn't talk about it, though. It was a very quiet, very long drive."

"No clues? Nothing about whose it might have been? Someone who might not have been happy about it?"

"Mr. Laid-Back wanted to raise the baby as his. How does that work?" Nick said. "And even though she picked up the occasional date in Charlottesville . . ." His brief pause was an obvious comment on the similarity of his and Karin's situations. "Her latest conquest was definitely local. We had coffee late one morning last week, and she said she had to meet someone in fifteen minutes. She had a look about her that told me that it wasn't a business meeting. You know what that means?"

"Tell me," Lucas said.

"Gerard was going to have to see the baby-daddy around town. Creepy, don't you think?"

"You think he changed his mind and killed her?"

Nick shook his head. "He's got his problems, but he's not a wife-killer."

"So, what about the baby-daddy?"

"Love's complicated ways," Nick said. "I think Karin was afraid of whoever it was, even though she wouldn't tell me anything at all about him. Not even after a few drinks. But she was definitely shaken up the day I took her to the clinic."

"Again, Nick. You've got no guess at all as to who the father might have been?"

"Yes, I have thoughts. Lots of thoughts."

"Maybe you could share those with me," Lucas said.

"I don't think so, Detective. Thoughts aren't something you can use in a court of law, anyway." He smiled. The slick lawyer was back. He put down a ten for the waitress.

"You wouldn't want to obstruct justice," Lucas said.

"My guesses—and that's all they are—could end up looking like slander if they got around. I know you wouldn't want me to get in any kind of trouble." He smiled again. "If you want to drop by the house later, I'll be home. We can have a drink." He took his car keys from his pants pocket.

Lucas noticed the flashy BMW fob that matched the dark sedan in the parking lot. Did Nick actually have more information, or was he just playing a game? Lucas hated games.

"Maybe another time," he said.

Chapter 38

Ariel shone the flashlight on her watch. It was after eight o'clock and it would soon be getting dark outside. Had her mother come back to the ballroom looking for her? It gave her a tiny thrill of satisfaction to imagine her mother thinking that she'd disappeared.

The air in the tunnel was mostly still, but Ariel noticed that when she raised her hand close to the low ceiling, she could feel a kind of faint draft. Somewhere there were openings to the outside. She just didn't know how to find them.

When she heard a sound far ahead of her, Ariel shone her flashlight forward.

"Who's there?" She looked over her shoulder into the opaque dark, trying to decide if she should run away from the sound or not.

The only answer was the sound of heavy footsteps. She wanted to squeeze her eyes shut and wake up back in her old bedroom, almost a thousand miles from Bliss House.

Knowing she was taking a chance, she switched off her flashlight. Now, whoever it was couldn't see where she stood. But she couldn't see them, either.

The footsteps stopped. She caught an even fainter sound—maybe a door closing.

Turning her flashlight on, she hurried toward what was surely the beginning of the tunnel. She had no idea how far she was from the stairway and the sealed door. Knowing that there was something else ahead of her kept her moving forward.

"Hello?" she said. Her own voice echoed back to her. The flashlight exposed twenty feet of gray walls and ceiling. She wished her mother had given her a better, more penetrating flashlight. When she reached the door a minute later, she felt hugely relieved.

This door was short—not much taller than she was—and the metal hinges were mounted on the inside of it. The handle, a sort of wrought iron lever, was set high, almost level with her chest.

She jerked up the lever and pulled.

She heard the sound of moving water. Pulling harder, she opened the door wide enough for her to pass through sideways.

Was she outside? Inside? A dusky light filtered through broken stone walls, casting everything in gray.

She stepped into a jumbled mess of stones and broken furniture and boards from which the paint was peeling. Instead of the fetid damp of the tunnel, the air smelled of fresh water and grass. Looking up at the cracked wooden ceiling, she could see that it was painted with some kind of bird. It looked as though it had once been brightly painted, but now there was a little, but faint, suggestion of feathers, stick-like legs, and a long, intricately feathered tail. One of the bird's clawed feet ended in a large brass hook. There was a hole in the ceiling beside it that looked as though it had held a second hook. The bird's narrow head sat atop a graceful curved neck and wore a feathered crown. A peacock.

"Amazing, isn't it? This is where they hung the meat and kept the milk."

Ariel dropped the flashlight at the sound of Jefferson's voice. It shone down into a chaotic pile of wood and metal, leaving them in the graying sunlight.

She bent for the flashlight, but Jefferson hopped down from the rock on which he sat and picked it up.

"Scared you again," he said, holding it out to her.

Ariel took it from him, but found it hard to speak. Jefferson seemed older, and it suddenly struck her that she'd never been outside with him. She hadn't really been outside the house at all in over a month. Mosquitos buzzed near her ear, the sound amplified and disturbing. It all felt so strange. She trembled with cold even though it must have been eighty degrees. Or was she just afraid?

"Hey, you're freezing," Jefferson said. "Take my jacket."

He eased out of his denim jacket and laid it over her shoulders. It smelled like him—the same mix of beer and cologne that had hovered around him the night of the party. "You want to sit?"

"Where are we?" Ariel said, remaining standing. "Where's the house?"

"Up there. You'll see," he said, taking her by the elbow. "Cut that light." They climbed up a few feet to stand beneath the remains of an arch. The crumbling wall on which they stood was more dirt than stone.

"There," he said.

She could see the back of Bliss House five or six hundred feet away, the blurred glow of the kitchen light marking the distance.

Chapter 39

As Bertie drove through town, she felt a strong sense of regret about leaving the book club meeting early. It wasn't that she was missing anything important. The recipes in between the chapters were her favorite part, and she had bought her own copy of the book. She felt bad about lying to her friends, telling them she had to leave because she had to get up early. She would have to lie to the Judge, too, if he asked how long the meeting had gone. The lies were piling up, burying her soul.

Her prickly conscience was one of the reasons she had never really wanted to go out in the world and get a real job. She was certain people would just try to take advantage of her. But sometimes she wondered what she might have become if her father hadn't supported her desire to leave college and find a husband. Like Rainey, she loved art and beautiful things. No one had ever—at least to Bertie's knowledge—suggested to Rainey that she couldn't have a career, couldn't spend her days and evenings making the world a lovelier place, and helping people acquire things that made them happy. It had occurred to Bertie that if she couldn't talk Rainey out of leaving Bliss House (which would really be the best thing), then Rainey was going to need some help. Lots of spiritual help and support, yes, but also someone to answer her business phone, make appointments, and order things. Maybe even help with clients. Bertie could do all those things in addition to bringing in many of those clients. It would all take place in the daytime, of course. Bad things didn't happen in the daytime. The idea of working with Rainey at Bliss House gave her a thrill, as though she were contemplating taking a lover.

What would the Judge say if she went to work? He hadn't even wanted her to take on the garden club presidency the previous year. But there was something about Rainey that made her feel brave, and willing to face down the Judge's opinions about what she should do with her time.

Rainey was her friend, now, as well as part of the family, and she even felt partly responsible for Rainey's unhappiness—at least the unhappiness she'd experienced since moving to Old Gate. The housewarming party had been her idea, and she'd practically written the guest list. The very least she could do was help Rainey deal with all the unpleasantness surrounding the Powell woman's death. The Judge would just have to understand.

It was bravado, she knew, talking inside her head. The visit she was about to make might confirm her worst fears, and all of her hopes could evaporate in an instant, just like Karin Powell's had. Outwardly, she and Karin Powell had so little in common. Sometimes it was the hidden things, like lies and secrets, that bound people together.

⌒

Nick slid the patio door closed with one elbow, his hands well-occupied with two tall glasses of white wine.

"This will bring a smile to your face, dear Bertie."

Thanking him, Bertie took one of the glasses and settled back in the cushioned wicker chair. She hadn't known until late in the evening that she would be stopping by Nick's house. Something one of the gossipy women at the book club had said about Karin Powell, about the way she dressed and the makeup she wore, had started her thinking. And those thoughts had led to truly uncomfortable thoughts. She had to share them with Rainey, but Nick was the person she needed right now.

Nick sat down in the opposite chair, framed by a fragrant butterfly bush that was heavy with lilac-colored flowers. "Cheers," he said, raising his glass to her.

They drank.

Nick's garden made her happy all year 'round, no matter how she was feeling when she walked into it. He held an annual Christmas open house, and even in winter the garden was bright with holly berries and boxwoods, crown-shaped tufts of decorative grass turned the color of hay. Now the small yard around the patio was crowded with green leaves and late-summer bloomers: black-eyed Susans, foxgloves, bold clematis clinging to a trellis, and tightly-closed chrysanthemums tipped with oxblood and gold. Seeing the chrysanthemums, she remembered that Nick had been an undergraduate at Virginia Tech, whose colors were similar.

Nick only did a small amount of his own gardening. The garden was meticulously tended and carefully mulched—not the garden of a hobbyist, and definitely not a garden tended exclusively by a busy lawyer with a busy social life. That he had someone take care of it for him didn't lessen its charm.

He lit a cigarette and offered it to her as though it were 1950-something and they were in a black and white film. That image suited Nick. He reminded her a little of William Powell—if William Powell had been short and discreetly homosexual.

She leaned forward and took the cigarette with a little giggle, and held it carefully to her lips. Inhaling, she managed to exhale the smoke again without coughing.

Nick laughed. "Nicely done." He reached out and took the cigarette back. "You don't have to smoke any more of it. I just wanted to see if you had it in you."

Bertie was about to protest that she wanted the rest of it, but stopped. She'd smoked cigarettes in high school for a while, like most of the other girls in her group. Then her mother had found them in her purse and had threatened to take her car away, and that had been that. Nick just always seemed to bring out the naughty in her.

"It's not like you to be out on the loose in the evening without your friends," he said. "Or your husband." Ignoring the pink lipstick stain on the filter, he took a drag and put the cigarette down in the ashtray on the glass-topped table between them. "What's up?"

Bertie liked Nick's forthright manner. She knew that some people in town considered him slightly disreputable, but she saw the honesty behind his snarky gaze. She trusted him.

Bertie took a large swallow of wine, then picked up her handbag from beside the chair. She laid a neatly folded tissue on the table between them, and carefully unfolded it.

She waited as Nick picked up the thing on the tissue, his face illuminated by the lighted tiki torches planted on either side of the patio.

When he looked at her again, there was understanding in his eyes.

"Ah, poor Bertie." He took her hand. "Tell me everything."

Nick walked Bertie to her car. It was late enough that the crickets had started their nightly song, but the nearby houses were still glowing with light, and they heard laughter from a house across the street.

When Bertie held out her hand to say goodnight, Nick took it and pulled her gently toward him. Breathing against him, she smelled a little of Pinot Grigio and smoke—probably from the torches. She was fleshy and soft and had a generous heart, like his mother. Maybe that was why he liked her so much.

Pulling away, he looked down into her face, which even in the glow from the streetlamp was slightly pink with wine—and what else? Relief?

If it was relief, he was glad to see it.

"Feel better?"

"Much," she said, getting in the car. She looked up at him, her eyes moist with emotion. "Thank you, Nick. I knew I could come to you."

"You be careful going home. I don't want to have to come bail you out of county."

She smiled back at him, and he stepped away from the car. He stood waving after her until her car turned the corner and was out of sight.

Back on the patio, he extinguished the tiki torches and sat down in the darkness. He lit a cigarette, and smoke filled the still air around him, covering the achingly rich scent of the butterfly bush.

Why do people work so hard to fuck up their own lives?

It was a question that he found himself pondering almost every day. Though, if they didn't, he supposed he'd be out of a job. And he liked his job, as complicated and unpleasant as it sometimes was. The laws within which he worked were like the people who made them: arbitrary and subjective and always, in their deepest hearts, surprising. But sometimes they were strangely malleable. The challenge was to find their weak points. That was the part of his job that he truly loved.

He finished the cigarette, thinking. Inside the house, after tucking the dirty glasses into the dishwasher, he went to his bedroom and picked up his phone to make a call.

Chapter 40

"I wondered when you'd figure it out," Jefferson said.

Ariel pulled the jacket closer around her, still chilled.

"My mom told me there was a springhouse out here some-where," she said. "I could see something from the third floor, but I didn't know this was what it was."

Jefferson jumped down from the broken wall.

"No," he said. "I meant the tunnels. How did you find them?"

"There's more than one?" she asked. She'd known there was something behind the metal door, but had imagined it would be a single room. Nothing more. She couldn't quite wrap her mind around the idea that there were tunnels, maybe rooms, or vaults, or perhaps a kind of dungeon beneath Bliss House. But it made sense, didn't it? There was so much to know about the house. That it seemed to be growing right in front of her shouldn't have been a surprise. Bliss House had reached out from its heart, sending out the tunnels like extra limbs that could only grow in darkness. Or had it been the other way around? She'd read that the nearby mountains were some of the oldest, most enchanted on earth. Maybe the house hadn't been built by people at all, but had actually pushed itself out of the depths of the ground, rising up from the dark, cold dirt.

"You couldn't get through the other door, could you?" Jefferson said. His face wore a look of amused satisfaction. He was teasing her.

But she wasn't in the mood to be teased, even if she was a little glad to see him. The evening air was like acid on her skin, and her leg hurt. A lot.

"At least I know how you've been getting into the house, and it creeps me out," she said. "The night of the party, you were in the ballroom, weren't you?"

"You've lived here five minutes," Jefferson said. "I've known this house . . ." He stopped. "My father knows this house. He told me how to get into it. So what?"

Ariel shrugged the jacket off. It didn't matter that she'd be cold. She tossed the jacket at him, but when he didn't bother to try to catch it, it fell to the ground. "So we own the house now, and you have to stay out of it," she said. "My mother's going to freak when she sees the tunnel."

"Do you really want her to know?" he said, carefully making his way over to her.

"I need to go," Ariel said.

"It didn't scare you, did it?" he said.

What does he mean? The kiss? The tunnel? She was so confused.

"I don't know," she said.

It was getting harder to see his face in the fading light. The burned side of her own face was itching so badly that she felt like it was on fire. She *really* needed to go.

"It's not scary in a bad way," Jefferson said, taking her hand. "Bliss House belongs to my old man. At least it should have been his. But I promise it's really okay if you're here. You're not somebody who's just supposed to pass through Bliss House. You're family. You're *my* family."

Oh, God. He was going to kiss her again. And what he'd just said about her being his family . . . Maybe kissing him was wrong. Really wrong.

Before she could finish the thought, they heard her mother calling her name.

"Guess you're busted."

"What if she asks where I've been?" Ariel said, panicking. Her mother would have so many questions.

"You went out for a walk," Jefferson said, dropping her hand. "No big deal."

"I should go back in through the house," Ariel said. She meant it. She had to get back inside so the pain would stop.

"That's a mistake. She'll think it's weird you didn't answer her before she came outside. Listen to her voice. She's scared. You don't want to scare her more, or she'll start hassling you. She might even freak out and take you away." He paused, appraising her. "Unless that's what you want."

He touched her chin. "You wouldn't want to have to leave, would you?"

No, I don't want to leave! But she couldn't say it out loud. Ariel stepped back, away from him, almost tripping on a fallen board.

He didn't press her further about it. "Go on," he said. "She doesn't know anything. You can do it."

She hesitated for a second, wishing with all her might that it was her father she was running to. Then she impulsively kissed Jefferson on one closely-shaven cheek, and turned to hurry away without looking back. She ran as best she could toward her mother's voice.

Chapter 41

Gerard let Ellie in the house ahead of him. She trotted straight for her water bowl in the kitchen, and drank until she had to come up for air. Finding Gerard nearby, she leaned against him happily, staining his pants with water.

"Let's get you fed," he told her, scratching her behind the ear.

They'd spent the night in a rough hunting cabin that he knew about in the hills overlooking Old Gate. There had been a few pieces of sealed jerky and a couple of bottles of water in the room's single cabinet. That was all the food, but there was a worn plastic bag with a pack of rolling papers and a couple of joints' worth of pot in the cabinet, pushed off to the side. He'd split the jerky with Ellie, and that was all the food they'd had since he'd walked out on Molly.

The evening was temperate, and he and Ellie spent much of it sitting on the cabin's canted porch, listening to crickets, frogs, and night-birds. When Ellie found a raccoon skull in the brush at the edge of the cabin's small dirt yard, he let her keep it. She tried to play with it, nosing it awkwardly up the slope of the porch floor as though it might, at last, move on its own. Finally, she pushed it into a hole in the boards, where it disappeared. After a few minutes of whining, she went back to where Gerard sat and lay on the floor with a disappointed sigh. At five years old, she was still very much like a puppy. Gerard didn't want to imagine how lonesome he'd be without her, now that Karin was gone.

In the fading light he rolled a joint, then realized he had no matches to light it with. *So much for that.* He didn't really need it to disengage from reality, anyway. The woods were enough. They had taken away his ability to concentrate on anything but the sounds around him and the rumble in his stomach. Karin, Molly, the police . . . they were a long way off.

When he found himself nodding off in the uncomfortable chair, he went inside to lie down, thinking it would be just for a couple of hours. He let Ellie up onto the camp bed to sleep with him, preferring her warmth to that of the dubious wool blanket piled at the bed's foot. It was well past dawn when they awoke to the sound of noisier birds, and started for home.

Gerard splashed water on his face at the kitchen sink, and wiped it off with the towel lying nearby.

"I wiped down the counter with that after supper last night," Molly said.

"Yeah," Gerard said.

Molly's curls were piled on top of her head in a clip. She wore clingy yoga pants and a Biltmore Estate T-shirt he recognized as belonging to Karin. Like Karin, she'd chosen to wear it without a bra. Despite the teasing motion of her breasts, and the pronounced curves at her waist, he felt no physical desire for her. If it was there, he'd shoved it so far down into the depths of his being that he couldn't see it.

She'd been in the bedroom, touching Karin's things. *What else did she find?* But hadn't he done the same thing himself? He supposed he would have to decide what to do with them. He wasn't in the mood to just give them to Molly, which was what Karin probably would've wanted.

"Whatever," Molly said.

The scene was too much like the one from the day before, though he had seen Karin's parents' car in the drive when he got back to the house.

"Mom and Dad wanted to know where you were last night. They were worried."

So, that's how it was going to be between them. All was forgotten, except that she was going to bait him until it wasn't forgotten anymore. Gerard dumped Ellie's kibble into her bowl, and she began to bolt it.

"I'm sure you took good care of them." Gerard was as hungry as Ellie, but he wasn't going to give Molly the satisfaction of letting her know. "I'm going to get a shower."

As he left the room, he could feel her staring after him, inchoate with anger and probably pain, but he couldn't bear to look at her face, which was so like Karin's. It hurt too damn much.

He knew he should say something to Karin's parents about his absence, but he procrastinated. After he got cleaned up, he returned the rash of work-related phone calls that had come in his absence and got his work crews going for the day. There was one vague message from Rainey Adams that had come the day before as well. He decided he would go out and see her instead of calling her back, knowing that it wasn't her so much that he wanted to see. It was that damned house. Bliss House. The house where Karin would always be.

⌣⌢

He found Molly and her parents in the kitchen. Her mother, Ingrid, sat at the table, absently stirring a cup of tea. She was fair, with a permanent look of fragility about her, so different from her ruddy, energetic husband and daughters. Her hair was bleached or colored to an elegant platinum—what Karin had called *rich lady blond*—her diamond-heavy fingers precisely manicured. Even though her eyes were slightly reddened and her face puffy, she looked as though she'd just had her makeup done by a professional. Karin had never once complained about her with stories of small cruelties or meanness. She was the perfect mother-in-law, too. She never criticized or questioned his judgment.

How strange it was that Ingrid moved so lightly through life, barely touching it. Never objecting. Always just floating along, leaving no wake.

Barron, her husband, simmered beside her, fire to his wife's vaporous cool.

"Where the hell have you been?" Barron said. "People have been looking for you. We have to take care of Karin. Make arrangements. You can't just walk out on this, son."

Son. Barron wasn't the kind of father any boy would want. He'd made it clear from the first day Gerard and Karin had moved in together that he thought Gerard was an unemployable loser and not fit for his eldest daughter. The success of Gerard's contracting business hadn't softened him a bit. Since he'd arrived, he'd spent half of his time on his cell phone dealing with his chain of furniture stores, and the other half in a tight cluster of grief with Molly and Ingrid. He wasn't interested in Gerard's pain.

"Molly didn't tell you?" Gerard pulled a twist of grapes from the bowl on the island and popped a couple into his mouth, hoping no one would notice how his hand was shaking. He wasn't quite sure what he was going to say next, but he knew he was going to have to put a tight rein on it if he wanted things to stay civil.

Molly had retreated across the room to stand by her mother. Her hand rested on her mother's shoulder protectively—or was *she* the one looking for protection?

"What?" Her voice had gone from cold to cautious.

Both parents looked up at her.

"She thought I needed to get away," Gerard said. "I got some bad news."

"Stop it," Molly said.

Ingrid flinched under her tightening grip.

"What in the hell could be worse news than your wife dying?" Barron said, standing up. "This had better not be one of your bullshit mind games."

Molly moved quickly, stepping in front of her parents. "Why won't you leave it alone? When did you turn into such an asshole?" Her eyes were hard with anger.

There was something inside him that was pushing him to be cruel to these sad people, people who had—to all appearances—loved Karin very much. He wanted to shout that they hadn't known her at all, that they had no idea what she was really like, that they hadn't managed to pass on even half of their upstanding, middle-class moral code to their oldest daughter. From the beginning they'd refused to believe in Karin's addiction, and it had hurt her.

"Maybe it started when Karin told me she was pregnant with another man's child," he said.

The words were spoken, then disappeared into the tense silence. For a confused second, Gerard wondered if he'd said them at all. Beside him, Ellie whined.

Barron fell back a step. Ingrid put her hand to her throat, as though stifling the cry that Gerard knew was aching to come out.

Molly turned back to her father. "Daddy?"

Barron slumped onto a chair beside his wife. Ingrid quickly grabbed his hand and squeezed it. They were one person, Gerard saw. The girls didn't matter so much as their parents did to one another. He was jealous for a moment. Something he'd never have. Something he should have had, but didn't.

He was about to turn and leave, almost regretting the scene he'd caused. *Almost.*

"You."

Ingrid rose from the table, pointing one of her pink-tipped fingers at him.

"*You* did this, Gerard. You killed her with what you couldn't give her. You told her she'd make a terrible mother. You told her she didn't have a bone of genuine kindness in her body. What kind of man says those things to his wife?"

She didn't wait for an answer. The diamonds in her rings caught the morning light as her hand trembled, shooting a spray of transparent stars across the ceiling.

"Karin *begged* me to tell her what to do. It was the one thing she wanted, Gerard. A child. First you couldn't give it to her, and then you *wouldn't*. And she'd finally decided. She was going to try to have a baby regardless of whether you—or anyone else—wanted her to."

What was she saying? His head felt fuzzy. He knew it was the lack of food, but he felt like he might never eat again, his stomach churned so.

"I want you to know that it was me, Gerard. Me." She put a delicate hand to her chest. "I told Karin that she deserved to be happy, no matter how you tried to break her, and break her heart."

Molly tried to put her hand on her mother's arm, but Ingrid brushed her away, impatient.

Recovering himself, Gerard interrupted. "It never occurred to you for a moment that she'd lied to you about me? She lied to you about everything her whole life! It was part of the illness you refused to believe in. You don't even know what you're saying."

"She said you didn't care if she slept with other men," Ingrid said. "You didn't, did you? Did you ever even love her? God help her, she thought you did. If she went ahead and got pregnant in spite of you, it was because she knew she couldn't trust you. It was your own fault!"

Witnessing Ingrid's shrill attack was like discovering that a furious Ellie had suddenly turned into a pit bull. Sweet, gentle Ingrid. Sweet, gentle Ingrid and her brutal words.

"We were going to raise that child together," Gerard said. "She didn't tell you that, did she? She didn't tell you that I was going to raise it as my own, whoever it belonged to. No, that wouldn't fit, would it? That would make me look human, and not like the monster you people want me to be."

He glanced at Molly. "Tell her, Molly. Tell them what a liar she was."

Molly gave him a snide smile and shrugged. "What do I know, Gerard?"

Behind her, Barron had begun to stir, roused from his shock.

For the briefest sliver of time—a millisecond or a nanosecond—Gerard saw the three of them crushed together, broken. Dead quiet. The force of his hatred for them at that moment tensed every muscle in his body. All he wanted was for them to shut up.

"Don't try to put words in Molly's mouth," Ingrid said, jabbing a finger at him again. "She told me you tried to hurt her too, Gerard. If you come near any of us we'll call the police. We'll tell them that we believe that you killed Karin and that poor baby."

Gerard stared at the people he thought he'd known. They were strangers in his house. Hostile strangers. If he didn't get away from them, he wouldn't be able to stop himself from saying or doing something he'd end up regretting the rest of his life.

"Molly, I'll let *you* tell them what actually happened to that 'poor baby'," he said. "You people don't want to hear anything I have to say. Then, all of you get the hell out of my house. I want you gone by the time I get back. I'll deal with my wife's body without your sanctimonious bullshit help."

Chapter 42

Rainey listened to Bertie's phone message as she did her breakfast dishes. Bertie was her breathless, cheerful self, asking if Rainey could come by for coffee and pecan coffee cake around ten-thirty. It wasn't something that Rainey was excited about doing, but the idea of cooling off away from Ariel for a while appealed to her. She was tired of Ariel's games, and her sneaking out of the ballroom and wandering outside had been the last straw.

The previous night, after spending an hour of angry energy to try to organize her office, and another hour trying to read a novel that was making no sense to her because she kept thinking about Ariel's accusations, Rainey had knocked on the door of the ballroom. She hated being so emotionally separated from Ariel. They'd both been angry. Hurt. But *she* was the adult, and it was up to her to make things work. Ariel was suffering. Possibly delusional. She knew she had to help her.

Behind the doors of the ballroom, the music had stopped.

At first, when Ariel didn't answer the knock or respond to her through-the-door apology, she'd been certain that Ariel had fallen asleep. Then she knew—*she knew*—that Ariel wasn't answering because something was wrong, and she began pounding on the door. Of course, she hadn't known the day that the worst had happened, had she? Her feelings weren't reliable. Maybe her fears were just guilt. But this was the room she never should've agreed to let Ariel use. Whatever happened to Ariel in there was her fault. *I never should have let her come in here!*

Finally, she tried to slide open the doors and discovered that they weren't even locked. Finding the room empty had been a surprise, but she was somewhat relieved to find that Ariel wasn't inside, hurt. She searched the house, calling Ariel's name, her panic rising each time her own voice came back to her, unanswered.

When Ariel finally appeared, a black-swathed wraith hurrying across the grass behind the house, she wanted to scream at her, scold her. Make her understand what kind of hell she'd put her through in the last half hour. Instead, neither of them spoke when they met in the driveway. Ariel limped past Rainey, hurrying, and obviously in some kind of physical pain. Her scars were reddened again, and her mouth was drawn in a tight, fierce line as she stared ahead, focused on the path to the house.

Rainey had followed her as far as the front hall and watched as Ariel made her halting way up the front stairs. Her bedroom door slammed shut behind her. Rainey sighed.

At least her daughter was safe.

⌒

Rainey changed out of her shorts and T-shirt and into a bright, casual sundress. Since the party, she hadn't paid much attention to what she was wearing. After brushing some fullness into her hair, she pulled it back with a pretty barrette, and put on some mascara and lipstick. Looking in the mirror, she even tried a smile. It was weak, but she felt a lot better than she had in days. Bertie would be flattered that she'd taken so much care.

On her way out of the house, she tapped on Ariel's door to tell her where she was going. She had to say Ariel's name twice to get her to answer, but finally she heard a dull *okay* from inside the bedroom. It was enough.

⌒

Bertie's house sat in the county's fertile bottomlands, exactly where Bertie had said it would be in her message. It was smaller than Bliss House, but grand in its own way, a white two-story plantation-style house nestled in the green countryside, with columned porches on both floors, jutting from the front. The windows were tall, topped with transoms to let in fresh air and framed by black shutters that were perfect in their hand-hewn imperfection. Two sets of chimneys bookended the house proper.

Bertie had filled the tree-spotted front yard with azaleas and rhododendrons, and it was early enough in the day that a few of the shaded bushes were still slick with dew. Their blooms were long spent, but Bertie had replaced their color with hundreds of red and white New Guinea impatiens. Rainey knew that Bertie's perennial garden—where she grew flowers for cutting—was in the back. Out front, the focus was on the house itself.

Seeing her house made Rainey like Bertie even more than she had before. The simple colors of the flowers and the lack of pretension showed a restraint Rainey couldn't have imagined before.

She parked in a gravel-covered rectangle off the main part of the driveway, and stood for a moment beneath one of the spreading oak trees. It was peaceful here, just like out at Bliss House. But it was a different quality of peace. Where Bliss House emanated lonesomeness and dignity, Bertie's house spoke of contentment.

On her way up the steps, she saw a small tabby cat sitting pressed against a sidelight window.

"Hello, kitty," she said. "How pretty you are." She went over to scratch it behind one ear. Maybe Ariel would like a cat. They certainly had the room for it. Bertie had said to expect field mice in the late fall.

The cat meowed and twisted its head to nip at her fingers.

"Hey, that wasn't very nice," Rainey said.

The cat jumped down the few inches to the floorboards and ran to the front door. It looked up at her expectantly.

"Now you want to be my friend? That's just like a cat."

Rainey pressed the doorbell, and a faint series of chimes, notes from a classical piece whose name she couldn't remember, came back to her. The cat meowed, impatient. No one came. Rainey hesitated to ring the bell again. She didn't want to seem rude. She listened for footsteps. Heard none.

The cat rubbed the length of its body against her leg.

"Okay," she said. She rang the bell again, and waited. It was twenty minutes before eleven.

She was about to tell the cat that they were both out of luck, when the door opened. A sleep-tousled Jefferson, clad only in boxer shorts, answered the door.

But there was something much more alarming than sleepiness in his face.

"What's wrong?" Rainey said.

"My mother. I found her," he mumbled. "I have to call somebody."

Rainey pushed open the door, making him step away. He stared out into the front yard as though looking for someone.

"Bertie?" Rainey called. She was weighed with the same dread that she'd experienced when she'd gone to tell Ariel about finding Karin's body. It was worse than déjà vu. This felt too, too real.

"Jefferson! Where is your mother?"

He turned without speaking and headed down the hallway that ran through the center of the house. Rainey barely noticed the fine rugs they crossed and the antique family portraits and photographs crowding the walls. She had an impression of cheerful, expensive clutter.

The hallway ended at the doorway to an enormous kitchen that was bright with sunshine. Inside, they passed a stone fireplace that was tall and deep enough for several people to stand in. She caught the scent of old cooking fires and animal fat. Outside the windows along the opposite wall, crowded, colorful spikes of foxglove filled the glass. Their brilliance reminded Rainey of one of Bertie's colorful skirts. *No, I have to focus!* She realized she was trying to think about anything except the words "I found her."

Please, God, don't let Bertie be dead.

There on the floor, not far from the kitchen sink, lay Bertie. Rainey gasped, dropping to her knees, heedless of the blood around her. Bertie's eyes were closed, which seemed to Rainey to be a good sign.

What does that mean? A good sign? Perhaps she isn't dead. God, she looks dead!

"Go call 911," she said to Jefferson. "I need to see if she's breathing."

This time, Jefferson responded immediately, sprinting for the telephone on the other side of the room.

Rainey leaned down to place her cheek close to Bertie's bruised face to listen for her breath. Hearing nothing, she grabbed for one of her friend's well-fleshed wrists. At first it was hard to distinguish between her own mad heartbeat and whatever pulse was coming from Bertie. But she willed herself to breathe. To concentrate. Then she felt something beneath her fingertips. Not anything very strong, but definitely something.

Chapter 43

Allison didn't care what the other man looked like. She didn't care that he never spoke to her, because she didn't have anything to say to him. All that mattered to Allison was that the way he touched her, the way he laid with her, was never cruel. Because Michael didn't change. He never changed. Now, soon after his worst visits—the ones that left her bleeding, or torn, or feeling completely hopeless—the other one always seemed to show up. Usually he brought something with him, like toothpaste or more candles (she was burning more and more of them since the electric light had gone away). Michael had never mentioned the absence of the light on the wall, but always made her light any unlighted candles when he came in. Sometimes the room was so full of smoke that she couldn't breathe. And sometimes she wished that the smoke would suck out all the air in the room and she would die. But that was only sometimes.

She still would stand on the chair to press her face against one of the grates to feel the air against her cheek, but she did it automatically, out of habit, the same way she would tie up the plastic bag in the toilet bucket after she used it, so that Michael could take it away. Or the way she would read all the ingredients on the RC soda cans or bread bags every time she thought of it. (Though, now, words didn't always make sense. She knew that they were words, but sometimes she would fix on one and wonder exactly what the letters meant.) Or the same way she ate only one slice of bread a day if it got down to the end of the bag, in case Michael forgot to bring her food. It had only happened once, and she had been hungry for a while. But it hadn't been so bad.

Now, it didn't matter how little she ate. There was something growing inside her, and she didn't want food to take up more space. The thing needed to grow.

It had told her so.

It spoke most often when she finally lay down to sleep, which she seemed to be doing more and more frequently. (There were times when she would wake to Michael tying one of her arms to the bedpost. Why did he bother to do that? It made no sense to her. But she didn't judge. Those were Hell In His Eyes days. She hadn't forgotten that. She couldn't remember when she first knew he had hell in his eyes. She only knew that she hadn't forgotten it.) The thing inside her didn't make the same sounds as whatever was in the hallway, or the rooms nearby (there had to be other rooms because she heard doors slamming). The thing inside her made gentler sounds. Friendly sounds, as though it were stroking her with its voice. She liked the idea that whatever was inside her was kind. It made her feel like she could be kind, too. It made her happy that she had the other man to be kind to. She didn't have to be kind to Michael. She just had to cooperate with him.

She hadn't believed in the thing inside her at first. It was like a creature out of a movie—a really scary movie. But she wasn't afraid of it. No! It was growing inside her, fast, like a baby might. It was alive, and had a soul. It was real.

It sometimes woke her out of a deep sleep to tell her secrets. The first secret was that she needed to keep working on the blanket, no matter what happened. Michael and the other man couldn't know that she'd finished it. It was important that she keep working, working, working. If she got to the end of the yarn, and they saw, they would take her away. They would take the thing inside her away. And if they took away the thing inside her, she would be alone forever.

She regarded these things as revelations, and they were more sacred to her than anything that she had read in the Bible.

Each time she finished the blanket, she'd quickly light a candle—she was deft enough now to crochet in the dark if she chose—and unravel the blanket to the last knot she'd worked. Then she would untie the knot and pull more stitches. And more. Until the entire thing lay in a curled pile of yarn on the floor.

Chapter 44

Lucas and Deputy Tim Hatcher sat parked in the space reserved for official vehicles in the lot near the hospital's emergency room entrance.

"I know this might be out of line, sir. But if we go in there right now, won't we look like major assholes?" Tim said. "They only brought Judge Bliss's wife here an hour ago. She might not even be alive."

"So we should go away and wait for her to die? Or maybe we'll just wait until your county compadres are finished up," Lucas said.

"I'm just thinking about Judge Bliss," Tim said. "He can be pretty touchy."

"So you're worried about your job."

"It's just that he's kind of a big deal. One of those old family, old money guys. I've always wondered why he's not a federal judge or something. Why is he stuck here in Nowhere, Virginia, and not in the legislature or in some cushy law office in Charlottesville or Richmond? Why just our little old county seat?"

"Seems like you and I live pretty close to Nowhere, Virginia," Lucas said.

"Oh, I know. And I wouldn't live anywhere else. But the Blisses were a big deal for a long time."

"Things change," Lucas said.

"Even back when my great-grandparents worked for them, they were weird," Tim said. "Or that's what my family said. But the Blisses knew lots of famous people and had big parties in that creepy house."

"What kind of vibe did you get from Judge Bliss's wife when you interviewed her?" Lucas asked.

"Mrs. Bliss? She seems really nice. Tried to get me to eat chocolate chip cookies and milk like I was a little kid or something."

Lucas drummed his fingers on the steering wheel. "I hate coincidences. She was there for the whole party, beginning to end. There's a chance she saw or heard something relevant that we missed. We need her to tell us more—including the name of the person who attacked her." He leaned forward to get a better look through the windshield. "Hey, that's the Adams woman coming out. What do you think she's doing here?"

"Really?" Tim said. "She got here fast."

"I wonder if she came in with the victim," Lucas said. "She looks pretty shook up."

Rainey Adams, in her flower-covered sundress, espadrilles, and oversized sunglasses holding back her shining blond hair, was an anomaly in the collection of wilted and injured humanity entering or leaving the emergency room. They watched as she stood outside the automatic doors, digging into her large handbag, perhaps looking for her keys or her phone.

Lucas reached for the door handle.

"Do you think you should talk to her now, Detective?" Tim said. "She does look upset."

Lucas knew exactly what the kid meant, but ignored him anyway and got out of the car.

When Rainey saw the detective coming toward her, she assumed he was there to talk to her about Bertie and was glad. She'd just left the waiting room where Jefferson was sitting, his eyes closed, waiting for news. Randolph had been picked up at the courthouse in a police car and had arrived at the hospital at the same time as the ambulance, ahead of Jefferson and her. The hospital staff had let Randolph stay nearby in the emergency room while they worked. They expected to have her in intensive care within the hour.

Bertie had remained unconscious and had looked utterly helpless lying on the EMT's gurney. Rainey found herself thrown immediately back to the first hours and days after the explosion that had nearly killed Ariel.

Death had definitely followed them here.

But she told herself that Bertie *wasn't* dead. Her next thought was: *At least it didn't happen at the house.*

"Mrs. Adams?" Lucas said.

"Have you found out who attacked Bertie?" Rainey said. She couldn't see the detective's eyes behind his sunglasses. He looked cool in his neatly pressed suit despite the wicked heat of the afternoon.

"What about you? Are you all right?" he asked. He indicated the splotches of dried blood around the bottom of her dress.

Rainey looked down. She'd forgotten about the blood. "I found her," she said. "With Jefferson."

"Was he in the house when it happened?"

"He was asleep, and found her when he woke up. Just before I got there," Rainey said. "Shouldn't you be asking him? He's inside. The police who came with the EMTs already questioned him."

"The county is putting their own team on the investigation."

"So why are you here?" Rainey was genuinely puzzled.

"I was hoping to ask her some questions." Lucas finally took off his sunglasses.

His eyes were perfectly clear, a pure green. She'd been too upset the two times he'd come out to the house to notice much beyond his café au lait skin color, his clothes, and the way he seemed to want to bully her daughter. But then she hadn't been in the habit of noticing what men looked like and how they might affect her for a very, very long time. It might only have been a few seconds that had gone by, but she suddenly realized she was staring at him, and felt self-conscious. Taken off guard.

God, what is wrong with me? She thought of Bertie lying in the emergency room.

"You're not going to be able to talk to her," she said. "Randolph says it's probably someone who wants to get back at him for something. He said things like that happen to judges and prosecutors all the time."

"I'm sure they'll look closely at that. Did Mrs. Bliss say anything to you about what happened to Karin Powell? Had she been to see you?"

"What do you mean? What does that matter?"

"She might have . . ."

Rainey finally understood. "You think what happened to Bertie had something to do with Karin's death? That's not possible. Karin committed suicide. Bertie didn't even know her that well."

"There's a very strong possibility that Karin Powell was murdered. The actual cause of death was the fall, but our investigation is leading us to believe that suicide is unlikely."

"I don't believe it. Not in my house." But as she said it, she knew it was possible.

Lucas looked regretful, but also resolute. Rainey understood that if Karin had been murdered, whoever had done it was still free to kill someone else.

"I have to call my daughter," she said, turning her attention back to her purse to search for her phone.

Lucas put his sunglasses back on. "We're doing everything we can to get this wrapped up, Mrs. Adams. I promise I'll keep you posted."

"Yes," Rainey said. "Do that."

To her surprise the detective turned and went back to his car instead of going on into the hospital.

⌒

Tim shut off his phone as Lucas got into the car, leading Lucas to think he'd probably been playing some game. He started the ignition.

"We're not going in?" Tim said.

Lucas shook his head. "She's still not conscious. We've got plenty of other things to do."

As they drove out of the parking lot, he glanced at Rainey, whose head was bowed as she talked on her phone. Sunshine washed serenely over her bare arms and blood-spattered dress as though nothing was wrong with the picture at all.

Chapter 45

His in-laws had listened. When Gerard returned from checking on the crew he had at an apartment complex project near the community college, both Molly's and her parents' cars were gone from the driveway. Relief welled inside him, pushing tears into his eyes. He cleared his throat, embarrassed, even though he was alone with Ellie in the truck. Ellie watched him, panting and obviously worried, her eyes searching his face.

"It's okay, girl," he said, rubbing her gently behind the ear.

Consoled, she licked his cheek, then shifted her attention to the front window where she could see a squirrel burying something in the garden mulch. She whined to get out.

"Girl, you've got a one track mind," he said, opening his door. She scrambled over his lap to get at the squirrel, but it was long gone.

Inside the house, it was as though Karin's family had never been there. The kitchen was still spotless, the floors swept. The only evidence was a slight rumpling of their beds, which they'd surely made as soon as they'd arisen. They were those sorts of people. Clean. Rule-abiding. He almost wished they'd done something bizarre, like dump the contents of the refrigerator out onto the floor, or tear down some curtains. Something childish and mean. But Ingrid had spent all her meanness on him. She'd gone for his throat in a way that reminded him of Karin when she was feeling threatened. Ingrid thought she'd been keeping Karin's secrets, when Karin had been playing her all along. That had to sting. He wondered what her revenge on him would be. Would they really go to the police?

But the police had beaten her to it. They had been the first ones to expose him.

Cuckold. Asshole. Fool.

He'd let Karin set him up. He'd set himself up.

Why didn't I see it coming?

Had Karin lied to him about wanting the three of them to be a family? The evidence said she had. He was starting to see that he'd never really known her at all.

Never trust an addict in the throes of her addiction. Everything he'd read had told him that, but he'd thought she was handling it, thought a child would change things. He'd even mentally staked out an area not far from the kitchen patio that was flat enough for a swingset.

He stood in their bedroom. Everything about it spoke of Karin: the careful mix of contemporary and expensive antique furniture, the expansive view of the hillside framed in the window, the plush, deep carpet under his feet. Karin was everywhere.

He wanted to hate her memory, but he couldn't. They'd had a marriage, even if it wasn't the kind of marriage other people had.

There were so many things he would never know. Information and explanations that had died with her. But there was someone living who knew the answer to at least one important question.

He remembered the phone.

He went out to the truck, Ellie following close behind.

When Karin hadn't come back from the party by one o'clock, it had started him wondering. Something about that house, and how she'd looked while she was there. Like she was a part of the place, like she was the grand dame, and Rainey Adams had just been another guest who faded into the background. Karin *possessed* whatever room she was in. People watched her. Women either hated her or wanted to be like her. Every time the two of them had been together in Bliss House, she had seemed completely at home there, as though she belonged.

He'd gone back that night to look for her, not really expecting to find her. But her car was still parked in the shadows of the driveway.

Bliss House was far enough away from town that the stars were bright above him. They, with the moon, were the only light. He'd walked confidently around the outside of the house, which stood looking solid and stately against the night sky. Rainey's bedroom was dark, and so was the girl's. Gerard was comfortable enough at Bliss House, even though he didn't like the place. The renovation had gone very, very well, as though the house had just been waiting for its close-up, for new paint and new fixtures and shinier floors. Rainey was trying to restore what she imagined was its graciousness, but he suspected that Bliss House had never quite been gracious. It was too severe. If Bliss House had a soul—and he strongly believed that if any house conceived in the mind of a man (or woman) had one, this one did—it was a stone, bottomless pit of a soul.

At the back of the house, he had tried the door to the mudroom. The new handle didn't budge. There was a nightlight on in the kitchen, but nothing moving inside.

Heading back around to the front, a sound from the bush-hogged meadow far behind the house stopped him. Rainey hadn't wanted him to deal with the springhouse far at the back of the property. It was a ruin, and he'd gotten the impression that she liked it that way, that she found it romantic. He didn't really blame her. If there was any person who deserved a little lightness in her life, it was Rainey Adams. But at that moment, he'd still been embarrassed by the way he and Karin had behaved at the party, and didn't like to think of her.

Now, four days later, digging in the paper- and tool-stuffed console of his truck, he wished he'd paid more attention to what he'd heard out in the meadow. He'd brushed off the sound as the human-like vocalizations of a coyote, but now he wondered if it hadn't been a person he'd heard. A person nearly hysterical with laughter. The thought chilled him.

Feeling around, he finally came up with a phone. Karin's phone.

He turned it on, realizing as he did that it was something he'd never done before. How could you be married to someone and not ever touch the phone that they kept with them twenty-four seven? Karin's phone was her lifeline, but she hadn't had it with her at the party, and that puzzled him.

Not finding Karin at Bliss House that night, he'd taken her phone from her purse where he'd found it, turned off, in her car. He wasn't sure what had made him keep it from the police. If they discovered he had it, they wouldn't like it. They would think he was guilty of something—maybe even Karin's murder.

He hadn't turned it on knowing that if the police were tracking her account they might be alerted that someone was using it. And they would find it with him.

The message icon said she had fourteen messages. One of them was a text.

He recognized most of the names as clients and the phone numbers of her coworkers. There was a block of calls to and from Nick Cunetta. Not surprising, since Nick had been one of her closest friends for the past two years. For a time he'd suspected that Nick wasn't gay, but walked both sides of the street. When he suggested it to Karin, she'd nearly choked with laughter on the wine she was drinking.

"You're jealous!" she'd said. "Jealous of a man who's been effectively out of the closet since grad school? Really, Gerry. Your gaydar sucks." She'd kissed him on the cheek with affection. "But you're adorable."

Three calls between them had gone back and forth in the hours before the party. There was nothing he could judge from that. They were always talking, and Nick had been at the party.

Disappointed, he was about to turn the phone off when he thought to open the text message.

WHERE ARE YOU? I'M UPSTAIRS. HAVE TO LEAVE SOON. MOM'S GETTING DRUNK.

The text wasn't signed, but the sender's name had been recorded by Karin's phone: JEFFERSONB.

If there were other texts between them, they'd been erased.

Gerard didn't need to see any more. He shut the phone down.

Chapter 46

By the time Rainey and Jefferson got back to the house from the hospital, the police were gone. Randolph was still at the hospital, and had asked her to keep an eye on Jefferson, who seemed to be in an uncomprehending daze. She told Jefferson to go upstairs and lie down for a while. He'd been quiet in the car, and obeyed her without speaking.

Not knowing what else to do, she went to the kitchen and started to clean. Neither Randolph nor Bertie should have to come back to a kitchen made untidy by a half-dozen cops or a floor stained with blood. As she searched for supplies, she found herself stopping frequently, distracted by the image of Bertie looking small and still on the ambulance gurney, her mouth and nose covered with an oxygen mask.

Why would anyone want to hurt Bertie, who hadn't even known Karin Powell all that well? Rainey told herself that the detective had to be wrong. There was no connection.

When the doorbell rang, Rainey had just finished scrubbing the tile floor for the third time, trying to get the last of the bloodstains out. But it wasn't happening.

She hurried to the door in case the doorbell disturbed Jefferson's sleep.

Looking out the long sidelight, she saw Gerard.

What is he doing here? Did he already hear about Bertie?

"Gerard," she said, opening the door a foot or so and keeping her voice low.

He looked confused at seeing her. His hands were shoved into his pockets and, for once, he wasn't wearing a hat. The dark circles beneath his eyes told her he wasn't sleeping well.

Taking his hands from his pockets, he put one on the door as though he would push it open. Rainey let him inside.

"Where's the kid? Where's Jefferson?" He raised his voice to a shout. "I know you're here, Jefferson Bliss!"

"What in the world are you doing?" she asked. "This is a really bad time, Gerard."

"This has nothing to do with you." He paced the hall as though trying to decide where to go next.

Rainey hadn't seen him since taking the food to his house. He looked much worse, and he was certainly angrier. She stood in front of him, unintimidated. "I don't know what's wrong with you, but you can't be here. Jefferson's resting and can't see anyone right now."

"He's upstairs?" Gerard went to stand at the bottom of the curving balustrade leading up to the second floor. "Get your ass down here, you son-of-a-bitch!" He looked as though he might spring up the stairs any second.

Rainey quickly took off her plastic gloves and dropped them on a chair. She touched Gerard's arm, hoping to get through to him. He flinched away.

"Gerard, if you don't go, I'll have to call the police. God knows they've already been here once today, but I'll make sure they take you with them. Bertie's in the hospital, and this family doesn't need today to be any more of a nightmare. What's wrong with you?"

She could see he didn't know what she was talking about. He was focused on one thing and one thing only. Before she could explain, he darted up the stairs, again yelling for Jefferson.

A door near the top of the stairs opened.

"What the hell?" Jefferson came out of his room, naked to the waist. When he saw Gerard, his eyes widened and he turned to run back inside.

But Gerard was faster. He laid both hands on Jefferson's shoulders and threw him onto the floor as Rainey ran up the stairs after them. She screamed for Gerard to stop. Jefferson was screaming as well, cursing and telling Gerard to get off of him.

Gerard dragged Jefferson farther out into the hallway, beneath the portrait gaze of the first Randolph Bliss's porcelain-skinned wife, Amelia, and told him to "fucking stand up, instead of acting like the weasely douchebag that you are." He stepped back while Jefferson awkwardly rose to his feet. Blood coursed from Jefferson's nose, running onto his mouth and chin. He smeared the blood away from his mouth with his hand and shook it to the floor.

"Come on, shit-heel," Gerard said.

Rainey screamed for Jefferson to get away, but no one listened to her.

"Yes, I fucked her," Jefferson said. "And you're a moron if you think I was the only one!"

Rainey was stunned, but when she looked at Gerard, she saw no surprise. He launched himself at Jefferson, whose face had turned mocking. Full of hate. He was shorter than Gerard, but more muscular with a lower center of gravity. He looked ready for a fight.

Gerard launched himself at him, going for his gut.

Knowing that she couldn't stop them, Rainey fumbled for the phone in her pocket and dialed 911 as she ran down the stairs.

As soon as the dispatcher answered, she gave them the address, telling them whose house it was. The woman kept trying to ask her questions, but Rainey ignored her and told her just to get the police there. Then she hung up.

Above her there wasn't much sound except for the grunts of the two men who seemed to be bent on killing each other. It was like some strange, bloody performance art. When she called up to them, again begging them to stop, her voice sounded shrill and lonesome in the big hall.

But by the time the sound of the sirens reached her, the men had separated. Jefferson sat slumped in his bedroom doorway, breathing hard, his head bent to his chest. Gerard had started down the staircase, only to stop, sinking down to sit, marking the pristine white wall with his blood and sweat as he rested his head against it.

Chapter 47

"You're damn lucky I didn't take the afternoon off like I planned," Nick said, following Gerard down the courthouse steps.

"Save it," Gerard said over his shoulder. He was moving slowly, still stiff from the fight. "You didn't do me any favor getting me out of there. They could have kept me overnight for hitting the son of a bitch. It was worth it."

Nick laughed. "You made quite an impression on our friend Rainey. Imagine having to call the cops on your handsome contractor."

Gerard stopped at the bottom of the steps. It was evening, and the cooling air felt good on his skin, though he wouldn't have given Nick the satisfaction of saying so. After refusing medical attention beyond a few swabs of disinfectant and some small bandages, he'd spent the entire afternoon in police custody for the first time in his life. It wasn't the only first of the day—he'd never ridden in the back of a police car or been handled roughly by a cop either.

"Listen," he said. "She almost didn't have to. They've been watching me since they questioned me about Karin. They were there two minutes after she got on the phone. You know they think I killed Karin."

"Your temper's not a big secret from me," Nick said, serious.

"Fuck you," Gerard said.

Nick smiled, but it was weak. "I know Karin's death wasn't your fault. Not directly, anyway."

Before Gerard could respond, Nick held his hand up.

"You listen. Karin was my best friend, and I knew things about her. Shit she wouldn't tell you in a thousand years. Why she continued to love you even after she figured out there were plenty of men who understood and appreciated her better than you did, I'll never know." He continued in a voice that was a remarkable imitation of Karin's own: "He's my soul mate, Nick. I belong with him."

Instead of angering him, as it was probably meant to, Gerard found himself unable to reply.

"Maybe she was doing that punk mama's boy you beat the shit out of," Nick said. "All I know is that she was stressed out like I've never seen her, and scared. I think half the reason she stayed with you is she saw you as some kind of white knight who would always save her no matter what she did."

"Until now?" Gerard said. "This time I fucked up and let her down. That's what you're saying?" His hands balled into fists at his sides. Punching Jefferson Bliss had given him a sick kind of satisfaction. It was something he was afraid he could get used to, and Nick was handy. "Our business is over. Send me a bill."

"You're damned lucky his daddy talked the kid into not pressing charges. You screwed with the wrong mother's son. And on a day when that mother—*also my friend*—was in a coma."

"Yeah, well, I didn't know that, did I? It doesn't change the fact that Jefferson Bliss was probably the one who got Karin pregnant and killed her." He looked for surprise on Nick's face and saw none. "You knew she was pregnant. Of course you knew." The words felt like lead in his mouth.

Cuckold. Asshole. Fool.

"What happened?" Gerard continued. "If she really did tell you everything, you knew we planned for the pregnancy to go ahead. It was not a problem for me. I certainly didn't kill her because of it."

A well-dressed tourist couple on an evening stroll stepped off the curb to walk around them. The woman glanced back at them curiously after they were past. Gerard, his face badly bruised and his lip swollen, nodded at her out of habit, and she quickly turned away. He looked at Nick.

"Well?"

"I told you I don't know for sure. I think she was scared of something," Nick said. "She had her reasons, but she wouldn't tell me what they were."

They stood by the street, evening falling around them. Gerard was exhausted. He felt as though he were living some alternate reality, in a town he didn't know, among strangers. He thought of Ellie at home. She'd missed dinner and certainly needed to get out of the house.

Nick changed the subject. "As soon as they figure out who assaulted Bertie, everyone will forget this little incident. Judge Bliss is a reasonable guy, and with you just losing your wife, and considering what you found out about Karin and Jefferson, you had a decent excuse."

"I should apologize to Rainey," Gerard said.

"Not right away. Give it some time. There's enough going on. They're not sure Bertie's going to make it. Life is pretty raw for that family right now. It's bad enough Rainey lives in that damned house with her freak show kid. You couldn't pay me to live in that murder hole for five minutes."

"No. I've got to talk to her. I want to make her understand."

"You're going to understand yourself right into a jail cell. Seriously."

Gerard shook his head. "I don't need your permission, man."

Nick sighed. "Fine. If you insist on going out there, at least let me go with you. I owe Karin that much. We'll take your truck, and you can drop me back here."

Chapter 48

"Is Bertie going to die?"

Ariel and Rainey sat at the kitchen table. The food Rainey had brought home from Gourmet Away sat untouched on their plates.

Rainey answered carefully, not wanting to give her false hope. "She was in a coma for most of the day, but that was her brain's way of protecting itself." Hesitating, she added, "You know how it works. They put you into one with drugs, remember?"

Ariel's face darkened. "I don't remember that. You know I can't remember."

Rainey reached out to touch Ariel's hand. This time she didn't move it away.

"I know, baby. I think Bertie's going to be okay. She's just too full of joy to let this . . ." She struggled for the words. "To let this terrible thing mean the end of her sweet life. Bertie is Bertie. Everyone likes her. I can't believe that someone could do this." Her voice broke on her last couple of words.

It was Ariel's turn to comfort her mother.

"She'll be okay, Mom. It has to be okay."

Rainey couldn't know that Ariel was thinking more of Jefferson than his mother.

After she'd gotten the call from her mom about Bertie, Jefferson had texted her:

I THINK MY MOM'S GOING TO DIE. SOMEONE TRIED TO KILL HER.

She had answered him, but never got a response. No matter how weird and secretive he'd been, he didn't deserve to have his mother die.

Her mother's tears reminded her of the first days she'd been awake, when her mother had told her that her father was dead. Ariel wanted to believe—to truly *believe*—that it was really her father who was here in the house with them, and not some other *thing*, like whatever had pushed her down the stairs and tried to hurt her in the ballroom. Or what was behind the door in the tunnel. The huge house was crowded with terrifying possibilities. Even the thought of seeing her father again frightened her. A little.

When the front door knocker broke the silence, they both jumped.

"God," Rainey said. "I hope that's not the police again. I can't deal with them anymore today."

Ariel stood. "I'll make them go away."

Rainey started to get up, but Ariel put her hand on her mother's arm.

"It's okay," Ariel said. "Drink your tea."

Rainey sank back down onto the hard chair, grateful for its solidity. She didn't even watch Ariel leave the kitchen.

⌢

Gerard hardly recognized the injured girl that only a few weeks earlier had hidden behind her mother in the upstairs hallway. Her attitude was the difference: she seemed taller, and walked without self-consciousness. She wore a silk dressing gown that looked like it should belong to someone much older. But it didn't look like something Rainey would wear. It covered her scars, but she didn't seem to be hiding them intentionally. Her hair was styled in a way that did a decent job of hiding what she didn't want anyone to see. Now he had a better idea of how truly lovely she had been before the accident.

Nick held out his left hand for her to shake, and she took it. "We haven't met," he said. "I'm Nick Cunetta. A friend of your mom's."

"I know who you are. No worries. Mom's in the kitchen. You guys should probably see her in there." She pointed to the open paneled door.

She seemed to want them to go ahead of her, so Gerard started across the big hall, with Nick following. Bliss House was much less brightly lit than it had been the night of the party. It took every bit of mental strength Gerard had not to stare at the rug where his wife had lain just a few days earlier. Was Nick trying not to look as well? It was, of course, the first time Nick had been here since the party. He had to be thinking of Karin, too. When they reached the doorway, Gerard sent Nick in ahead of him, and turned to thank the girl. But she was gone.

Their footsteps must have been too quiet, because when Rainey looked up from the kitchen table, she seemed startled. In the stark overhead lights, she was hideously pale and looked even more exhausted than she had that afternoon.

"What are you doing here?" she asked. "Nick?"

Gerard fell back a step. Nick had been right. It was way too soon. She would probably try to take out a restraining order against him. He felt like an idiot.

"I didn't know you would be at their house," he said. "I'm sorry. I had no idea about the judge's wife. I'm sorry, Rainey. Very sorry."

Nick touched his arm, signaling him to be quiet.

"I know it's late, Rainey," he said. "It's been a very long day for you, and I know this is an imposition."

"Gerard, the police told you to stay away from all of us. This isn't staying away." She stood up. "And I still don't know what you're doing here, Nick. Are you trying to apologize for him?"

Nick shook his head. "I'm here as his friend. You know that Karin and I were close."

Even with Nick beside him, Gerard couldn't help himself. He wanted Rainey to understand why he'd beaten up her cousin. Why Jefferson Bliss had to be responsible for Karin's death. Should he tell her the whole truth?

No, I can't do it. Not yet.

"Please," Gerard said. "I need you to understand. I'm not proud of it, but I want you to know they were lovers. Jefferson and Karin. Maybe even in this house. If he had something to do with her death, we all need to know the truth."

"Isn't that what the police are for, Gerard? You could've told *them*. He's not even twenty years old. You might have killed him. How could you?"

"He did okay for himself," Gerard said. "He's no kid."

Beside him, Nick tensed. "We'll have Detective Chappell look into whatever involvement he had, right away. I think Gerard just wanted to tell you . . ."

"It was all so wrong," Rainey said. "If you could've seen Jefferson after he discovered Bertie, you'd know how wrong it was, no matter what he did with Karin. It's going to break Bertie's heart when she comes out of this and learns what you did, on top of everything else. How are you going to face her, Gerard?"

The exasperated tenderness in her voice surprised Gerard and made him feel like more of an asshole. He should've taken the phone to the police and offered it as evidence.

Surprise! Look what I found! Now, arrest that little silver-spoon turd who was screwing my wife.

No. It would never have happened that way. He couldn't expect Rainey to fully understand.

"You're right. I shouldn't have gone after him," he said. "It was a mistake."

He didn't hear the girl come into the kitchen, but he saw Rainey's eyes cut past him.

"My mom wants you guys to leave." Ariel's voice sounded deeper, more mature than it had when they first arrived. "I think you'd better go."

She was taller than her mother, but still well short of his six feet. Her manner wasn't agitated, but it was clear she felt like she had some authority.

"That's a good idea." Nick looked pointedly at Gerard. "Everybody needs a chance to do some healing, here. It's time to go."

"We'll talk in a few days?" Gerard said to Rainey. He hadn't gotten to say all that he wanted to say, but he knew that hanging around was only going to make everything worse.

"You'll apologize to Bertie?" she said. "What you did to Jefferson wasn't just unfair to him."

"I will."

"We'll see ourselves out," Nick said. "Good night." He gave Gerard a nod and headed for the door.

Gerard said good night to Rainey and followed Nick. But something made him stop in the doorway.

"Ariel, Jefferson was here the night of the party," he said. "Did you see him? Upstairs, maybe? Did you see him with my wife?"

Something flickered in the girl's eyes.

"You did see him," he said.

"I didn't see anyone," she said. "I didn't see anyone all night except . . ."

"Except who?" Gerard couldn't keep the hope from his voice.

Ariel smiled her strange, lopsided smile. "My mother, of course."

"My wife is dead," Gerard said. "I want to know why she died."

Without warning, Ariel put her own hand on Gerard's upper arm.

"What did you do to Jefferson?" she asked.

They all stared at her.

"Tell me." There was a threat in her voice.

"Ariel?" Rainey said, alarmed at the sudden change in her daughter.

Behind Rainey, a glass rattled in the sink, and Gerard felt the foundation of the house shake, like the aftershock of an earthquake.

"Jefferson's okay, honey," Rainey said.

"You said he almost killed him," Ariel said, staring at Gerard.

Gerard didn't like what he saw in the girl's eyes. She looked crazed, maybe dangerous. He had to remind himself that she was only fourteen and no threat to him.

"This isn't your problem or your business," he told her. "This is between Jefferson and me. No one else."

"You'd better leave," Rainey said softly. "Honey, let's sit down. I'll tell you what's going on. You don't need to worry."

"Your wife was a slut," Ariel said. "That's what your problem is. She was a slut who got herself killed, and you want to blame someone else." She smiled. Her facial scars were flaming red now, making her look strange. Frightening.

"Ariel!" Rainey said, approaching her daughter. "You shouldn't be in here."

It took every ounce of willpower Gerard had not to slap the smile off of the girl's face. He hated how he felt and acted in this house. Ever since he'd arrived for the housewarming party, it had made him edgy. He wondered what sort of people Ariel and Rainey had been before they moved in.

"Gerard, let's go," Nick said. "Right now."

"Excuse me," Gerard said, walking around her. "I'll be in touch, Rainey."

Ariel turned around to watch him go, the same hideous smile on her face, her eyes shining with malice. Rainey was speechless.

As Gerard followed Nick through the hall, he felt a breeze like a cold sigh on his neck. His hands were shaking, and he was glad

Nick was there to get them out of the house. Outside, a silver-white curtain of moths shimmered over the light beside the walkway. Gerard was watching them, distracted, when the foundations of the house shook again. His foot slipped on the loose brick on the front steps, and he fell onto the walk, his ankle twisting awkwardly beneath him.

At the same moment, inside the house, a speechless Rainey caught Ariel by the arms as her daughter collapsed, fainting, to the floor.

Chapter 49

Ariel woke on the floor, opening her eyes to her mother's worried face. Her head throbbed.

"Oh, God, you're awake," Rainey said. "Don't get up yet. I want to call an ambulance."

Ariel held onto her mother's arm. "Don't. I'm not dying." She struggled to sit up. Her head felt like it weighed a thousand pounds.

"Ariel, please."

"No, Mom!" Ariel's own voice made her head throb, but she didn't want to see any dumb EMT people or the inside of a hospital ever again. "Why am I on the floor? Why am I in the kitchen?"

She closed her eyes. "I went to answer the door, and it was that contractor guy."

"They're gone," Rainey said, helping Ariel slowly to her feet. "He's going to stay away for a while." To hear herself say it made Rainey feel regretful. She'd been angry, but a part of her still pitied him. Unlike the police, she didn't think for a minute that he'd killed Karin, and everything that he'd done since that night could be traced back to the tragedy. What thoughtless, stupid things had she done since Will's death? And *that* had actually been her fault.

She walked Ariel to a chair. Ariel sat down and let her head fall onto her folded arms, blocking out the light.

Rainey stood looking down at her. She'd seen someone else in Ariel's eyes when she was talking to Gerard. Someone who scared the hell out of her. This wasn't her precious child who had flown across the lawn wet from the sprinkler to greet her when she came home from work, and who cried when her best friend's parakeet died.

So many changes. So much pain. She hated the helpless feeling she got when she thought about this Ariel, who was barely even a teenager let alone someone who had nearly died in agony. It was like there was someone else inside of her. She looked at the elaborate robe she was wearing, the one she had found, and wished she could sneak it away and get it out of the house.

"Honey, what are you feeling right now?" she said. "Can you tell me?"

As used as she was to therapists and her mother trying to draw her out, the question took Ariel by surprise. She lifted her head.

"I feel like someone hit me on the head and then ran away. I feel empty."

"What do you mean by empty? Like something's missing?"

Ariel searched her mother's eyes. "I'm not sure what I mean."

What am I trying to ask? Are you possessed, sweetie? Do you think there's someone inside you, someone who wants you to look different? Sound different? Do and say things that hurt other people?

"Do you feel like yourself? Does that make any sense?" Rainey shook her head, dissatisfied with her own question. "Did you know that the house shook right before you passed out?"

Now Ariel understood. Just when she was sure her mother didn't know her at all, didn't have any clue who she was or what she was like, her mother pulled out something like this. Like she could see right through her.

The tears came fast, unbidden and unwelcome.

"Mommy," she said with a rush of emotion. Fear. "Help me, Mommy."

Rainey fell to her knees.

She wrapped her arms around Ariel and buried her face in her daughter's hair. Ariel smelled of soap and warm perspiration. If she could have, she would've absorbed her daughter into her own body to hide her and keep her safe.

"I'm so sorry, baby. I'm so sorry this is happening to you. I'm sorry I brought you to this place." She rocked Ariel gently. "I was selfish. And you needed me to take care of you."

Ariel's shoulders shook with sobs. Her frame was so slight, so slender, that Rainey feared she might crush her by holding her so close.

"I want Daddy," Ariel said, her voice clotted with tears. At that moment, she wanted to see her father more than anything she'd ever wanted in her life. Not the strange shade that had appeared in her room, but her real flesh-and-blood father. The missing point of their broken triangle.

"Yes," Rainey said. "Yes, baby. I know. I miss him every minute."

"I don't know if I believe you," Ariel whispered.

The words broke Rainey's heart in two. She could feel real pain burning and suffocating her as it spread through her body.

How can you? she wanted to say. But of course Ariel could say that. When was the last time either of them had mentioned Will's name without fighting? They were both guilty of—not exactly forgetting him, but of not keeping him alive between them.

"We never should have come to this place," Rainey said, unwilling to draw Will's memory into their pain. "We should've stayed in St. Louis where we knew people. Where some new, terrible thing wasn't happening every day." She seemed almost to be talking to herself. She stood, leaving one hand touching her daughter's hair so they would at least be connected. "It's this house, isn't it? If we hadn't come here, Gerard's wife wouldn't be dead, and Bertie wouldn't be dying."

Ariel lifted her head slowly. "And I wouldn't be healing," she said. "You knew it was happening just as much as I did."

"You've made some progress, yes." Rainey stopped.

"Look at me!" Ariel said, raising her voice. "Look at my face. Look at my hand." She took Rainey's hand and held it up to her cheek. "Feel it. Feel how soft it is. It's new skin. New. I'm becoming new."

Rainey didn't know what to say. She heard the manic joy in Ariel's voice, but she just couldn't see what Ariel saw.

"Why don't I need my cane anymore? Why can I see out of this eye almost as well as I could before the accident? Why won't you admit it?"

Rainey shook her head. "I don't want you to get hurt anymore, baby."

"I'm living some kind of miracle, and you're worried about me getting hurt? That's crazy, Mommy. Plain crazy."

"They said there would be some healing. We need to get you to the new doctors. We're not going to miss that appointment."

Ariel shook her head forcefully, even though doing so caused the pain inside to ratchet back and forth.

"No doctors. Not anymore," she said. "I'm through. They did enough to me already."

"I don't want to have to make you go, honey. Please don't make me."

"Then don't," Ariel said. "Tell me what happened before I passed out. Please stop acting like it's some kind of secret. You asked me, but I can't remember. You know something! It's me, remember? I'm the same person I was two days, two months ago. You have to trust me, Mommy. If I say I'm okay, then I'm okay. I promise. I'm not a little kid anymore. Stuff has happened to me."

Rainey couldn't bear the pleading in her daughter's voice. "You are different," she said. "I believe you. I see it."

"Then tell me why you looked like you saw a ghost or something when you looked at me a minute ago. Tell me why you're afraid of me. What did I do to make you afraid?" Ariel squeezed Rainey's hand. "It's not how I look, is it?" she said, feeling like it was the first truly adult thing she'd ever said to her mother. "There's something else. I know there is, and you don't trust me enough to tell me."

Rainey wanted to tell her something, but had no idea what to say.

Chapter 50

Gerard stopped his truck in front of Nick's office, and Nick got out.

"You're sure you don't want me to drop you at your house?" Gerard said.

"I want to walk. Call me if you need me. Please, just stay away from everybody named Bliss for a while, okay?"

"Smart ass," Gerard said. His cheek and jaw were still swollen, so it was hard for Nick to read his face, but he thought he saw the hint of a sardonic smile.

He watched the truck drive off, its taillights the only color in the darkness.

Poor bastard.

Karin had really left a mess behind her. She'd screwed with her husband's head for so long that he didn't know which way was up. The collapse of that arrangement had been overdue for a long, long time. He wondered what had made her so reluctant to dump the guy. Had she really loved him that much?

It seemed to Nick that a woman who really loved her husband wouldn't spend so much of her time making him look like a dickless wimp. They had both deserved much better. She'd never have found what she needed in Old Gate, of course, which was a damned shame. Sometimes he thought about leaving this place, where the chances for his own happiness were getting slimmer every day. Charlottesville wasn't far away, but it seemed like the men he met there just got younger and younger, while he couldn't help getting older.

It had been more than three years since he'd felt anything but mild contempt for a lover. He'd lost his chance for happily-ever-after.

Scott Selden hadn't been classically handsome, but his smile and gentle manner had caused Nick to look beyond his rather plain Anglo features and tall, softly rounded body to discover the person who might complete him. He was wholly Nick's opposite: where Nick was polished to a shine, Scott was relaxed and down-to-earth. Where Nick was sarcastic, Scott was forgiving and optimistic. When they traveled—the only time they could comfortably be out together as a couple—Nick had noticed more than a few frankly curious looks from other men. He ignored them and held Scott more tightly when they were alone. Back home, they kept their affair deeply buried. Scott worked as a partner in his father's law office in Culpeper, and Nick—while he didn't hide the fact that he was gay—preferred to keep his sex life discreet.

After they'd been together a year, Scott told Nick that he wanted to come out to his family, to at least let them know how happy he was. Nick didn't think it was a good idea, but they never got a chance to find out. Scott was at the office one Tuesday afternoon when his appendix burst. His father got him to the hospital, where they performed surgery, but Scott also picked up a vicious staph infection. He was dead within the week.

Unable to get anywhere near the room where Scott lay in isolation, Nick had to settle for a couple of late night phone calls, the last of which had been the day before Scott died. After the nurse helped Scott end their last call, Nick sat holding the phone, staring at the empty fireplace grate, until sleep temporarily released him from the hideous knowledge that Scott wasn't going to recover.

There was no real goodbye. Only a brief memorial in the gracious garden behind Scott's parents' home, an urn with Scott's ashes lonely in a sea of white roses and boxwood. Nick was just another in a line of lawyers, clients, and old school friends who waited to shake the parents' hands. Scott's mother accepted his sympathies with kind eyes that moved on to the next guest even as her hand slipped from his. Afterward, Nick went to the studio apartment he kept in Charlottesville (which Karin had used so frequently that it often smelled of her perfume) and drank and slept for days.

It was a ten-minute walk from the courthouse to Nick's cottage, which, like his office, was in Old Gate's official historic district. The houses on Botetourt Street weren't the oldest in town—those were over on the west side near the Presbyterian and Anglican churches—but dated from the late nineteenth century. Their low wrought iron fences had been grandfathered in during the 1950s, when the historians in town began to worry about outsiders moving in and ruining the town's historic character, and put fence restrictions in place. Nick had narrowly avoided being named to the Old Gate Historic Commission more than once in the past two decades, but he thought he might try it when he stopped practicing law.

He'd been drawn to Old Gate's low-key, civilized atmosphere after graduating from Georgetown Law School. It hadn't hurt that his uncle had had a practice here from which he wanted to retire. But most of his clients came to him because he'd done his undergrad degree at Virginia Tech. It made him a kind of rebel, given the town's proximity to UVA. He nurtured that persona publicly, and had given himself a reputation for being a little loud, occasionally a little déclassé. He liked to keep his private life private. And quiet. These days, he was spending less and less time at his apartment in Charlottesville, preferring the cottage in Old Gate. Sometimes he worried that he was just getting old.

The dusk-to-dawn front porch light was on, drawing moths and other flying annoyances to his doorway. Otherwise, the cottage was dark. His car was in the driveway where he'd left it.

He jangled the keys in his pocket—a habit that Scott had always teased him about, telling him he was turning into a country lawyer like his old man—and debated whether he should get in the car and go (he didn't have any morning appointments), or call it a night. The evening was fair, and it would have been pleasant to sit in one of Charlottesville's outdoor cafés or in the bar up at the Grange, have dinner, maybe drink a half-bottle of something decent, then see where it took him.

But thinking about Scott had made him sad, and he was too tired to drive the forty-five minutes into Charlottesville. He swung open the wrought gate at the end of the walk and went into the house to see what he could find for dinner.

The house was welcoming, but markedly empty. He thought briefly about the detective, Lucas. The sex with him in Charlottesville had been great, but they were awkward together afterwards. Lucas had enormous charm and, like Karin, a pleasing, aggressive sexuality. But although he and Lucas had law and order in common, they didn't have much else. Still, sometimes any company was better than being alone. He held out a slender hope that Lucas might stop by again.

Locking the front door behind him and shutting off the porch light, Nick turned on a few lamps. He went straight to the freezer in the kitchen and pulled out a serving of some chili he'd made weeks earlier. Once it was heating in the microwave, he opened the refrigerator for a beer.

Inside, he found the bottle of wine he'd shared with Bertie. He'd made a quick trip to the hospital around lunchtime, but they were only letting family in to see her. Randolph Bliss was in intensive care watching over his wife, and the cretin son, Jefferson, was stalking the waiting room and had stopped just short of telling Nick that Bertie was none of his business. Poor Bertie, living her whole life with that pair of assholes.

Maybe you won't have to much longer, dear Bertie.

Nick undressed down to his socks, hung up his suit, and put on his robe. Usually he made himself sit down at the table to eat dinner, disinclined to slide the whole way into the incivility of permanent bachelorhood, but tonight he settled for eating on the couch, in front of the TV.

The beer was cold, and the television show ridiculous. He found that he wasn't all that hungry. Resting his head back on the couch, he closed his eyes.

What a shit of a week.

It was his last coherent thought.

The garrote caught him deftly beneath the Adam's apple, and his head was snapped forward so the thing could go all the way around his neck. Nick grabbed instinctively at his throat but quickly realized that clawing at it was useless, so he tried for the hands gripping it. Strong wrists, masculine. Forearms, hairless. Nothing to hold onto, to tear. His nails were short, but he scratched—something would be found beneath them! Whoever the man was, he was much stronger than Nick and kept him from thrashing enough to get him off balance, or pull him over the back of the couch.

Beyond the immediate pain was the feeling that the world outside him was imploding, sucking itself down to nothing, while the inside of his head was expanding exponentially. An imitation of the universe: airless, weightless, infinite.

At the last moment, a sob tried to escape his throat, but there was nowhere for it to go, and it died with him.

Chapter 51

When the gynecologist came into her office, Lucas stood politely. She didn't smile, but only nodded in greeting and told him to "please, sit down."

In the photographs of her with a pair of girl twins—holding them as infants, wearing a tired but obviously delighted smile, then building a miniature snowman with them, the ends of their blond curls escaping their matching toddler bunny hats—she looked like a different person. Today her thick blond curls had been tamed into a tight bun, and her lips were drawn in a serious line. She sat down in the chair behind her desk, not looking at all pleased to see him.

"You're going to have to convince me, Detective, that your having this information is really necessary. I can't be compelled to give it, and I'd just as soon make you convince a judge, first," she said.

The DA had been less than encouraging about the possibilities of getting a warrant, calling it a long shot. Lucas started there.

"To tell you the truth," he said, spreading his hands, "it's a long shot."

When she looked neither suitably impressed nor vindicated, he continued.

"Everyone we've spoken with insists that Mrs. Powell wasn't depressed. Which makes the idea of suicide less and less plausible. From her GP, we've already learned that she had a prescription for Lorazipam, in addition to her medications for her hypersexuality."

The doctor pursed her lips at the word.

"The ME says she had a significant amount of Lorazipam in her system when she died."

Now Erin P. McDonald, OB, GYN (as it said on the shiny wooden and brass block on her desk) held a poker face.

"So?" she said. "What does that have to do with her records here?"

"We know that she recently had a termination procedure at a clinic in Charlottesville."

"That's a decision that some women make," she said.

"It doesn't surprise you?" Lucas said.

Erin McDonald shrugged. "Why should it?"

Lucas looked at her more closely. *Why isn't she surprised?*

"There were two people that we know of, with some certainty, who were aware of the child," he said. "Her husband and her lawyer. The husband, Gerard Powell, knew about the pregnancy and fully believed that they were going to become parents. He had no idea that she'd terminated before her death. Her lawyer, as one of her closest friends, also knew, but she didn't give him any reason for the termination." He didn't add that Nick Cunetta had driven her to Charlottesville for the procedure.

"I still don't understand what this has to do with me or her death," she said.

Lucas shook his head. "Do you know why she terminated? Here's the thing: If there was some anomaly with the child, it would go a long way to explaining the why of it, considering—according to her husband—they were happy about the pregnancy." Maybe "happy" was an exaggeration, but he went with it.

At this, the doctor raised her eyebrows.

"What?" Lucas said. She'd opened the door, and he wasn't going to let her shut it again. "Did she say something about her husband?"

The doctor stayed silent.

"Listen," he said. "We know that he knows it wasn't his child. He's been open about that, as well as about her other sex partners."

The doctor's shoulders relaxed a little.

"I just want you to understand what's already been established," Lucas said.

Leaning back in her chair, the doctor said, "But you wouldn't be investigating her death just to confirm it was a suicide. Why are you really here? Do you think he killed her?"

"We haven't nailed down one particular suspect, if that's what you mean. That's not to say that murder isn't a real possibility. There were marks on her that implied that some kind of violence was done to her shortly before her death."

She seemed to consider him for a moment with her frank brown eyes. The office was silent. She'd shut the door behind her on her way in, which had told him that she was at least going to hear him out.

"So, you're telling me that it's a definite possibility that she might have been a victim of a crime? Why didn't you say that in the first place?"

She opened the small laptop that she'd brought into the room with her. "You people never get to the point."

Lucas knew better than to respond. He just wanted the information, not to be the winner of a pissing contest.

"Karin called my nurse saying she was spotting and had some cramping. We had her come in that afternoon," she said, looking at the screen. "She seemed calm enough. A lot of women would panic." She looked up at him from the laptop. "But in her case, panic was appropriate. There was no fetal heartbeat, and we immediately did an ultrasound."

"What happened?" Lucas asked.

269

Lucas left the office understanding Karin Powell better than he had. Rather than letting nature take its course, or having the D & C performed at the small local hospital, she'd opted to have Nick drive her to Charlottesville, where fewer people knew her. It seemed a small difference to him. But he wasn't a woman who had just lost a child. The news had seemed even more tragic to him when the doctor said that she and the radiologist had looked at the images later and determined that the baby had developed with a neural tube defect—probably anencephaly. The doctor hadn't had the chance to tell Karin Powell. As she was already dead, Lucas saw no need to put that in his report.

Chapter 52

For the second time in twenty-four hours, Ariel woke up with no immediate memory of how she'd gotten where she was. This time, her face was pressed into a blanket, and her head was filled with the smell of stale cigarette smoke and rot: old clothes, dust, decaying paper.

Before she woke, she'd been dreaming that she was at their old house in Kirkwood with her grandmother, mother, and father, and that they were playing Scrabble, one of her grandmother's favorite games. Ariel was losing as she always did. Without saying why, her father pulled out a violin from a box beneath his chair and started playing. He closed his eyes as he played, and his face was as pale as it had been when she had last seen his ghost in her bedroom. So pale, it was like he'd never been out in the sun. Even the mournful music coming from the violin sounded weak and transparent. Her mother helped Ariel's grandmother out of her chair so they could sway to the music together, slowly, Ariel's mother towering over her grandmother who was as small as a seven-year-old. They tried to get Ariel to dance with them, but she was embarrassed. The music receded as her father faded away, until it was finally replaced by the whiny hum of a nearby motor, and she woke.

Ariel rose onto her hands and knees and looked around, worried that she hadn't really woken up at all. In that moment of being not-quite-awake, she didn't yet panic.

She'd never been in a room like this: low-ceilinged and damp, the light from the sconces on the wall so faint that she couldn't even tell what color the paint was. Its surface was uneven, maybe some shade of gray, like burned-out charcoal. The humming noise came from a small refrigerator in one corner; there was a café table with two cane chairs crowded near it. The bed she was on was tall, like her mother's antique bed, but the headboard was carved with strange human and animal figures.

Seeing an open door to her left, she exhaled with relief. It meant she could leave anytime she wanted. The idea calmed her until she looked to the opposite wall and saw, a foot or so from the ceiling, an ornate brass curtain rod with bare hooks strung along its length. No curtain. No window, and no sign of there ever having been a window. It whispered of deceit to her. Someone had once played a trick on someone else, hanging a curtain there. A cruel trick in this secret place. Knowing that, Ariel was far more frightened that when she'd first awakened.

She remembered. Not much, but something.

Remembered getting quietly out of her mother's bed, making her way through the room by the nightlight. Walking into the hallway of the sleeping house, the big clock ticking downstairs, measuring her steps. Laughter. She remembered that she had laughed out loud, as though she were embarking on some fun adventure.

No, not me. It wasn't me. I wanted to sleep!

No, it was another girl who had laughed. Another girl, wearing Ariel's robe, who was making her way upstairs to the ballroom. Who opened the door and went across to the fireplace and found, even in the darkness, the flashlight that Ariel had left there. It wasn't Ariel who opened the door beside the fireplace and, pulling it closed behind her, went down the hidden stairway, unconcerned that someone might hear her. There was no one to hear her.

And at the bottom of the stairs? The door. She reached up and pressed the first tile, then the last in the row, then pressed the first again. The door swung open, silent on its hidden hinges.

Now Ariel knew how to get into this place beneath the house. But how did she know? Who else knew about it?

Jefferson knew, and had practically challenged her to find her way inside. Looking around, she found it hard to imagine him in the dim, musty room. This was like a room in a museum. The furniture was worn out, but the refrigerator looked like it was almost new. How did things age here? Was there even time in this place? Carefully climbing down from the bed, she crossed the oriental rug covering most of the floor and opened the refrigerator door. Inside, she found two beers, several bottles of water, some dried-up cheese loosely wrapped, and an uncorked bottle of wine.

Ariel closed the door nervously, feeling like she was trespassing on someone else's life.

What is this place?

She tried to tell herself that she wasn't afraid, but she was suddenly anxious to be upstairs, out of this room. Reaching for the flashlight on the bedside table, she knocked a shiny paper box on the floor. Quickly bending to pick it up, she saw it was an open box of condoms. She blushed and dropped it on the table. Maybe Jefferson brought girls here. The idea made her feel slightly sick to her stomach.

She turned on the flashlight and stepped out into the hallway. Her heart beat hard in her chest.

Expecting to see the door leading to the outer tunnel right in front of her, she was startled to see that she was actually in a long hallway. Yes, the big door was to her right, but shining the flashlight to her left, she saw the hallway went on. It wasn't like the tunnel on the other side of the door that led out to the springhouse, but more like a hallway in a house. The walls were rough but painted, decorated with a strip of wainscoting. There were also two more doorways.

Ariel took a couple of slow steps, the flashlight making the hallway loom larger in front of her. She thought about the ghost-hunting show one of the nurses had gotten her hooked on in the hospital, and how her light looked much the same as theirs did. They were always listening for sounds, and now she found herself listening for the faintest sounds too. In the room she'd just left, the tiny refrigerator clicked off with a distant whine. Now there was real silence. She quickly turned her back on the rooms beyond the light, her free hand already reaching for the door into the outer tunnel.

It was there, a few feet away.

Finding it closed, Ariel dropped the flashlight and threw herself against it, pounding it with her palms.

"Who's there?" she cried. "Let me out! Let me out!"

When there was no answer, she grabbed up the flashlight again and shone it above the door. Yes, there was a row of tiles identical to the ones she remembered being on the outside. Closing her eyes, she whispered to herself, trying to recall the order in which she'd touched them to get in.

How did I know?

Whatever, whoever, had guided her down here had known how to get in.

But the same combination wasn't working. Ariel pressed the first and last tiles again and again. Nothing happened.

She began to sob in frustration. Maybe whoever had brought her here hadn't known how to get out either.

Chapter 53

"What's wrong with you?" Michael said. "You didn't eat any of the food I brought the other day." He took Allison by the arm and spun her about to face him. He hadn't been to see her in a long time. Now that she'd stopped eating, she couldn't count by meals—in fact she hadn't made actual meals since she could remember.

"Take that robe off."

Allison crossed her arms over her chest and took a few steps back. Her body felt light. There were times now when she thought she might be able to float from one part of the room to another. When she last awoke, she found that a tooth was loose in her mouth. It had come out easily. As a joke, she'd put it under one of her pillows so that Michael might find it. Now she wished she still had it in her hand so she could slip it in his pocket when he wasn't paying attention. The idea made her smile, but she kept her smile small so as not to reveal the hole in her mouth. He would notice soon enough.

He didn't look so frightening to her in the candlelight. She'd gotten so used to seeing him that she hadn't noticed that he was starting to lose his hair at the sides, around his widow's peak. It made his nose look even larger. He was starting to look like an old man.

"Allison. Come here."

But she wouldn't. She knew he wanted to look inside her.

"I don't want to play," she said, her voice hoarse with disuse. "I don't want to play anymore, Michael." That's what they were doing, and had been doing. It was a game, and she had other things to think about now. She was finished playing.

"But I'll eat something if you want," she said. "I just haven't been hungry." In fact, the idea of food repelled her. She had eaten one of the apples not too long ago, but it had made her sick and she'd vomited into the bucket. "Here, I'll show you."

She turned to the cooler—which hadn't held anything cold since she'd tried to escape—and bent to take out a piece of bread. Surely she could eat a piece of bread, couldn't she? Then he would stop asking questions, do whatever he wanted to do to her, and go away.

But he grabbed her around the waist and pulled her to him.

"I said I want the robe off, my love."

She obeyed, and let him untie the flowered silk robe that the silent man had brought to her. Michael never mentioned him, but he had to know about him, didn't he?

He pushed the robe off of her shoulders and it fell to the floor. She shivered, as she always did. The damp had entered her bones, had become a part of her very being. Turning her sideways, he put his hand on the place where the thing inside her was growing. There was the rise in the flesh, a taut mound that fit his hand as though it were a ball he might palm.

"Jesus Christ," he said roughly. "You little shit."

Now he knew. She didn't say anything. That had been the second secret the thing had told her: that Michael wasn't going to hurt her anymore. She'd become immune to him. The thing was there to protect her.

Inside, she felt it move and stretch and speak its soothing, special language.

All will be well, it told her. *All manner of things will be well.*

It was a long time before Michael came back again. But the other man came, wearing his balaclava. She never asked him to take it off. Sometimes she imagined that the man was really Michael, pretending to be someone else. What other reason could he have for covering his face? He wore different clothes from Michael, and was thinner at the waist. There was a bulge in the back of the balaclava that she thought might be a ponytail. Was there some weird magic in his mask? Was it part of the game? It made a strange kind of sense. Sometimes she suspected that there might not be any other men in the world anymore besides Michael and the other man.

When the other man next came to her, he brought a Thermos with a milky drink in it. The drink was like chalk in her mouth, and made her cough. He pulled a clean handkerchief from his pocket and wiped her cheek.

As soon as she was calm, he spoke.

It wasn't Michael's voice. It was deeper than she expected, but just as kind as she'd thought it might be.

"Allison," he said. "You know you're going to have a baby, don't you?"

She laughed. The candle on the bedside table flickered.

"You can't stay here anymore," he said. "We have to think about taking you somewhere else."

At his words, the thing inside her spun like it had been cut loose from a rope at which it had been straining. It hit the wall of her gut, and she doubled over in pain.

"What is it?" he said, touching her arm gingerly.

When she looked up at him again, she saw that he had lifted the balaclava from the front of his face and pushed it up to his forehead. In the candlelight, he looked a lot like Michael.

She shook her head and pushed him away. "Go away," she said. "Leave us alone." She hadn't wanted to speak to him, but this was important.

"This isn't any kind of place for a baby. I shouldn't have let this go on so long," he said. "You're sick, Allison."

There was kindness in his voice, in his words. But there was no question of her leaving. The thing inside her, the thing that loved her, had told her not to worry. They would be together, but they could only be together in this place. If they were together, neither of them would ever, ever be alone again. All his talk about a baby was just made up. It wasn't a baby. It was her other half. Maybe even her twin. It was her responsibility to take care of it. And she couldn't do that out there, where she was before. There was only here!

She looked around the little room. Soon she wouldn't even need Michael or this other man to come to her. She'd drunk whatever he'd brought her in a moment of weakness, but she knew she couldn't be weak anymore.

"Allison. What are you thinking?"

She reached a hand out to stroke his face in the same way he had stroked hers that first time he had come to her room. Her castle.

He took her hand and held it for a moment, then brought it to his lips. "I'm sorry," he said.

His face was rough with whiskers in a way that Michael's never was. She liked that. Inside her, the thing purred its happiness. It was comforted. Taking her hand away, she climbed onto the bed. She tugged on the man's faded, hooded sweatshirt, wanting him to come to her. She was always happy to give him what Michael took from her each time he came to her.

He made a small move toward her, and the thing inside her was happy. She was happy.

But then he got up from the bed and turned away.

"Wait!" she said. Scrambling off the bed on the other side, she ducked beneath it and pulled out the blanket. Lifting it before her, she spread her arms so he could see the width of it, but it only hung down to her thighs. "It's not finished. I'm not finished yet. We can't leave!"

"What is that? Did you make it?"

She sighed. He would understand.

"It's nice, Allison."

For some reason, his praise embarrassed her. She hung her head shyly. Inside her, the thing sighed too.

"Listen. Drink all of that stuff I brought," he said. "Not right away. Wait a little while. I don't want it to make you sick."

At the door—which was unlocked, as it always was while he was in the room—he turned back to her.

"I'm coming back," he said.

But he didn't come back for a long, long time.

Chapter 54

Lucas left a late morning meeting with his supervisor at the State Police post and headed back to Old Gate and the sheriff's office. There were few things he disliked more than having to justify his running of an investigation. He'd met with a lot of skepticism about the Roberta Bliss assault being linked to the death of Karin Powell, but after he'd emphasized the fact that Roberta Bliss was a judge's wife, he got a little more cooperation. His supervisor was no stranger to pressure. Judge Bliss had many friends in the police bureaucracy and among policy makers around the state. He was a UVA man as well, and that counted for a lot.

"This is starting to look like a clusterfuck candy bar and we're the soft nougaty inside," Lucas said.

"Sir?" Deputy Tim Hatcher looked up from his work.

Lucas laughed. "Wake up, Deputy. We've got to get our asses in gear on this case. What does Roberta Bliss have in common with Karin Powell?"

Tim furrowed his broad, freckled brow. "Rainey Adams? I don't really see her whacking her cousin-by-marriage in the back of the head. No obvious motive."

"Someone from the party? Or a complete stranger?" Lucas said. "Both the front and back doors of the judge's house were unlocked. Word is that Roberta Bliss was known to be a soft touch for a handout."

"But the judge didn't say anything was stolen, did he?" Tim said.

"The kid said everything looked okay. I don't think the judge has even been home since it happened," Lucas said. "I wonder about him. Do you—or your grandmother, or whoever—know anything about what kind of guy he is? Is he a good family man? I know he's not exactly a hanging judge."

"After his mother died, he started giving away his parents' money, and got to be everyone's favorite lawyer," Tim said. "Creepy house. Creepy family. But I don't know that I believe in that haunted stuff, though. Do you?"

Lucas took a moment to answer. When he'd first seen Bliss House five years ago, he'd believed it to be nothing more than a testament to some psycho Yankee's vanity. But soon enough, he was standing on the cusp of the then-weedy driveway of Bliss House, watching as Peter Brodsky, the house's last owner, was led outside, his wrists cuffed, his eyes shining with madness. He couldn't forget the way Brodsky had laughed as his wife's body was loaded into the ambulance. He'd laughed as the ambulance crunched slowly over the gravel, its flashing lights barely visible in the harsh morning sun. His laughter stopped for just a moment as he was pushed—with less than necessary care—into the back of the car that would take him to jail. Once the door was shut on him, he resumed laughing, louder this time, so that Lucas could hear him even as the car began pulling away.

Then, about a week after he was arrested and jailed without bond, Peter Brodsky changed. He was beyond remorseful about his wife's death, refusing to eat, weeping loudly, crying out her name. Gone was the cocky, joking demeanor, the lewd comments about the female officers and—shockingly—his dead wife. He attempted suicide using a bed sheet.

The psychiatrists said he had entered a guilt phase. Lucas had a different explanation.

Brodsky was away from Bliss House. He would never see it again, never stand inside it. The house had been inside his head. But when he got away from it, it let him go. It was finished with *him*.

Tim was watching Lucas, waiting for an answer.

Lucas didn't want to get sucked into the memory of that investigation. Every time he entered or even passed the sheltered drive of Bliss House, he felt himself being sucked back in. Helpless. He didn't do very well with feeling helpless.

"We're covering all our bases. We've got someone researching for lawsuits and complaints on both Karin Powell and Mrs. Bliss. We've got the psychiatric files on Karin Powell. Maybe she was in denial about losing the baby and started feeling guilty about how it all happened. Do we have any information on whether she was the religious type?"

The deputy shrugged. Just then, Lucas thought that he probably should've asked to have another ranking detective put on the case days ago. His partner, Brandon, would be back in less than a week, but Lucas had little hope of getting more answers before then.

"Does a person have to be religious to have a conscience?" Tim said.

"Yeah, we're not going to go there." Lucas got up to pace. "So, we've got a missing phone, missing fingernails, a house full of people who said Karin Powell was her bright and cheerful self up until she had words with the contractor husband. Then we've got a woman from the same party being attacked in her own kitchen. And that woman's son getting the shit beat out of him by one of the suspects, in front of the woman who owns the house where the first woman was killed."

"Wow," Tim said. "It's a bad time to be a Bliss."

"Looks more like it's a bad day to be Gerard Powell," he said. He had stopped in the doorway, where he had a view of the reception area. "The sister-in-law is here, and she doesn't look happy."

⌒

"What I don't understand is why you let him go."

Neither Molly nor her parents had heard about Gerard's being taken into custody, and she was angry that she'd had to learn about it from Lucas.

"Mr. Cunetta, Mr. Powell's lawyer, works fast, and the victim decided not to press charges," Lucas said. "Certainly none of us expected he'd be out so quickly." He was surprised to see her, and a little taken aback by her anger. Up to now, the family hadn't even hinted that they thought Gerard Powell had killed his wife.

"My sister was pregnant with some other man's baby," Molly said. "Wouldn't you want to kill your wife if she did that to you?"

Lucas let that one go. "Mr. Powell and your sister had a kind of understanding because of her addiction, yes?"

"That's because he's a creep. Why shouldn't she get what she needed somewhere else?"

Lucas wondered at her ability to equate suffering an addiction with simple need. "Did she tell you whose child it was?" he asked.

Molly reddened. "She didn't tell me about the baby," she said.

"Was your sister afraid to tell you?" Lucas asked. "Had she spoken to you about being afraid?"

"She might have been afraid. I'm sure he only messes with people he thinks can't fight back."

"Like Jefferson Bliss?" Lucas said, unable to hide the incredulity from his voice. "I gather that the younger Mr. Bliss got in a punch or two."

"There's always an exception," Molly said. "That's not my fault."

"But you said your sister could take care of herself. Did she ever say he threatened her? Or injured her? When I interviewed you with your parents, you specifically said that you didn't think Gerard Powell had anything to do with her death. What happened to change your mind?"

"Didn't someone say they were fighting the night of the party?" Molly said. "And you already know he didn't care if she slept with other people."

Lucas nodded. "That would speak to a certain degree of tolerance rather than a propensity to violence, wouldn't it?" Her agitation and heightened color told him he was getting to her.

What in the hell is she here for?

"I think he wanted to punish her." As she talked, she began to unbutton her cotton blouse. "I think he changed his mind when there was suddenly real evidence—the baby—that he couldn't make Karin happy. I think he wants to punish all of us."

Tim had been silent up to this point, sitting motionless in his chair. Listening. Now, he gave a nervous cough. He glanced at Lucas for confirmation that what was happening was really happening, but Lucas was looking steadily at Molly. She stopped unbuttoning with two buttons left to go, and pushed the blouse back over one shoulder. Her peaches-and-cream breasts were bare. She wore no bra or jewelry.

"Ma'am," Lucas said, "please don't do that."

Molly said, "Look at this. Look what he did to me." She turned so they could see the four gray bruises on the back of her shoulder. "And here." She turned back again and pointed to the dark oval of a fifth bruise at the front. Staring at them defiantly, she waited for some kind of response.

"Put your shirt back on, please. If you don't I'll be forced to write you up for indecent exposure," Lucas said.

She re-buttoned it slowly, watching him.

"We're not playing games here, Ms. Schroeter," he said. "Are you making a charge against someone?"

"He attacked me. I think he was going to rape me."

"Any assault is a very serious charge," Lucas said. "But if someone attempted to rape you, that puts the assault at a whole different level. Maybe you'd be more comfortable with a female officer in the room?"

"You're not taking me seriously. Gerard attacked me at his house. He hates us. He hates me!"

"We'll need to have you checked out by a doctor and have some photos taken of your injuries. Before that, though, we'll have one of the officers work on an incident report with you."

Molly stood. "Why in the hell don't you just get the son-of-a-bitch in here? He should be locked up. I don't understand. I show you what he did to me and you're going to blow me off? Make it seem like it's no big deal? What is wrong with you people?"

Lucas stood as well, and the deputy copied him.

"I'm sorry for your distress, Ms. Schroeter. Let me get a female officer in here. We also have a counselor you can speak with at the hospital."

"You're trying to get rid of me," Molly said. "You think I'm lying, don't you?"

"Ms. Schroeter, no one said that we don't believe you. We just have a system for dealing with situations like this. If we don't follow procedure, there can be problems getting a conviction, or even getting charges brought. I promise that we're taking this very seriously. Did you have an argument with Mr. Powell?"

"Of course I had an argument with him! Is this blame-the-victim time? Is that how you do it in this stupid little town? Karin told me the cops around here were morons."

"Do you want to make a formal complaint?" Lucas was wearying of the woman's game. Gerard Powell wasn't any more a rapist than he was. Something had obviously occurred between the two of them, but he suspected that it hadn't gone nearly as far as she was implying.

"Detective Chappell," Tim said, his voice cautious. "Do you think maybe we should let Ms. Schroeter have a few minutes alone to collect her thoughts?"

Molly looked vaguely triumphant. Lucas didn't look away from her, though he was sorely tempted to tell Tim to shut the hell up.

"Please sit back down, ma'am," Lucas said to Molly. His voice had a sharp edge to it.

"I don't think so," Molly said.

"Fine. Don't sit, then. Just stand there and listen."

"I don't have to listen to anything you have to say," she said.

"I don't know how you got those bruises, Ms. Schroeter. I suspect that you did get them from Mr. Powell, but I don't think he attempted to rape you. I think you got into an argument and things got unpleasant. He'd just lost his wife and you'd lost your sister and neither of you was thinking clearly. Things got out of hand, you got angry with him, and then you decided to come to us and screw him over. You may even now believe that he's responsible for your sister's death. I can't give you an answer on that one, but we're working on it."

Molly's face darkened.

"Are you finished?"

"I believe that covers it. Shall I call an officer in to make a report?"

"You prick. The only report I want to make is about you and the way you've treated me today."

"You could do that, ma'am," Lucas said. "That's your right."

She left without saying another word, not following the arrow markers to the reception area but weaving her way through the desks and low cubicles, ignoring the stares of most of the station.

When she was out the door, Lucas heard one of the men give a slow whistle.

Lucas turned to Tim, who was still staring dumbly after her. "Don't ever do that again," he said.

Tim looked for a moment like he might try to explain, but he thought better of it. It was a brief struggle. "Yes, sir."

"She has a thing for the contractor," Lucas said. "I doubt her parents have a clue. I don't even know that Powell suspected it before they had their knock-down drag-out."

"How do you know? That is, if you don't mind me asking."

"When I interviewed her right after Karin's death, she was too high on him. Very defensive. But now he's let her down. Her sister's dead, and he still doesn't want her. Life's a bitch." He couldn't let Tim see how relieved he was that he'd been right. It had been a huge risk. "It still doesn't clear the Powell guy of anything else, in my book. But, son-of-a-bitch, could this day get any worse?"

Chapter 55

After checking on his crews first thing, Gerard headed for the funeral home. The woman he dealt with was organized and responsive to what he wanted. There would be no maudlin hours of visitation or long speeches. Just a short service in the main parlor of the big house that was now the funeral home, then Karin's body would be taken, unaccompanied, to their off-site cremation operation. He gave her Karin's parents' address for the delivery of the ashes. Karin's memory, and the things she'd touched, would be all around him, every day, for a long time. He didn't need a Porcelain Elegance Keepsake urn full of dust and teeth to remind him of her.

Dust and teeth. Karin would've been horrified at the image.

Leaving the funeral home, he looked across the street to see the day care center—another renovated old house—where the wealthier people in town sent their kids to play with other privileged kids. Karin would have insisted that their child go there while she worked. Maybe he couldn't have handled looking at the other dads' faces when he came to pick their son or daughter up, constantly wondering if one of them were its real father. He would never know for certain.

Walking to his car, he looked for the blue sedan that had been dogging his steps for the past few days, but didn't see it. Had they given up now that he'd actually done something that had landed him in custody?

All of his jobs were a few days behind schedule, but no one would fire him in the end, because of Karin's—*I have to say it. Think it.*—death. Instead, he headed to Nick Cunetta's office a block from the courthouse, stopping to pick up a coffee on the way. The pretty brunette at the coffee house's counter smiled at him and self-consciously tucked a thick curl of hair behind one ear. Gerard guessed that she'd seen him pull up out front, because she had his usual order ready.

"I'm sorry about your wife," she said, sliding his cup across the counter. "She was really nice."

"Yeah," he said quickly.

When he saw her face fall, he immediately felt bad about being so short with her. She was a good kid working her way through nursing school.

"It's been kind of rough," he said. "Thanks."

When she smiled again, it hit him that he was now single. No longer was he married to one of the town's most visible women. For years he'd ignored the not-so-subtle advances of the attractive, bored women who were often his clients. Advances that flattered him but also made him uncomfortable. It wasn't that Karin would've complained. She'd had no right to complain. But she had taken all his energy—emotional energy, anyway. And he could see in the eyes of this particular girl that emotional energy was what she was looking for.

⁓

When he got to Nick's office, he found Nick's secretary closing and locking the front door. A quaint BACK IN 10 MINUTES sign hung on the other side of the glass was swinging to a stop.

"Is Nick in?" Gerard said.

Nick's secretary was as quaint as her sign, with bifocals dangling from a jeweled chain around her neck and a slight stoop to her shoulders. Gerard vaguely remembered meeting her at one of Nick's holiday parties.

"Oh, no," she said. "I've been messaging him all morning, and he has court this afternoon. You don't have an appointment, do you?"

Gerard introduced himself, but there was no responding flicker of recognition in her eyes. "No appointment."

"I'm going to pop over to the house and make sure he hasn't overslept. Sometimes he does that." She shook her head like an indulgent mother. "Silly thing."

Raised to be his mother's idea of a gentleman, Gerard told the secretary that he'd be glad to drive her over, or go and knock on Nick's door himself. When she insisted that she wanted to walk, he asked her if she didn't mind if he went along. He didn't tell her that he was anxious to put more pressure on her boss. Nick's insistence that the Bliss kid wasn't Karin's lover—or at least not the lover who had gotten her pregnant—felt false to him, and he wanted more answers.

A few minutes later, standing in the fraught silence of Nick's meticulously kept house, he wished he'd just gone to check on his jobs as he'd planned.

Chapter 56

"Clusterfuck, like I said." Lucas stretched a pair of Latex gloves onto his hands.

Nick Cunetta's garroted body lay sprawled across one of the two couches in his silent living room. The satellite company's logo drifted across his television screen. In the kitchen, an EMT was treating his secretary for shock. Gerard Powell sat a few feet away from her, silent, looking like he might never be able to speak again. There was a uniform standing nearby in case he did. Or in case he tried to leave.

Lucas could hardly blame him if he did. It looked bad. He knew the temptation killers experienced wanting to be around their victims and their crime scenes, but he still didn't think the guy had it in him. Gerard Powell was aggressive, as he'd proved by beating up the Bliss kid. But he'd had a damned good reason—even if his response was way out of line. How many times had Lucas had to keep his own temper in check? And Powell couldn't have been worried that his wife had been sleeping with Cunetta. At least that was out of play. Nick Cunetta hadn't had a heterosexual bone in his body.

A deputation of state crime scene techs were unloading their gear and hauling it into the house. Neighbors had begun to gather outside, a few of them in tears.

He lifted one of the dead man's badly injured hands. The smell of bleach was strong around the body, and the soft leather of the couch and much of Nick Cunetta's bathrobe were splotched, drained of color. Getting any DNA from his hands or from under his nails would be nearly impossible.

The deputy, Tim, came in from the kitchen. "What did our contractor have to say?" Lucas asked.

"Says he just wanted a word with his lawyer. Stopped by the office and found the secretary was on her way over here. The door was locked, but the lady had a key."

Lucas looked up to see Gerard Powell standing in the doorway from the kitchen. Another county deputy hovered behind him. Why the hell wasn't he doing his job, keeping Powell and the woman away?

"You're going to take me in, aren't you?" Gerard said.

Lucas heard the tremor in his voice. Not so much the tough guy now. Powell had lost his wife, been taken in for assault, practically accused of murder, and had walked in on a dead man who'd been murdered in a thoroughly nasty way. It sucked to be him, and it showed. There were a couple of days' growth of beard on his face, and the skin beneath his eyes sagged. His eyes were almost more red than hazel. If he'd slept more than two or three hours in the past twenty-four, Lucas would've been surprised. But the more worn down he was, the more they'd get out of him. If there was anything to get.

"We'll need a statement," Lucas said. "And that'll be done more easily at the office. We'll drive over there as soon as we're finished here, and give you a ride back to your truck later. You two walked over here, right?"

"I think he knew," Gerard said, looking past Tim to Nick's body.

"Knew what?" Lucas said.

It was as though Gerard couldn't look away from Nick, at the man he'd disliked for so long. The man his wife had trusted with her life and her secrets. If he could only shake him, get him to speak, to give up what he knew.

"I think he knew who killed Karin. Who she was sleeping with. He acted like he didn't, but I think he did."

"Mr. Cunetta was an officer of the court. You don't think he would've told us if he knew who killed your wife?"

Gerard looked from Nick to Lucas. "I knew him a hell of a lot better than you people. He had his own agenda, and it mostly had to do with what Nick wanted."

"Did he make a pass at you or something?" Lucas said. "Maybe he had different ideas about what was wrong between you and your wife?"

Powell didn't flinch. "You think this was about Nick being gay?" he said quietly. "I don't give a shit who he spent his nights with, Detective. It's none of my business. He never tried to get me in the sack, if that's what you're asking. We didn't like each other very much. I've got no reason to hide that fact."

"Yet he helped you out yesterday when you might have ended up in jail," Lucas said, curious. He wondered if Cunetta had felt as sorry for the guy as he did. Or maybe he had done it because of the dead wife.

"What's your point?"

"Why don't you tell us what made you decide that Jefferson Bliss was the one spending time with your wife?"

A cough at the other end of the room brought their attention to the waiting forensics team. It was as though the three men in the room had forgotten the fourth—the dead man.

⌒

Lucas and Tim searched the house and discovered that a casement window in one of the three bedrooms had been pried open. It was one of the tougher types of windows to open from the outside, but the double-paned glass had been neatly cut and the window pulled open, so that the killer could pop the indoor screen from its place. Because it was still open, there was no indication that the killer hadn't left that way as well.

When Tim returned from directing the forensics team to search for evidence outside the forced window, he found Lucas checking out the closet.

It was a strange exercise for Lucas. He'd known plenty of men who had died, but he'd never spent the night with any of them. Together, the neatly hung suits, sportcoats, and pants gave him a more complete picture of the man, but strangely enough it was the careful way that he'd arranged his shoes that affected him. Each pair was in a clear, labeled storage box: Boat Shoes-Tan; Boat Shoes-Chestnut; Wing-Tips-Black; Wing-Tips-High Shine-Black; Loafers-Tassel-Tan; Loafers-Tassel-Gray; Loafers-Drivers-Pebble Brown; Loafers-Penny-Oxblood. There were fifteen or twenty more boxes, but on the box with the penny loafers' label, another hand had written, in smaller print: *Ha! Such a dork!—xo*. The tenderness of the comment took him by surprise. Someone had been in the closet and wanted to tease Nick. Had it been Karin Powell? Lucas didn't think it was her style.

He'd liked Nick well enough. But he'd gotten the vibe that Nick was looking for more. That somebody had cut off any possible future that Nick might have had by strangling the life out of him made Lucas angry. He would have to work to keep his anger from messing with the investigation.

"Whoa. This guy had a boatload of clothes," Tim said. "There's stuff in here with the tags still on it."

"Do you have kids?" Lucas asked.

"Two," Tim said. "Four and two."

"If you were a lawyer in your forties, unmarried with kids, you could afford a closet full of suits, too. Hey, you didn't tell Powell what I found out at the doc's this morning, did you? About his wife's miscarriage?"

"No, sir. Why would I do that?"

Lucas shrugged. "I don't think he needs to know just yet. Now that we've got this . . ." He gestured toward the living room where Nick Cunetta's body was still on the couch. "We want to see where it goes."

He walked over to the custom-built desk that took up most of one bedroom wall. It had three monitors, all dark, sitting in a comfortable arc in its center. The high-end desk chair sitting in front of them looked as though it probably cost at least a month of Lucas's state salary. He passed a gloved hand near the computer's mouse pad, gently nudging it. The computer built into the center monitor hummed, and all three monitors blinked to life.

"Shouldn't we wait for a warrant?" Tim said.

"Oops," Lucas said.

"Why would someone need three computer monitors?" Tim asked.

"Gaming? It's a pretty sweet setup for that."

"Got it," Tim said. He came closer. "You don't think there's a bunch of porn on there, do you?"

Lucas glanced back at him. "We'll do what we have to do, yeah? I mean, the guy's dead. It's our job. I guess you never worked vice, either."

Tim blushed.

Lucas smiled and turned back to the computer.

"Sometimes I think if it weren't for dumb luck, no murder would ever get solved," he said.

The center monitor was covered with neat rows of application icons on top of a photo of a smiling Nick Cunetta in sunglasses, shirtless on a rocky beach, his arm around a taller and slightly younger blond man whose smile seemed tentative but nonetheless genuine. The left-hand monitor had a photo software program open, with an image of an old barn that Cunetta had been editing. But it was the third monitor that grabbed and held their attention.

It was a split screen. One box held an image of Nick Cunetta's bedroom—specifically the bed, which was covered with a simple brown spread and had an opulent pile of pillows at its head. The second was of the front step of the house. It was a fish-eye view, and they could even see the front fence and a bit of the forensics van. The third box looked like a scene from a television crime show.

A forensics tech was bagging Nick Cunetta's burned hands, her face not far from his, just as the murderer's must have been.

"You're fucking kidding me," Lucas said, unable to suppress his astonishment. There had been nothing about Nick Cunetta that suggested he might like to record himself—or himself with others. The bedroom camera spoke to Nick's obvious loneliness. The same thing that had almost sent Lucas to Nick's doorstep the previous night. He'd even slowed the car as he'd approached the neat little house. If he *had* stopped by, he might have saved Nick's life.

Holy shit.

"Wow," Tim said. "I think we may be the luckiest bastards on the planet."

Lucas closed his eyes and took a deep breath. *Maybe.*

Chapter 57

Rainey threw a forearm over her eyes to block out the sun. She swore unintelligibly in her half-sleep then caught herself, remembering that Ariel had come to bed with her. Rolling onto her side to check on her daughter, she saw the other half of the bed was empty. She also saw that it was after noon. No wonder Ariel was already out of bed.

Sleeping so late wasn't like her at all. The previous day had been insane, with one terrible event after another, and then the haunted, unfamiliar look in Ariel's eyes. The fear in her voice. But there had been that moment of relief at the end, when Ariel had broken down and allowed herself to be vulnerable to her, and huddled close as she drifted off to sleep, just as she had when she was five or six. It gave Rainey hope that—despite the strange things that had happened to them since Karin's death—they might have some kind of normal relationship.

She called for Ariel, thinking she might be in the bathroom. No answer. That the bedroom curtains were open confused her. It was her habit to shut them at night just like she'd done back in St. Louis, even though they lived far out in the country. In one of her very few light moments, Ariel had teased her about it.

"Really, Mom? You think there are wild turkeys in the trees, or bears trying to spy on us?"

Rainey had laughed, telling Ariel that she'd heard the local black bears were famous peeping toms. But in the back of her mind she had been thinking about Mr. Brodsky, who'd killed his wife out in the woods. Sometimes she couldn't stop thinking about it. She was glad Ariel hadn't brought it up lately.

The sudden appearance of a dark streak in her sweet Ariel worried her. Was it that she'd grown up too fast since the accident? The way she'd spoken to Gerard, with that vicious, predatory look in her eyes, had been alarming. Even her voice was different: older, more confident. Not just confident, but commanding. This was an Ariel who terrified her. It was wrong that she should be frightened by her own daughter.

Perhaps there really was a sinister presence in the house. One that was stealing Ariel away.

No! I've got to stop this.

She squeezed her eyes shut, once again forcing the thought from her mind. She had to focus on Ariel and what was going on here and now. Her friend Bertie was hurt, and a woman had died—*was probably murdered*—in her house. She knew *she* hadn't killed Karin Powell, and neither had Ariel. But there had been someone besides Karin in the house after the party. Someone who had either stayed behind to kill Karin, or had come into the house later.

This house. So much I don't know about it.

Bliss House had been the biggest impulse purchase of her life. She had only wanted to get away, to get out of St. Louis and go somewhere safe and different and engrossing enough to consume all of her guilty energy.

No. It couldn't be the house. It was anger possessing Ariel. That was all. Ariel couldn't let it go. And, obviously, neither could she.

But she could help Ariel let it go, couldn't she? If she loved her enough, she could make it happen. She just had to try harder.

"Honey?" she called. "Ariel, sweetie?"

Rainey used the bathroom and threw on a new robe that she'd hung on the back of the bathroom door. The rich turquoise color was one that Will had loved to see on her, so she felt special while wearing it. Sunny, like the day outside the window.

Out in the hall, she looked across to see if Ariel's bedroom door was open. Seeing that it was, she was relieved. Perhaps she'd already gone downstairs for breakfast.

What had really happened in the kitchen last night?

Her fragile mood fell.

Across the gallery, Ariel's door slammed.

"Ariel?" she cried.

Behind her, her own door also slammed shut, causing her to jump. She looked back, stiff with fear, to see the heavy door standing closed and silent as though it had been that way all morning.

But it wasn't over. She heard other doors in the house slamming—doors above her and below—and pounding footsteps, as though several people were racing to shut them, as though they were playing a great, noisy game.

She crouched there in the hall, covering her ears, her eyes shut as tightly as she could make them. Waiting, waiting, waiting for it to stop.

⌒

Rainey was still shaking. Even after she heard the front door slam, she stayed where she was until the vibration beneath her feet stopped as well.

Opening her eyes, she stood. She had to find Ariel.

She ran for Ariel's room. Every door she passed was now open. Even Ariel's was open, just as it had been when she first came out of her own bedroom.

Sweet Jesus, what's happening?

"Ariel!"

Ariel's bed was empty and unmade, but then Ariel never made her bed anymore. The en suite bathroom, and the rest of the room: empty.

"Where are you, honey?"

The house had a late-morning stillness about it. Above Rainey, the painted stars looked down, mute and unconcerned.

Chapter 58

Allison leaned against the headboard, her legs curled beneath her to keep her feet warm. Even with the socks and extra blanket the other man had brought her a long time ago, she couldn't get warm. The candlelight was so dim that another person might find it difficult to see where the crochet needle ended and the last bit of blue yarn began, but she could see well enough. She even fancied that she could see in the darkness almost as well as a cat. There were times when she woke up in the blackness and made her way to the sink without even lighting a candle.

She had almost come to the end of the yarn and was in a hurry to finish so she could tie it off, and then untie it and unravel it again. The only thing that troubled her was untying the tiny knots when she came to the end of each skein. It hadn't been as hard when the yarn was new, but now it was wearing thin in some places. Some bits were so worn that she let them break, chewed away the weak parts, tied the yarn back together, and started again.

The work was making her anxious in a way she'd never been anxious before. The thing inside her was worried, too, and wasn't able to soothe her any longer. It was much bigger now, and fretted and rolled and nibbled at her, often waking her from sleep. Yet it hardly spoke at all. Had it sensed something that she couldn't? Was it time? She wanted to tell it not to worry, that they wouldn't have to leave, but she knew she couldn't lie.

Then one day, Michael told her that the other man had gone away, and that he wouldn't ever come back to try to take *her* away. That this was where she belonged.

"Yes! Yes!" she said, taking her hands in his and covering them with kisses.

Why did he look at her so strangely? Had she done something wrong? No. He always told her right away when she messed up. Still, it worried her. If he was unhappy, he might decide to make her leave after all.

Then he laid a dainty set of pearl-handled scissors across her palm, and she felt the weak, happy approval of the thing inside her. When she caressed them with her other hand, the thing inside rolled about with some of its old familiar joy.

"You'll know what to do with these when the time comes," Michael said.

The scissors were so light that she could hardly imagine they would cut anything. What had he meant about knowing what to do with them? She thought of the blanket she'd stuffed beneath the bed when she heard him coming in. Her teeth hurt sometimes from chewing off the bits of the yarn. The scissors would be helpful. But the scissors also brought other thoughts that she couldn't bear to examine too closely. Thoughts that brought a strange, mirthful smile to the thing inside her.

When Michael was gone, she took them from the side table where she had laid them aside, folded them closed, and hid them beneath her pillow.

Chapter 59

Ariel knew no one could hear her, but she continued screaming for her mother and pounding on the door until she could barely lift her arms.

No one knows I'm here. No one knows.

She sank to the floor. Closing her eyes, she willed it to be a bad dream. Her mother would wake her by gently shaking her shoulder, and they would have breakfast together, and she would never be cruel to her mother again. She would forgive her, and stop punishing her for letting her father die. She would go to the doctor just like she'd asked. They would be friends, like they were before. She would even help her set up her business, and try to make new friends now that she didn't look so much like a freak. It would all be different.

I promise I'll be good. Mommy, I promise, promise, promise!

Her mother loved her. They would be happy.

Then she remembered.

Jefferson.

Jefferson would find her. If he had a girlfriend he was bringing here, he would definitely be back.

Newly hopeful, she went back into the bedroom and took a long drink from one of the water bottles in the refrigerator. She was hungry, too, but the cheese didn't look appetizing at all.

She wished she had her phone. He'd never answered her text about his mother, but surely he would try to, soon. When she didn't answer, he'd come looking for her and would know to look here.

What was she going to do here until someone found her? She perched on the edge of the bed. There were the other rooms down the hall. Their doors were closed, and something had to be inside them. Maybe a way out?

No. I won't look.

But she couldn't stand it, sitting there like some kind of prisoner. Stupid door! It was probably just jammed.

She got up and went back to the hallway. This time, instead of banging, she tried to tease the door handle, just like her dad had showed her to tease a cork out of a bottle when he let her be their *sommelier* at dinner. Putting her ear to the monstrously thick wood, she listened for the lock's inner-workings. *Nothing.* The handle turned easily but it was as though it wasn't connected to anything.

"Daddy," she whispered. "Daddy, if you're here, please help me."

She knew she was being childish. The memory of him appearing in her room was getting dimmer all the time. The memory of his face smiling at her, the memory of him laughing at some stupid joke she'd told him on the way home from dance class that day. It was all fading away.

She couldn't remember anything that happened after she pulled the mail from the box in St. Louis. The world had just ended. Now it was as though she'd been transported from that moment to here, in this hidden place. Nothing had happened in between. That time was lost.

"I'm sorry, Daddy," she said to the darkness. "I wish you were here with me."

The answering voice might have been a distant sigh.

"Button."

Chapter 60

It was the second day in a row Gerard had spent time at the sheriff's office, and he was grateful to leave. As soon as he got back to his truck, he took out his phone to call the funeral home to tell them to just go ahead and cremate Karin without a service.

Screw Molly and her parents.

When he'd signed in at the sheriff's office front desk that morning, he'd noticed Molly's name just two lines above his. The detective told him not to worry about it, but wouldn't give him any information. Which told him that she'd come by to make his life harder. She and her parents deserved zero consideration. *Such a bitch!* What in the hell had he ever done to her?

But he knew it was what he *hadn't* done. He hadn't looked to her for consolation. He'd known for a long time that she had been interested in him long before he and Karin were married. Molly wasn't as forward as Karin was. She had a lot of issues that were the exact opposite of Karin's. If Karin couldn't keep her hands to herself, Molly couldn't figure out what to do with hers. So lovely, but so awkward. Her crush on him had been almost charming a few years earlier, but now it was just a problem. It wasn't his fault that he wasn't attracted to her. It *was* his fault that he hadn't been able to judge the depth and inappropriateness of her feelings. In her mind, he'd treated her badly. Now she was going to make him pay. Hadn't she told him as much?

He looked down at the phone. No, he wasn't going to call the funeral home. He couldn't do it.

I'm not that much of an asshole.

His own parents were on a missionary trip in Turkey with a doctors' charity. They had been fond of Karin, but they wouldn't be able to get back for the service. It was only right that Karin's parents should be there to mourn their daughter.

Instead of calling the funeral home, he listened to the messages that had piled up on his voicemail. The last was a polite, formal message from one of Karin's clients who had planned to sign a contract with him to build a house, but was now canceling. "In light of recent events . . ."

Recent events.

He'd been wrong in thinking that he was going to be cut some professional slack because of Karin's death. It was going to screw him up in every possible way. It was even possible that his business— which up to now had been incredibly solid—could fail. His work was the only thing he truly gave a damn about now besides Ellie.

There was a temptation to let it go, to just give up, and maybe leave Old Gate. Leave Virginia altogether. Start somewhere new. He'd never been one to give up on things. Look how long he'd stayed with Karin, even in the face of the crap he'd been dealing with for years. Maybe it was time.

But what did he have left to give?

What had he given Karin? Cover? Maybe legitimacy. Affection. Companionship. An amazing house. A strong base to live from. Love? Yes, he had loved her.

What had she given him? Loyalty? No. Affection? Yes. Companionship? Some. Sex? Definitely. Maybe even love. He was no longer certain of it. Her addiction had controlled her. In the end, Karin was always about Karin. In her line of work, she had had to make it appear that other people's emotions and desires were important to her, and she'd gotten good at faking it.

Like she'd faked it with him. He'd let her get away with it, even encouraged it.

What kind of man am I? What have I done?

Were all women like Karin?

He pictured Rainey Adams's cheerful smile the first day she'd opened the door to him at Bliss House, her look of interested concentration when they worked together on the remodeling plans, the fear and worry in her eyes when she felt she had to protect her daughter from him.

No. Not all women. But did he even deserve to be with a woman who wasn't like Karin, no matter who she was?

On his way home, he drove past the hospital. Poor Bertie Bliss was still inside. Rainey had been right to give him shit about beating up Jefferson just hours after someone had attacked his mother. It didn't matter that he hadn't known when he went over there. He should have listened when Rainey tried to stop him. But he hadn't been able to stop. It was as though the violence was gaining momentum. Three major acts of violence in a little less than a week, and all of them attached to him in some way. Three acts of violence, beginning with Karin's death.

But the trouble for him had started before that. It had started with the pregnancy, and Karin's silence.

Karin didn't trust me any more than I trusted her.

That was a fact he could never change.

Chapter 61

Bertie was freezing, but she couldn't tell anyone she wanted a blanket. She'd listened to chatter about her blood pressure and pulse and the color of the contents of the embarrassing catheter bag attached to the side of the bed. But nothing about helping her *feel* better. Her head ached as though the top of it had been sawed off and her brains scrambled with a large metal fork. She could think, but only barely. Images came slowly. Painfully. She wasn't sure if she would even be able to speak. Right now, though, she wasn't at all certain that she wanted to make the effort ever again.

The Judge was nearby, talking to someone else in the room. He was being just as bossy with the nurse as he always was with her. Her mother had warned her how it would be.

"It comes naturally to men like Randolph, even when they're young," she'd said.

Bertie had laughed. "I just let him *think* he's in charge."

Her mother had been tight-lipped after that, waiting for Bertie to come around. To understand. But it was her mother who didn't understand. Bertie's many friends didn't understand either. Over the years, they all imagined that she'd begun to see herself through the Judge's eyes. They didn't understand that she was content. She had everything she'd ever wanted. She didn't need their approval or appreciation. Nor the Judge's. She knew he loved her as much as he was capable of loving anyone. It might not have been enough for another woman, but it had been enough for her. And she had Jefferson, who (almost) never disappointed her.

The truth was that her expectations for Jefferson weren't terribly high. His academics weren't impressive like his father's (hers had been less than stellar, so why should she judge him?), and he seemed satisfied with his life in Old Gate. That surprised her. So many children wanted to get away as fast as they could.

But there was a problem. Some terrible complication was about to tear down everything she had worked so hard to build: her comfortable marriage, her position in the community, her social standing and extensive circle of friends. Her home. Her only problem was remembering what it was. The only thing she could do was lie here and think and keep trying to remember.

She'd come downstairs later than usual. The Judge had said he would get breakfast in town and had already left the house by the time she got up. Rainey was coming over for coffee because there was something she wanted to talk to Rainey about. It had been important, and she'd wanted both the Judge and Jefferson out of the house. Jefferson . . . what had Jefferson been doing? Was he still asleep?

Damn it. What was it? What did I need to say?

Oh, Lord. Her head hurt so badly. She wanted to touch her hand to it but couldn't lift her arm. It was something about Rainey and the house and someone else. More than one someone else.

You'll be a Bliss, Bertie! Bliss, as in happily ever after. Forever. And the house, Bertie. Maybe you can get the Judge to buy Bliss House back. There were always Blisses in that house.

Her friends. What did they know? She'd been so young when she married the Judge.

Of course she'd imagined bringing the house back into the family, even after the tragedies there. Then her mother-in-law had come to visit one day when Bertie was pregnant with Jefferson, and told her that it was absolutely out of the question. She'd told her the truth about Michael, too. Bertie had listened and was almost convinced. Then her mother-in-law died, and there was the business with the doctor who'd bought the house from her. And not so long ago that awful Peter Brodsky had killed his sweet wife, Mim. Finally, Bertie understood that it wasn't him, but the house, that was really responsible.

Rainey, Rainey, Rainey! Why couldn't you stay away? That house means heartache for you. There are hidden things. Horrible things.

Why can't anyone hear me?

Bertie tried to turn her head, to open her eyes. Open her mouth. But nothing happened. Then she remembered:

She'd been in the kitchen, making a cinnamon raisin braid for Rainey's visit. Jefferson was upstairs, sleeping. He always slept late when he was home, just as deeply as he had when he was a toddler. There was a wasp at the window, flying at it, trying to get out. The kitchen was already warm with sunshine, and the oven was heating, and she'd gone to adjust the thermostat in the front hallway down a degree or two. When she'd come back, there was a man in the kitchen.

His face was covered with some kind of wooly balaclava, which made him look ridiculous against the flowers and sunshine at the garden window. But she didn't laugh. Despite the mask, he seemed familiar. Something about the sunshine and the windows made her think she knew him. But he was obviously there to rob them or do them some kind of harm, so she opened her mouth to scream. Before she could make more than a squeak, he jumped at her, knocking her down.

Her knees hit the floor first, then her breasts and belly. The stone kitchen floor had never seemed harder, and the man pressed his knee into her back to keep her there.

Not in my own kitchen!

She tried to roll away from him, to get him off of her, but he had her by the hair. How many times had she been afraid when she and the Judge were in DC, or even Charlottesville, walking at night? How was it possible that this was happening here on her own floor?

He pushed her face into the stone, once, twice, and she felt something break. Pain seared in her head, and blood flooded her mouth and sinuses.

He got off of her, but she couldn't move or make any sound. She heard him moving around the kitchen. Not quietly. He was messing with the pots and pans hanging from the rack above the stove. The pain in her head made her feel confused, but she wondered what he might be doing. No one robbed people of their pots and pans. The rattling stopped and she heard his shoes scuffing lightly across the stone.

She had to get away, to get up and call for Jefferson, but the blood in her mouth kept her from speaking. Dragging herself to her knees, she reached for the cabinet to steady herself, but she missed it.

The man came to stand over her, one of her precious antique copper kettles in his hand—the one she'd bought in London and had such a problem shipping home. She shrank away, still reaching fruitlessly for the cabinet, the wall, anything. By God's mercy, she'd felt only the first blow.

In her hospital bed, she jerked in alarm, as though he were standing over her still.

Take me away from this place! Someone take me away, please!

The voices across the room stopped, as though the Judge and the nurse had heard Bertie's cry.

Please. Please. Please. I don't belong here. I have to tell Rainey.

A machine somewhere above her head had begun a frantic electronic bleating, and Bertie's own voice, the voice in her head, was drowning in it. Her mouth opened as she choked on the slender tube that ran from her nose to deep inside her body. She thought she would never breathe a free breath again, and her hands clenched and unclenched the insufficient blankets.

"She's coding!" a nurse said.

Bertie didn't hear any more for the roaring in her head.

"Judge Bliss, please step outside the room."

"Is she dying?" Randolph said. "What's happening?"

They shoved past him as he stood watching his wife's life fleeing from her as though it couldn't get away quickly enough.

Chapter 62

After searching the entire downstairs as well as the second floor bedrooms, Rainey paused in the front hall, breathing hard and close to tears. She looked up. The dome stared back at her, unseeing. If it were a sort of lens, it would take in the entire house, and maybe reflect her daughter back to her. The dome had been one of the things that had drawn her to the house. It spoke to her of European art and romance. History. Whimsy. Things she loved. But it was only a decoration. It couldn't help her.

Before she started back up the stairs, she checked her cell phone for recent calls. Nothing. She tried Ariel's number, counting the seconds while the call tried to connect. Again, nothing. It didn't even connect to voicemail. Reluctantly she pressed the locator button, already knowing what it would tell her.

LOCATION NOT AVAILABLE.

Her heart sank. She was going to have to go up to the third floor. Maybe even the roof. She'd already checked the cellar, which had been padlocked since their arrival, and she had the only key. The place was swept clean and completely empty, except for the furnaces and the old coal bin.

The theater was directly above her bedroom. Sometimes, as she lay in her bed at night, she imagined she could hear slow footsteps crossing the floor. She'd told herself that they weren't actually footsteps, but just sounds that an old house might make. Karin had rushed her through the theater when she showed her the house, but Bertie had told her about traveling troupes, prohibitionists, and visiting preachers who had appeared there. The family had invited townspeople out to hear them, and many people came. Some, of course, had just wanted to see the inside of the impressive, mysterious house.

The ballroom wasn't a favorite of Rainey's either, but she checked it first because it would be easy, and because she was procrastinating. She didn't at all understand what attracted Ariel to it. Then, Ariel was a teenager. Rainey too had reveled in being completely shut off from the world when she was a teenager, but she'd managed to be satisfied with a reading nook in her walk-in closet. Finding nothing inside the room, she quickly closed the doors behind her.

Crossing the gallery, she opened the doors to the theater room and called Ariel's name.

Her heart jumped when she heard an answering thud.

"Ariel, are you here?"

The sound came from the stage. Rather than using the steps, Rainey climbed directly up the front, grazing her leg on a metal finial on the stage's base. The stage was empty except for a pair of wooden folding chairs that looked like they wouldn't even hold her slight weight. Turning, surprised by a movement to her left, she saw a terrified blond woman who looked as though she had been running for her life. It was her own image, distorted by a cloudy mirror.

"Mommy, let me out! Please, Mommy! I promise I'll be good!"

The voice was muffled, but sounded farther away.

Rainey hurried toward it. "I'm coming, baby!"

"Mommy!"

Rainey heard terror in her daughter's voice, the same terror that had come with a year of nightmares after the explosion.

"Baby, I'm coming. Where are you?"

"Mommy! They're hurting me!"

Rainey banged on the panels of the wall behind the stage, screaming Ariel's name. Her head was full of noise, and she thought she would explode with frustration. In her panic, she almost missed the small, burnished doorplate at the edge of one of the panels. Finding it, she pushed. Hard. Nothing happened. Again. It wasn't until she pushed more gently that the thing opened.

"Ariel!" She fumbled along the wall for a light. Finally, she found one of the old-fashioned push-button switches, like the one in the ballroom. Just one of the ancient bulbs in a sconce on the wall came on, its timid, wavering glow barely piercing the dark.

Had she expected to find Ariel in here, on the other side of the wall? A part of her had. Ariel hiding. Ariel playing a game. Instead, all that came back to her was the dead sound of her own voice hitting the walls of the room.

The room was filled with the shadows of furniture pushed to the sides, and smelled of decaying rugs and dust and wood. It was the kind of place that she would have delighted in as a child—or even now, under different circumstances. Antiques were her passion. But this place might be her daughter's prison.

In the quiet, she calmed some.

"Honey? Are you in here?"

She heard sobbing coming from a far corner of the room. She walked slowly toward it.

"Ariel!" Her fear put an edge of anger in her voice. "Come out. Stop this. Please!"

Was Ariel playing some kind of trick on her? Thinking it was fun to make her worry, fun to scare her? After the incident with the doors—*No! I didn't dream the doors slamming. The footsteps. I swear I didn't!*—she was frightened. If Ariel *were* playing games with her,

315

it would make everything worse. She thought for a moment about simply leaving the room to let Ariel come out on her own. But her gut told her she was wrong. Those screams had been real. Ariel was here, and in some kind of danger.

In her pocket, her cell phone rang. Ariel's ringtone. Excited, she pulled it out to see Ariel's smiling, uninjured face of two years earlier looking back at her.

She touched ANSWER.

"Honey!" she said, expecting to hear Ariel's voice.

Even though she'd tried to answer, the phone continued to ring. She pressed ANSWER again. The song, a snippet of music from Tchaikovsky's *Romeo and Juliet*, Ariel's favorite, started over.

Why? Why is this happening?

Nothing on the phone would respond when she touched it. Her heart broke to see Ariel's lovely face, her eyes playful in a way Rainey hadn't seen them in a long, long time.

The ringing was maddening. Was Ariel really trying to reach her through the phone? She had to be! And yet she'd heard her say that someone was hurting her. Rainey felt helpless with the phone in her hand. Ariel seemed close, but it was as if there were an invisible wall between them. In the second before she was about to throw the phone to the floor in frustration, she screamed for it to *stop!*

It did.

Over in the corner, something—or someone—began pounding on a trunk or wooden chest. It was loud and not quite rhythmic. Below the pounding, another cry:

"Mommy! Mommy, please!"

Stuffing the phone back into the pocket of her robe, the instinct to rescue her daughter sent her to a trunk in a dark corner. Ariel was sobbing and crying, "Mommy! Mommy!" over and over.

Rainey pulled the heavy trunk as far away from the wall as she could so she could have the advantage of the triangle of light coming from the open doorway. She tried to reassure Ariel that she would be out right away as she slid the trunk, but the girl was hysterical. Rainey sobbed with frustration.

The trunk was lashed with thick leather straps secured by tarnished brass buckles. Unnerved by fear and the terrified—and terrifying—sounds coming from the trunk, Rainey's hands shook as she tried to undo the straps.

"I'm getting you out, honey! It's okay!"

Rainey finally got all three buckles undone. Relieved and grateful, she knelt to open the trunk, trying not to think about the fact that someone had *locked* her daughter inside.

She lifted the heavy lid with both hands and had to stand to get it all the way open.

As she looked down, a rush of frigid air blew out of the empty trunk, passing through her body as though she were made of linen. The force knocked her back, onto the floor. The pounding was replaced by the sound of childish footsteps running from the room.

"Mommymommymommymommymommy!"

The voice melted into a child's mocking laughter as it faded away.

Chapter 63

"The video is set up to record for three days, then dump the data."
Ginny, the post's computer tech, slid a flash drive across the desk
to Lucas. "I put each camera on a separate file for your viewing
pleasure."

"Three days?" Lucas asked. "Just three days?"

"Best that I can tell, unless he backed it up somewhere else
before he died. I'll see if he's got cloud back up, but try to be patient,
okay? You just handed it to me an hour ago."

"So there could be a record going back further, then.
Somewhere."

"Could be," she said. "I'll let you know." She turned back to
her screen without further comment.

Lucas watched the silent video of Nick sitting on the couch,
half-dozing as he watched television in the darkened living room.
On the screen, he saw what Nick hadn't been able to see: a shadow
crossing the room, clinging close to the wall, then appearing right
behind him. The garrote was hard to make out on the screen, so

it almost looked as though the men were engaged in pantomime. Nick jerked back, the killer bent forward, his arms taut while Nick flailed and clutched at him. Almost three agonizing minutes passed.

It wasn't until the killer began pouring the bleach over Nick that Lucas averted his gaze. He would have to watch it many times and knew it wasn't going to get easier.

Fortunately, the preceding days' footage was unremarkable in comparison. He started at the beginning and watched as Nick came and went. When he reached the last couple of hours recorded two days earlier, he saw Roberta Bliss standing on the front porch. She touched her hair and adjusted her skirt while she waited for Nick to open the door. When he finally did, he gathered her in a warm embrace.

Lucas made a note: 9:05 P.M., after interview at the Waffle House.

When Nick and Roberta Bliss disappeared from the screen, Lucas switched to the file with the living room camera footage. After a brief conversation, Roberta Bliss went out the patio door, and Nick disappeared into the kitchen. A few moments later, Nick returned carrying an open bottle of wine and two glasses and went outside as well.

Roberta Bliss didn't show up again on any of the files, so Lucas guessed she must have left from the patio. But the bedroom video showed that, twenty-five minutes after he'd gone outside with the wine, Nick made a cell phone call that lasted about ten minutes. He paced as he talked, and his lips were too close to the phone to read. When he hung up, he was wearing a grim smile.

The rest of the videos, up until the murder, showed only Nick, and an hour and a half of a woman who let herself in to clean the house.

Now they had at least a tentative link between Roberta Bliss's assault and Nick's murder. Lucas called Tim Hatcher in to see if he'd started researching Nick's phone records.

Chapter 64

Gerard sat in his truck in front of the house. He saw now that there was no returning to normal life, because screwed-up was the new normal for him. He couldn't get Nick's agonized, waxen face out of his mind. All he wanted to do was sleep, but he knew it wouldn't happen anytime soon.

He was so dazed that it took him a moment to realize Ellie was barking at him through the dining room window, dancing her paws back and forth across the windowsill. The sill was covered with deep scratch marks, evidence of her perpetual excitability.

There was a game he and Karin played sometimes when they came home, going close to the window, peering in on Ellie.

"What do you think she's trying to say?"

"Ball! Ball! Ball!"

"Maybe 'Let me out! Let me out! Let me out!'"

The more they talked about her in front of the window, the more excited she got, her barks turning into frantic whines.

"I think she's saying, 'Dammit! Dammit! Dammit!'"

"She gets that from you, not me," Karin would say.

Thank God for Ellie.

He let Ellie outside to do her business, and when she was done he grabbed a tennis ball from a basket by the front door and threw it for her until she tired. She signaled that she was finished by lying down in the grass to mouth the thing while rolling on her back. How many ball covers had she chewed off? Hundreds, certainly. He kept a case of cheap tennis balls in the garage just for her.

"Ellie girl, where's your dignity?" he called to her.

Hearing her name, she jumped up and ran over to him. He knew that dogs weren't supposed to be able to smile but with the ball in her mouth she seemed to be wearing a happy, foolish grin.

"You're shameless," he said, scratching her behind the ear.

In answer, she dropped the ball at his feet and rubbed her face—drooly mouth and all—against his blue jeans.

At least Ellie's life was back to some kind of normal.

Even though Karin was going to be cremated and would have no visitation, the undertaker had talked him into at least providing a dress and shoes for her to wear in the casket. The notion had seemed ridiculous to him at first. No one would see her. But the undertaker had said, "You will know. You will think about it, later." It was a strange thing for her to say, and maybe that bothered him more than anything else.

He didn't like to think about the dead Karin. What that empty body was wearing when it went into the thousand-degree chamber of fire, to burn and burn, meant nothing to him. He went to her closet—*not thinking, not thinking*—and laid his hand on the shoulder of a dress. Any dress. It happened that it was bright blue silk, the color of the indigo buntings that came to the feeders in spring, a blue as bright as a child's Easter egg. It was a dress he'd seen her in many times. Not a special occasion dress, but one that turned people's heads on the street on any given day. In it, she looked like she owned the town, especially when her hair was brushed up and away from her face, yet loose around her shoulders. A powerful, sensual mane. That was the Karin he would remember.

Had she met one of her lovers while wearing that dress? The dress had no zipper or buttons, but stretched so that it caressed her even as a man might. Had some other man helped her take it off, carefully lifting, sliding it over her hips, her breasts, her lips, and, finally, her hair?

Gerard could go no further. He turned to the shelves of shoes and reached for a pair of blue heels. They weren't the same color as the dress, and he suspected that Karin would've mocked his choice. He was about to pick another when the phone in his pocket rang. Grabbing the first shoes, he quickly laid them on the bed with the dress, and took out the phone. He recognized the number.

He answered, but there was only a hollow silence on the other end.

"Mrs. Adams?" he said. "Rainey?" His leg still ached because he'd tripped on the loose brick just outside of Bliss House. It had been a strange, embarrassing moment, and he'd been sorry that Nick was there.

When there was still no answer from her, he waited, listening. If it wasn't Rainey herself, then surely it was her daughter playing some kind of trick on him. He said her name again. Nothing.

He hung up the phone. It rang again immediately. When he answered this time, there was static, rising and fading.

What in the hell?

The cell reception at his house wasn't the best, but it was never this bad.

"Rainey?"

"*Gerry.*" A whisper inside the static.

He told himself that he hadn't heard it.

"*Gerry.*" Only one person had ever called him that.

"What is this bullshit?" he said, anger almost disguising the fear in his gut. It was Karin's voice, or some simulacrum of it that made

322

him want to scream obscenities down the phone line to whoever was on the other end of it.

God, no. Please, no.

"Gerard, it's me. Rainey." The static was gone. "I didn't know who else to call."

"Why did you call me that?" he said. "Who told you to call me that?"

How did you know?

"I don't know what you mean," Rainey said.

"Who told you?" he repeated. "Is this your way of fucking with my head? You think this is funny?" The idea that she could be so cruel stunned him. He'd been on the receiving end of her justifiable anger, but he'd never imagined her to be cruel.

Rainey barely heard him.

"Please help me find Ariel, Gerard. She's gone."

Chapter 65

"I know neither of us wants to deal with them, but we have to call the police," Gerard said. They stood in the woods beyond the maze. He looked past Rainey, through the trees, to see the house standing silent and ponderous in the sun. An historic house. An inexplicable house. He'd helped it become what it now was. No longer a feared object of infamy, but a home for Rainey Adams and her daughter. He'd made it so. Or, up to this minute, he'd thought he had.

Once he'd seen Rainey Adams's tear-streaked face, he forgot the strange voice on the phone. She'd come running out of the house to meet him at his truck, dressed carelessly in a pair of shorts, sandals, and a loose T-shirt. In her vulnerability, she looked no more than a decade older than her missing daughter. Despite the recent tension between them, he felt a sudden urge to touch her. Hold her. But he resisted the impulse. Karin had told him that his habit of wanting to be the compassionate hero to every woman he met would eventually get him into trouble. How ironic that she had been so concerned about *his* reputation.

"She didn't take anything with her. Not her phone. Money. Nothing," she said.

They were searching the woods, oblivious to the swarms of gnats that descended wherever they stopped. Gerard was certain that they weren't going to find Ariel anywhere outside the house. It didn't feel right to him. He'd brought Rainey outside to calm her, to get her to stop running up and down the stairs, checking the same places over and over. She'd tried to tell him what had happened to her up on the third floor, but it hadn't made any sense to him.

He'd felt a palpable hesitation hanging in the air inside the house. It was waiting for something.

"What if someone took her?" Rainey said, turning to face him.

Did you take her? Do you hate her that much?

Gerard understood what she was thinking. She didn't know him. She had a right to ask.

He touched her arm and she didn't jerk away.

"I think she's still here." He looked down into her tired, worried eyes. *Because we found Karin here.* He couldn't, wouldn't say it out loud. Instead, he said, "Tell me what happened after I left."

Rainey sank onto a fallen log and told him about Ariel's need to be with her in her bed, like a little girl. How she'd fallen asleep listening to her daughter's even breathing, as she had so many times before. "She even snored a little," she said.

Gerard smiled. "Sure."

"It wasn't like she was happy. But not unhappy, either. She was just herself."

"Not like she was earlier? Down in the kitchen?"

Rainey put her face in her hands. "That wasn't her," she said. "I swear to God, that wasn't her."

Which led him also to wonder who it might have been that had animated Ariel, twisting her words, giving her the aspect of a suspicious, disturbed woman instead of a teenage girl.

"What will the police say? They'll think I'm insane," Rainey said.

"I'm sure she's in the house or somewhere very close."

Rainey nodded.

"I loved this place," she said, staring past Gerard to the house. Then she turned to him, changing the subject. "Listen. There's something else you need to know."

Chapter 66

He'd called her *Button* again. Her father's special name for her.

But her father couldn't really be here because he couldn't be anywhere. Dead was dead.

Only it isn't, is it?

"If you're my father, then you wouldn't be trying to scare me," she called out. "Whatever you are, I'm not going to believe that you're him anymore. Do you hear me?"

This time the answer was a laugh that was more like a child's laugh than a man's. But the fact that the voice was young didn't make her feel any better. She thought of the hands that had pushed her, chasing her from the ballroom. Her leg had been sore for days from the bruising she'd taken on the stairs.

How much would she have given to know that the voice was real, that her father was in one of the rooms down the hallway, body, heart, and soul? Would she give her life? She was becoming more and more certain that they weren't going to find her alive down here.

What am I doing, looking for whatever is down here with me?

Although she'd always been the first one to drag her friends into Halloween haunted houses, she could only do it because she hadn't really believed that spirits or demons or whatever could hurt her in any way. Now she knew better. She thought of Gerard's wife. If something had made Karin Powell fall to her death, couldn't it kill *her*?

"*Button, button, where's my button?*"

Now the voice was a vicious parody of her father's, and it echoed in the hallway.

"Stop it!" She almost flung the flashlight in the direction of the voice, but then clung to it. It was the only thing that her sleep-walking self had brought with her from the world above.

"*Button, button, found my button.*"

"You're not him! You're not!"

Against every instinct, she moved down the hallway, toward the voice. There was nowhere else to go. She might have tried to hide in the room in which she awoke, but she knew it would be useless. At least there was a chance that she could find a way out that she didn't yet know about. She imagined herself driving back whatever thing was in the darkness ahead of her.

"If you're stuck," her father had said, "sometimes you don't need to go back where you started and begin again. There's always more than one answer."

As she approached the voice, the air around her became even more still. She thought of church and the peaceful sunrise masses her grandmother had made her attend when she slept over on Saturday nights. But there was no peace here. So focused was she on finding the source of the voice that it took her a long moment—a moment that she couldn't think about later without being dragged into despair—to realize that the more significant, more earthly sound was behind her after all.

The door to the tunnel had opened. She turned around.

The light from her own flashlight and that from the light held by the person standing in the doorway made the space between them a bright river of black and white.

"I knew you'd come!" Ariel said.

Overwhelmed with relief, she dropped her flashlight where she stood and ran at Jefferson, ready to launch herself into his arms as she might have her father's.

But before she could reach the doorway, Jefferson pulled the door shut, plunging her back into semi-darkness.

⌒

Ariel lay on the bed, staring up at the lace of brown cracks on the ceiling without seeing them. What she saw was Jefferson's face: mouth open in shock, sudden recognition in his eyes. *Fear.*

Why was he afraid? He'd teased her about getting inside, practically challenged her to do it. And now he'd shut her back in here, leaving her alone. Had she done something wrong? The last time she'd seen him, things had been awkward, but had she made him angry? It was *her* house to explore. Maybe he was jealous or angry that she'd found her own way in.

The irony was that she hadn't really found her own way in. Something had led her here and had shown her how to get inside. All she'd had was a wish. A desire to know what was behind the door. It was a part of what was going on in the house, and had everything to do with her. Now she understood Jefferson was a part of it too.

It made her sick to think about it. He'd left her behind the door to die. He wasn't her friend. No more than whatever was calling her from the hallway was her friend.

"Button," it said again. *"Find me, baby."*

Chapter 67

In a quiet corner of the hospital cafeteria, Randolph Bliss, the judge who apparently scared the hell out of every prosecutor in several surrounding counties, looked like just another old man worried about his sick wife. The worn canvas jacket he wore over his white dress shirt looked like it spent most of its time in the cab of a farmer's pickup truck, and he briefly chewed at a thumbnail—a new habit, given the pristine state of his other nails. The sagging skin beneath his eyes had a translucent, bluish tint. His shoulders hunched over his paper cup of tea as though it would offer warmth.

"What have you found out?" the judge said. "I hope you're here to tell me you're about to make an arrest?"

When Lucas had asked Randolph if he could speak to him away from his wife's hospital room, it hadn't occurred to him that the judge would assume he was there about his wife. They were about to get off on the very wrong foot.

It was the son, Jefferson, about whom Lucas had questions. No one could find him: he wasn't answering his phone, and wasn't at the family home. Lucas's quick call to Nick's distressed former secretary had told him that the kid had no professional business that she knew of with her dead boss. She didn't speculate on whether or not they had a private connection. Chances were that she had routinely endured that kind of prurient interest, and there was nothing telling Lucas that he needed to go there.

"The scene at your house was processed, sir. The sheriff's deputies are working with your staff to explore the possibility that your wife was attacked to get your attention," Lucas said.

While this was technically the truth, Lucas wasn't certain how quickly it was happening. Nick Cunetta was dead, and death was his first priority.

"Next you're going to tell me that there was no sign of forced entry and my wife's dressing room and jewelry box were in disarray," he said, his voice conversational. Low. "Did you even spend five minutes in my house? The sheriff has called me three times today already. Perhaps you would like to know that they believe they've found traces of blood on a copper tea kettle," he said. "My wife is fond of copper tea kettles. She has seven or eight. Two are from Ireland. One is Spanish. One we picked up in London."

Lucas suddenly understood why the defense attorneys and prosecutors were afraid of Randolph Bliss: he was a sophisticated bully. But the old man didn't bother him a bit.

"Why are you here, wasting my time?" Randolph said. "There's nothing you have to say that I can't hear from more involved parties."

"I'm looking for your son."

Randolph leaned forward. "My son was assaulted."

"Yes, sir."

"And you imagine my son assaulted his mother?"

"Absolutely not, sir," Lucas said. "No one is implying that."

He was trying not to pass judgment on the kid too quickly. He wanted to think he was able to look beyond Jefferson Bliss's rich-boy looks and demeanor. God knew he'd had to deal with enough guys like him at college in North Carolina. Spoiled, but clever and arrogant. Especially when they were as embarrassed as Bliss had been after the contractor beat the crap out of him.

"Then why am I down here?" Randolph said. He indicated the artificially bright room whose walls were absurdly painted with enormous orange flowers. "My wife just had a cardiac event related to an assault by God knows whom, and you've brought me down here for some kind of masturbatory exercise."

"I need to know if your son had any dealings with Nick Cunetta. Mr. Cunetta called him shortly after your wife left his house."

"What do you mean, 'after my wife left his house'?"

"Your wife was seen at his house the night before she was attacked."

Randolph gave him a wan smile. "You think my wife was spending evenings with Nick Cunetta. You know how ridiculous that is, don't you, Detective?"

"If you say so," Lucas said, returning the smile. *You old bastard.*

Randolph's smile disappeared. "My son had nothing to do with Nick Cunetta's death."

"We're looking at all possibilities surrounding Mr. Cunetta's murder. We're taking his clients into consideration, just as we're looking at people you've had issues with. *All* possibilities. It just happened that he called your son soon after your wife left his house."

"You know this how?" Randolph said.

"Phone records."

"My wife was at a book club meeting that night. Who says she was at Nick's house?"

He was going to have to tell him about the video. He was going to find out sooner or later. Everyone would. Even the murderer.

The pager the nurse had given Randolph vibrated, moving itself a few centimeters across the tabletop. They both stared at it a moment until Randolph grabbed it. He stood up.

"If my wife went to Nick's, she was probably looking for a shoulder to cry on. She's been overly upset about the death of that young woman in my family's former home. Roberta's too kindhearted for her own good. It's her greatest fault," he said. "It makes sense that Nick would call one of us to let us know. I'll talk to my son."

Lucas watched him leave the cafeteria looking less like a despairing old man than like a man with some kind of purpose.

"Prick," he said under his breath.

Chapter 68

Allison groaned as a contraction woke her. In the fog of waking, she thought at first that Michael had come in and done something to her belly, maybe wrapped something tightly around it. But when she opened her eyes, she knew she was alone except for the thing inside her.

The thing inside her wanted out. She waited for the pain to subside, knowing that it would eventually. The squeezing pain had been happening on-and-off for a long time now.

Stay! Stay! There's nothing out here for you.

It wouldn't respond, and she knew the silence meant it wasn't listening to her.

Whatever Michael had told her to do when the thing (he kept calling it a baby, but she didn't believe that it was) came out had escaped her memory. What would the thing be like? What would it want? She was going to have to share her food with it, she guessed. Michael would have to bring more.

She lighted the candle on the bedside table. As she tried to get up, she found that the sheet and bedclothes around her were cold and wet, and she wondered if she'd urinated in her sleep. She sighed. It was so hard to wash the sheets in the tiny sink.

But Michael had brought her a tall pile of new white towels (she'd read the attached tags hungrily: 100% Cotton/Coton, Machine wash in hot water, Tumble dry, Made in U.S.A, Carolina Mills, Inc.) and more of the lovely-smelling jasmine soap.

Stripping off the gown, she got off of the bed to light the candle on the wall, but another contraction overtook her. She dropped to her knees.

The thing's silence was even deeper as it fought its way out.

But Allison couldn't be silent. She cried out, calling for her mother, whom she could only remember as love and warmth and laughter.

After another wave of pain, she felt the urge to bear down on the thing as it tried to escape her.

Allison groaned as her body seemed to split open. She felt the thing's head and hands and claws and teeth as they rent her. It was so angry. So mean. But she knew she needed to help it get out. This needed to end!

With one great, final grunt and push, the thing was out, a coated, silent mass of gore and pink flesh. When Allison regained her breath, she fell back on her bottom. On the floor in front of her, the thing opened its black eyes, and opened its tiny mouth as if to speak, but it couldn't make any sound. She stared at it, marveling at its silence, and its lack of claws. Was this the thing at all?

She picked it up, her hands uncertain as they tried to grasp the slick body. Without thinking about what she was doing, she used her fingers to sweep out its mouth. It began to make sounds. A choked whimper at first, then a full-throated, angry cry.

"You're so tiny," she said. "And where are your teeth?"

The thing didn't respond but continued to cry, as though it had forgotten how to talk.

Shifting the thing in her arms, she felt an unpleasant tug inside her, and noticed the cord coming out of the thing's belly. She was exhausted, but she reached as far as she could up on the bed and felt for the scissors that Michael had given her. She almost dropped the thing, trying to hold it in one arm, but she kept it close to her body.

When she got hold of the scissors, she laid them on the floor next to her, then gently rested the thing beside them. Its body shivered violently with its cries, and Allison felt a response deep, deep inside her, as though she might start crying as well.

"Shhhhh. It's okay. It's going to be okay."

Allison took one of the towels and laid it over the soiled, wet bedsheet. The rest of the towels were piled by the door, no longer white or new. She settled herself on the towel, her pillows pushed against the headboard so that she might recline but not lie down completely. The thing had stopped crying and lay sleeping in a nest she had made on the bed out of the blue crocheted blanket. It occurred to her how lucky they were that she hadn't yet gotten to the end this time or it would've just been a pile of loose yarn.

She picked up the thing and laid it on her stomach, then covered them both with the blanket. The thing was warm against her skin. Michael and the other man were warm as well but they weren't nearly as soft, and neither of them would ever lie still with her for long.

Allison closed her eyes. Right then, there were no sounds coming from outside the room. No banging, no laughter, no running footsteps out in the hall. She felt calmer and less confused than she'd felt in a long time. After a while she slept, and woke only a little when the thing latched blindly onto her small pale breast and suckled.

Chapter 69

The other man tried to catch her sleeping, but the thing lying in its nest beside her woke her, crying, as he came in the door. She opened her eyes to the painfully bright beam of his flashlight and quickly squeezed them shut again. The thing cried louder, and she knew it was trying to get her to make the other man go away. But Allison's mouth was so dry that when she tried to speak, nothing emerged.

"It's time to go," he said, looking down at her and the screaming thing. He laid his hand on the thing's forehead. "It's so tiny. How is it even alive?"

Turning away from the light, she shook her head "no."

"You both have to leave. I'll help you, Allison."

He rested the flashlight on the bedclothes, and when the thing noticed the light shining on the wall, its cries subsided. He unscrewed the cap from a Thermos. Putting his fingers gently behind Allison's shoulder, he brought her forward and raised the Thermos to her lips.

She recognized the smell of chocolate, and with it came a merciless flood of feeling. She drank and drank.

"Slow down," the other man said. "It's hot."

The drink comforted her throat. It dribbled onto her chin and her gown, but she didn't care. When the man tried to take it away, Allison grabbed his forearm to keep him still.

As she drank the last, the words *hot chocolate* finally came to her. They came to her with images of a fireplace, of a shining metal pan. Voices. Happy voices that didn't frighten her. Her mother's face!

So many things that she'd forgotten.

How could I have forgotten?

The man set the Thermos on the bedside table next to the wooden box that had been empty of coke and pot for so long now. He used an edge of the wool blanket to wipe her mouth, then let her rest a moment. He smiled at her and she smiled stiffly back at him.

"It's okay," he said. He wasn't wearing the balaclava and, yes, his hair was long, pulled back into a ponytail.

While he was retrieving the robe with the large peony flowers from its nail, she felt beneath her pillow for the little scissors. Finding them, she made a fist around them.

When he brought the robe to her, she was standing shakily by the bed. He helped her into the robe and tied the belt around her so it wouldn't gape open. The sleeves were so long that they hid her hands.

"You don't have any shoes, do you?" he asked.

She looked at him blankly.

"Doesn't matter," he said.

When she reached to scoop the thing up in its blanket nest, he stopped her.

"It's too big," he said. "Too much blanket." He looked around the room and found one of the towels she had washed in the sink and hung up to dry. After he laid it across the bed beside the blue blanket, he gently pushed the folds of the blanket aside and carefully picked up the thing, cradling its head in his hands. It looked up at him, away from the light, but it didn't make a sound.

"It looks healthy, Allison. You did a good job."

Allison didn't know why he was saying that, but it made her feel less worried.

He wrapped the baby tightly in the towel so that its arms and legs were bundled inside, but left a small flap of towel to rest over its head. Then he lifted it again and gave it to Allison.

Taking the flashlight in one hand, he took one of her hands in the other.

As he opened the door wide, a small amount of light and a strong draft of air rushed into the room.

Startled, she tried to pull away.

"You can do it," he said, pulling her close to his side. "We have to go, Allison."

She shook her head vehemently.

"It's okay. Just a few more steps, and I can carry you if I need to."

A wave of fatigue washed over her, and again she felt as though she might fall. When the man moved, she willed herself to follow, letting him be the force that kept her going forward.

They were in the hallway that she'd glimpsed for just those few seconds so long ago, when Michael had crushed her shoulder. Ahead, a door as thick as a wall stood open. Beyond it was only darkness. But she sensed that it wasn't a small darkness, like her room. This darkness was vast, possibly endless.

"It's just there," he whispered. "Not too far."

The word "there" held no specific meaning for her. "There" was everywhere that wasn't her room. Her legs weakened, and she stumbled. He held her up.

Before they'd gone more than a few feet, they heard a noise ahead. A door opening, shutting. She saw a second light.

"Shit!" the man whispered. He blinked off their flashlight.

The distant light bobbed through the darkness, coming toward them.

The man almost fell over her as he tried to maneuver her back-wards in the dark. She cried out when he stepped on her foot.

At the other end of the tunnel the response was immediate, as though she'd called it forth:

"Allison!"

Michael's voice. She knew it like the sound of her own heartbeat.

The man switched his flashlight on again. He was pulling her away from Michael without explanation or apology. She kept her eyes cast down, looking at the rough floor, which wasn't nearly so worn as the floor in her room. The thing in the towel began to whimper.

I'm sorry!

Now the man was dragging her up a staircase that climbed up, up into a different darkness. The walls pressed in, barely far enough apart to let them pass. She hadn't made it up ten of the steep, irregular steps before she flagged and almost fell backwards.

Down in the tunnel, Michael kept after them.

The flashlight's beam danced on the walls as the man bent to help her up. Her head scraped against the bricks more than once as they climbed, and she closed her eyes, trying to ignore the pain.

"Allison!"

Michael was closer. The thing cried out to him. But as weak as Allison was, she knew already that she couldn't ever go back to that dark, dark place, even if the light seared them both.

When there were no more stairs, they emerged into a room with electric lights like the one in the room she'd just left. But there were many, all glowing, casting a rich amber light. The walls were covered with women in antique Japanese dress, surrounded by blossoms.

Panicked, she cast around for a door and saw two wide, wooden panels that might have served as doors, but she wasn't certain. The only opening she saw was behind her, a narrow gap that seemed to be part of the fireplace. But she could hear what was coming behind them. Was she meant to stay in this place?

No! Not another prison!

The man with the long hair took her hand again and they ran across the room. The wooden panels did make up the door. He slid one of the panels aside, and she found herself in an enormous, sunny hall which seemed, oddly, open to a sky filled with stars.

Chapter 70

"We told the police that Ariel wasn't sure what she saw that night," Rainey said. "And that was true." She and Gerard had left the woods and come into the kitchen to get some water.

Gerard was sitting on one of the kitchen stools, while Rainey paced, restless.

"The woman she saw go over the railing didn't look like Karin. She was dressed differently and looked younger. To tell you the truth, it all kind of sounded like a dream, the way she explained it."

"She woke up in the middle of the night, right?" Gerard said. "Maybe she *was* dreaming."

Rainey shook her head. "She definitely saw Karin." Her voice got quiet. "After." It pained her to have to talk about Karin being dead. The way her body was exposed when she found her had shocked her, and she hated to think how much it had hurt Gerard. He looked exhausted. Miserable. His jaw was still swollen from the fight with Jefferson, and the cut beside his lip would take a while to heal.

"That just doesn't make sense," he said.

"But there was something else," Rainey said. "The part that really freaks me out."

Gerard waited.

"She said she saw my late husband Will standing outside my bedroom door, watching it all. She said he's appeared to her before. That he's been here all along. With us."

Now Rainey watched him, nervous. He took a moment before answering.

"I've never believed in ghosts. I think people get themselves overexcited and make stuff up."

When Rainey started to protest, he raised a hand to stop her.

"I didn't say that's what I think about what is going on here," he told her. "Maybe in some other place. But not here."

"You mean, you believe her?"

"Karin never thought there was anything supernatural going on here, and nothing happened to me while I was working on the house. But there *is* something wrong here, Rainey."

"That's why you think she's in the house."

This time, seeing the pain on her face, Gerard got up to put his arms around her.

They stood like that for a few moments until Rainey could breathe again. Around them, the kitchen was silent. The house was silent. She couldn't even hear the clock in the hallway. Had it stopped? It was as though the house were waiting for them to move. To make some sound. It shocked her how much she wanted to stay right there with his arms around her and her head against his chest, not moving, until Ariel appeared. She wouldn't ask any questions. She'd forgive Ariel anything.

She knew she was embarrassing herself, letting Gerard hold her this way. But there didn't seem to be anything in his embrace except compassion. And she was grateful.

Finally he pulled away, looking a little abashed.

"It's going to be okay," he said. "We'll find her."

Rainey nodded, trying not to cry. Crying was not allowed. She had to keep her shit together. The house always had its shit together, and she had to wrest Ariel from it.

"She didn't run away," Gerard said.

"No. She never wants to leave. She doesn't even like to be outside," Rainey said.

"Because of her scars?"

"Maybe. Do you think she looks any different from the first time you saw her?"

"I don't know. Maybe. I just thought she looked less afraid. She was pretty shaken up that day she fell upstairs."

Rainey leaned against the counter, her hair almost completely loosened from its tie. She looked spent. "She's got this idea that the house is healing her in a really dramatic way. I've seen her looking in the mirror when she didn't know I was watching. She touches her face like she's really happy with it. When we first got here, she wouldn't even have a mirror in her room. And you saw that big one we put in the ballroom. She's trying to start dancing again."

The ballroom. It creeped him out far more than any other space in the house. Even the strange, empty sheds up on the roof.

"But nothing's actually different?"

"Of course not," Rainey said. "She's not using her cane as much, and she's stopped wearing those hats. Sometimes she tries to use her right hand. But those are all things that the doctor encouraged her to do." She paused, watching his reaction. "What is it?"

"We need to call the police, Rainey. It's the only way. They need to do a wider search. You can have them comb through the house, too. Get some volunteers."

Rainy looked away, but she knew he was right.

Chapter 71

Demons, darkness, spiderwebs . . . these were all things Ariel might have expected to find after turning the ice-cold doorknob on the next room down the hallway. But she could see nothing at all for a moment because she was suddenly engulfed in blinding light and could barely open her eyes.

Sunshine streamed with a surreal intensity through the windows around the dome: pure, yellow, brilliant light as though the sun itself had exploded. She'd never seen so much light in the well of Bliss House. Heavy motes of dust hung suspended in its rays like shapeless snowflakes, and everything around her was bathed in shades of gold. She was standing on the third floor, outside the theater room. But there were pieces of furniture she didn't recognize: tables and chairs and lamps, a large cabinet, and paintings of landscapes that looked a lot like the Virginia countryside.

It wasn't the Bliss House she knew. Even *she* was not the Ariel she knew. She felt weightless, as though she might rise at any moment into a shaft of sunlight. It was all so impossible! Though her mind was telling her differently, she knew her real self was still in that unexplored room, far beyond the lowest floor of Bliss House.

She heard angry voices coming from the ballroom. The door flew open.

At first Ariel thought it was two women frozen in the doorway by the sun's brilliant assault, but she realized that one of them was a man with lank blond hair that hung to his shoulders. They didn't hesitate long. The man pulled the woman behind him onto the mezzanine. She was carrying something wrapped in a towel. Neither noticed Ariel standing opposite.

The girl hardly looked human. Her skin was white, bloodless, and she blinked against the light. Her stained robe billowed around her, but her arms and legs were so thin that Ariel wondered she could move at all without breaking. Her feet were bare. The man dragged her purposefully, as though she were a reluctant child. Ariel knew her, recognized the robe, the blazing red hair. It was the girl she'd seen fall the night that Karin Powell had died.

A second man emerged from the room, screaming after them. "Allison, stop!"

It was Jefferson. And yet it was not. This man was like him, but taller, much less stocky, and his wavy hair brushed the collar of his button-down shirt. His voice was deeper, too. Commanding, where the Jefferson she knew was less confident. Less frightening. She'd seen this man before, too.

"She's a whore, Michael," the man who looked like Jefferson said. "Look at her child!"

It was when his mouth was closed, though, that Ariel recognized him. Or recognized the man he was to eventually become: Randolph Bliss, Jefferson's father.

The man who was pulling the girl stopped. So this was Michael, the man with the ponytail, the brother who everyone said had run away. The brother they assumed was dead.

The girl stopped as well and looked up at the man who had hold of her. She clutched the bundle closer. Was that a baby she was carrying in the towel? Her voice was so weak that Ariel could barely hear her.

"What did he call you?" she asked. "Who are you?"

Run, Ariel whispered. *Just run.*

"You did this to her!" the man called Michael said. "You're an animal, Randolph. You've almost killed her." He looked down at the girl. "He wanted you to think he was me. But he's my brother, and his name is Randolph."

Already bone-pale, the girl seemed to fade in the sunlight. The only darkness about her was her eyes, and their seriousness aged her decades. She stared up at the man called Michael as though seeing him for the first time.

Whatever else the rooms beneath the house were, they had been hell on earth for the girl. How long had she been down there?

Run!

Ariel felt no danger for herself. And as fearful as she was for the girl, she understood that what she was seeing had happened long ago, and might happen again and again. Time didn't move, here, and nothing she did could change it.

"You fucked her, too, Michael," the young Randolph said. "Why didn't you take her away before now? She was good, wasn't she?"

He addressed the girl, Allison. "Ask him why he didn't rescue you. What was he getting out of it?"

Allison jerked her hand from Michael's. She took several steps back.

Her voice was hoarse, and broke with her words. "Why didn't you just kill me? Please, God, just kill me!"

"You know we can't let her go," Randolph said, a wheedling tone in his voice. "And she doesn't want to leave with you. She's our responsibility."

"Don't listen to him," Michael said, reaching out to her. "I'll help you."

But the girl shrank away.

"Michael wore a mask because he's a coward," Randolph said. "Where do you think he was for so long? He was getting laid by somebody else."

"Allison, I'm sorry! He's right. I was a coward. I shouldn't have gone away. Let me help you now."

Ariel understood. The place she'd been so curious to get into had been—and still was—a prison.

The sunlight flickered, momentarily throwing the scene into a blackness deeper than night, deeper than the blackness in the staircase leading down to the tunnel. But the three other people on the gallery didn't seem to notice.

"But *you're* Michael," the girl said, her voice barely a whisper. She pointed to the young Randolph.

"I was teasing you," Randolph said. "Like we were playing a game. I know you don't want to leave, Allison. You told me you want to stay here. You can stay here, and the baby can stay here if you want. Or you can let me take the baby. My mother will make sure it goes somewhere very, very safe."

Michael lunged, but Randolph was faster in retreat, and Michael was only able to tear the front of his shirt.

Randolph laughed. "You're such a pussy, Michael. Be a man for once."

Michael went after him again. The girl stared—not screaming, not reacting at all.

Someone was going to die in this shining place, and Ariel didn't want to watch. She told herself that all she had to do was to look away and it would all disappear.

In the second it had taken her to turn her head toward the sound of an explosion, their house was gone and so was her father. There had been nothing to see but a gray, nameless chaos of debris flying toward her, rising into the sky. But, no. There had been one thing . . . a single, bright blue bird of cast concrete. She'd bought it at a school tag sale for her mother, who had tucked it beneath a boxwood near the front door, as though it were

348

resting. That bird had sped by her, launched into the same oblivion that had absorbed her father.

Randolph and Michael grappled on the landing. Ariel had seen fights between brothers before, in school, and they were always more intense than fights between strangers. Beyond the anger, there was the history. Favoritism, jealousy. Pain. But there was insanity here.

Michael aimed his head at Randolph's stomach like a battering ram, and knocked him into a table. Now they were on the floor, rolling in a violent embrace. Michael screamed as Randolph grabbed his hair, jerking his head back until Ariel thought his neck would break. She felt her stomach jump as a handful of Michael's hair and scalp came away.

Still the girl stared, holding the bundle to her with one hand and tugging nervously at her own hair with the other.

Run!

This time, Ariel screamed at her. Not getting any reaction, she ran across the gallery, pressing herself against the wall—a wall that was solid, *real*—to avoid the brothers crashing one another into the furniture. The men's faces were bloody.

But Randolph's face was changing rapidly. Ariel saw a hundred other faces flash across it, as though he were a hundred different people, some hideously ugly, some terrified, some vicious and insane. Women, children, men. Michael froze in his brother's embrace. His face contorted, and Ariel knew that the sight of it was killing him. It had hold of his mind, of his heart, and was squeezing the life out of him. She could feel it reaching for her, too, digging deep, deep inside her.

It was the house. *This* house. It was holding all those faces—all those souls—captive. Innocent souls. Guilty souls. Not just men, but women, too. Children.

Ariel closed her eyes and heard Michael's moans. She prayed for the sounds to stop. For what was in front of her to stop. But when she opened her eyes again, it was still happening.

She forced herself to run past the men, toward the girl who was so pale and slight that Ariel could hardly believe she was still alive. Up close, the girl's skin was murky, like old snow. It hung loose on her bones, making her look much older than Ariel thought she probably was.

Ariel tried to grab her by the shoulders to shake her to get her attention, but couldn't get purchase. Beneath her hands the girl's body felt pliable and unpleasantly cold, like gelatin. To her disgust and fear, her fingers sank into it, and she quickly dropped her hands to her sides. She caught a glimpse of the baby's delicate face. It couldn't have weighed more than three or four pounds, and its eyes were still the indefinite black of a newborn's.

The girl's eyes were still fixed on the men a few feet away, but what little light was left in those eyes was quickly dying.

"Run, Allison!" Ariel screamed.

Behind her, there was a great roar that sounded like twenty men dying.

Ariel turned to see that Randolph had plunged his hand into Michael's chest as though his hand were a well-sharpened blade.

Randolph didn't pull his brother's heart from his chest, but Ariel understood that he was tearing it, wrenching it from where it was fixed. Randolph's face was his own again, and it was bloodied yet filled with beatific pleasure.

Ariel cried out.

As Michael died, his body slumped toward the floor. Randolph turned to look at Ariel.

He can see me!

She watched, stunned, as Randolph let his brother's body fall. He rose up on his knees and stretched out his hand to her. The triumph had left his face, and it now held a look nearly as miserable and used-up as the girl's.

"Allison!" he screamed.

No, he hadn't seen her. He was looking at the girl behind her.

The girl bent her head to kiss the forehead of the baby, then carefully laid the bundle on the floor. Feeling for the balustrade behind her, she gripped it and jumped up on it so that she was able to balance.

Ariel screamed for the girl to stop, and Randolph rushed toward them.

Before he could reach her, the girl smiled a perfectly lucid, happy smile. She wasn't looking at Randolph, or Ariel, or even Michael's still form. Her eyes were focused on the distance, beyond the carefully built walls that had helped to hide her. That had helped to ruin her. Ariel saw that she was pretty. Maybe even prettier than she had been when Randolph Bliss had first brought her here.

For the second time since Ariel had come to Bliss House, she watched Allison push herself backwards and fall into the rays of light that reached all the way to the enormous oriental rug spread across the front hall.

~

Before Ariel could take another breath or cry out, the gallery and everyone in it disappeared without so much as a sigh. Around her, the air that had been so charged with violence and pain and sunlight was now dense with a frigid calm. However horrible that place of death had been, it was far from where she was now, in the bowels of Bliss House.

A shudder moved through Ariel's body, rattling her chest. She hugged herself tightly, feeling as though she might fly apart.

I couldn't save her. I can't even save myself.

When she opened her eyes again, the first thing she saw was the flashlight lying on its side, its beam cutting a useless line across the floor of the small room. The great hall was gone. There were objects beyond the light's reach, but she didn't really want to know what they were. She bent quickly to pick up the flashlight, but her fingers brushed something ice cold. Shining the flashlight on it, she saw it was a set of scissors, not any longer than her palm. They had a bright white pearly handle but the blades were stained and rusted.

Still shaking, she picked them up and put them in the pocket of her robe.

Will I die here? Like she did?

The first answer to come to her mind was an emphatic *no. Please, please, please, no.*

She couldn't get Allison's image out of her head. Her arms and legs had been like those of a child, even though she'd been much older than Ariel. She thought of the pictures of Holocaust victims she'd seen.

Was the same thing going to happen to her?

Shooting the light around the room, she saw it was completely empty but for an orderly stack of woven baskets the size of the antique traveling trunks that her mother sometimes had around. The trunks had been a source of wonder to her as a kid and always made her think of Babar the elephant and his family and their travels. Safe thoughts. Happy thoughts.

But the little girl that she had been was far away from this horrible place. She would not look inside them.

Shining the flashlight ahead of her, she hurried out of the room, closing the door behind her with a dull thud. And almost walked into the man standing on the other side of it.

"Hello, Ariel."

Chapter 72

The massive door leading into the tunnel was wide open. Randolph was the only thing standing between Ariel and freedom.

"Jefferson told me you didn't look like one of us," Randolph said. "I never met your father. But he was a lawyer, wasn't he? I'm sure I would've liked him."

Unused as she'd become to moving quickly, Ariel propelled herself into the small space between the man and the hallway wall. There was no thinking to it. She didn't have to get a good look at him to know that he was the man she'd just seen murder his own brother all those years ago.

Before she could get past, he snaked out an arm and shoved her backwards onto the floor. She hit with an agonized cry. The flashlight fell to the floor and blinked out. The only light left in the hallway was the weak amber glow from the two lights on the wall. Still, it was enough light to see the cruelty in Randolph's face.

"You're hurt." Randolph's face changed with an alarming swiftness that belied the wrinkles there, and he put out a hand to help her up from the floor.

353

She took it. She had no other choice. But when she tried to stand, her legs gave out and she fell against him.

"You know who I am?" he asked, still supporting her.

She wasn't fooled by the kindness in his voice.

"I'm not stupid," she said.

Standing, but still unsteady, she jerked away.

"No," he said. He pulled her to him, locking her arms behind her.

As much as he was hurting her, Ariel bit back her fear. Knowing what he'd done to the two people she'd just seen, she continued to thrash, trying to pull free.

He was strong. Maybe as strong as her father.

I am going to die, just like them.

Randolph bent his head to speak just a few inches from her ear. "Did Jefferson bring you here? What did he tell you? Did he already do something to you?"

The nasty implication in his words made her more afraid.

She struggled, landing a heel on one of Randolph's shins. He grunted, but his grasp on her didn't loosen.

"Ariel," he said. "Stop!"

She jerked her head back, trying to hit him in the chest or neck, but he snaked his arm around her and squeezed. Once he had a firm hold on her, he dragged her into the bedroom, pushing her onto the bed.

"You've got to behave, Ariel."

She didn't want to die here, without seeing her mother again. Without the sunlight.

Not thinking, she let her eyes stray to the bright gold sandal lying on the chair across the room.

The man glanced that way as well, and she knew in that second that he had something to do with the Karin woman dying. She wasn't sure what it was. Had he been up on the balcony that night? Or had it been Jefferson there? Either was a horrible choice.

"She was vile," Randolph said, seeing where Ariel was looking. "She did the unthinkable to a child. She had it sucked out of her womb like so much trash. And then she lied about it."

"You were there when she died, weren't you?" Ariel said.

"She pretended to be so brave, so brash. She loved doing the things I did with her here. She got a kick out of Jefferson, too. Screwing the son after screwing the father. But I'm afraid Jefferson took it all too seriously. The poor boy fell in love with her."

He stepped nearer to the bed, so tall beneath the low ceiling of the room that he seemed like a giant. With that thought, Ariel suddenly had the sense that they weren't alone in the room. Someone else had been here—more than a single someone—and thought the same thing. The feeling overwhelmed her, and while her nerves were already at their limit, somehow it was okay. She felt less afraid. She wasn't alone. As much as she wished her father were there to help her, she understood that he had never really been there. Something had tricked her into thinking he was because she'd wanted it so badly. But *someone* was here. Someone who didn't want her to be hurt.

"She didn't even scream, did she?" Randolph said. "Just like the other one. As though they were afraid someone would hear them. Someone would know their shame."

"Get away from me," Ariel said.

"That was her robe. Allison's robe. You didn't know Allison. But you're young, like she was."

Randolph stroked her leg. Ariel flinched.

"You must have been pretty. The way you look must break your mama's heart." He looked around the room, as though enjoying some distant memory. "Your mother's been in this room, you know. But she wouldn't remember. So your being here makes a great deal of sense."

Ariel hardly heard him. All the panic she'd felt up to that moment dissipated. The walls of the room felt close and solid and, strangely, safe.

Randolph rested his fingertips on the edge of the bed and leaned forward.

She knew what he was capable of, but it didn't matter. She was not going to die.

Wait.

The voice that came to her was feminine. She had heard that voice before. It was weak, but this time it wasn't frightened.

When he reached for her again, she didn't resist, though every nerve in her body screamed for her to kick out, to do her best to get away. The robe had fallen away, and her undamaged leg was exposed, glaringly white. She felt gooseflesh rise on her leg as he touched her ankle, her thigh.

He was awkward climbing onto the bed.

Wait.

I don't know if I can!

He lowered himself onto her. He smelled like medicine and disinfectant from the hospital. And coffee.

His face is too close!

Except for her father and Jefferson, and the doctors and therapists working on her, no man had ever been so close to her. If he wondered why she no longer resisted him, he showed no sign.

Please! I can't!

But the voice had left her. Was she alone? With him?

She felt his belt buckle against her stomach, and something worse against the top of her thigh that made her want to scream. He pushed her robe aside, and his hand was sweaty on her skin.

She had to wait. Wait until he turned his head.

He stiffened when the scissors pierced his neck, and his mouth opened in a cry of agonized surprise.

Chapter 73

"Well, look who's awake."

The cheerful face of a very young nurse smiled down at Bertie. "Can you tell me today's date, Mrs. Bliss? I want us to give the doctor a good report."

When Bertie tried to speak, she felt like she was trying to talk from under water. "Where am I, dear?" she said slowly. "I feel like an elephant stepped on my head."

The nurse laughed. "That's a good start. We'll get that pain taken care of right away, don't you worry."

As the nurse started away, Bertie knew she had to stop her. She reached out and touched her arm.

"There's someone . . ." she said. She knew she had to talk to someone, and could visualize her phone. She was unsure about who it was she needed to call, but she was sure she would remember just as soon as she saw the phone. "I need my phone."

"I don't know that you have a phone here. They brought you into emergency a couple of days ago, and you didn't have anything with you."

Emergency? Bertie suddenly couldn't breathe. She could hardly focus on the nurse leaning so close for the pain in her chest and head. Nearby, a monitor went into alarm mode.

"It's all right, honey. Breathe!"

Bertie gasped, clutched at the sheets. She'd known by the look in his eyes that the man wanted to hurt her. Before he raised a hand to her, she had understood exactly why he wanted to hurt her. And it broke her heart.

The nurse flitted around her, finally put a mask over her face.

Oxygen eased its way into her nose and mouth, and she felt the pain in her chest relent.

That man. I know who it was.

"Better?" the nurse said.

Bertie breathed deeply.

Where is Randolph? She wanted to ask the nurse, but didn't have the energy.

"I'm going away for a minute." The nurse touched the monitor to turn off the alarm. "But I'll be right back. Okay?"

Bertie nodded. The oxygen was clearing her thoughts, but not the pain in her head.

Why can't I remember? Think, Roberta. Think!

Her father's voice. It was always his voice when she knew she was in trouble. When she was feeling pressured, she never could remember important things. Everything had been so simple when she was a girl. If she did well, her life was happy and calm. If she made a mistake, then she was punished. It had seemed to her that it was the way the world was supposed to work. She'd tried to raise Jefferson that way, God knew. Maybe there had been times when she should've punished him instead of looking the other way. But he'd been so good. Such an easy baby. It had been the Judge who was hard on him. She'd just wanted to make up for it. It wasn't Jefferson's fault that his father was sometimes cruel.

But he's never too cruel, is he? He never crosses the line. Not with me. Not with Jefferson.

Now she couldn't stop thinking about the three of them. Their life together.

Isn't it a good life?

It had been everything she had ever wanted. Everything that her parents had told her married life should be. Except her mother hadn't prepared her for Randolph's peculiar tastes in their marriage bed. Her mother had told her (rather proudly, Bertie thought) that she had always insisted that Bertie's father approach her only when the lights were off, and never, never, *never* at that particular time of the month. There had been girls from school, of course. Girls who weren't afraid to share that kind of information with each other. When she'd told her best friend and former roommate Mary Borgsmiller about what Randolph had required her to do—well, she had been so ashamed, but she'd had to tell somebody—Mary had giggled and told her that she was being a prude. "You should've watched more *Three's Company* and less *The Facts of Life*, Bertie!"

The truth was that he'd never *hurt* her. He teased her a lot, but he'd never humiliated her outside of the bedroom. Certainly their life had its pleasures.

Yes! It's been a good life!

But a thought pressed against the inside of her throbbing head. The hospital room smelled of disinfectant and was too chilly to be comfortable. The blanket resting on top of her was too thin to offer protection. She was alone, and she hated to be alone. If she had had her way, her house would've been filled with children: noisy, happy children on whom she could shower love and silliness and happiness. But there had only ever been Jefferson.

It was Jefferson she'd been thinking about. Until three or four years ago, Jefferson had been hers. Then he had changed. He still liked to be around her, but Randolph had put a kind of claim on him, taking him away unexpectedly on overnight trips, sharing jokes with him she wasn't in on. But the opposite had happened, too. Sudden, angry arguments between them that she never understood. Randolph fuming, Jefferson storming out of the house. She'd been relieved when he went to college. She loved him so much, but she knew now that she had failed to make him care about other people with the same intensity that she had. Randolph had interfered.

Her breath had calmed to almost normal; her heartbeat felt steady. That would make the nurse happy, and it meant she might remember things better.

Bertie gingerly touched her hand to her head and felt the bandages that swathed her like a nubby turban. The pain made her want to squeeze her eyes shut against the wan sunlight coming through the cheap vinyl blinds, and call for the nurse to bring her morphine or something else terribly strong. With the same hand (the other was attached to the IV), she reached for the bedside telephone and, with some effort, slid it closer.

⌒

"Mom?"

Bertie opened her eyes. Her darling boy!

Jefferson stood over her, tentative but concerned. At least he loved her, and she was glad of that.

"Mom, we thought . . ." he said.

"Will you give me that cup of water? My throat's dry."

Her head felt much better. The nurse had indeed eventually returned, trailing a rather bored looking male resident who shone an appallingly sharp light in her eyes, okayed some painkiller to be administered through her IV, and left without further comment. Still, she had called a weak "thank you" after him. Even if he didn't have any manners, she had managed to keep hers.

Jefferson picked up the cup of water and held its straw to her lips. When she was done drinking, she waved the cup away with some irritation.

"What's wrong? Do you want me to get the nurse?"

"A terrible thing has happened, Jefferson. I don't have my phone and I need you to get a message to Rainey when you leave here. I need you not to tell your father."

"That's crazy, Mom," he said. "Rainey can't do anything for you. Dad and I will take care of you. You need to stop worrying about other people like that and concentrate on feeling better."

"What I feel is devastated. And not a little afraid of the fact that some man broke into our house and tried to kill me."

He interrupted her.

"Did you see him? Do you know who he was? Dad says it was someone who wanted to get to him."

Of course Randolph would say that.

Bertie closed her eyes a moment to gather her thoughts. After she'd called Jefferson to the hospital, she'd had time to think about what she was going to say but hadn't come up with anything more clever than the truth.

"I know who it was, Jefferson, and I will certainly tell the police. But I'm very tired now, and I need you to tell me something." *Tired* didn't really begin to describe the way she felt.

"You're all upset. Maybe we shouldn't be talking about this stuff."

Jefferson was excellent at distracting her, but today she would have none of it. What if she died before she knew the answer? Her head was so damaged that she couldn't really think straight. Death still seemed like a distinct possibility. She knew now that no one had been arrested for what they'd done to her.

"What were you doing with that Karin Powell woman?"

She'd seen her son caught in lies before. Now, he simply looked as though she'd slapped him, which was something she'd never done.

"I found one of her ridiculous fingernails in your laundry after she was killed, and—don't try to argue with me—I know it was

361

definitely hers, and I know you disappeared for a long time during that party. Whether you were with her then or not doesn't matter. But I need to know if you had anything to do with her death."

"I can't believe you'd think I would kill someone!" He held up his hands as though he had to physically fend her off.

She shook her head with a painful effort. "I didn't say I thought you killed her. I just want to know if you were involved."

"You hate me."

"Don't be absurd, Jefferson. I told Nick that I didn't think you could have killed her, and he agreed. But I know you. I know you're very sensitive to, you know, women. And she was a very seductive kind of woman. Men seemed to like her, and I know you have certain needs that I do *not* care to discuss. That's why I gave Nick your number and asked him to call you about Karin."

"You don't know, do you?" Jefferson said. "When did you talk to Nick?"

"I went to talk to him the night before . . . well, before this happened." She gestured weakly to her bandages. "I think it was the night before. I had to talk to someone, and God knows I couldn't talk to your father."

Jefferson fidgeted with the collar of his Oxford cloth shirt, just like he had as an anxious little boy.

"Whatever Nick thought he knew about me doesn't matter, because somebody killed him," he said. "Strangled him inside that faggy little cottage of his."

Bertie couldn't speak. Maybe she hadn't woken up at all from whatever medicine the doctors had given her to make her sleep for so long. She'd slept, and had such terrible dreams, and woken to this!

"I guess you think I had something to do with that, too," he said. "What was it with that guy? Why did you talk to him about us?" His voice was getting shrill. Sweat had broken out along his hairline. "You and Karin. It was like he was some kind of girlfriend or something. You couldn't talk to Dad, but you could talk to *him*? No wonder Dad . . ."

"Stop it!" Bertie said. "Just stop it!" She could feel the tightness in her chest beginning all over again, despite all the medicine they'd given her.

"Why did you have to get involved?" he asked. "Why? It didn't have anything to do with you. That stupid Rainey and that stupid party. You just couldn't leave it alone. You never know when to leave things alone!"

"Don't. Please don't be so loud." Bertie's words were strained. The elephant was back on her chest.

"Why?" Now he was almost shouting. "Do you know what that faggot did? He called me. He called me and said he knew about the stupid fingernail, and that he knew about Karin and me, and that he thought I probably killed her. And it was you who messed it up, Mom. You messed it up, and Dad had to fix it. Why do you always do this?"

He turned and stalked the room once more, running his hands viciously through his hair. "Why, Mom?"

"Jefferson . . ."

He returned to her, looking determined. She'd seen the same look on his face when some other child had taken one of his favorite toys, a look she thought he'd grown out of when he was six or seven. Leaning over the edge of the bed, he put his hands around her neck, pressing his thumbs into the front of her throat. Tears started in his eyes and quickly welled over. As Bertie watched her son's face, one of the tears fell onto her cheek, and even through her rising panic she felt his anguish and was sorry for him. As he squeezed and her airway closed, it hurt less, but the bright room was quickly darkening.

"Hey!"

There was a roar of blood in Bertie's ears, but behind it she heard a woman's voice. It seemed to wake something in Jefferson, and he jerked his hands away. Bertie closed her eyes, heard Jefferson run from the room, heard the woman fall against the door as he pushed past her. Heard the woman scream for security.

Bertie knew that Jefferson was going to get away, out of the hospital, without being caught. As terrible as the thing he'd done to her was, she knew he hadn't really meant to do it.

Poor Jefferson. Poor Nick.

Now it was her turn to cry.

Chapter 74

Gerard kept his distance as he watched Rainey trying to calm her daughter. He coughed, once, as though it would hide his emotion.

Ariel was sprawled over the back porch steps, weeping into her mother's lap, the voluminous robe he'd seen her in the previous night trailing over them both. She was covered in blood and dirt.

Goddamn the person who did this.

Rainey had just gotten off the phone with someone at the state police who had promised to track down Detective Chappell, when they heard Ariel's incoherent screams coming from outside the house. They found her, collapsed at the bottom of the porch steps outside the mudroom.

Gerard looked away from the two of them, toward the orchards beyond. He thought he caught a movement, but the breeze had picked up, and he saw that it was a piece of trash, maybe a plastic grocery bag that had found its way from the road. He waited a few more moments for Ariel's sobs to subside before he spoke.

"Let's bring her inside."

The breeze was a hot one and he had begun to sweat. Something was very wrong all around them. The sun had dimmed, though there was no cloud in the sky, and the birds had gone quiet. He heard a car start somewhere in the distance, maybe on the other side of the woods. It was a normal sound. A sound that made sense.

"Gerry." A whisper.

He looked at Rainey and her daughter. Ariel lifted her face from her mother's lap to look at him. Her cheeks were plastered with tears and blood, and her lips were swollen and cracked.

"Gerry. Help me," she whispered, her voice clear but not her own. It was the voice from the phone. The voice he'd heard nearly every day of the past fourteen years.

Rainey looked down at Ariel, then at Gerard. She pulled her daughter closer, enfolding her until the girl's eyelids dropped closed, and she was either asleep or had fainted.

Chapter 75

Lucas passed through the front hall, headed for the kitchen so he could get some privacy to talk to the sheriff on the phone. The front door to Bliss House stood open, and an EMT tech walked hurriedly past him to the salon, where she and her partner were treating the girl.

By the time he'd arrived, expecting to have to talk Rainey Adams down because her kid had done a runner just like any other teenager might have done on a bad day, the EMT truck was already preceding him up the long driveway to Bliss House. It was a hell of a thing to stumble into: a fourteen-year-old girl bundled into a blanket half-naked, with blood on her arms and face, on top of her already dramatic scarring. Seeing her like that was one of the images he knew he'd never forget. She was a different person from the girl-with-attitude he'd interviewed only a few days earlier. She was awake, and wired, talking a thousand words a minute. Unfortunately, little of it was making sense. He'd encouraged Rainey Bliss to let the techs give the girl something to calm her down, but both the girl and the mother had refused.

Now he was left to tell the sheriff the freakish news about Judge Bliss.

"This is some kind of joke," the sheriff said.

"You'll need to get a few uniforms out here fast," Lucas said. "I've already contacted my post, but the closest folks we've got are twenty minutes away. Karin Powell's husband is having a hard time sitting on his hands. The girl says she thinks Judge Bliss is dead, because she stabbed him with some kind of magic scissors or something. She's definitely got somebody's blood all over her."

The sheriff cursed quietly. "That's too many people out there," he said. "We don't need this to get around before we even know if the judge is dead or not."

"Too late," Lucas said. God, he hated provincial politics. "She said the judge's kid is involved, too. We need a bulletin out on him."

"Hold on," the sheriff said. In the background, Lucas heard him calling in his chief deputy.

"I guess I don't have to tell you to keep your pants on until we get there," the sheriff said, returning to the phone. "If the girl didn't kill him, he's got nothing to lose because he's already killed one person. Maybe two. Did she say if he was armed? Shit. I'd never have thought it of him."

"No firearms that she knows of, but I'd bet he carries one concealed, at least," Lucas said.

"That he does," said the sheriff. "My daddy signed the order for it himself twenty or more years ago."

After he hung up, Lucas hurriedly looked through the cabinets to find a glass, then turned on the tap to fill it for the girl. The pipes groaned like some living thing.

This house. God, I hate this house.

He hurried back to the salon, where he handed the water to a grateful Rainey. She put it down in front of the girl, who was telling one of the EMTs that there was no way she was going to the hospital. Her eyes were shining. Glassy. She looked as though she might have a fever, but he suspected that she was just experiencing a delayed adrenaline rush.

Noticing him, she said, "Did you find him? Did you see him?" She leaned forward in the chair, her hands white-knuckled from gripping the arms. The EMT trying to take her blood pressure for a second time tried to gently push her back.

The late afternoon sun gave the room an uncharacteristically cozy appearance. Despite the people gathered, it was quiet and tense. The room and the house seemed to be filled with the same sense of anticipation as the girl.

"Where's Mr. Powell?" Lucas said, realizing that there were only four others in the room: the girl, her mother, the two EMTs.

A brief shadow of guilt passed over the mother's face.

"Where is he?" he repeated.

The girl answered. "He didn't say where he was going, but I heard him go upstairs. You didn't go with him. Why didn't you go with him?" Her voice rose, panicked. The mother put her hand on the girl's arm and said her name.

"What room? Where?" Lucas stared at the mother, wanting to curse her for her stupidity. "If the judge isn't dead, do you think he won't be soon if Powell finds him?"

"He didn't say anything," Rainey said. "And why shouldn't he go after him? You haven't done anything yet. Look what that man did to my daughter!"

One of the EMTs spoke up. "She said something about a ballroom."

Lucas nodded his thanks. "Does she need to be seen at the hospital? Because I want you all out of this house as soon as possible."

"We're just about done here," the EMT said. "I'd recommend we take her in. Depends on what mom here says. She's not in any danger, no."

"The sheriff's on his way with more officers," Lucas said to Rainey. "We're going to have to secure the house, so you need to leave here until I let you know it's safe to return. Do you understand?"

Rainey nodded, but the girl shouted her protest. "You can't make me leave, Mommy! You can't take me away from here! What about you? He said you'd been in that room, Mommy! You can't leave here either!"

Deciding that the girl was her mother's problem, Lucas headed upstairs.

To his mind, the ballroom was second only in creepiness to the bizarre theater across the hall. It made a kind of sense that there would be a secret passage somewhere inside of it. The girl had said there was also an entrance to the underground rooms out in the old springhouse on the property. Why hadn't they found it when they were investigating the Brodsky murder? So many secrets. He almost found Bliss House's ability to keep its secrets admirable. But to believe that, he would have to acknowledge that Bliss House was a living, practically breathing place. He didn't think he was that far gone. Yet.

From the stairs he could see that the pocket doors to the ballroom were open. He unholstered his Sig Sauer P220 and tactical light.

The room was empty except for a pair of tables and some exercise mats. As he turned toward the fireplace, the reflection of his light caught a tall mirror and made him jump.

Shit. He hated how freaked out this place made him feel.

The opening beside the fireplace was short, and he had to duck inside. He shone the light down stairs that were narrowly situated between rough brick walls, and steep as hell. Which is where, he figured, they probably led.

Shit and shit.

He kept his progress slow and careful. The field was narrow enough that he would have an easy shot at anyone he came upon who needed shooting, but he was equally vulnerable. Steep as the stairs were, by the time he reached the bottom after 107 steps (he'd always been a counter, particularly when he was nervous), he'd had to make at least four turns. This was not a basement. The angle and depth of the staircases told him they were below and outside the footprint of the house.

"Powell!" He stopped on the bottom stair before entering what seemed to be a cave-like tunnel. He could see a wall directly ahead of him, but his voice seemed to resound in a larger space.

"In here."

The voice came from the right, and he believed it was Powell's. A small amount of yellowish light came from that direction as well.

"Come out where I can see you," Lucas said.

"I think you better come and look at this," Powell said. "There's nobody else here."

Lucas entered the tunnel carefully, clearing the seemingly endless dark space to his left, then checking out the space to his right, which turned out to be a doorway. The tunnel extended beyond it but turned into more of a hallway, with smoother walls and a couple of low-wattage lights on the wall.

He felt his breath constrict in his chest. He hadn't been wrong. It looked like a hallway to hell.

There were three doors that opened onto the hallway on the left. He found Powell standing in the first room.

Working on a drug case early in his career, Lucas had busted a dealer who kept a couple of badly-used prostitutes in a secret room behind a wall in his basement. It had been a crude place, with concrete walls and bare mattresses on the floor. The stench had been sickening. The girls turned out to be North Carolina runaways who both ended up in the hospital for several weeks. The room in which he found Powell was less crude, but it had a similar prison-like feel. The low ceiling, rough walls, stained sink, and the curtain rod hung on a hopeless blank wall spoke a language of evil.

There was blood. It had stained the bedclothes and was smeared on the bedside table and the floor.

"Jesus Christ," Lucas said, looking down. Dark blots of fresh blood followed an irregular path past him and out the door. He stepped outside the room and followed the stains past the hallway and a short way into the darkness of the tunnel, which he now saw canted slightly upward toward the ground's surface. The judge had gone out that way, just as the girl had. He made a mental note to ask Ariel why she didn't go back into the house by the stairs. Turning around, he went back into the room where Powell waited. The exploration of the tunnel and the possible discovery of the stabbing victim (if he could be called a victim) could wait for the arrival of the other officers. They couldn't be far away, but there was no way to hear their approach. Wherever this place was, it was a universe away from the rest of the world.

"Was he here when you got down here?" Lucas asked, though he thought he knew the answer.

"If he had been, he'd be dead now," Powell said without emotion.

Despite the dramatics, Lucas didn't give him a hard time. The person who had assaulted the girl had probably killed the guy's wife as well. Lucas had to keep his head and not let Powell know how sure he was that the judge, or the judge's son, was his wife's killer. But after the disturbing interview he'd had with the judge at the hospital he understood that Randolph Bliss was a cold, cold bastard, and probably a very successful psychopath. If he was indeed their perp, there was plenty of evidence with the blood and whatever DNA was on the bed to nail him.

"We need to get out of here. I don't want this scene contaminated any more than it already is. Let's go."

Powell didn't respond.

"We'll get the crime scene techs down here. What is it?"

"It's Karin's," he said.

Lucas saw where Powell was pointing. A shiny gold sandal lay on a chair. He'd seen the other in the dining room after they found Karin Powell's body.

Chapter 76

Gerry.

God, he had hated it when Karin called him that. He hadn't had the heart to tell her in all the time they'd been together, and now that he was hearing it after she was dead, it felt unbearable to him.

But why was he hearing it now? Twice in one day?

There was no one to ask. He already knew the answer: It was all in his head. It was the guilt talking. The guilt from the knowledge that he'd let Karin get involved with a man like Randolph Bliss. A powerful man from an obviously sick family. But of course he hadn't known that Randolph Bliss was the one, before. And what about the kid, Jefferson? He certainly didn't put it past Karin to have been screwing them both. She was ambitious that way. If the baby had lived, it would've been a Bliss, certainly.

No. It wasn't Karin's ambition that had brought them to this point. It was her illness. She was sick. They both had known it soon after they got together, but he'd loved her enough to marry her in spite of her addiction. She'd wanted to love him. To be true to him. But she hadn't been willing to continue the counseling work to get herself to a place where that was even a remote possibility.

He'd been her husband, though, and they'd been through a lot of shit together. They'd understood one another. At least he'd believed that, once.

It killed him that he'd had to learn from Nick that she'd been afraid. That she'd felt threatened. Why hadn't she come to *him*?

Trust. She hadn't trusted him enough to share the secret that the baby was a Bliss.

Using Rainey's keys, he brought her Lexus around to the front of the house, parking as close as he could given the sudden increase in number of police vehicles in the circular driveway. He wouldn't miss being away from this place. The detective had insisted that Rainey and Ariel leave so that they could secure the scene. Who knew what else they would find in the hellhole where Ariel had been attacked.

He'd smelled Karin's perfume down there. He'd heard her voice: *Gerry.*

What if he'd hung around the house after the party? Knocked on the door when he drove back there that night and awakened Rainey and asked where his wife was? She probably wouldn't have known at that moment, but they would've been awake. They would've been there to stop whatever had happened. Stopped Karin's murder.

Nick Cunetta would be alive. Bertie Bliss might not be in the hospital. Ariel wouldn't have been assaulted.

I've got to stop this!

He slammed the door of the running Lexus so hard that it drew the attention of one of the uniforms standing nearby.

So fucking what! he wanted to say. *You people have made my life miserable enough already. Get over it!*

Inside, one of the troopers directed him to Rainey's bedroom where he found Rainey standing by the unmade bed. Ariel was curled into a fetal position, her back against the enormous pile of bed pillows, her face hidden.

Rainey looked up at him in surprise when he came through the door.

"She won't go," she said, her voice low. Miserable.

Ariel didn't move.

"Ariel, you don't want to stay in this place," Gerard said. "He could come back. It's not safe for you here."

He put a hand on Rainey's arm and pulled her gently to the side.

"Ariel," he said, sitting on the edge of the bed. "I need you to listen to me. I know you think I'm an asshole, and I apologize for the mean things I said to you. You didn't deserve them. And I'm not just telling you this because I feel bad about what just happened to you."

Ariel didn't respond. They could hear the police moving through the house, the occasional scratch of their radios, scraps of conversation. It was somehow worse than it was the day Karin had been found. Then, there had been a kind of surreal calm in the air. Today was frantic. They finally had someone to pursue, and it was as though they'd discovered a new kind of energy to keep things going.

He thought of touching Ariel, but stopped before he did it. It might push her over the edge.

"Did they tell you that you couldn't come back?" he said. "Is that why you don't want to leave?"

"Of course we're not going to . . ." Rainey stopped in midsentence when Gerard put a finger to his mouth, shushing her. He shook his head. He could tell she was leery of the next thing he might say, but she didn't finish her sentence.

"Is that it?" Gerard said.

"I can't leave," Ariel said, her voice muffled.

"I promise you can come back." Gerard knew he was clearly out of bounds, but he felt like he had to take the risk. He had to get her out somehow.

There was a sound of footsteps out in the hall, and Lucas Chappell came to stand in the doorway. This time it was Rainey's turn to shush. She hurried over, motioning for him to stay outside the room. As she pulled the door halfway shut behind them, Gerard could hear the detective telling her that they needed to leave right away.

He turned back to Ariel. "They're going to try to force you to go," he said. "But you'll get back here faster if you go without a fight."

"She's going to take me away, forever. She told me. She told me she's going to sell the house and move us back to Missouri." She sat up a little, but still wouldn't look at him. What he could see of her face was pale, and her undamaged eye was wide with panic.

"I know why you don't want to leave," Gerard said. *And God help me for the lie I'm about to tell*, he thought.

She looked at him suspiciously.

He looked away, toward the window onto the garden.

"I know how much the house has changed you," he said. "I know your mother either doesn't see it or doesn't want to admit it." Turning back to her, he said, "Am I right?"

Her sudden relief was like a palpable thing between them.

"It's real," she said. "It's all real. When I'm outside, it hurts again. I could feel the change right away, when we first moved in. I hated being here at first. But then things started to happen. I don't care what else happens to me here. It doesn't matter! Somebody will catch that horrible man."

He heard the fearful hope in her voice.

"Jefferson too," she added. Though she didn't sound as certain.

Whether she was certain or not didn't matter. Gerard was certain enough about Jefferson Bliss for the both of them.

"Your mother told me she was booking a room at the Grange."

Ariel shook her head vehemently. "I won't go."

"It's a cool place to stay, but I don't think it's the place for you right now. Too many people."

Out in the hall, Rainey's voice was rising with panic. The detective's response was quiet enough to be unintelligible. He could picture them trying to carry an unwilling Ariel out of the house. No way that was going to work.

"Did you ever meet my dog, Ellie?" he asked her. "She's funny as hell. Chases a ball like it's her life's mission. I've brought her out here a bunch of times, but maybe before you all got here, so you haven't had a chance to meet her yet. Karin loved her, even though she was always jumping up on her. We kind of sucked at training."

"We never had a dog," Ariel said.

"Listen. You and your mom can come and stay at my place until they arrest those guys. It's totally private. You can't even see the house from the road. Now that my in-laws are gone there's plenty of room."

Ariel looked at him steadily. He could see she was a nice kid. Before her accident had changed everything, she had obviously been the center of a very small, adoring world. He wondered what kind of woman she was going to be and hoped she wouldn't end up batshit crazy. That would definitely happen if she stayed in Bliss House for any long period of time. Right now, they just needed to save her life.

"Can they really make me leave?" She had been able to hear the detective as well, and she wasn't stupid.

"Yeah, they really can." God, she was just a little kid. He wanted to kill Randolph Bliss. He was a fucking demon.

"It doesn't feel fair to me," she said. "I'm the one he tried to hurt. I should be the one to decide."

"I agree," he said.

"I wish I could make them see. Maybe you could get my mom to make it look like we're leaving. Then we could come back when they're all gone. They can't keep us out of our own house. It's got to be against the law. I know they think he's not dead, but I swear he wasn't moving when I left him. Maybe Jefferson came and got him. Or maybe someone else was there, hiding."

She was so earnest that he wanted to encourage her. But it wasn't possible.

He shook his head. "Not going to happen. Even if you could keep him out—and I'm not saying that you're not right that he's dead, or maybe injured—the police aren't going to let anyone stay tonight. If they find him, they might let you and your mom come back tomorrow."

"I don't believe you. My mom is even more upset than the police."

"It would be stupid for me to lie to you," Gerard said. "You don't even really know me, I know. But this has been a kind of nightmare for all of us, Ariel. Maybe your mom would be pissed off if she knew I was saying this to you . . ."

She waited.

Gerard ran a hand self-consciously over his hair and looked away. He hadn't known that he would have to be more honest with the girl than he'd wanted to be.

"Everything you've seen—including Karin's death—tells us that this guy is responsible for more deaths than just hers. It's hell losing someone you love, and I know you know that better than anyone, Ariel. Your mom is scared she's going to lose you, too. I can't get my wife back any more than you and your mom can get your dad back."

"I thought he was here," Ariel said. "I think your wife is here. Someone helped me. I can't really explain it."

"Telling your mother that is just going to freak her out more," he said. "But I believe you."

"Why?"

"Listen. The police only deal in what they can prove. If they can get Judge Bliss and Jefferson they'll be happy. Or at least they won't care about you coming back here. Whatever else is going on . . . I don't know, Ariel. There's a lot of weird stuff that has gone on at this house. I kind of agree with your mom that this is maybe not the best place for you. But I know it's important to you right now. You're not a stupid person."

"No," she said quietly.

"We just have to let the police do their job. Stay out of their way. It won't be for long."

He didn't look away from her gaze. She was uncertain of him, but perhaps there was a small amount of trust. He wondered how long it would last.

"One night," he said. "Maybe two. It's not like nobody knows who Judge Bliss and his son are. They can't hide for long."

Ariel fidgeted with the edge of the hem of the plain pink T-shirt she wore. The police had taken away the bloody robe as evidence.

"If I go, do you think Ellie would stay in the room with me at night? Does that sound dumb?"

What she sounded like was the kid that she was. He smiled. "I think she'll want to climb up and put her head on your pillow. But I've got to warn you: she's a blanket hog."

Because of the tight skin on one side of her face, Ariel's smile was awkward. But it was a genuine smile, and he knew he would be sad not to see it after she realized he had betrayed her. It was going to be a long time before she and Rainey ever came back to Bliss House.

She sat up even more and smoothed her hair. "All right," she said. "Just for a day or two, but then I have to come back here. You have to make my mom understand how important it is."

"You bet." Gerard got up from the bed quickly to go and speak to Rainey before Ariel could change her mind. He couldn't bear to look at the girl's trusting eyes anymore. How many lies had he told her? Two? Three? He knew his Bible well enough to be grateful that there weren't any fowl near Bliss House, lest he hear a cock start crowing.

Chapter 77

Lucas was in the middle of the hall bringing the team of state troopers up to speed when his phone rang. It was Tim Hatcher, the deputy. Lucas excused himself to answer.

"Why aren't you here?" he asked by way of a hello.

"I was about to leave the office when we got a call from the hospital, sir."

"And?"

"Mrs. Bliss woke up. The judge wasn't with her, obviously, because he was there at the house, right? The sheriff said the judge is in some deep shit. Is it true?"

"I don't have time to go into it now, Deputy," Lucas said. "But yes. Deep shit describes it. Did she say anything?"

"Well, I was just getting ready to call you anyway because we got a hit on the fingerprint from Nick Cunetta's window. And all hell broke loose at the hospital because Mrs. Bliss's son, Jefferson Bliss, showed up there and tried to strangle her. I went over there right away."

Lucas exhaled sharply. "Jesus H. Christ, Deputy. Where in the hell did you go to academy that you make a report like that?

Because you're not making any sense, and I've got a house full of cops here tripping all over each other and a state judge running around bleeding like a stuck pig. So please think very carefully before saying whatever you're going to say next."

There was a pause, and Lucas thought that the deputy might just have given up in confusion. He silently cursed the sheriff for giving him such a rookie to work with.

"Mrs. Bliss said that she knew who attacked her in her kitchen. She's pretty sure it was a guy named DeRoy Lee, who works at Fauquier's Bookstore." He took a breath. "I looked him up real quick. He did a year in county lock-up. Works at the bookstore in town. Assault. Possession. He's in some special parole program run by the county."

"Okay," Lucas said. "That's a nice surprise. She's sure?"

"But there's more. She said he's the judge's second cousin by marriage, or something like that. Also that her son freaked out because she asked him if he had something to do with Karin Powell's death. She told Nick Cunetta she had a fingernail belonging to Karin Powell that she found in her son's pocket."

"You're doing better," Lucas said. "So she's saying there's some connection between her son and Nick Cunetta?"

"The son told her Nick Cunetta called him and threatened him because of it."

"Did some helpful member of the staff tackle the kid after he hit his mother, I hope?"

"They didn't. Security says they probably have him on video, though."

"Great," Lucas said. "Security's a shitload of help. Maybe we can get them to keep an eye out to see if he comes back and detain him. Since they know what he looks like now."

"You want me to tell them that?" Tim said, sounding serious.

Lucas was being sarcastic, but the deputy didn't catch the nuance. "You can tell them, but they won't notice shit." He was about to hang up when he remembered something else the deputy had said. "So, what about the fingerprint?"

"That's the best part." Tim paused for dramatic effect. "The fingerprint also belongs to DeRoy Lee. So it looks like he attacked Mrs. Bliss *and* might have killed Nick Cunetta."

If Tim Hatcher, Deputy First Class, had been there in the room, Lucas would've given him a big, unprofessional kiss on the lips.

"Get the paperwork started and interrupt some District Attorney's dinner. I need a warrant so we can visit Mr. DeRoy Lee right away. Call me."

Lucas took two officers, one with a video camera, down into the underground rooms via the ballroom's staircase, while another team headed outside for the springhouse tunnel. Both teams carried large battery-powered lights.

The troopers with Lucas hadn't yet seen the rooms and were vocal about their disgust.

"It's like some kind of creepy love nest," Lucas said. "Condoms, wine, mini-fridge, a sink. A covered bucket for the necessary stuff."

"The furniture down here isn't new," one of the troopers said. "It's like my crazy great-aunt's house in Danville."

"Man, remind me not to come to Sunday dinner with your family," said the one with the camera.

"Just get the footage," Lucas said. "Nobody wants to stay down here all night. Let's do what we came to do and make sure there's no imminent threat. We can get the forensics teams down here first thing in the morning."

They recorded the first room easily enough, careful to stay out of each other's way.

Lucas thought about the judge. This was where he'd chosen to spend his spare time. And now the Adams girl had said that the son had showed up. What about Karin Powell? Would they find her DNA here? Her shoe was still where Gerard had pointed it out. He knew the answer was probably yes, given her habits. She was probably screwing the son as well. Three people who could well have afforded expensive hotel rooms or even apartments had chosen to hide their activities in this dank hellhole.

Lucas noted that the officer doing the recording had done a lingering shot of the blank wall with its useless curtain rod. Once upon a time, someone had hung a curtain there. Why? Lucas was sure it had been some psychopath's joke.

What if the girl hadn't escaped? How many others had the judge and his son had down here? Looking at the grubby, and now bloody, bedcoverings, Lucas felt his stomach churn.

"I'm going next door," he said.

"We'll be there in just a minute," said the officer with the camera.

Going into the hallway, Lucas wondered at the weak electric lights on the wall. The bulbs looked old, as though they'd been screwed in decades earlier and just hadn't burned out. And how had they gotten electricity all the way down here? It spoke of planning. Of history. This place had been in use for a very, very long time.

The contents of one of the baskets in the second room had spilled over the floor: It was all porn, and not gentleman's porn either. Disgusted, Lucas used one gloved hand to sort through the pile. Given the vintage, it had probably belonged to the judge.

"Dirty, dirty Judge Bliss," Lucas said.

He moved on to the other baskets. Opened them.

There were two people inside. At least he thought they were people.

Each looked like an enormous doll washed of all colors except black and gray, their torsos and heads bloated and waxy, their eye sockets empty holes.

He'd seen figures like these before. Never at a crime scene, but when he was in training at a medical forensics class. *Adipocere* was the name for what had happened to whoever the people had been. The decomposition of the fat in their bodies had transformed them, preserved them like carnival mummies. People who had become corpses and were hidden away. Most likely for years.

Chapter 78

Rainey busied herself with changing the sheets in the bedroom that Gerard's in-laws had vacated. The room had been left exceedingly clean, leading her to wonder what sort of people they'd been and where they'd gone. Gerard had spoken to her very briefly out of Ariel's earshot, saying only that he'd had a disagreement with them. She couldn't imagine what they would think if they knew that strangers related to their daughter's death were sleeping in their daughter's house. The idea had made her uncomfortable at first, but not uncomfortable enough to insist that she and Ariel could find somewhere else to stay. The thought of going to even a nice hotel with Ariel right now sounded like a new nightmare. Now that a high-profile person like her cousin Randolph was the target of a manhunt linked to perhaps two murders—she had been stunned to learn of Nick's death from Gerard—the press and other unwelcome parties would again start circling. She would sleep in a den of actual snakes if it meant she could protect Ariel from that kind of exposure.

The detectives hadn't yet shown her the underground room where Ariel had been attacked. There hadn't been time. She told herself that it was a good thing because Ariel needed all of her attention right now. But she couldn't look at Ariel without wondering what it had been like. What her daughter had felt. How terrified she'd been. It sickened Rainey that she hadn't known about the room and hadn't understood the house, or the danger Ariel had been in.

Once again, she'd done nothing to protect her daughter. She'd twice put Ariel's life in danger because she'd put her own selfish desires first. What kind of mother did that?

Right now, she both wanted to grab Ariel and hold her to try to keep her safe, and stay far, far away from her lest she screw up again. By coming here to Gerard's house, relying on Gerard, she felt like she was abdicating responsibility for taking care of Ariel. She was relying on Gerard in the same way she might have relied on Will. He was taking care of them both, and it embarrassed her. But what else could she do? The police hadn't really offered her any alternatives but to say that they'd have an officer keep watch near wherever Ariel was staying. It was hardly a comfort. Randolph was supposed to be one of the good guys, too, and look what he'd done.

When she was finished making the bed, she went into the next room to check on Ariel. Gerard had been right about his Golden Retriever, Ellie. She lay on the bed with Ariel, settled comfortably beneath the sleeping girl's extended arm. It was such a natural, happy sight, almost as though that terrible thing hadn't happened to Ariel just a few hours earlier. Almost as though nothing terrible had ever happened to Ariel. Except that the arm lying over Ellie was pink with scarring, and the hand misshapen.

Of course she should have gotten Ariel a puppy before now, but she hadn't wanted to deal with training it.

Selfish. So selfish.

A few minutes later, she found Gerard cleaning up after the meal the three of them had shared in the large, high-ceilinged kitchen.

The homemade soup and local bakery bread had been fresh and satisfying, and they'd all eaten hungrily, like people who hadn't eaten in days. And in truth, maybe they hadn't. Rainey couldn't remember the last time she'd sat down to an actual meal.

"Dinner was delicious," she said to Gerard.

Like Ellie, he looked like he belonged in this place, with its mellow surfaces of granite and slate tile. The kitchen's ceiling was raised and peaked, open to the other common rooms in the house. With its tall windows—now dark—that looked out on the ridge, it seemed as much suited to contemplation and inspiration as cooking. She could imagine having coffee at the long hand-hewn table at the end of the room, watching the morning light illuminate the mountains, working on sketches or planning her day. Will had often talked of building a place down in the Ozarks, on a lake. Nothing as large as this house, but something with lots of light and a view of the mountains.

"My mother-in-law keeps her cooking pretty simple," he said. "The soup took some doctoring, but not too much. Do you want a glass of wine? I could use one, but I didn't want to get it out in front of Ariel."

"Sure," she said. "Sounds good."

He opened one of the several doors in the wine storage compartment in the kitchen's island and, after pulling a couple out and putting them back, finally selected a California pinot noir.

"This won't suffer too much if we don't decant it."

When it was opened, he took the bottle and a pair of glasses and led her into the family room on the other side of the kitchen fireplace. Again, she was surprised to find how relaxed yet sophisticated the furnishings were. Karin had seemed to be anything but relaxed. From the mix of neutral suede-covered furniture arranged over the old-wood floors and contemporary rugs, Rainey chose one of a pair of deep-seated chairs close to the fireplace and sank into it.

Taking a glass from Gerard, Rainey realized her hand was trembling. The simple act of sitting down in this comfortable room seemed like such a normal thing to do. It shook her.

"God, I'm a mess," Rainey said, embarrassed. "I'm sorry."

"Hey, it's okay. It's been a hell of a day. Maybe you just should've gone to bed after Ariel."

"I'm not usually such a wimp." Rainey took a shaky sip of the wine, and then another larger one.

Gerard sat across from her. Ellie appeared seemingly from out of nowhere, plodding across the room to collapse with a weary sigh at his feet. When Rainey sat forward, looking anxiously in the direction from which the dog had come, Gerard said, "She's fine. She's asleep. It's what she needs right now."

Rainey retreated into the chair. They sat in silence for a few moments, listening to Ellie's breathing deepen as she relaxed close to her master.

"We can't go back to the house," she said finally. "I don't know what in the hell we're going to do, Gerard. It's . . ."

"Sick," Gerard said. He hunched forward, suddenly animated, as though he'd been waiting to speak. "That house has a sickness. I always felt like something was strange but never grasped it, never understood it. I don't know what kind of man Randolph Bliss is or what his family was like, but either he corrupted that house or it corrupted him. And it got to Karin. I know it got to Karin. Or he did, the bastard."

Rainey didn't know how to respond. Gerard took her silence as reprobation.

"I'm sorry. That was stupid."

"It wasn't anything I haven't thought already. Randolph is *my* family. Ariel's family, too. Maybe that's why we're—I don't know. Maybe it's why we're so involved. If we hadn't bought the place from Karin, maybe she wouldn't have gone back there."

Gerard took a long draught of wine, set the glass firmly on the table between them.

"Whatever happened to Karin was going to happen to her regardless of who lived in the house. If it had still been empty, it would've happened anyway. She was pregnant by either that animal or his son, and one of them killed her because of it. Or because she'd aborted it. There's no way to tell, unless one of them confesses."

"Oh, my God, Gerard. I didn't know. That doesn't even sound possible."

"Hypersexual disorder," he said. "Her parents and her sister, Molly, refused to believe it. Karin tried to tell them, but they thought she was being dramatic—even after she told them she'd gotten a clinical diagnosis. She did her best to keep it in check with drugs and spent a lot of time in therapy. But she couldn't control it for very long. There were times when I had to come and get her from places . . . well, they weren't the kind of places you or I would ever think of going. The way she was made her vulnerable to stuff. You'd think she'd be aggressive—and she was, in business—but not necessarily when it came to sex. She was compulsive and lived for the rush. Being in that house, I guess with the judge in the beginning, satisfied that compulsion. It made sense that she later took on the son. Probably just to mess with the judge's head."

Rainey's stomach clenched. *That room.* Where Randolph had attacked Ariel, her little girl. Karin had been her parents' little girl, too. She'd wondered at Karin's always-seductive appearance, but there'd been nothing about her to suggest that she'd been ill in that way. The idea that Karin had been obsessed with sex seemed so strange, so foreign to her.

"When did you know?"

"That she was pregnant? I'd known for a few weeks. But I didn't know about the abortion. We'd agreed that we would keep the baby. Raise it together, no matter whose it was. I had no idea that the father was one of those assholes. I've had a medical thing since I was eighteen that means I can't have kids of my own, but half of that baby would've come from Karin, and that meant something to me."

He shook his head, picked up his wine glass but didn't drink from it. "I sound like some kind of loser, don't I? That's what Karin saw. That's what she had to see."

His voice was bitter.

Seeing him in this house, knowing how laid back he was most of the time, Rainey believed he could've raised another man's child and been a terrific parent.

"She was sick. Her judgment was pretty skewed, Gerard."

"I was giving her a hard time about drinking at the party. That's what we were fighting about. She said I wasn't the only one giving her shit about it, so I guessed that whoever had gotten her pregnant was at the party too. No one else knew. But there was no baby by then. She just hadn't told me. I don't know what she was waiting for."

"You have to forgive her for that."

"Forgive her?"

"She must have had a reason. She didn't deserve to die because she was keeping secrets from you. But she's beyond your anger about it. If you hold onto it, it's only going to be harder on you."

"You don't understand. I don't blame her for anything. I just thought you should know what had been going on between us," he said. "How Karin's weakness made her vulnerable to that man and that house. Randolph Bliss is evil. What he was affected her."

"We still don't know anything about the *why* part. You can't just say that the house is bad and Randolph is evil. That Karin died because he's evil—not mentally ill, but *actually* evil. Is that even possible?"

Gerard sat, quiet, for a moment. Then he looked into Rainey's eyes, and she saw he was serious. "Yeah. I think it's definitely possible."

The silence broadened between them as they finished their wine. Rainey thought about the implications of his words. *Evil.*

Was it a state of being? What about her own selfishness? Had her insistence that they have the antique gas stove been a kind of evil? Maybe she'd helped to bring on what was happening to them now because her selfishness demanded it. She was the one who had insisted on moving into and staying in a house with a dubious reputation. She hadn't been thinking of Ariel but only of herself. And if she was honest with herself, she knew she'd been the one running away, wanting to feel better, wanting to be around new people. New possibilities. Her selfishness was, perhaps, a lesser evil. But her weakness had allowed the greater evil to creep in. She'd made them vulnerable.

"If you don't mind, I'm going to go shut things down for the night." Gerard got up and called Ellie to him. They went to the kitchen, and Rainey heard him moving around then opening the back door to take Ellie outside.

She poured a bit more wine into her empty glass and drank it in two swallows. Sitting back in her chair, she realized she was a little drunk. Will had often teased her about what a lightweight drinker she was. Now, a part of her wanted to drink more, to finish off a bottle and sink into a state where she didn't have to think about evil or regrets or how much danger Ariel was in. A memory of one of her mother's uncles, telling her ten-year-old self that she was a spoiled brat after she'd refused a piece of his daughter's birthday cake because it didn't have enough icing on it, floated into her mind. *Spoiled.* Maybe that was her problem.

But Jefferson. Hadn't he been spoiled from the beginning? It was obvious that Bertie doted on him, and Bertie had probably never had an evil thought. Her son had turned on her. A man, a boy, who could turn on a woman like Bertie? Yes, that was evil.

After another splash of wine, Rainey decided she'd had enough. She knew self-reflection wasn't one of her strong points, and although she'd made Ariel go to therapy after the accident, she didn't believe in it for herself. The mental work of getting from

Point A to Point B without falling into some kind of self-pity trap frustrated her too much. She had enough to deal with keeping Ariel alive and herself half-sane.

When she heard Gerard come back inside, she took the nearly-empty bottle and her glass into the kitchen. He took the bottle with a polite *thanks* and didn't even seem to note how much was left. Rainey set the glass in the sink.

"You remember where your room is?"

Rainey nodded. He looked tired and thinner than when she first arrived in Old Gate. She remembered seeing him the night of the party, standing beside Karin who looked devastating in her tight dress, sex incarnate. He had looked so normal, so calm. But now she knew the truth. Despite the hell Karin's death had put him through he was still calm. Handling everything. He'd lost his temper with Jefferson, but everyone knew a man could only be pushed so far. She respected him, appreciated that he wasn't perfect.

Before she left the kitchen, she stopped in front of him and raised her hand to his unshaven cheek. She thought it was to his credit that he looked a little surprised, but didn't push her away. Standing on her toes, she kissed his other cheek and whispered *thank you*.

She checked on Ariel, who was sleeping soundly, and went to her own room. She fell asleep, deeply and without dreams, and if anyone paused outside her bedroom door, she didn't hear.

Chapter 79

The warrant hadn't yet arrived. Lucas stood in the weed-pocked gravel driveway in front of DeRoy Lee's trailer with Deputy Tim and a state police response team, waiting. He was a fan of big gestures when it came to getting the bad guys. It made an impression on them, as well as on the public. Usually it paid off. He had a good feeling about DeRoy Lee. Nick Cunetta was tied too closely to Karin Powell's death, as well as Roberta Bliss and her family, for his murder to be a coincidence. A local ex-con who had been in both the state and county penal systems was a reasonable suspect.

He knew he shouldn't have been as happy as he'd been to leave Bliss House before everyone else had left for the night. At least one team would hang around until morning, guarding what was becoming an ever-intensifying crime scene. But the truth was he didn't mind leaving to stand in the moonlight outside DeRoy Lee's shitty trailer, waiting for the bastard to come outside. At least he could breathe out here.

The wildly incautious part of his brain was hoping that DeRoy Lee had been the murderer of Karin Powell as well as Nick Cunetta. But he didn't want to get ahead of himself.

The trailer sat among a small collection of six in a field well south of Old Gate, near the county line. It was an area that bred meth labs, fighting dogs, and bare-knuckle brawlers against a backdrop of hidden pot fields. Lucas was more comfortable with urban landscapes, like his hometown of Richmond. But after six years in the sticks, he was getting used to it.

Under the response team's lights, the trailer was a long once-white affair with brown shutters, a rotting set of stairs without a landing leading to the front door, and a lidless barbeque grill with a bent set of tongs and an open bag of charcoal that looked lonesome without a rusting can of lighter fluid beside it. A child's pink tricycle lay on its side, visible beneath the trailer, and a motorcycle, half-covered by a blue tarp, sat a few yards into the grass. The trailer's windows were blacked out with curtains from the inside.

No one from the response team was expecting trouble, but they were suited up for it.

The captain of the team pounded on the door, calling for Lee to come out.

Lucas stood over near the car. He knew the captain preferred to keep the detectives as uninvolved as possible in the tactical stuff. He didn't take it personally.

There was no glass in the trailer's door, and no activity at the windows. The captain shouted again for *DeRoy Lee* to come out of the house. They just wanted him to answer some questions at the station.

As far away as he was, Lucas heard the quick, muffled response from inside the trailer.

"Hey, I'm coming out! Don't freak!"

"Open the door, slowly. Come out with your hands where we can see them."

In a moment, DeRoy Lee was down the stairs and standing barefoot in the weedy gravel, looking way more relaxed than any man involved in killing people deserved to look. His blond-gray hair lay softly about his shoulders like a woman's; he was beard-less, and his relaxed cotton T-shirt and—*dear Lord*, were those yoga pants?—pants hung loose on his muscled body. He looked like a trainer at a less than prosperous health spa.

"You caught me in *savasana*," he said with a beatific smile after Lucas introduced himself.

"Corpse pose?" Lucas said. "How appropriate."

"All you had to do was give me a call, and I'm happy to come and talk to you people. You don't need to send an armored invita-tion. Now, what do you want? It's air-conditioned inside, and it's irritatingly hot out here."

"You inviting us in?"

DeRoy Lee's face was impassive. "Sorry. There's not room for the whole crew." Then he smiled. His teeth were yellowed and only slightly crowded, as though he'd once had braces, but his bite was slowly returning to its original shape.

"Detective Chappell!"

While they'd been talking, the captain had been checking out the surrounding area with a couple of other officers. The inhabit-ants of the other trailers were slowly opening their doors, curious at seeing the uniforms stand down.

"There's clotted blood around the door and step in the back," he said, coming to stand a few feet behind DeRoy.

"Have you injured yourself, Mr. Lee?" Lucas said. "You look pretty healthy to me."

DeRoy shrugged. "Neighbor kids. They play rough with each other."

Lucas opened his eyes wide, in mock surprise. "If you have injured children in your trailer, they could need medical attention. We can be of some help."

A scowl creased the other man's features for the briefest of moments before the calm returned. "I don't let those kids in the trailer. They're my sister's kids, and they like to play tricks on their old uncle DeRoy sometimes. So, no worries."

Lucas pointed at the trailer. "Captain, did you hear any sounds of distress inside?"

"I believe I heard some whining. Like someone was in some kind of health trouble. Could definitely have been a kid."

"Fuckers. Too lazy to get a warrant?"

Lucas shook his head. "Really, man. We just came to invite you to come in and answer a few questions pertaining to the death of Nick Cunetta, a local lawyer. He wasn't your lawyer, by any chance?"

"See, all you had to do was ask," DeRoy said. "No, he wasn't. Don't know him. You can go home now."

"That's a great start. You're a helpful guy, Mr. Lee. Now . . ." Lucas didn't bother to finish his sentence. A cruiser, its lights and sirens going, turned into the trailer park. He smiled. "Great. Our invitation has arrived. I promise we won't step on your yoga mat."

The first of the three troopers to enter the trailer for the search came back to the open front door. The look on his face told Lucas it wasn't good news.

"We're secure, sir. But you need to come inside."

Lucas glanced back at the trooper standing beside the cruiser in which DeRoy Lee was sitting. "Keep him here until we see what's what."

Inside, the trailer was spartan and much cleaner than its grubby outer structure implied. The walls were painted a cheerful yellow, the furnishings were light oak and of the assemble-it-yourself type but with lean, stylish lines. They'd apparently caught DeRoy Lee in the middle of a leisurely meal: a plate of bacon, eggs, and peanut butter toast sat on a restored antique trunk that served as coffee table, beside an open book lying spine up: *Dream It! Be It! 7 Steps to Personal Growth Through Dream Analysis*. The television blared an episode of a TV psychologist's talk show. It didn't surprise Lucas that he'd lied about doing yoga when they arrived. The guy was obviously vain about his habits.

"There's nobody else here?" Lucas addressed the trooper who had led them in.

"I wouldn't say that."

The air inside the trailer was thick and humid, barely chilled by the rattling air conditioner in the front room. It stank, too, and not just of bacon, mold, and peanut butter.

An acrid slaughterhouse smell. Blood.

Instinctively, Lucas felt in his front pocket for the handkerchief he always carried. He didn't yet take it out, but it was there, ready.

They walked through the kitchen and down a short hallway whose walls were lined with carefully trimmed magazine images of elaborate sunsets and tropical beaches populated by shore birds and nearly naked teenage girls. The pictures were sensual but naively tame, like a preteen boy's idea of sexy. That didn't jibe at all with Lucas's idea of what a killer would have on his trailer walls, but he didn't have time to dwell on it.

Before he even got inside the bedroom at the end of the hall, Lucas could see Randolph Bliss's body slumped over the edge of the bed as though it might fall onto the floor at the slightest touch. Blood covered the sheets and had soaked into the room's thin striped carpet. From the impressive size of the wound covering his back, and the physical matter on the wall behind him, it looked as though he'd been shot in the stomach or chest, then had tried to lunge forward, toward his attacker. But his heart and brain had stopped, and gravity had frozen him in his place.

The captain gestured and the trooper went to the body to check for signs of life. A party of flies danced above the judge's head.

"Best thing that could've happened to the son-of-a-bitch," the captain said. "He would've had to spend the rest of his life in solitary, if he'd made it out of county at all."

Lucas took in the bandage wrappers, bloody cloths, scissors, and other detritus piled on the bedside table beside a nearly-empty bottle of Jim Beam. The bandages had been applied to the judge's neck. A plastic tumbler lay on the floor, not far from the judge's outstretched arm, as though he had reached for it before dying.

Lucas couldn't help but think of the superior attitude the judge had taken on when interviewed in the hospital cafeteria. His smug little smile.

Condescending asshole.

"Anyone see a weapon?"

"The guys are checking out the rest of the place," the trooper said, standing up after checking the judge. "He hasn't been dead too long. Rigor hasn't relaxed yet."

"That's just fine. Will someone please give dispatch a shout and get the medical examiner out here? Let's get this ball rolling."

In the living room, the television host was shouting at one of his guests. Lucas left the trailer to a chorus of boos from the audience.

Walking to the cruiser, he kept his eye on DeRoy Lee. Now there was a fucked-up guy. He'd gotten himself an innocuous job in a bookstore (and what was that about? how did that happen?), groomed himself like a West Coast health nut, and yet had not only continued his criminal ways but escalated them. No doubt the judge had made it worth his while.

He nodded to the trooper monitoring the cruiser.

DeRoy didn't bother to get out when he opened the door. A sly smile lit up his clear gray eyes.

"Where's the weapon?" Lucas said.

"With the person who used it."

"What kind of bullshit answer is that?"

"The only answer you get until after I spend some quality time with my lawyer."

"Why the games, Mr. Lee? Is there someone who's so worth your time that you want to spend the next few years of your life trying to convince the courts that you didn't kill an officer of the court? I'm sure that will buy you plenty of cred in prison, but is it worth it? We already know about Nick Cunetta. Now it just looks like Randolph threatened to expose you, so you killed him. Quit wasting my time, and yours."

DeRoy grinned. "If I offer you that information now, it ceases to be useful to me."

"I already know who it was," Lucas said.

"Fuck me. Then you win."

"It was the kid," Lucas said. "And he used his old man's own gun."

DeRoy was silent half a beat too long.

"Thanks." Lucas stepped back from the cruiser.

Now they just had to find that kid.

Chapter 80

Ariel awoke to moonlight coming through the tall windows across from the bed. For a moment she had no idea where she was, and then she remembered the comforting feel of the dog cuddled beside her. Now the dog was gone, and she was alone.

Her cell phone vibrated beside her, bathed in a white puddle of light.

There was a text message right on the front of the screen, waiting for her. Before she could talk herself out of it, she texted an answer as quickly as she could. When a response came back, she read it then lay down with the phone beneath her, her heart pounding against the screen.

Chapter 81

Rainey stood at the nurses' station, waiting for permission to see Bertie. Lucas Chappell had called her cell phone just after 8 A.M. to tell her and Gerard they'd found Randolph dead. The sheriff had been to the hospital first thing to tell Bertie, and Rainey was worried about her. The nurse at the desk wasn't being particularly helpful, and no one seemed to be sure if she would even be allowed to see Bertie. The events with Jefferson, plus the presence of a deputy outside Bertie's room, had complicated things.

It had been hard enough to leave Ariel at Gerard's house. She'd roused Ariel briefly to tell her about Randolph, but wished that she hadn't. Ariel's face was drawn, and she looked as though she'd hardly slept at all. Yet she had insisted that Rainey go to the hospital; they were both relieved that Bertie was awake. Rainey wasn't sure that the news that Randolph was dead had really hit either of them yet.

Rainey trusted Gerard. She really did. They'd had a good talk, and while they hadn't come to any conclusions about Bliss House and what to do about it, she didn't feel quite as helpless as she had before. Her head was so much clearer, as though she were recovering from some long illness.

She was about to text Gerard to see how things were going when she saw Detective Chappell come through the double doors across from the nurses' station. As he headed down the hallway toward Bertie's room, she called after him. To her surprise he waved her forward, indicating she should follow.

Chapter 82

Bertie felt grateful to have Rainey there to hold her hand and give her strength as Detective Chappell—the handsome dark-skinned officer—interviewed her. And where was Jefferson? They were saying Jefferson had killed his daddy. She prayed it wasn't so. How could she bear to live without them both?

It all had something to do with those strange appendages to Bliss House that had been only rumored to exist. Randolph had laughed at her when she'd asked him about them years ago.

"Fairy tales," he'd said. "Foolishness."

She wondered if he'd believed in ghosts at the end. She wondered if he was in Hell. If he'd hurt Ariel the way the detective said he had, that was where he deserved to be. Her years of loving him now felt strangely worthless.

The detective refused to sit, saying he'd stay as long as he needed to, but that every available officer needed to be out looking for Jefferson.

My love. My baby son, what have you done?

But there was more death. Bodies in one of the underground rooms. A man and a woman.

More death.

Finally, Rainey spoke. "Bertie, I know this is hard right now. But it's important. Last night, Ariel was trying to tell us about some kind of vision she had when she went into that room." She described how Ariel had been certain she'd seen another version of the judge. A younger version who, while she watched, killed another man and drove a red-headed girl to throw herself over the balcony.

"Just like Karin Powell," Lucas said.

They both looked at him.

"Yes? That's the implication, right?"

"But Ariel also said earlier . . ." Rainey shook her head. "No. It couldn't be."

"I told the Judge that Ariel thought she saw a man up there in the gallery too. Did she see something else?" Bertie asked. Her teary voice shook. She kept a wad of tissues pressed to her face.

Lucas put a hand up. "Wait. You told the judge that Ariel saw a man with Karin Powell?"

"Ariel didn't know what she saw!" Taking her hand from Bertie's, Rainey crossed her arms protectively in front of her chest. "She was half-asleep. Confused. She told me that when it was all over, she thought she saw Will, my husband. My *dead* husband."

"Oh, that poor precious thing," Bertie said.

After a moment's silence, Lucas spoke: "It's important that I'm clear. The judge believed Ariel saw a man up on the third floor balcony with Karin Powell? A fact that was never shared with us?"

Bertie nodded. "I think so. It was the day I found that poor woman's fingernail in Jefferson's laundry. I gave it to Nick because I didn't know what else to do. He was going to help me."

Bertie twisted her hands together, anxious. She thought she heard the detective whisper a curse word.

"I was going to tell Rainey about it when she came over. I was going to tell her I didn't think it was safe for her to have Jefferson at the house. My own son! He had something to do with that woman. And what if he killed her? What if my own son killed her? She needed to know!"

Her chest was tight, but *no!* she wasn't going to let them give her medicine that would knock her out again.

Concerned, Rainey bent over her and smoothed her hair—which was a mess, Bertie knew. But she couldn't think about that. It wasn't a time for vanity.

"Should I get a nurse?" Lucas asked Rainey. "I was afraid this would be too much for her today. But we have to know how Jefferson and his father were involved."

Bertie breathed deeply. *I will get control.* She was not going to lose her dignity, too.

Poor Nick was dead. The Judge—a man so strong she thought he might live forever—was dead. And a monster. Her son had turned into a criminal.

Mother Bliss had been on her mind ever since Rainey had moved into the house. How she had refused to talk about their time living there to anyone outside the family, except to make historical references, to properly place her family in the pantheon of Blisses who had owned the house for most of the past hundred years. She'd sold Bliss House when Michael disappeared, and never looked back. But he'd left one thing behind.

"I'm all right," she said, looking up at Rainey. "I'm all right."

"We can come back." The uncertain tone in the detective's voice told Bertie he didn't really want to leave.

"There are things that must be said," she told him. "Those bodies in the basement. I don't know who the woman is, but I think the man must be Michael, Randolph's brother. There were times when I almost guessed. Randolph cried in his sleep sometimes. He had terrible, terrible dreams. Drenched the bed in sweat. He would never tell me what they were about." She closed her eyes for a moment. "But I didn't really want to know."

"Of course, one couldn't know for sure," Rainey said. "He fooled you. He fooled everyone."

"When Michael's friends started calling, asking where he was, Mother Bliss—well, I didn't know her as that then, just Mrs. Bliss—went up to Charlottesville. The police got involved, but it was like he just disappeared off the face of the earth. People were looking everywhere, and it was in all the newspapers for a while. It wasn't until all that died down a few weeks later that they noticed his passport and several thousand dollars were missing from the safe at the house."

"If it *is* his body," Lucas said, "that information will go a long way to identifying it, as well as lining out the circumstances. Maybe the girl's, too."

"I didn't think about her," Rainey said. "I wonder who she was?"

Bertie knew she was thinking about Ariel. What had Randolph done to that baby girl? What had he meant to do? Neither Rainey nor the detective had gone into specifics, and she'd been deeply grateful. The truth would come out soon enough.

Detective Chappell looked at his watch. "I need to get moving. Our priority is to get your son safely into custody, Mrs. Bliss."

Oh, my God, my God, when will it end?

"We just want to make sure he's okay, get him somewhere so there's not a chance for whatever has already happened to escalate."

"Escalate?" Bertie said. "You're not going to kill him, are you? There's such a thing as due process. Whatever he's done, *whatever* Jefferson has done, he has to be given a chance to make it right!" She couldn't look at Rainey. If her child had done something equally horrible, she would understand the need to take things slowly. "You have to gather all the facts."

Really, Roberta? The facts? It was Randolph's voice in her head. *No one judges on facts. Don't be naïve.*

Rainey and the detective exchanged skeptical looks.

"Of course," Lucas said. "That goes without saying. But I need to know if there's somewhere he might go to hide. Do you think he'll stay around here? Do you have a vacation home somewhere? Friends who would hide him?"

"I hope they wouldn't," Bertie said.

He tried to reassure her again, but he could tell she was completely worn out. After he confirmed she'd given the fingernail to Nick for safekeeping—having pretended to put it in the garbage in front of her husband and Jefferson—he nodded and told her to get some rest.

"I'll be in touch," he told Rainey. "We can talk more later today about your daughter. I'd like to interview her again."

When Rainey started to protest, he put up a hand. "Later. I still don't want the two of you back at the house until Jefferson Bliss is found. I hope we'll be done gathering evidence today."

"I don't know about going back. Ever. It doesn't feel safe."

Lucas didn't comment, but closed his notebook.

When the detective was gone, Bertie asked Rainey to come and sit beside her on the bed. Rainey took her hand again.

"Bertie, I just don't know what to say. I feel like our coming here has just meant one disaster after another. I've told Ariel I think we should sell the house if we can and go back to St. Louis as soon as possible. I'm afraid we've messed up everything."

Bertie was weak, but she squeezed Rainey's hand as hard as she could.

"That's foolishness, honey. You and your little girl have brought love and sunshine into that house, and I wouldn't trade you for anything. You belong here. Much more than you know."

"I loved it here, at first," Rainey said. "But I don't think I can keep Ariel safe here anymore, Bertie."

Bertie cautiously moved her other hand, the one with the IV needle attached, onto one of Rainey's hands so they could both have something to hold on to. "I need you to be very, very strong when I tell you this."

Rainey almost pulled her hand away, but didn't. She didn't need any more surprises.

407

"I mean it," Bertie said.

"Why are you trying to scare me?"

Bertie shook her head. "I'm just telling you the truth. This is a terrible day for all of us, but I think everything needs to be out in the open right away."

Rainey forced a smile. "People always want unpleasant things 'out in the open.'"

"This is serious. This will be a shock, Rainey. But I know for a fact that the people who raised you weren't your real parents. The woman who raised you was a Bliss, as you are, but she wasn't your real mother."

Rainey laughed. "That's ridiculous, Bertie. That man really did hurt your head."

"For once in my life, I'm not being ridiculous at all. It's my strong belief that you are the child of Michael Bliss and the poor girl who died with him in those rooms years and years ago."

"No. That's not possible." She tried to pull her hand away, but Bertie held tight. "My real parents are buried in St. Louis."

"They went to St. Louis because they had to leave Virginia. Mother Bliss knew they wanted a child but couldn't conceive, and she had one who needed to be taken away. She couldn't risk having you raised anywhere near Old Gate."

"Stop! That's insane." This time Rainey pulled her hands away and stood.

"I won't," Bertie said. "Not until you've heard the truth. Randolph came to Mother Bliss with a baby, and you were that baby. He said Michael told him the baby was a product of a failed affair, and that Michael had left the baby with him and run away. He talked like Michael wasn't coming back but wanted to make sure the baby was placed in a good home. My heart tells me that Randolph lied, Rainey. Now, I believe Randolph murdered your biological parents and left their bodies in that room or whatever it is down there."

Rainey shook her head vehemently. "I don't believe it. And I'm sure there's plenty of DNA to prove that those dead people weren't my real parents." Seeing Bertie's distress, she lowered her voice. "I hate to tell you I think you're wrong. I'm sorry that all this has happened to you, but I just can't see how it has anything to do with me."

"I hate that my husband was a murderer. I hate that he killed your parents, leaving you alone."

"I don't know how to go forward from here." Rainey spoke quickly. Her slender hands trembled as she picked up her purse to leave. "What I do know is that I need to be with Ariel right now. She needs me."

"We're going to get through this. I promise," Bertie said. "We can make things better. So much better."

⁓

As Rainey hurried to her car, anxious to be away from Bertie and her outrageous claim about her birth, she was suddenly struck by the memory of Ariel screaming at her when the EMT was treating her.

He said that you had been in the room, too.

Chapter 83

Ariel pulled on some blue jeans, a cami, and her bright orange hoodie. She hadn't packed much, so the selection was slim. But it didn't matter because she'd be home in a matter of hours. Home, with all of her things. Home, with mirrors she could look into. Home, with its thick, sheltering walls. Home. Where she belonged.

As she sat down on the bench at the end of the bed to put on her shoes, Ellie came into the room and nosed her arm.

"You're such a dorky dog." Ariel scratched Ellie's head, and Ellie squeezed her eyes shut with pleasure.

When Ariel leaned her face close to Ellie's, she felt the dog's warm breath on her cheek. "You could come with me. You could sleep in my room. Even up on my bed, and it wouldn't matter at all what anybody said about it. Do you want to come?"

Ellie licked her face. Ariel let her hand trail across the dog's back as it moved away, toward the window. Finding a wide rectangle of sunshine on the rug, Ellie lay down and watched Ariel finish dressing.

When she was done, she looked around. There was no door to the outside in this room. Her mother's room had a door that led outside, but Ariel wasn't sure where it went because it had been dark last night when she saw it. Did she dare take the time to check it out? Her mother had just texted that she'd be back in about an hour. She decided she would chance it, and get something to eat first.

Checking her front jeans pocket to make sure she had her cell phone, she headed for the bedroom door. Before she reached it, Ellie was up and ahead of her, leading the way to the kitchen as though she'd read her mind.

Ariel's progress was slow and painful. Her cane, which she hadn't had to use all week, was back at the house.

"Hey, can I fix you some breakfast?"

Gerard stood at a desk in the corner of the kitchen, holding some papers. She hadn't noticed before how tanned he was, but not like he'd gone to the beach. His worn blue jeans looked like they spent a lot of time being dusty.

She wanted to dislike him as much as she had when he'd first been in her face about his wife, but then he'd really seemed to understand her. Here in this house she liked him even better. Here there were no voices in her head telling her not to trust him. She wondered about his dead wife and what their life together had been like. She'd found rows of clothes in the closet of the room she was staying in. Expensive winter clothes: coats trimmed in fur, long-sleeved beaded gowns, knee-length sweaters of cashmere and silky weaves of fine wool. Everything was hung with perfect neatness and looked recently cleaned. The clothes were beautiful, but they didn't seem to be at home here the way that Gerard did.

Ellie stood in front of him and barked. Once.

"The one useful thing we trained her to do. She needs to go out. Want to take her?"

Ariel hung back in the shadow of a tall cabinet. "No, thanks. I'll get myself something to eat."

"Sure thing."

As he and Ellie left the room, she felt an unexpected swell of gratitude. Now that she'd slept more hours in a row than she had in weeks, she was thinking more clearly. Agreeing to leave Bliss House had been a huge mistake. It was a mistake she could *feel* in every injured inch of her body. Particularly in her right leg, which wasn't working at all the way it should.

After checking the time, she opened the giant glass canister on the counter that held the bagels and took out one with poppy seeds. In the refrigerator, she found several bottles of her favorite brand of mango and strawberry smoothie. Had Gerard bought them just for her? When?

The thought that he might have bought them before he even knew for sure she was coming here disturbed her. *No. He couldn't have.*

She was being paranoid. Putting down her drink and bagel on the counter for a moment, she pulled out her phone and sent a quick text. The answer was almost immediate.

All will be well, she told herself. *It has to be.*

⌒

When Gerard brought Ellie back into the house, she ran first for the water bowl and then down the hall to the guest bedrooms. He smiled to think he'd been right about Ariel and Ellie hitting it off. It had been a crapshoot, bringing Rainey and Ariel here. No one had seemed excited about the idea, though no one had offered a better alternative. Rainey had trusted him, which was more than he could say for his in-laws who had already left half a dozen calls on his cell phone. But he wasn't going to go there. Right now his job was to keep Jefferson Bliss away from Ariel, to make sure she didn't risk her life as Karin had risked—and lost—hers. He badly wished he'd been there to see Randolph Bliss die.

But he had to stay here and wait. In the meantime there was plenty of paperwork to catch up on, and many *mea culpa* work phone

412

calls to make. As he picked up some papers at the kitchen desk, he heard a faint but clearly recognizable whining coming from the other end of the house. Following it, he found Ellie sitting in front of the closed door of the bedroom where Rainey had slept the night before. He could hear the sound of a television coming from inside. Ellie inclined her head back to him and whined again.

"Come on, girl," he whispered. "She'll come out and play with you later. She just needs to be alone for a while." Smiling, he hooked a finger beneath Ellie's collar to lead her away.

Chapter 84

"Damn, girl. Why didn't you just wrap yourself up in Christmas lights? I could see you coming through the trees half a mile away." Jefferson downshifted, slowing the old Jeep as they took a particularly tight curve.

"Sorry." Ariel's response was little more than a mumble. She felt stupid about wearing the brightly-colored jacket. She'd been wearing it the day he kissed her, and it made her feel happy. Secure. Plus, it was good for hiding her face, and kept Jefferson from seeing what she looked like away from the house. But of course he had already seen her at the party, when things had just started to change, and only a few nights earlier at the springhouse.

"There's a hat and a blanket on the backseat. Put those on."

As much as she wanted to tell him to *shut up* and stop telling her what to do, she quickly obeyed. He was doing her a huge favor by getting her back into the house. Once she was there no one could make her leave again.

He'd texted her overnight, apologizing for leaving her there in the underground room. He'd freaked out, he told her, and was going to come back and get her, but then his father had told him he should hide out for a while because the police were looking for him.

It's not my fault my old man's crazy, he'd texted. I'M SORRY!

He'd attached a picture of himself with a big, sad frown on his face. She'd smiled there in the dark, alone in that strange bedroom.

He might be a jerk, but he was her only friend. She had to trust him. Going back to the house was the only thing that was going to make her feel better, and if he was the only way to get there then that was how it had to be. If he knew his father was dead, he wasn't saying. Should she tell him? She didn't feel like she should be the one to do it, but she knew she would want to know right away.

After she put the grubby golf hat on and hurriedly wrapped the blanket around her, she sank low in the seat without being asked. It was noisy inside the old Jeep. The ragtop was torn in places and hot August air rumbled through. Outside the window the landscape was unlike the Missouri countryside she knew. It looked more like the backroads of Kentucky she'd driven with her parents on the way to the Kentucky Horse Park, with the road hugging the hillsides, the tree branches leaning close so that she thought she might be able to open the window and touch them.

She'd been allowed to ride in the backseat of her mother's Lexus without a seatbelt, lying down, playing her portable video game or reading or watching a film. Her parents joked around in the front or her father sang. Her mother used the road atlas and GPS to find more interesting routes to get where they were going. They'd strayed close enough to Mammoth Cave to decide to make a detour and spend the night at a funny little hotel with a miniature golf course in the huge basement.

How old had she been? Eight? Just after third grade.

Daddy, where did you go? I miss you.

She understood that he wasn't at the house as she'd imagined. The house had tried to trick her, but she wasn't that naïve anymore. Her father was gone, and she had only herself left to depend on.

She'd seen how her mother had smiled at Gerard the night before, and wondered if she was glad his wife was dead.

Maybe she's glad Daddy's dead, too.

No! That couldn't be true. She wasn't stupid. She knew her mother had made herself sick with guilt over the explosion. She wasn't a bad person. She just didn't understand.

⁓

"I don't see them near the house," Jefferson said.

They were crouched in the woods not more than two hundred feet away on the garden side of the house, Jefferson's backpack on the ground between them. The leaves on the trees scattered sunlight back and forth over the canvas, making it look almost alive. It reminded Ariel of something, and not in a good way.

"They've got their trucks and stuff parked out by the springhouse. I think they're just too fucking scared to use the stairs to get down there."

"You don't need to come in with me," she said. Her leg throbbed. Because she was no longer wrapped in the blanket, the top half of her body was barely covered. The cami hid nothing. She felt like some hideous thing exposed to the eyes of the world. She couldn't wait to get into the house where she was safe.

"That's the thing about a house with a bad reputation," Jefferson said, lowering his compact binoculars. "Nobody wants to mess with it."

From this vantage point Bliss House looked benign but lonesome. Sure, there were things about it that frightened her, but she knew she could handle them. The worst threats had come from actual human beings.

While they waited a few minutes to make sure there really wasn't anyone at the house, Jefferson told her his father wasn't going to bother her anymore. He was "pretty sure" that he'd killed Karin Powell, and was mixed up with Nick Cunetta's death, too.

Worse, he believed his father had something to do with the attack on his mom.

As he told her these things she realized he either didn't know his father was dead or was a very good liar.

"What kind of person tries to have his wife killed?" he asked her. "I should kill him myself."

Seeing the look of sincerity in his face, a chill went through her. She knew he meant it.

He picked up the binoculars and again checked out the house.

"I think we're good to go. Welcome home."

Chapter 85

Gerard found Ellie pressed up against the closed bedroom door where Ariel was resting. The television inside was tuned to a reality show he recognized as one that Karin had watched. Ellie looked up at him and gave a little whimper. She hated to be away from the most interesting thing going on in the house, and now that Karin was gone she'd decided Ariel was it.

"I bet she just forgot about you." He bent to scratch her behind the ear, but she got up ready to go inside the room.

Gerard tapped lightly on the door. When there was no answer he tapped louder. Ellie whimpered again.

"Hey, Ariel. Can I let Ellie in to hang out with you?"

When there was no response or corresponding change in the TV volume, he considered going outside and peering in the door that opened on the garden, but dismissed the idea as being too creepy. He knocked one more time and waited, wondering if he should open the door a crack to check on her or just leave her alone.

He decided Rainey would definitely want him to open the door.

He'd only opened it a few inches, calling Ariel's name, when Ellie pushed through the crack, forcing it open all the way.

The TV was playing to an empty room. On the other side of the bed the garden doors stood open, and the room's temperature had risen several degrees above that of the rest of the house. The bed was neatly made. There was no sign anyone had been there except for the blaring TV, and Rainey's overnight bag on the suitcase stand.

Ellie lifted her nose, sniffing as she walked around the bed. Gerard followed her into the bathroom, but there was no one inside.

"Maybe she's outside?"

Hearing the word "outside" Ellie went to stand in the doorway to the garden. When a mayfly flew over her on its way inside, she lifted her head and gave it a desultory *snap*.

Gerard called Ariel's name again, hoping against hope that she was just outside looking at flowers or catching butterflies or whatever a fourteen-year-old girl did to pass the time the day after she'd been assaulted by an insane county judge.

"Shit," he said. He double-checked the garden knowing that she wasn't there, then called Ellie in and closed and locked the doors.

There was no question about where she'd gone. But how was she getting there? The only answer that came to him was one that made his gut go cold.

Before going to his truck he went to the safe in his bedroom and grabbed the Glock 9mm he used as a carry piece when traveling. He tucked it into his waistband and pulled his shirt down over it, praying he wouldn't have to use it.

⁓

Rainey answered on the first ring.

"I was just getting ready to call you," she said, already sounding frantic. "I've been trying to reach Ariel, but her phone seems to be off. Will you check on her?"

When Gerard hesitated, she got louder.

"What's wrong with her? What's going on?" In the background Gerard heard a distant siren, and he knew she probably hadn't yet left the hospital.

"I'm driving to your house right now," he said. "Ariel left. I don't know when. But that has to be where she's going."

"How could you let her . . ."

Gerard cut her off. "I'm sorry. She got breakfast and went back to your room and shut the door. I'm sorry, Rainey. I'll find her."

"We never should've made her leave the house. We should've stayed there and protected her, where she felt safe."

"She wasn't safe. She's not safe at all in that house."

"She's obviously not any safer with you."

It stung, but he knew she was right.

"I'm on the way to my car. I'll be there soon," she said and hung up before he could say another word.

Chapter 86

Lucas parked his car at the end of the pavement near the carriage house. The ME's van and the crime scene people had driven through the grass to park their SUVs close to the springhouse. The generators they'd set up hummed across the distance. The scene investigators had discovered that the third underground room contained a closed-off entrance to what looked to be a second tunnel. So far they hadn't gone into it because it looked like it hadn't been used in at least several decades.

God, how he hated this place.

He took off his jacket and left it on the passenger seat before heading across the grass. The day was already as humid as a wet dishrag. The only thing he was looking forward to about going underground was the relative chill of the tunnel.

Since the previous night the tunnel had been filled with portable lights. Moving deeper inside he could see the careful detail of the tunnel's construction. Not plaster, but some kind of mudding method made the earthen walls smooth and obviously stable. How old the walls were, they would have to figure out.

At the end of the tunnel where the rooms were, the lights were even brighter. All the furnishings had been dusted for prints, anything fabric had been removed and was stacked in large clear evidence bags. The top one contained a blue blanket or afghan of some sort. Obviously handmade. He tried to imagine the hands that made it and wondered if they were the hands of one of the victims who was being prepared for transport to the morgue.

Lucas found Silas Hamrick, the ME, in the second room with a pair of technicians. Silas looked up. He said something to the female member of his team and came out into the narrow hallway. He looked delighted.

"Haven't seen one of these cases in twenty years. Exciting as hell. My money's on the male being the judge's brother. He went missing over thirty years ago. Everyone said he ran off with a girl. But it's obvious he didn't run too far."

Lucas frowned. "The judge's wife said the same thing an hour or two ago."

"You hang around long enough, you remember things," Silas said. "I need to get out of here. I'm supposed to be at my nephew's confirmation party, and I haven't seen my family in a week. The kids can wrap this up. I have to say I'm getting pretty damn sick of seeing you, Detective."

"The feeling's mutual, Silas. Maybe after these two, we get a break?"

Silas pressed his hands together in a mock prayer of supplication and looked up. "Your mouth to God's ear."

Chapter 87

As she walked through the front hall, Ariel thought she could feel the house sigh with happiness. Or was the happiness just inside her? Already the ache in her leg was subsiding. She'd hidden it from Jefferson, but she'd almost been in tears as they'd hiked through the woods from where they'd parked the Jeep.

The idea that the police might have done something to the house had worried her. But inside it was just the same as when they'd left the day before. Maybe even better because now she had come home to it, just as Jefferson had said. He'd been right. Most people didn't want to have anything to do with a house like Bliss House. And that was fine with her.

On reaching the Jeep she'd turned off her phone. Within thirty seconds of turning it back on, two voicemails and two texts from her mother popped up. Of course she was freaking out. Ariel knew she wasn't supposed to leave Gerard's house. Her mother could come and find her if she wanted to, but there was no way she could make her leave again. She deleted the texts and the voicemails.

Jefferson had gone upstairs to wash up, saying he was feeling nasty. They hadn't yet come to any conclusion about where he should go next. She wanted to help him escape, but only because he had helped her.

Before going into the kitchen, she stopped in the powder room off the main hall and turned on the light. Looking in the mirror, she took off the ridiculous golf hat and turned her face slightly. She touched the scars with her hand.

Nothing yet. She didn't see the same improvement she'd noticed before. Why? What had happened? She closed her eyes, breathed deeply. She told herself she'd just gotten home. All would be well soon. The house would take care of her. She just had to be patient. Her leg already felt better, didn't it?

In the kitchen she was careful not to get too close to the windows. She could just see the police vehicles out by the springhouse, and there were probably more cars parked by the carriage house. She was more concerned for Jefferson than she was for herself, and knew she might get in trouble for helping him. But what could they really do to her?

While she was assembling a snack on a tray—the antique metal tray with the tole-painted yellow and green flowers that was her favorite—her phone vibrated again. She almost didn't look, thinking it was her mother.

The text read:

HURRY UP! I HAVE A SURPRISE FOR YOU!

Ariel smiled, but her smile slowly faded. The text was from Jefferson. She remembered how he had surprised her in the tunnel, and the sudden way he'd appeared on the third floor the night of the party and insisted on talking to her. She didn't mind helping him, but she didn't know if she wanted anything to do with his surprises.

Chapter 88

There were no sounds coming from her mother's room, where Jefferson said he was waiting. Why was he in there? Ariel listened for the television. Some normal, everyday sound. Anything. When there was nothing but silence she knew she'd made a mistake coming upstairs. The noontime sun shining through the windows around the dome cast everything in the well of the house in stark relief. She and Jefferson were alone in the house. Her mother was at the hospital, and the police were down in the underground rooms a world away.

She noticed Jefferson's backpack lying open on the gallery rug, empty of whatever had filled it earlier.

Don't open it, Button. It's full of fire.

Jefferson stood in the doorway of her mother's room. He looked different than he had just a few minutes before, but Ariel wasn't quite sure why. Something about the way he was watching her.

"What is it? You're too funny, texting me when I was just down-stairs." She laughed nervously. Where *was* he going to go? He needed a hiding place. She thought of the underground rooms. Just the memory that they even existed—let alone that she had almost died there—made her tense. But right then it was suddenly important that she not let him know what she was feeling. Out of that confusion of feelings grew a single strange thought: she never wanted him to kiss her again. In fact she never wanted to be close to him again. What had changed?

The change was in Jefferson's eyes. How he was looking at her. The times she'd been with him before today, he'd always had a hint of amusement in his eyes, as though he never took anything too seriously. As though he believed that while things might not be great at that moment, they were sure to turn out okay. She hadn't trusted him at first, but had put that down to her own worries. Seeing him across the gallery—the very same gallery in her vision—she saw his father's eyes. Sharp and cruel. Mocking. She was jolted by the memory of young Randolph twisting his own brother's heart in his chest. Fear shimmered over her skin like tongues of fire. The sunlight had formed a kind of halo around Jefferson and he didn't look like an older teenager anymore, someone who might have been the brother of a friend, someone to hero-worship and crush on. He looked like a man.

"It's better here, isn't it? Karin thought so," he said.

Ariel felt frozen where she stood and found herself waiting for him to approach her. But he stayed where he was.

"She liked to do it everywhere in this house, not just in that creepy room downstairs." Jefferson's voice was hard, but there was a note of sadness in it. "My father liked it down there. She said she didn't, but maybe she was lying. She was like that."

Now he did take a few steps toward her so that he blocked the stairway. It was as though he were sleepwalking, not really paying attention to her. Her mind told her to run, but she knew he was much faster than she, even if she could get past him. She'd never make it downstairs and outside.

The air around them thickened.

"I didn't give a shit that she was a liar, you know? She was good to me. My old man's girlfriend," he said mockingly. "*Mistress,* he called her, like it was something to be proud of. He thought it was a joke, telling me I should fuck her. That she would like it. He thought *she* was a joke. He thought everyone around him was a joke, the arrogant fucker. I guess your old man wasn't like that, huh? I wasn't a lucky cunt like you."

Ariel wasn't sure he wanted an answer. Unable to look at his hate-filled eyes any longer, she glanced away. He was carrying something, holding it at his side, almost behind him. A can of some sort. Was this the surprise?

"I'm not lucky," she whispered. His face didn't change. Had he even heard her?

Someone, *something* had heard her. The air changed again. A low rumble like thunder sounded around them, incongruous with the midday sunshine.

"I wanted a dad like that. But that's not what I got. I got a fucking narcissist, *a sadist* who played God with everybody he ever knew. Fifteen!" He was shouting now, his face red, twisting with pain. "I was fifteen fucking years old when he showed me that room. He told me what he did to the women he brought down there, how he drugged them and fucked them till they bled. Fifteen! What in the hell was I supposed to do with that?"

"I'm sorry." It was all Ariel could think to say. It wasn't her fault she'd been born to people who cared about her. Loved her.

Where are you, Mom? Find me, please.

She'd gotten away from the father. Now she had to get away from the son. He was watching her too closely.

The rumbling echoed through the house, but seemed to be coming from above. Ariel hoped against hope that someone was up there. *Someone alive.* Maybe one of the cops. But they were all far away in the tunnel. There was nothing here for them inside the house.

Unwilling to wait for someone to save her, Ariel turned and ran as fast as she could for the back stairway. *Up* was her only chance.

Chapter 89

Rainey pulled up in front of the house.

As she shut off the car her eyes were on Gerard, who was fumbling with opening the front door of Bliss House.

There were no police to be seen, except for a single car at the carriage house. The rest of the vehicles were presumably far out on the property, near the springhouse.

So much for protection.

As she hurried up the front stairs, shouting for Gerard to get the door open, she stumbled.

Bliss House didn't want them inside.

⁓

Hamrick's techs worked without chatter. Lucas suspected they, like Hamrick, were in a state of awe over the find of the bodies. They wore protective masks and white hazard suits, and while they'd left the door to the room with the bodies open, they wouldn't let him inside. He was anxious to see if either of the victims had any sort of identification on them, and was most curious about the female. The male was almost certainly Michael

Bliss. The presumption was they'd been murdered. The male had obviously sustained some kind of chest injury, but the details of the female's death were less evident.

He hadn't gotten to the house soon enough to hear all of Ariel's story right after she'd been attacked. But piecing it together with the interview he'd done with her in the library, he suspected the unidentified female might have been the woman she'd seen go over the balcony the night Karin Powell died. And now Ariel had mentioned a baby, too. He made a note to ask Hamrick if there was a baby involved somehow. Would it even be possible to check for signs of pregnancy in the female's body, given its state? Science needed to give them the answers—especially since so many of the major players in this mystery were dead, and the only witness (if you could call having visions being a witness) was a child who might be half out of her mind.

Lucas sat down on the bed's bare mattress. The place was practically airless, the stuff of claustrophobic nightmares. What in the hell had these walls, and this barbaric headboard with its bloodthirsty hunters, witnessed? How many generations of degradation? This was no cozy nest for lovebirds, even if the judge and his son had been screwing the lovely Karin Powell here. And it was no hidden playroom for the kiddies, or housing for servants. Whoever had carved it out of the dirt had had very specific, very unpleasant motives in mind. But who would ever know what they were?

Creeped out by his own thoughts on the room, he decided to take one more look around, and mention the female's possible pregnancy directly to one of Hamrick's techs instead of waiting to talk to the doc himself before heading up to the main part of Bliss House by the fireplace staircase to see if he could learn anything else there.

The lever on the front door's lock moved, but the door wouldn't budge. Gerard's shoulder ached from shoving against it, and he cursed, not wanting to believe that there was no rational reason for the door not to open. The fact that there was no give at all told him nothing had been pushed against it, and he doubted Ariel would've had the strength to move anything that heavy anyway. Rainey had stood by for a minute or two while he'd tried her key, but then she'd lost what small amount of patience she had left and took off to try the nearest doors and windows. Gerard suspected it was fruitless. The house was secure. Ironically, he and Rainey had made it so.

He rested a moment, breathing hard, and watched Rainey hurry around the corner of the house. A charged stillness had settled over everything, and though she was running she seemed hampered by the thick humidity of the summer afternoon. It killed him to see the way she was suffering, worrying about her daughter. He felt responsible for what was happening. *His* work had made it possible for her and her daughter to move in here. *His* wife had brought her here, had allowed herself to become entwined with Randolph Bliss and his twisted son. Worse, he knew he hadn't watched over Ariel the way he should have. It was his fault she was here and in danger. Even if they found her safe inside, any friendship he might have had with Rainey was certainly spoiled.

He'd gone to bed the night before thinking about her voice in his ear, the way her petite body fit against him as she kissed his cheek. At first it had felt strange and disloyal to think of her as he was lying there on sheets that still smelled of Karin. But he'd let his mind go there, and didn't regret it.

Giving up on the front door, he ran after her.

Chapter 90

Jefferson tackled Ariel on the back stairs, grabbing her around the waist. Her forehead hit a step with a *crack* that vibrated through her skull. She didn't lose consciousness, and felt the blood, slick against the wood. Perhaps stunned by his success in knocking her down, he momentarily loosened his hold and she scrabbled away, clawing at the stairs, propelling herself up, up to the third floor. To some kind of imagined safety. She was driven by a need, a certainty that she was going in the right direction. The third floor was the heart of the house. How strange. How unbalanced. Her life might be slipping away, but all she could think about was the house. It had let her down. Betrayed her.

She made it to the last riser and groped for the floor above it. This hallway was where she'd been pushed weeks ago, and now she'd found her way back up those stairs. A few more inches was all she needed.

Why had he let go? She didn't dare look back—that much she knew. She kept going forward, keeping her mind focused on getting to the ballroom. There had to be safety there, if nothing more than the stairs beside the fireplace that would take her to any police who were left. Yes, they were a long way down, but she could scream, couldn't she?

But it wasn't to be. She'd stumbled only a few feet toward the front hall when she felt something cold on her unprotected back.

"This is for you, you little bitch. You freak!"

When she turned she got a second blast of—oh, God, what was it? It burned!

"This should feel familiar," Jefferson said. "Getting burned out there in St. Louis. Good times, yeah? Hot times!" He laughed at his own joke, squeezing the metal can over and over, squirting charcoal lighter fluid over her skin like it was water.

When the fluid first touched her it was cold, but it quickly began to sear. The pain in her eye was unbearable.

Please, God! Not again!

It was as though she were still on the front lawn, lying in the smoking grass, her eardrums nearly shattered, her skin on fire.

As he poured and poured the stuff on her, he called her hideous names.

"Your fault, you little cunt! You and your cunt of a mother! Everything is your fault!"

Still she kept crawling, stumbling to the hallway despite the pain. The smell of the stuff threatened to overwhelm her, and Jefferson himself was like some ponderous animal dogging her. He ranted like a madman, but she would not give in to him! Too much had been taken away from her already. He wasn't going to take her life. They moved forward as one writhing, violent beast until they could go no farther. The air in front of them had thickened to a point that movement wasn't possible. *Is this what death feels like?* Ariel could barely form the thought. Some invisible force shoved them backwards so they were driven apart, the abruptness of it causing Jefferson to soak himself with a long stream of lighter fluid he'd meant for Ariel.

Ariel landed on her back near the ballroom's open doorway. The massive pain inside her head and the burn of the chemical made her want to curl into a ball and disappear. Or die. It didn't matter to her.

The motionless air was filled with the rumbling sound that might have been thunder. The house shook.

Enraged, Jefferson stood and let out an inhuman roar of frustration. Through eyes narrowed with pain, Ariel saw him hurl himself toward her, his handsome face a hideous mask of fury.

Not knowing what instinct compelled her, Ariel drew back her knees. When he was just inches away she closed her eyes and kicked out, making contact. While she would never know exactly where she'd landed her kick, his cry of surprise told her she'd done something right. Not wanting to wait to see what he would do, she rolled onto her side to get up, half-anticipating that he would be attacking again.

But when she looked, Jefferson wasn't the first thing she saw.

Rainey reached the herb garden outside the kitchen. She paused, noticing Lucas's car parked at the end of the drive. Several other vehicles were parked in the grass near the remains of the spring-house. Hearing something behind her, she glanced back to see Gerard catching up with her.

"Maybe Ariel's with them." Rainey said the words, knowing she was wrong.

Rainey hadn't wanted to see the place where her daughter had been trapped. As far as she was concerned, she never would, unless Ariel wanted her to. But she knew it was unlikely she could avoid it. She owned the property, and there would probably be some kind of inquiry. She would need to know the details because the place was, ultimately, her responsibility.

"No. I think she's inside the house." Gerard said. "Come on."

They went to the porch where, only the day before, Ariel had come to them. Rainey carefully avoided looking at the warped smear of Randolph's blood Ariel had left behind on the porch.

Gerard tried the back door, and Rainey went to the window that looked into the butler's pantry. Nothing.

433

"What about the servants' entrance?" Gerard crossed the porch, tested the door. Locked.

"I don't carry that key," Rainey said.

"We're going to have to break in. Unless one of us runs out to the springhouse and goes up through the stairway." Gerard stopped. The porch beneath them began to shake, slowly at first, then more violently. Neither of them was knocked over, but Rainey grabbed onto the porch railing for support.

There was the sound of glass shattering, and Rainey turned to see the window in the upper half of the mudroom door splinter in its frame and fall to the ground.

Gerard leapt to Rainey's side, curving his body around hers protectively. But he couldn't protect her from the sounds emanating from the new opening in the door. A deep rumbling coursed through the house in waves as though the earth had opened, revealing its terrible heartbeat. Rainey started to cover her ears, but when she heard the scream and unintelligible shouting, she knew she had to listen. They had to go inside.

There was nothing in his head but a red, burning rage. Rage beyond which he couldn't see. It was a heavy curtain, hiding everything he'd ever known except this moment. He had some idea of where he was. The walls, the balustrades, the open ballroom—they were familiar, but they felt distant. He knew the girl lying on the floor. The cripple. The one he hated. The one he knew he had to kill. To do that, he had to go forward, toward her. But each step was agony. The floor was unstable, and he could hardly breathe. Any air that got into his lungs was hot and felt as though it was melting his flesh as he drew it inside.

But it was the sight of the two women flanking the girl that brought him to a halt. One of them was small and about his age, but very like a child. The other, taller. So familiar, so alive that the sight of her made him want to weep. Their hair was red and gold, like tendrils of flame. Yes. Their hair wasn't hair at all, but flame. Soft, crackling flames that released no smoke, but only heat.

A hot stream of urine ran down Jefferson's leg, into his shoe.

There were more people beyond the women, moving around the ballroom. But they didn't seem quite so real. They were strangers. Women and children. Young children. A man and a boy. They seemed lost. Aimless.

But these two women weren't lost. They were coming toward him, their shining eyes focused on him. The younger one seemed frail in her pretty robe, but he somehow knew that she was the more dangerous of the two. He wanted to beg for their mercy, but his body was so paralyzed that he couldn't free the words from his mouth.

One of them was reaching out for him. He said her name out loud. *Karin.* Over and over. Begging. He didn't want her to see him cry, but he couldn't stop himself.

There was so much he wanted to tell her. She needed to understand that he would've stopped his father if he'd known he was going to hurt her. That he, Jefferson, had never wanted to hurt her. Or anybody! Not even the crippled girl. He had just lost his head. For so long he'd just wanted to please his father. But hadn't he killed his father for her as some kind of retribution? Hadn't that counted as something?

When she brought one of her long fingers to his chest, a single finger whose nail was pale and broken, a sad thing beside the rest of her perfect bronze nails, he hardly recoiled. And when the flames— so warm, so beautiful—traveled down her arm to her hand, igniting the lighter fluid soaking his shirt, he tried not to scream.

He saw a hint of forgiveness in her eyes when she embraced him. The flames licked his throat, his chin, his cheek. Still, he didn't make a sound. He would accept her, return her embrace. Even when she took him over the balustrade of the gallery, propelling him to the ground, the only sound was Rainey's anguished cry of disbelief as she watched from below.

Chapter 91

Lucas held up the shirt that the hospital staff had dutifully bagged for him on his admission for smoke inhalation. He didn't need to hold it any closer than arm's length to know it was unwearable. Worse, the smell of it suffused him with dread. He stuffed it back into the bag with the rest of his belongings.

"Damn, I take one little vacation, and you end up burning down a house and getting locked up in the hospital. What gives, Chappell?"

Brandon Stuart, his work partner, stood in the doorway of the hospital room holding a plastic shopping bag in one hand and an oversized coffee mug with the words *Life's Waaaaaay Better at Virginia Beach* in the other. He held up the mug. "Got you a souvenir. Gayle wanted to get you some candle with shells stuck on it, but I thought it was fruity." He tossed the shopping bag onto the bed.

"What would I do without you to protect my masculinity, Stuart? Once again you've saved me from your wife's excellent taste. These my clothes?" He opened the bag on the bed and was relieved to see the pair of blue jeans, sandals, and polo shirt he kept in his work locker. They didn't smell anything like smoke. "Hey, shut that door."

Brandon shut the door, and Lucas undid the hospital gown he wore and slipped it off. His own clothes felt good. The shirt was soft and comfortable. He was just as glad he'd had no clean dress shirts left in his locker. He would have to replenish them, though, ASAP.

When all the proper forms were signed, he and Brandon left the hospital and went to Brandon's waiting cruiser.

"We got your car from the Bliss place—or what's left of it, anyway. So, Judge Bliss's kid burned it down? Can't say I'm sorry to see it go. County had to block off the driveway. Lots of folks wanting to check it out."

"Yeah, it was something like that." Lucas stared out the window, watching the landscape go by. A late summer thunderstorm had passed through that morning. Most of the rain had dried, but any leaves still in the shade shimmered with water. He was glad for the sunshine. When he thought about the house, the opaque darkness of the stairway filling with smoke as he blindly made his way down to warn the techs, both his throat and his mind constricted. In the hospital they'd had to sedate him so he could sleep. The judge's kid had died, but the girl, Ariel, hadn't needed to be hospitalized at all. That was a mystery he knew he'd never have an answer to.

He answered all of Brandon's questions he could, filling him in on the deaths of the real estate agent, the judge, and Nick Cunetta, and how they were all connected.

"The woman, Rainey Adams, who moved into the house with her kid didn't seem to be personally involved, at first. All she had in common with them was . . ."

Brandon cut him off. "That damn house."

"That damn house," Lucas said.

Brandon was still technically on vacation, so he dropped Lucas off at the state police post with his bag of smoky clothes and the coffee mug. Before he drove away, he asked Lucas if he would see him in the office the next day.

Lucas nodded. "Might as well get started on the paperwork. I'm sure DeRoy Lee has a shiny lawyer all lined up."

"Yeah, but no judge to help him out."

"There's that."

On his way into the post Lucas paused by the large covered trashcan near the front door and stuffed the bag of clothes inside. He didn't need a souvenir.

Epilogue

Bertie was glad to be done with the trial of DeRoy Lee. Almost a year to the day after Nick's death he was found guilty of first-degree murder, after cutting a plea deal over his assault on her. He had—inexplicably—pleaded *not guilty* to killing dear Nick, despite there being several minutes of video that showed him committing the murder. The sentencing wouldn't be for another couple of weeks, but she would be in the courtroom for that, too. She watched as the bailiff led him away, looking twenty pounds heavier and much less satisfied with himself than he had when he worked at the bookstore. The glamorous silver-blond ponytail was gone. The prosecutor, whom she had known for many years, had told her that DeRoy had had a particularly nasty case of lice that required him to shave his head. Bertie thought the lice couldn't have made a better choice of victims.

"Are you okay?" Rainey touched her arm. Around them, the other spectators were filing out of the courtroom.

Bertie noticed that quite a few of them were staring rudely. Most were curiosity-seekers (Randolph had called people like them *trial junkies*), not people she knew. People like Ethan Fauquier, who had employed DeRoy at her husband's suggestion, avoided her eye, but she knew Ethan in particular would surely be on his phone as soon as he got out of the building. Nick's secretary and his sister were being shepherded out by the assistant prosecutor, their heads bowed. The sister shared Nick's coloring and sleek black hair, and had wept openly when the jury was shown photos of the crime scene.

Bertie didn't care if people wondered why the wife of the man who had hired DeRoy Lee to kill Nick was at the trial even on the days she hadn't been called as a witness. The things she heard about her husband and son caused her to cry into her pillow each night, but she was strong at the trial because she wanted to honor Nick's memory. He deserved so much better than to have died that way. If only he hadn't called Jefferson right away! She wasn't sure what she'd expected when she'd taken the fingernail to him. Maybe just advice. Maybe just to know she wasn't alone in her knowledge that Jefferson was involved in Karin's death. But Nick had surprised them all, and been killed for it.

At first, right after the Judge and Jefferson died, her closest friends had rallied around her, sharing her grief and disbelief. But after the salacious details of the Judge's and Jefferson's involvement with Karin Powell had been spread by the newspapers and gossips, they'd all fallen away. While her feelings had been terribly hurt, she understood that they just didn't know what to say to her anymore. If she'd been in their place, what would she have said?

I'm so sorry your husband was a monster who murdered two people and tried to have you killed. What a tragedy that your son was as crazy as his father.

But it was all going to be okay. She was making new friends and she had Rainey and Ariel, who were settled in Charlottesville for the time being. Bliss House had been a complete loss, and the insurance company had arranged for the shell to be knocked down. Any undamaged brick and iron had been sold for salvage. Now, the whole estate was once again up for sale.

Bertie took Rainey's too-thin hand in her own. "Perfect," she said. "Let's go to lunch. We deserve a little celebration." She peeked around Rainey to address Ariel. "Shall we get out of here, sweetie?"

Ariel looked up from her phone. "Just a sec. I'm coming."

It did Bertie's heart good to see Ariel texting. She'd made friends with another teenage girl at the hospital in Charlottesville, where she'd had four or five operations so far.

The surgeons had been able to completely restore the sight in the eye that had been burned by the lighter fluid and improved the vision in the other. And while she would never win any beauty pageants (it was an unfortunate description, but it was the one that always came to Bertie's mind), the surgeons had been able to help her feel comfortable enough with the way she looked to go out in public. Though she still balked at going to school. It had been more than three years since she'd set foot in one, and Bertie didn't blame her. School was never her favorite thing, either.

Rainey started to admonish Ariel, but Bertie interrupted her. "Here comes Detective Chappell."

Bertie put on a warm smile for the detective. Rainey looked uncomfortable at his approach, and Bertie felt bad for her. She'd never quite gotten over the feeling that the police had mistrusted her, and that their mistrust had endangered Ariel's life. Bertie didn't try to dissuade her. She'd learned quickly after first getting to know her the previous summer that it was impossible to argue with Rainey. She was stubborn—particularly when it came to protecting her daughter.

If only I'd been that stubborn in protecting Jefferson from Randolph.

"Mrs. Bliss."

Lucas took Bertie's hand as though he were going to shake it, but stepped closer and gently embraced her. His simple act brought tears to Bertie's eyes. Even on the days he wasn't testifying, he'd been at the trial as much as his job would allow, watching DeRoy Lee like a cat who wasn't about to let his prey get away. Before letting go of her completely, he told her he was very sorry for everything she'd lost and hoped things were going well for her. He seemed to understand that DeRoy's trial meant a kind of closure, even though she hadn't been the victim of the crime for which he was being prosecuted.

"Oh, my," she said. "So many people lost so much, Detective. I pray every day that the people my husband hurt will find some peace." She put an arm around Rainey.

"I'll be here for the sentencing. You can count on it." He looked to Rainey. "Let me escort you all out the staff door. There are too many reporters outside."

Rainey looked relieved. It had been a very rough year for her, and the trial had brought the reporters out of the woodwork.

After escaping the burning house and being checked by paramedics, Gerard had taken Ariel and Rainey back to his house where—for the second time in as many years—they realized they were homeless. This time it was Ariel who was the strong one, who brought Rainey cup after cup of herbal tea, slept close against her while she had fitful dreams, read to her when she felt too tired to get out of bed. Gerard had fended off the press and their insinuations about the coincidence of Rainey staying with the man whose wife had been murdered in her house. Someone in the police department leaked the details of how Ariel had seen a vision of a young Randolph Bliss kill his brother and captive girlfriend, and the history of Bliss House and the Brodsky murder and earlier deaths there were once again front page news in the area. Ghost hunters flocked to the ruined property, and Rainey had to hire security to keep them away.

It was a month before things died down. Ariel blossomed in the sunshine, taking Ellie for walks once the professionally curious stopped staking out Gerard's home. Karin was cremated and, after a very private memorial service, Ariel helped Gerard pack up her jewelry and clothes to send to her sister.

But while Ariel and Gerard formed a strong bond of friendship, Rainey held herself back. Her losses felt too raw: the house, the family she'd thought she would have with Randolph, Bertie, and Jefferson, the plans she'd made for restarting her career.

When she felt strong enough, and had her finances in some semblance of order, she decided it was time to leave Old Gate. Not surprisingly, Ariel didn't object. But neither one of them wanted to return to St. Louis. They settled on an apartment in Charlottesville for the time being, so they wouldn't be too far from Bertie.

The name "Allison" had been matched to a decades-old Charlottesville missing persons case. The girl's mother had tentatively identified her daughter's partially-decayed body, but DNA tests had confirmed her identity. Rainey had seen the heartbreaking images of the corpse and knew it must have taken a great deal of courage to identify it. But the woman wouldn't see Rainey, and didn't want Bertie's apologies. Through Detective Chappell, she said she didn't want anything to do with anyone from the Bliss family, and that she certainly didn't believe anything some child had thought she'd seen in a dream.

An autopsy of Michael's body had revealed that his chest had, indeed, been crudely torn open, his heart twisted and crushed. And his DNA had revealed—several months later—that Rainey was probably his daughter.

⌒

The house where Bertie had lived with her husband and son for half her life was in too much disarray to go back to for lunch. It had sold two months earlier, but she had been spending the time since then sorting and boxing things up, sending a few items to scattered family members, donating even more to charity. She was downsizing.

Rainey had looked surprised when she told her she'd bought Nick's cottage, but she seemed to have come round. Ariel had said she thought it was a really nice thing to do, and couldn't wait to help her move in. All of Nick's belongings were gone, of course, and she'd had it completely renovated (not by Gerard, who had declined) so the whole situation was less macabre. She hoped to have the house and its precious garden in shape for a New Year's open house.

When they got to the Lettuce Leaf, a new hostess greeted them with a professional lack of curiosity. Bertie was grateful for the temporary anonymity. She had felt gawked at for too long in her hometown.

"This way." The hostess started to lead them to an empty table at the back of the restaurant.

"Wait," Ariel said, tucking her phone into her purse. "Let's sit over there." She took off her sunglasses and started toward a sunny table near the front window.

Bertie was happy to see that Ariel was now completely unselfconscious about her limp. She moved quite nimbly, without hesitation.

"Oh, no," Rainey said.

Ariel stopped at a table for four that already had one person seated at it. Gerard Powell stood up.

"Gerard!" Bertie threw her arms around him and kissed him on the cheek. "How wonderful to see you."

"Do you mind if I join you?" Gerard was addressing her, but Bertie saw him cast an awkward glance at Rainey.

He had spent two hours testifying at the trial earlier in the week but had left immediately afterwards, and neither Bertie nor Rainey had talked to him. The months had been kind to him, and he looked like he had come to a better place after his wife's death.

Bertie wondered if Rainey was ready to forgive him for not watching Ariel more carefully that dreadful day. Yet Bertie felt that no one at the table carried more blame than she herself did.

God knows, sometimes we all make terrible choices.

"I invited him." Ariel turned to Gerard, looking very proud of herself. "I'm so glad to see you."

Bertie noticed that the girl's quick, impulsive hug seemed to please him, and she liked him all the better for it. Even Rainey smiled a little.

"Shall we sit?" Bertie said.

Gateshead Country Estates Realty, Ltd.

Available now: Sixty-two acres of prime farmland and orchards in south-central Virginia, located less than an hour from Charlottesville. Beautiful home site, valley views. Water, electric, and cable available. Quaint carriage house with apartment and four bay garage suitable for vehicles or equipment storage.

Attractively priced.

Acknowledgements

With Deepest Gratitude To . . .

Susan Raihofer, my dear, indefatigable Agent Susan of The David Black Literary Agency, who has never said the words *that sounds crazy* to me. She makes my dreams real in the real world, and does it with a brilliant ferocity that would scare the hell out of me if I didn't know what a sweetheart she really is.

Eleanora Benedict, the first and most beloved reader of my every manuscript, who fills my life with music and wit. She keeps me grounded with her favorite question: "you're kidding, right?"

J. T. Ellison, wielder of tough love, wise words and a killer golf swing. Her generous spirit and extraordinary work ethic inspire me every single day. It is no exaggeration to say that I would never have finished *Bliss House* without her telling me again and again that it could be done.

Maggie Caldwell, who always makes a difference with her California sunshine positivity, boundless determination, and subtle wit. Everyone she touches grows through her encouragement and kindness. I'm so proud to call her my friend—and I don't just say that so she won't spill all my secrets.

Yolanda Gunzel, who listens and guides and makes me laugh.

Kevin Winchester, Sue Spina, and Ruth Mercer for responding enthusiastically to my Facebook call for a few select character names, and letting me use their suggestions.

Anneliese and Alexander Wilmsen, who made the summer brighter and shared their great ideas.

Kermit Moore, one of my favorite humans, for his keen reader's eye and always-generous advice on firearms, police matters, and all things ghost-hunting.

Cleveland Benedict II, who not only endured a lot of late dinners and cheered me up when I got stuck, but also made it through middle school over the course of the writing of *Bliss House*. He had the tougher job.

The lovely folks at Pegasus who gave *Bliss House* a happy home: Publisher Claiborne Hancock, and Jessica Case, Associate Publisher and editrix extraordinaire, who asked all the right questions and gently demanded answers that would make the story whole. Also Maria Fernandez, who made it beautiful with her interior design and typesetting, and Deb Anderson, for her excellent proofreading.

You, the reader, for letting my work occupy your mind for a while. You've given me such a gift. Thank you for trusting me.

Pinckney, who is first, last, and always.